Titles by K S Ferguson

River Madden series:

Touching Madness

Undercover Madness

Rafe & Kama series:

Calculated Risk

Hostile Takeover

Family Owned

The Hellhound series:

No Place Like Hell

Novella:

Puncher's Chance
(with James Grayson)

Touching Madness

Copyright © 2012 by K S Ferguson

Contact the publisher: http://www.ksferguson.net

ISBN: 1-938179-19-6
ISBN-13: 978-1-938179-19-8

Touching Madness

K S Ferguson

Published by

K S FERGUSON

Dedication

To my mother, whose descent into the madness of Alzheimers inspired this book.

Acknowledgments

I would like to thank the many people who assisted with this novel. First, thanks to my daughter for her unfailing support and thoughtful suggestions. Then thanks to my writing partner, primary beta reader, and copy editor, James Grayson, for his sharp eye and dedication to quality storytelling. Thanks to my crit group, Critical Maass, for their valuable feedback.

I'd also like to thank my readers, without whom there'd be little point in writing. If you enjoy this book, please consider leaving a review at the retailer or library site of your choice. Reviews are an enormous help to authors.

If you would like to be notified when the next book in the Madness series becomes available, please sign up at http://www.ksferguson.net/sign-up-for-news.html. I won't sell your contact information to anyone for any reason.

1

~~~~~~~

My feet sped over the jogging path beside the river, a madman in hoodie, jeans, and backpack, racing toward the setting sun. Winds of change gusted behind my eyes, and the world tilted off kilter. The ribbon of asphalt that lead back to Centralia, Kansas city center disintegrated into a storm of silver glitter. *Aw, hell. Another psychotic break coming to a neighborhood near me.*

The Dark Place sucked me in. Fire peeled back my flesh until my skin melted away. Then muscles scorched, enveloping me in a sickening stench. Heat bent my bones, shattering them into a thousand shards. Only my hysterical thoughts remained. Songs of demons wailed in my consciousness, and I wondered if this time I'd go permanently insane. Maybe I already was.

"Not real," I chanted, clinging to sanity through the hellish pain. "Not real, not real."

The tattooed runes that circled both my wrists itched worse than a million spider bites. Clouds of nightmares scudded away from hideous fairytale trolls, giant two-headed snakes, and a three-headed dog. They all fled from an enormous demon I thought might be Satan himself. He strode on cloven hooves through a landscape of fire and crystal and inside-out structures that couldn't possibly exist, where up was down and down was up, but none of that mattered because the creatures inhabiting the space simply ignored gravity.

"Not real. Survive. Done it before, do it again," I whispered as I streaked through the aberrant landscape.

After what seemed eternity, another onslaught of blinding silver glitter whirled around me. Like a kaleidoscope being twisted, the glitter showed first a late autumn pasture, then a dark, rain-swept alley, followed by an apocalyptic cityscape, all soot-covered ruins. One of them was real; the others not. Which one?

"Please let it be the pasture," I prayed. "I like cows. Cows are nice."

A bruising thump against my chest signaled the return of sanity. It could have been worse—I could have landed on the asphalt of the rainy alley instead of the garbage pile. Cannon blasts of pain throbbed through my head, a trickle of blood ran from my nose, and my heart raced. I waited. Right on cue, my stomach arrived, twisting in contortions that made me retch.

I rolled over on a mountain of garbage-stuffed plastic bags surrounding an overflowing dumpster that backed up against a two-story brick building, typical of the style in Centralia's older downtown district. Yep, garbage collectors out on strike again. Lucky me. The rain turned to sleet, and I shivered, my toes and fingers aching from the chill. Despite the cold and the need to get up, I lay there unmoving, too exhausted to make the effort.

Down the alley to the west, a single light above a door marked *Soo Ling's Chinese Take-away* struggled valiantly against the darkness, and I took stock, just to reassure myself that I was intact. Two feet, long toes. Two scrawny white legs none the worse for wear. Hip bones jutting against skin, stark ribs you could play a tune on. Thin arms, dark blue wrist tattoos still itching like mad. Male body parts intact, not that I had any chance with girls. What woman would date a psychotic schizophrenic who woke up naked in alleys wondering where he was and how he'd gotten there?

"Don't go there, River," I said. "Think survival. Clothes first."

Why did I always end up in the buff after a damn break? What the heck did I do with my clothes while I was crazy? How long was I loony? It had been sunset when I left reality, and now it was pitch black—maybe a different day. Was I even in Centralia? Once I'd awoken halfway across the country from the town I'd been in before the break, but I couldn't remember how I'd gotten there.

Across the alley and off to the east, the back wall of another brick building shimmered with a coating of silver sparkles. Shadows moved where the wall should be, and glimpses of the darkening cow pasture overlaid the broken city. I shivered again, the smell of my burning flesh still clinging to my memory.

"Not real."

As I gathered the strength to rise, the demon stepped through the shimmery wall. I sucked in freezing air and choked. He looked even bigger than he had in the Dark Place, all of eight feet. Fur or dense black hair wrapped the legs and hips above his cloven hooves. Chest and arm muscles bulged under ruddy skin. The fingers ended in long, sharp talons. His face looked like a bull's head. Curly mountain goat horns graced each side of it, and a third, stumpy horn stuck up off the top of his skull like a stubborn cowlick. Glassy black eyes looked straight at me, while little puffs of smoke whispered from bovine nostrils with each powerful breath.

"Not real," I reminded myself uselessly, because he sure *seemed* real, and my nervous system responded like he *was* real. Generally, my demonic hallucinations took the shape of three-foot tall gargoyles that crossed the edges of my vision, disappearing when I turned to look, not huge suckers like this one, standing in plain view. *Damn, what a fine imagination I have*, I thought as I tried to breathe normally. Too bad I didn't have paper and pencil handy. A sketch of him would sell for a couple of bucks to the Goth kids who hung around the park.

The demon turned his massive head toward the west end of the alley up past Soo Ling's, as though listening for something. Then he twisted it to the wall he'd just stepped through and listened again. Big streams of smoke snorted from his nostrils, and the corners of his mouth curved in a smile. *But cows can't smile.* With a last look at me, he trotted off to the east. His hooves clip-clopped against the asphalt as he receded into the darkness. My lungs drew in a deep breath at last.

"Stop staring at things that aren't there, River," I advised myself, "and get some covering before you freeze to death."

Plenty to choose from, a veritable scrounger's feast. I picked up the garbage sacks one after another with a connoisseur's eye, inspecting each for holes and the ripeness of their contents. Finding nothing to my liking, I minced over to another mountain of bin bags burying a second dumpster beside Soo Ling's door. I wouldn't go east toward the sparkly wall. Something about it called to me in a way I didn't like.

The first time I'd woken up naked after a psychotic episode, I looked for help before I covered myself. Six delightful months in a mental ward convinced me I'd always wrap in *something* before venturing into the world. Cops were much less sympathetic to the mentally ill than to a homeless twenty-something who passed for sixteen and dressed in garbage bags while he claimed to have been mugged for his clothes.

I found a lovely cinch-style bag that, with the bottom torn open, made a knee-length skirt I could tighten at my waist. It smelled mildly of rotten vegetables. Over my head, the light bulb sang *Frosty the Snowman* off-key while I shook harder. I hated light bulbs. Tone deaf the lot of them. I scrubbed at my scalp where a hundred thousand tiny ant feet did the Cha Cha in waves.

"Not real," I growled. "No ants." But the feet danced on undeterred.

I completed my glossy, all-black ensemble with a second bag in which I tore head and arm holes. I tried not to gag on the odor of sour milk emanating from the plastic, but at least it protected me from the biting wind. If only someone had tossed out a pair of trainers and a watch cap, I'd be in heaven. Thank goodness my tattoos no longer itched.

I was scrounging for a final bag to use as a hood and cape when the alley blazed with light. I pulled back into the darkness beside the dumpster, assuming a passing squad car had turned its spotlight toward me. The light went out, and I heard people, real ones. Or at least I thought they were real.

"Gear up," a gruff male voice ordered. "Keep the noise down so we don't attract a black-and-white. We don't want the local precinct on our case, and remember—no witnesses. Stun whoever you see whether they're a talent or not."

"Yes, sir," two voices answered in unison, one male, and one female. Both sounded young and excited. Oh, joy, overeager trainees out to prove how tough they were. Not a good night for the denizens of the streets.

"And don't get too close to the fracture. It's a big one. Sammie, you have the cuffs ready?"

The chipper female voice replied, "Yes, sir."

I peeked around the edge of the dumpster, expecting to see a patrol cruiser. At the mouth of the alley to the west, a floating stone tablet six inches thick and maybe seven feet across hovered above the pavement. Hieroglyphs ringed its edges, pulsing with faint light. A little mushroom thingy rose up a couple of feet in the center, and a large dog that wasn't quite a dog sat with its front paws resting on the mushroom cap. *Impossible*, I thought. *It's a police car.* The light bulb above the restaurant door began to hum the *Dragnet* theme.

An escapee from a costume party stood on the stone platform beside the dog. He wasn't any taller than me, maybe five foot eight, but probably weighed twice what I did. He wore a ludicrous ankle-length gold lamé robe and a matching hat that belonged on a Roman Catholic cardinal. He had a tall, softly glowing staff in his right hand, and he tapped it on the edge of the platform in time with the pulsing light. Outside my psychotic breaks, I didn't normally have such large and complex hallucinations. I worried that I might be losing it.

Three silhouettes advanced on me. I could barely make them out in the darkness of the alley. Two tall and one rather short, they wore all black—berets, uniform shirts, loose pants, and soft shoes. The clothing didn't look right for regular officers. Berets on city cops? No shiny badges or buttons? Maybe they were SWAT?

Oh, hell! My throat closed. Had I wandered into the middle of a drug bust? Or was some suspect holed up in one of the buildings along the alley, maybe with a hostage? But where were their rifles? They swung flashlights and carried what looked like plastic wands from a magic shop. The wands were too thin to be either billy clubs or cattle prods, both of which I'd experienced during my fifteen years on the streets.

I eyed the dark alley behind me as tingling fear climbed up my spine. I needed to either get out of there or hide. Sometimes I saw imaginary things; sometimes I saw real things differently from how they were. Whoever these people were, my brain thought they were a threat, or I wouldn't visualize them as cops. Johnny Law was no friend of mine.

Garbage bags rustled across the alley. A lightning bolt leaped from a wand and cracked against a dumpster near the sound. A calico cat screeched and tore away into the darkness. I ducked low. The after-image of the bolt burned on my retinas and my knees shook.

"You'll never live that one down, Griff," the female officer laughed.

"That's enough," the older officer said. "Griff, identify your target before you shoot. Unnecessary weapons' fire attracts attention we're trying to avoid."

They were too close for me to sprint away. Besides, the sparkly wall was down the alley. I eased back, intending to wedge myself between the dumpster and the building, where my attire would camouflage me nicely. I was doing great until I brushed against a loose bag, and it rolled down the heap to crash on the asphalt. Oops.

"What's that?" the one called Griff asked, pointing his wand my way.

"Sammie, take lead," the older officer said. "Watch your tracker. If the talent's running hot, back off. You don't want to get sucked into a new fracture."

Footsteps pattered along the alley, and flashlight beams swung my direction. I crouched among the bags, uncertain whether to raise my hands and come forward. I opted to hunker lower and put a bag on my head.

"Meow," I crooned, doing my best cat imitation.

A flashlight beam passed too close for comfort, and someone waded through the trash, kicking it aside. A clicking sound tapped faster the closer it got to me. I held my breath, my heart pounding like a demented drummer in a heavy metal band. I had my back to the wall and no place to go. My pursuer reached the dumpster and stopped not three feet away.

"It's okay," Sammie's soft female voice assured. "We've come to take you home. You'll be safe now."

Home? How would she manage that when I didn't have one? But her voice: so kind, so caring. No one had spoken to me that way before. No one had made me safe—not even Jimmy—through all the years. Something inside me ached.

"Whoever it is can't understand you, Sammie. They're crazy, remember? Just stun 'em and get the cuffs on so we can get out of here," Griff grumbled. "Wish we'd worn our slickers."

"We're looking for a lost human being, one who deserves respect and dignified treatment, not some feral animal," she replied.

"Get your minds on the mission, or you'll both be on report," the sergeant ordered. "Can you see the talent? Is it male or female?"

"Can't tell," she said. "Seems to be buried in the trash."

Sammie stood in the dim pool of illumination from Soo Ling's light and swept her left arm in front of her. Dark hair pulled back into a short ponytail accentuated her oval face. Thin brows angled down in concentration over exotic Asian eyes, a cute button nose, and a narrow, pouty mouth. All she lacked were pointy ears to make her an elfin princess.

The clicking came from a black lump on her wrist. Her arm pointed my direction, and the clicking grew louder and faster. The young cop moved to back her up.

"Come on out," she soothed. "I won't hurt you." She took a step forward.

A deafening boom ripped from the east end of the alley, blasting her sideways against the metal container with a sickening thud. She slumped on the bags in front of me.

Three cloaked men looking like Harry Potter wannabes strode out of the darkness down by the sparkly wall. I could see only half their faces under their hoods. Banana-shaped... *somethings* in their hands pointed at the cops. *There must be a Halloween party in the neighborhood,* I thought. *Or maybe it's a full moon and all the crazies are out.*

One of them extended his banana gun, and a second boom followed the first. The young male cop flew backward and slammed down on the pavement. My blood turned to ice. Voices shouted, and streaks of electricity arced from the third cop's wand toward the new arrivals. The new guys continued their forward march unfazed, long black robes swaying with their steps.

"Retreat!" ordered a parrot voice, complete with clicks and whistles. It came from the cruiser at the end of the alley.

Feet ran toward the patrol car, followed by another ear-splitting boom. Blinding light flashed, and the black robes stopped. One of them chuckled.

"Enough," said another, walking toward the cop who now lay deathly still in the middle of the alley. "Take the DC's tracker and find the talent. He's still here, or the collection team would have been gone already."

The chuckler waded into the garbage. When he reached Sammie, he knelt beside her and unstrapped the black lump from her wrist. It was too big for a watch—more the size of a cell phone. He extended it in my direction, and the clicking became a blur of static, like a Geiger counter.

"Found him," he called to his compatriot. "This DC's still alive."

"Finish her and get the talent back to the fracture," the first black robe replied.

Finish? As in *kill?* Where the hell was her sergeant? What about the officer with the dog at the patrol car? Why weren't they helping their fallen comrade? Fear squeezed my chest. I couldn't let this happen and live with myself, but I was unarmed and useless in a fight. She seemed so nice, so caring. He pointed his sonic banana gun at her. As I tensed to spring, the third black robe screamed.

The demon towered behind the third black robe, his nostrils billowing smoke and his talons planted deep in the man's head. He extracted his claws and licked globs of shiny white goo from them while the man stood paralyzed. My stomach flip-flopped, and I shrank lower.

The demon bent close and whispered in his victim's ear. His victim fired his weapon, and the chuckler's head ripped through the back of his hood, splattering blood, brains, and scraps of fabric on the wall above me. The edge of the shock wave blew my garbage bag hat off, and my ears ached from the sound.

The first black robe fired at the demon and his prey, and the poor guy burst like an overripe watermelon dropped from a great height. The demon roared, uninjured, his heavy bull nose wrinkling to bare pointy un-cow-like teeth.

This couldn't be real. I might see gargoyles, but I knew they didn't exist. Neither did eight-foot demons or banana guns that shot killer sonic waves. The demon took a step toward me, his eyes intent on the female officer.

The back door of the Chinese restaurant opened, and a wizened old Asian man shuffled through, garbage in hand. He saw the chuckler's body and stopped. Then he looked at the remaining black robe and dropped his bag, oblivious to the demon clopping toward us. So Black Robe at least was real. I'd sort out the demon later.

I rose from the garbage, scooped the cop onto my shoulder, and pushed through the open door. Thank goodness she was small, probably not more than ninety-five pounds soaking wet, which she was. The old man grabbed my arm and tried to toss me out, but I shrugged him off.

"Muggers!" I screamed. "Gang fight! Lock the friggin' door!"

As I charged through the kitchen, I heard the door slam behind me. I plunged into the main seating area, thinly sprinkled with staring, open-mouthed customers. Downtown Centralia—if that's where I was— didn't have a lot of nightlife. They'd probably get charged extra for my entertainment value. A boom echoed from the kitchen as I reached the front entrance, followed by the crash of the back door hitting something. I hoped the old guy had gotten clear.

I snatched a trench coat from the rack by the door, exited, and made a right, half jogging, half staggering past the restaurant windows with Sammie on my shoulder. Amazing how a good jolt of adrenaline could increase strength. Another boom and the window glass exploded, spraying me. My bare feet slid on the sleet-coated sidewalk. My legs burned, and my back bowed lower with every step. I gulped air and stumbled faster toward the end of the block, but I knew it wouldn't be fast enough, not carrying the cop. I couldn't leave her. Black Robe wanted her dead.

Storefronts dropped away, replaced by a corner parking lot with an attendant kiosk standing by the far exit. I race-walked across the lot to the kiosk. To my relief, the little building was unlocked. I plunked her on the floor as gently as I could, dragged on the too-big trench coat, and stepped out, closing the door. A city bus rolled past on the cross street and pulled over at the corner to pick up a passenger. I ran like hell for the bus stop.

Black Robe arrived at the parking lot in time to see me leap onto the bus. His banana gun fired, the side of the bus near the front dented in, and half the windows burst. The driver stared, first at the windows, and then at me.

"Mugger!" I shouted. "Drive!"

The bus lurched forward, dumping me on the floor. I looked up into the face of a thirty-something businessman sitting behind the driver, and fear looked back. His bloodless face matched the white dress shirt under his business suit. He clutched a fat blue gym bag to his stomach and glanced over his shoulder where wind whistled in the broken windows.

Someone huddled on the floor between the seats about halfway down, and a striking blonde woman hunkered in a seat near the back. She wore a waitress uniform, and despite the glass speckling her clothes and hair, peered down the aisle at me with such confidence and intensity that it scared me. *Lunatic*, I thought. *Thrill seeker*. She probably gawked at road wrecks.

"Stay down!" I yelled, scrambling to my feet to look out the back. Black Robe pounded past the kiosk without glancing at it. I squatted beside the driver, thrilled with my brilliant planning. Crazy didn't mean stupid.

The engine roared for a block, and then the driver backed off as he approached a red light.

"Keep going!" I shouted. "Go, go!"

Another boom took out the back window and the bus driver's head. Gore splattered the windshield. The driver's headless body slumped onto the steering wheel. The bus wobbled along the street. I swore. What a fool I'd been to gloat over my cleverness.

I hauled the dead driver's torso back with one hand and spun the steering wheel with the other, my knuckles white on the wheel. I kicked his foot from the accelerator and pressed down with my own. We flew around a corner too fast, clipped a parked car with a screech of metal, and zig-zagged on down the street. As we crossed our second intersection, a car t-boned us. The bus spun like a ballerina on the icy street until it crashed into the front window of a carpet shop.

My shoulder smashed against the windshield. I looked around, trying to get my bearings. The businessman had thumped his forehead against the driver's seat and appeared dazed. He'd dropped the gym bag beside his shiny dress shoes. A gym bag meant workout clothes, and no one wore dress shoes in a gym, did they? We'd only gained a block or two on Black Robe. If I was going to lead him away from the cop lady, I needed shoes. My feet ached from the cold.

I slammed the door control open and snatched the gym bag. The damn thing was heavier than I expected. I didn't have time to worry about it. Sirens wailed in the distance, and running down the center of the street barely a block and a half behind came Black Robe. No time to dig out shoes.

I vaulted from the bus and sprinted along the sidewalk, trying to keep parked cars between Black Robe and me until I could get around a corner. Black Robe's gun thundered once, rocking me with a near miss and setting off a cacophony of car alarms. I hurtled south at the next cross street, my shoulder blades crawling in expectation of another shot.

I headed though a business district toward a seedy residential neighborhood where I could give my pursuer the slip once I'd led him far, far from the police woman. She'd be safe. I'd be a hero. I smiled, regaining my confidence. Then I remembered the dead bus driver. My fault. My hands clenched on the handle of my stolen bag, and I ran faster.

Turning another corner, I pulled up under a street lamp and peeked back. Black Robe labored on at a dog trot, tiring badly. My feet were killing me. I needed shoes, and now I had time to put them on. I dropped the gym bag on the sidewalk and unzipped it.

No shoes.

Just stacks and stacks of money.

2

God hated me. He didn't talk to me, but I got the message. The bag held enough money to buy every pair of trainers in the city—if only shoe shops were open all night. And somewhere out there, a man wanted his cash back, probably a man with a lousy sense of humor who didn't want to hear about a homeless guy desperate for footwear.

Who carried a million bucks in a gym bag? Some rich lawyer paying a ransom for his kidnapped child? A politician buying off a blackmailer? Maybe a crime lord's minion on his way to a drug purchase? An environmentally minded minion with an eye on the bottom line, one who rode public transport? *Yeah, right.*

I considered leaving the bag right there on the sidewalk. But the bagman had seen me, and I wasn't leaving town until I checked on the lady cop. If he caught me, I'd be in marginally less hot water if I could return the money. Maybe he'd only break my arms and legs.

This wasn't the neighborhood to flash cash. Every shabby shadowed doorway suddenly seemed like a hiding place for muggers and thugs; every darkened parked car filled with watchers waiting for me to trot past so they could whip out and whisk away the bag. I shivered, and not from the cold wind soughing down the pavement.

The sound of running feet came to me over the distant wail of police sirens, ambulances, and fire trucks. *Shit, Black Robe.* I bolted down the middle of the street where I had more hope of avoiding broken glass and spotting lurkers. I needed to stay far enough ahead of my pursuer that he couldn't pop me with his sonic banana gun, but not so far ahead that he gave up the chase. The farther he followed me, the safer the cute lady officer in the kiosk would be. I worried about her. She'd hit that dumpster hard. What if she needed medical attention? What if she died because no one found her? I had to protect her from Black Robe first, and then I could think about helping her.

The sleet turned to rain. I ran on past increasingly decrepit businesses and a flea-bag hotel. A couple of prostitutes huddled in the doorway, seeking refuge from the miserable weather. At least *I* was suitably attired in the latest waterproof fashion. Black Robe followed, but he'd stopped shooting. I hoped he was out of ammo.

My garbage bag outfit became a sauna, but my toes were numb from the slush melting on the street. The gym bag got heavier by the minute, and the dark sky seemed to hunker down on the streetlights. The city must be having an air quality alert. Not-quite smoke mixed with not-quite fog and wafted over the rooftops. Or maybe I was hallucinating the amorphous black clouds the same as I glimpsed the occasional gargoyle hidden behind a fire hydrant or disappearing into a doorway.

I was pretty sure I wasn't hallucinating the guy slumped on the pavement under an awning, laughing maniacally to himself. Or the half-dressed couple having slow-motion sex on a car hood despite the cold and wet. Their heads turned to watch me pass, but their eyes had a glazed, unfocused look. I didn't remember Centralia having quite such a drug problem. I drew the trench coat tighter to ward off the strangeness.

I wanted some decent clothes and a dry place to sleep for the night so the hallucinations would abate. Then maybe I could think straight about what I'd seen in the alley. But I also wanted to check on the lady cop. Who was she? Why were they all looking for me? I wasn't getting what I wanted until I ditched my shadow a safe distance from city center. Just my luck to be chased by a bad guy so out of shape I had to work to not lose him.

We slow-trotted south out of the business district through a neighborhood of ancient hovels with unkempt yards decorated by junked-out autos, broken appliances, and knee-high weeds. A red sports car roared by and pulled to the curb at a ruined house in the next block. The car horn sounded, and a teenage boy loped out to do business with the driver while two hoodlums lounged on the porch, watching. Their transaction complete, the car sped away, and the boy darted into the house again. I'd found the local crack house and veered away to avoid contact with any lookouts.

After another half mile, I sprinted ahead and into an alley. Halfway down, I ducked into the shadow of a leaning garage and looked back the way I'd come. I scrubbed at my scalp where the ants still danced. If I didn't get a hat soon, I'd go psycho. Well, more psycho.

Black Robe wobbled past the alley without stopping, gasping like a guy headed for a coronary. I waited, holding my breath. In a moment, he was back, swiveling one way and another. He looked down at something in his hands, and I could hear the faint slow tick, the same tick I'd heard coming from the police woman. *What the hell?* They had some kind of crazy homeless man detector? My heart rate went into overdrive.

Risking life, limbs, and the soles of my feet, I cut through a back yard and out to the street. If Black Robe could find me half a block away, I had some serious running to do to lose him permanently. I'd been chased by the best: skinheads seeking sport, an angel dust addict armed with an ax, and cops cruising for emotional release through therapeutic beatings of bums. Nobody caught me. Ever.

I continued south and east through the blighted houses for a mile or more before turning north, still running hard and looking back every few minutes. Black Robe had to be far behind. He'd be searching the slums for me for hours.

I found a ramshackle house, door and windows boarded up, and roof losing shingles. A detached single-car garage stood at the back of the property, nearly swallowed by weeds, alone and forlorn in the dark and rain.

The garage door stood ajar. I slipped inside, glad to be out of the weather and standing on a dry floor, even if it was dirt. The neighbor's back porch light shone through a cracked window. I caught a snatch of *Singing in the Rain*. Great. A halogen with incandescent wit.

I crouched on the floor and rocked. Should I call the cops? In my experience, they were more interested in closing cases to make their numbers look good than in catching the guilty party. As someone with a mental illness, I'd be a prime candidate to take the blame for the deaths in the alley. I could see the headline: Schizophrenic flips out, kills three. At least I had witnesses to what happened to the bus driver.

Then there was the problem of the money. If the bagman had a legitimate reason for carrying all that cash, he'd report me, and I'd be guilty as charged. They'd put me away forever. If it was dirty money, the moment I came forward, the owner would know who I was and where to find me. For my own safety, I needed to avoid the police and get out of town.

Most troubling, what the hell did Black Robe and the lady cop want? Had I done something bad—something criminal—while I'd been in the throes of the psychotic break? I wished I could remember. That didn't explain why two groups seemed to be willing to fight to the death over possession of me, or why the first group didn't want the local police to know they were there. Had I stolen a top-secret rocket formula? Overheard a powerful politician plotting a hit?

I had no answers, but the lady cop waiting in the kiosk did. Dare I approach her? If she didn't know whether I was male or female, would she recognize me? What did she know about me? Could she tell me who I was, or why my family abandoned me? No, I didn't care about my past anymore. I'd left it behind fifteen years ago, and I wouldn't look back. I pushed away a haunting longing and scrubbed at my scalp where the ants still partied.

I didn't know how bad the lady cop was injured. If no one found her and she died, her death would be on my hands. I couldn't bear that. Maybe the guys with her were jerks, but she'd seemed so kind. Bad enough her team left her behind; I wouldn't do the same. I had to check on her, get her medical help if she needed it. Get her to tell me what she knew before I headed south.

By standing on a workbench nailed to the garage wall, I could just reach some sheets of plywood stored overhead on the ceiling joists. I pulled a wad of bills from a stack and wrestled the gym bag and its remaining booty onto the plywood, out of sight.

Without the bag, I jetted toward the business district, stopping once to stare at a hulking, burned-out manufacturing plant that marked the edge of the residential area. Built at the turn of the century as a foundry, the high-ceilinged interior was crisscrossed with huge beams used to support suspended trolleys and conveyor belts. Then it got converted to a pie factory. But when had it burned? I always had memory problems after a break. Names changed, buildings moved. It rattled me. What else had I forgotten?

The Salvation Army Thrift Store was exactly where it should be and intact. Relief swelled in me. It wasn't open in the middle of the night, but I'd shopped its discards before. I scoped out the place, then jogged across the parking lot to two enormous dumpsters.

One of the dumpsters contained a lot of broken junk 'donated' by cheapskates who didn't want to pay tipping fees at the dump. The other was packed with clothing donations too badly worn out to sell. I climbed in. Five minutes of scrounging and I wore jeans torn out in the knees and frayed at the hems, a faded gray t-shirt with a rip in the right armpit, and a red, threadbare hooded sweatshirt with holes in the elbows. Delightful.

I dug nearly to the bottom before I came across some cheap tennis shoes a size too big. I ripped up my garbage bag skirt and stuffed wads of plastic in the toes, and then I used the leftover cinch tie as a belt. I prided myself on my recycling. A grungy brown backpack with the front pocket torn off caught my eye, and I snatched it.

I emerged from the dumpster feeling human again. After checking to be sure no one watched, I pulled out my roll of bills and looked at it under the parking lot lights. Great. Nothing but hundreds. Those wouldn't attract *any* attention coming from a guy dressed in rags. I stuffed a few under the insole of each shoe, in my sweatshirt and jeans pockets, and in the backpack. I took that old adage about eggs and baskets seriously. I tossed the bloodstained trench coat in the dumpster.

My next stop was the Night Owl Pharmacy, a place ready to service the suddenly sick or those who remembered an anniversary in the middle of the night. I guess they didn't worry about getting robbed despite their late business hours.

The clerk, a fat guy going prematurely bald, gave me the evil eye while I browsed. I picked up a bottle of water, aspirin for my still-throbbing head, two pairs of socks, and a cheap plastic rain poncho in a little snap pouch. Then I splurged on two granola bars. Oh, the decadence!

In the personal care aisle, I snatched a hairbrush, toothbrush, and little travel tube of toothpaste. No shaving tackle required—I'd never grown hair on my face, a blessing when I wanted to pass for a kid, and a curse when I needed a disguise. I plucked a black watch cap off a display near the registers, dumped the whole mess on the counter, and waited while the clerk rang it up. The four rows of fluorescent lights hummed a funeral dirge.

When I handed the clerk a hundred, his eyes popped open despite the late hour. He crinkled the bill, held it up to the light, checked it against something under the counter, and stared at me.

"Last of my disability check," I said.

"I can't change something this big this time of night," he replied, but he didn't hand the bill back.

"Oh." I gazed around the store, wandered the aisles, and returned with two space blankets over-priced at nearly seven bucks each.

The clerk added them to my purchase, frowned at the total, and shook his head. "Nope, still can't do it."

The ants formed a conga line on my head and danced happily across my scalp. I knew for an absolute fact that if I didn't get socks—two pairs—on soon, my feet would develop some horrible fungal rot and disintegrate. I wasn't good with confrontation.

"How about if you keep a ten spot for a tip?" I said, thinking he could use it to buy Rogaine and turn his love life around. If only mine were that easily fixed.

He leered at me, punched open the register, and proffered my change.

When he'd swept all my stuff into bags, he said, "Big wreck couple blocks west. Somebody grabbed a bus. Lots of cops crawling the streets looking for the hijacker. They say he's some punk kid high on drugs. He killed the driver."

Wanted for murder. How could that be? I wasn't the one shooting up the neighborhood. I guess the passengers on the bus hadn't set the cops straight about what happened. I was so distraught I wandered two blocks east before remembering that I needed to put on the watch cap and socks. I stepped into the doorway of a tattoo parlor with garish dragons painted on the window and donned the new apparel.

I hadn't killed the driver, but as someone with a mental illness, I'd be an easy target for the blame. Who'd believe me when I said a creep in wizard robes murdered the poor guy? *Geez, I hope the driver doesn't have a family waiting at home.* Energy drained away from me like water down a sewer pipe. I needed to get out of town, but I stood frozen on the sidewalk.

Keep moving, River. They can't get you if you just keep running. But what about the lady cop? She could be dying in that kiosk, and that was a death I could prevent. I should find a pay phone, dial 9-1-1, and send an ambulance. Then I should leave before the cops caught me. Or the owner of all that cash. Or Black Robe. Yeah, that would work. My feet remained glued to the concrete.

I dug out the aspirin and washed two tablets down with a swig from the water bottle, adjusted my cap, fussed with the poncho, and rocked back and forth, back and forth. By now, the lady cop's team should have come back for her. But would they? They were untrustworthy; they'd abandoned her without a fight. No one deserved to be abandoned by those they relied on.

I should call the police. But her sergeant said they didn't want the police involved. Maybe they were on some covert mission, and I'd blow it if I turned her in. What would the mission matter if she died? What were they looking for in the alley? Why did they have a device that reacted to my presence? I was no one special. I had to know.

Drawing a deep breath, I plotted a course that would take me to First Avenue, a few blocks east from where I'd wrecked the bus. My feet moved slowly, and then they accelerated into a steady run that didn't stop until I reached my destination. I peeked around the corner and saw controlled pandemonium.

Yards and yards of yellow tape fluttered in the breeze, as though some gigantic mad spider had woven a web around the buildings, the cars, and the bus. Blue lights rotated on top of cop cruisers that blocked both ends of the street, preventing any hapless drivers from wandering into the spider's trap. Racks of portable lights shone on and inside the bus, where forensic cops gathered evidence. A hulking great tow truck waited with its own flashing red turret, prepared to haul away the dead carcass of the bus.

Even being three blocks away from all those cops sent an electric shock up my spine. I couldn't outrun a bullet. I put my head down and crossed the street heading north. I also kept my eyes peeled for Black Robe. I didn't know what range he had on his little device, and I didn't want to find out the hard way.

Two minutes of steady walking, and I'd looped around to approach the parking lot from the north side, away from all the activity around the bus. I stepped into the shadow under a coffee shop awning and looked south. The cruiser idled up by First, but nothing stirred near the corner lot where I'd stashed the officer.

On cat's feet, I slipped up the street. My blood pounded in my ears, and the rain poncho made so much rustling I thought they could hear it in New York. I stopped to remove it.

A dark shape lurched out of the alley, and I jumped away, slamming into a parking meter, heart racing. A bleary-eyed drunk stared at me, saluted with a bottle wrapped in a paper bag, and meandered away, oblivious to the drizzle and the evening's excitement. When my heart stopped hammering, I eased up to the corner.

A police van sat in front of Soo Ling's. Lights still shone inside the restaurant, and more yellow tape decorated the storefront. A crime tech dressed in blue overalls came out to the van, deposited a big case, and went back in.

Were they packing up? Should I wait until they left? If they saw me running across the intersection, they'd be on me like wasps on a soda can. I wasn't sure I had the courage for it. My hands shook; my knees knocked. The risk might be for nothing. The lady cop might have recovered and left. Or she might have been discovered and taken away. Her team might have returned with reinforcements and found her. I'd been gone an hour at least. Heck, she might be dead, and I didn't want to explain yet another body.

My brain screamed at me to run away. Running served me well. It kept me safe and distant from harm, from caring, from loss. But my feet were deaf and marched across the intersection. I didn't breathe the whole way. I slid through the kiosk door and closed it behind me, then ducked to the floor.

The cop lay curled in the shadows, a fairy-tale sleeping beauty. Her chest rose and fell in a quiet rhythm, giving me hope for her health, but it would do the same if she were in a coma. She shivered every minute or so. The kiosk wasn't warm, and she'd been soaked through when I dumped her there. I didn't know what to do. I stared and rocked.

After five minutes, she shifted position a little and mumbled something. I brightened. I'd roomed with a few coma patients in the mental ward, and none of them ever moved like she had. Maybe she didn't need a trip to emergency. Maybe she'd wake up and tell me what was going on. Or maybe she'd grab me and call the cops. At least she'd lost her wand in the alley.

I'd stay for an hour to make sure she was okay, but then I'd go. I was too tired to head out now, fatigued from the psychotic episode and all the running in the cold. And the cops were still out there; they might spot me if I left the kiosk. But Black Robe could return, or her team, and I didn't want to be around for that. One hour, no more, and I'd go, whether she'd woken up or not.

I covered her with a space blanket and the poncho. She stirred and rubbed her cheek where the blanket grazed it, but she didn't open her eyes. Her long dark eyelashes lay against her skin like ostrich feathers on beige silk. The sight of her made my stomach tighten. So beautiful. I wished I had pencil and paper to draw her.

I wrapped the other blanket around myself and wedged into the corner, keeping my distance from her, and started to count off the minutes. My eyelids felt like steel shutters determined to lock down for the night. I'd close them just for a minute... or maybe two...

3

I cowered at the hooves of the eight-foot tall demon, wallowing in the soot and debris of the apocalyptic cityscape. He frowned at me, and his mouth formed words, but I couldn't understand him. Hoards of translucent black cloud nightmares rose and fell through cracks in the scarred ground, widening the fissures with each pass. They roiled around us, cutting off light coming from a source that I couldn't identify. I opened my mouth to scream, and one of the nightmare clouds poured in, clogging my throat, filling my lungs with ash, and shooting burning cinders up through my brain. I thrashed, trying to get to my feet so I could run, but I no longer had legs.

I jerked awake, thoroughly tangled in the space blanket, my legs numb, and looked into a pair of amber eyes that stared back at me along the blade of a big, scary military-type knife pointed at my throat. I swallowed hard. Boy, had I screwed up.

"Hi," I said.

She didn't blink. My God, she was beautiful in the pre-dawn light glowing through the windows. No human looked that perfect. Was she real? I freed my right hand and ever so slowly raised my index finger to the tip of the blade while she watched. When I pressed lightly against the point, it pricked my skin. I pulled my hand back. Blood welled from the tiny cut. Yep, real. *Shit*. She'd taken me prisoner.

"We're surrounded by cops," I said. "If you stick me, I'll scream like a girl."

Ah, crap, why'd I used *that* expression? She probably screamed like an Amazon warrior. How'd she even lift a knife that big? She was such a tiny thing. All the cops I'd met were big louts. But she had the drop on me, and the knife was a lot more threatening than her wand thingy.

"Who are you? Where are we? How'd I get here?" she asked. The taut muscles around her eyes telegraphed fear, and the knife trembled in her hand.

I rubbed my prickling wrist tattoos against my jeans and caught a whiff of something burnt. I glanced around the kiosk. Up near the ceiling, a trace of shapeless sooty cloud leaked out through the crack around the door. My mouth opened, closed.

"Do you smoke?" I asked, hoping she'd tell me she did. The cloud could have been cigarette smoke even if it didn't smell like tobacco... purposeful cigarette smoke, on the dark side. A hallucination. *Not real.*

A frown joined her stare. Oops. I'd wandered off topic. What had she asked? *Who are you?* But her team had that tracking device that reacted to me. How could she be looking for me but not recognize me?

"I brought you here so they wouldn't shoot you. I had to hide you while I led him away." I gave her a tentative smile and waited for her to gush her thanks for saving her life. Maybe she'd be so grateful, she'd tell me about the tracking device—and point that big knife some other direction. Then I could get away before she figured out who I was.

She added narrowed eyes to the stare and the frown. I chewed my lower lip. Maybe I wasn't communicating as well as I'd hoped. I felt woefully inadequate talking to someone as lovely as her, especially someone carrying a dangerous weapon. It could have been worse—at least I hadn't degenerated into word salad or spoken in rhymes.

"Let's start with your name," she said, enunciating each word.

"River," I replied. "River Madden."

"River," she repeated. "That's an interesting name. Were you named after River Phoenix, the actor?"

Heat crawled up my face. "Um... no."

"How old are you, River?"

"Sixteen," I lied automatically. I was always sixteen. Sixteen was old enough to be on the streets without supervision, and young enough that if they locked you up, you went to juvie instead of real jail.

"My name's Sammie. Can you tell me how we met, River?"

Her questions were now moronically simple, and I resented her implication that I was somehow mentally deficient. Crazy, not stupid.

"I found you unconscious in the alley." I gestured toward the alley behind the parking lot. "Some... gang bangers were getting ready to kill you. I interrupted them."

"How did I end up unconscious?"

What could I tell her? The bad guy missed his shot, or I wouldn't be talking to her now. She'd never believe sonic banana guns. Making up stories on the fly wasn't my strong suit. Hell, describing reality wasn't my strong suit, either. I never told anyone about the schizophrenia. Better to keep interactions with others brief and pass for normal. Why had I thought talking to her was a good idea? A trickle of sweat crept from my armpits down my ribs.

"I don't know. You were on the ground when I found you."

"What about the people I was with?"

"What people?" I felt guilty for not telling her the whole story. She'd worry about her buddies. That's what friends did. I didn't have any, but I knew that's how it worked. She must have friends, lots and lots of friends.

"You didn't see anyone with me?"

"Just the gang bangers." I bumped my back against the wall of the kiosk and wondered when I'd started to rock. I balled my hands into fists and forced myself to stop.

"And how do you know they were getting ready to kill me?"

"Because the gang leader said to take your... um... watch, and then to finish you." Exasperation edged my voice. How stupid did she think I was?

Her mouth opened in surprise, and then she looked to her left wrist. Panic flared behind her amber eyes, just for a moment, to be replaced with steely resolve.

"You didn't see anyone else in the alley?"

I shook my head. How was I going to ask about her device? How did they use it to track me? It had to be something internal. I'd arrived in the alley in my birthday suit. Did I have some kind of implant? Geez, I was starting to think like one of those alien abduction weirdos.

"You're sure you didn't see anyone?" she asked again. "You didn't see someone who maybe acted crazy, kind of gibbering and drooling? Someone who wasn't wearing clothes?"

Someone who wasn't wearing clothes. It's possible I gibbered and drooled before I came to my senses. I didn't know anyone in that alley last night. How did they know me? But if they knew me, why didn't she recognize me now? It all made my still-throbbing head hurt a little more. She started to get suspicious because I'd been so slow to answer. I screwed up my face in disgust.

"You mean like a flasher? A pervert? Is that why you were there? To arrest them?" I went on the attack. "Are you a cop? Because you don't have any insignias on your uniform, and you haven't shown me your badge."

She'd pegged me for a retard and scrambled to answer. "I work for the government in an agency you haven't heard of. We're entrusted with the security of the nation. I can't tell you about the mission we were on."

I'd read somewhere that the most successful relationships were between equals. If that was true, Sammie and I were destined for bliss; we were equally wretched liars.

"Perverts are a national security risk?" I pressed. "Since when?"

"Don't you have to go to school or something?" she asked, replacing the knife in a leg sheath.

"Curriculum day," I snapped, determined to make her tell me what she and her team were doing in the alley, especially now that she'd put away the knife.

"This is Wednesday. Aren't those usually on Fridays?" She pushed the blanket and poncho to one side.

No one in the world gave a rat's ass about me. No one even knew I existed. And yet two groups had been after me in that alley last night, and at least one of them was willing to kill to get me. What did they want? I was just a homeless wacko. No super powers or anything.

Maybe I should tell her who I really was. She'd seemed nice, talking in that sweet voice when she searched for me. No, scratch that. Her sergeant said to stun me. Whatever they wanted, they didn't expect me to cooperate. I burned to know more, but I didn't want her team to catch me. Or Black Robe. Or the bagman from the bus. I'd certainly become a popular guy.

Sammie rose enough to peek through the windows, verifying that she didn't want to be seen by the cops. Satisfied, she straightened and reached for the door. I scrambled up beside her, blocking the exit.

"Wait, you can't go. There's a guy trying to kill you. I should go with you." At her dubious look, I added, "For protection."

She gave me a reassuring smile, and for a moment, I thought she intended to pat my head. "Don't worry about me, River. I'm a trained agent. I can handle myself. But if this is a dangerous neighborhood, you should go home. I'm sure your parents are worried about you."

She brushed past me but stopped just outside the door.

"Is there a hardware store nearby?"

A hardware store? Did she plan to whip up a suit of armor or some new secret weapon? Maybe replace her magic wand? *Or put together a new device to track me?* That thought made me uneasy. But why wasn't she rushing to rejoin her team? Why weren't they here looking for her? What kind of buddies were they that they left a fallen comrade behind?

"I could show you," I offered. If we stayed together longer, she might let something slip.

"Directions will do," she replied.

I ground my teeth and pointed. "Four blocks west to Lincoln, then turn south up the hill. There's a hardware store on the corner of Fifteenth. But it won't open until nine."

"Thanks." She waved and walked away up the street.

I rocked. If she didn't know where the hardware store was, she probably wasn't meeting her team there. I'd be no more likely to encounter Black Robe, the bagman, or the police on the way to the store than anywhere else. Maybe if I followed her, I could learn something. If that didn't pan out, I'd leave town.

I hustled to stuff the blankets and poncho into the backpack. I couldn't tail her. She'd see me, especially this early with so little traffic out. Rush hour wouldn't start for at least another half hour. I didn't know whether police still lingered around the bus crash site or Soo Ling's. I'd have to head north again, cross over to the west, and leg it up the hill on Monroe, parallel to her path up Lincoln. If I hurried, I could beat her there.

###

I lounged against a tree in a yard half a block down the street from the hardware store, wondering whether she'd deliberately thrown me off her track by asking for the directions. I'd run like the wind an extra six blocks just to get into position before she arrived, and now she hadn't shown up. How slow did government agents walk? She must get paid by the hour.

The hardware store occupied the left half of a long, narrow building set down with its parking lot smack in the middle of a nice, older residential neighborhood on busy Lincoln Street, a main arterial leading from the posh South Hill down to city center.

The right half of the building housed a Starbucks, and they did a brisk business on this chilly, misty Fall morning. I had enough walking-around money to get one of their over-priced hot chocolates while I waited for Sammie to show up, but I didn't want her to spot me, so I blended in with the drippy maple tree and pretended I was a yard gnome. Everybody knows that gnomes don't drink hot chocolate.

I peered up through the tree branches trying to figure out why the morning light didn't seem right. The wind and rain should have washed the pollution from the air, but the sky seemed grimy, like an LA thermal inversion, which we didn't typically see here in Kansas.

The hardware store turned on its open sign, and still no Sammie. I'd been a fool not to follow her. How would I find her again? With its population of a hundred thousand, Centralia wasn't small. She could be anywhere. I glanced around, keeping an eye out for Black Robe. And the bagman from the bus.

Maybe she'd met up with her team. Yeah, that made more sense than trekking off to a hardware store at the crack of dawn. Why hadn't I thought of that sooner? A couple hours' sleep in the kiosk wasn't doing much for my brain. I should just head out and stop worrying about why everyone wanted me. If they couldn't find me, they couldn't make me do anything I didn't want to.

I'd pushed away from the tree with every intention of leaving town when I spotted her. She limped a bit, like she ached all over. Her hair looked a fright, and her once-crisp uniform sported wrinkles and creases.

I mentally kicked myself for sending her on such an uphill climb. I'd forgotten her crash against the steel dumpster. I should have thought of someplace easier to get to. At least she was still alone.

She hobbled into the hardware store, and I jogged closer. A quick fish in the garbage bin outside the Starbucks and I had a discarded cup. I leaned my shoulder against the edge of the hardware store window and looked inside while I pretended to enjoy my coffee. I didn't want her to see me and think I was some kind of demented stalker. Well, okay, maybe I was a demented stalker, but I had a good reason.

She headed toward the back. When she'd disappeared between the rows, the gray-haired lady manning the register snapped her fingers to get the attention of a younger clerk stocking a display of Halloween lights, and then she jerked her head in the direction Sammie had gone. Uh-oh. They'd decided she was a shoplifter. Were they in for a surprise. She'd probably dazzle them with a fancy platinum credit card issued to Uncle Sam.

A van pulled up in front. On the side, a starving wolf with big teeth crouched under the words *Snappy Plumbing.* A guy in work clothes hopped out and hustled into the store. Sammie wandered into view. She picked up and replaced one item after another in just about every department as she worked her way closer to the door. When the plumber walked up to the cash register with a couple lengths of pipe, she made her move to leave, a can of something and a small brush in her hand.

I'd never seen a more blatant shoplift so badly done. Maybe her agency didn't train her how to steal. And why was a government agent shoplifting in the first place? Wasn't she supposed to be upholding the law? Had she lied about working for the government? That would explain her sergeant's desire to avoid police attention.

The young stock clerk had her by the elbow as she pulled the door open. He dragged her back, his face promising trouble. The old lady looked up from her transaction with the plumber and scowled. *Crap.* If the cops picked her up, I had no chance to find out what she wanted with me. I had to do something. I ditched the cup and charged for the door.

"—is a criminal offense, and we prosecute to the full extent of the law," the young clerk lectured. He clutched the can and brush in one hand while he gripped her arm with the other.

"Hey, sweetie," I sang as I sailed up and snatched the can from his hand. "Is this it?"

Sammie and the clerk both stared at me open-mouthed. I rolled the can around to read the label. White paint. She'd shoplifted white paint. *What the hell?*

"You know, I don't think this is the right shade. Needs to be more eggshell. Doesn't it?" I glanced out the window to the parking lot and saw a soccer mom walking away from a white SUV. I turned to the clerk. "Here, you look."

I dragged the clerk out the door, which I propped open while I held the can up pretending to compare the dab of white on the label to the car on the far side of the lot.

"What do you think?" I asked. "Does it match? We've got a heck of a scratch. I'm not paying a body shop hundreds to fix it. Not when I can buy a can of paint for—" I checked the label "—three ninety-five. But the last can wasn't the right shade. I want to be sure this one matches. No looking at the label under those store lights, I told Sammie. They always change the color. We gotta see the label in real daylight. So what do you think?"

The clerk looked at me like I'd escaped from the loony bin, and he wasn't far wrong. Sammie looked terrified. We needed to be out of there before the soccer mom returned with her latte and my scam blew up in my face.

"All right," I said, not waiting for his reply. "I think this one's a match. Here's a twenty. We're running late. You keep the change."

I swapped the bill for the brush the clerk still held, grabbed Sammie around the shoulders, and waltzed away trembling all over. I expected a hand on my collar at any moment.

I steered us to the far side of the SUV where I gesticulated at the imaginary scratch until the clerk stepped back inside. Then I dragged Sammie down the hill as fast as she could manage.

"I would have loaned you money for paint," I said. "All you had to do was ask."

She dissolved into tears.

4

"The stupid manual doesn't cover half this stuff," Sammie wailed. "'Get paint,' it says. How the hell do I get paint with no money?"

She sniffled and wiped the heels of her hands over her tear-filled eyes. I walked beside her feeling completely helpless. Never in my life had I dealt with a crying woman, and I had no idea what to do. I couldn't even offer her a tissue because I hadn't thought to buy any. Talk about needing a manual.

"'Don't fraternize with the natives,' it says. Better to just blunder around getting in trouble on your own." Her tone had taken on a sarcastic edge. "'Don't lose your tech,' but they don't cover stolen, do they? No, because that could never happen. My dad will be so pissed when he finds out how I've screwed up."

"You could have been killed. Won't he be glad you're okay?"

She got a thousand-yard stare and went very quiet.

I dug out the aspirin and the water bottle and offered her both. She'd looked so sore coming up the hill, it was the least I could do. She glanced at the aspirin. Then rueful laughter burst from her.

"You didn't tell me you were a doctor," she said, managing the start of a smile. When I looked perplexed, she added, "Take two aspirins and call me in the morning?"

I had no idea what she meant, but at least she wasn't sobbing. "I'm sorry I don't have an unopened water bottle."

"Ah, River, you're the best. Here you are trying to cheer me up and I haven't even thanked you for getting me out of the mess at the store." She popped two aspirins and washed them down with a long pull of water. I did the same. Maybe understanding women wasn't as hard as I'd heard.

We walked down Lincoln to Third Avenue in companionable silence. That seemed safest since I didn't know what had set off her crying in the first place. I offered to buy her breakfast at the IHOP on the corner, and

she agreed. Worried that they wouldn't let us in the door looking like
we did, but concerned that she might be insulted, I handed her the hair
brush so she could tidy up. She accepted the offer graciously, and my
confidence inched up another notch. I was pretty good with women. Now
if she'd just tell me what she was doing in the alley.

The place was nearly empty. A waitress showed us to a booth by the
windows and took our order. Sammie wanted one egg over medium with
a side of toast, and I ordered pancakes and hot chocolate. I'd never eaten
in a sit-down restaurant where someone brought the food, and I hadn't
had pancakes since Easter breakfast at a Gospel Mission five or six years
ago. I wasn't sure about the protocol. Did I need to ask for syrup and
butter? Did I have to pay up front? That's how it worked at McDonalds,
not that I ever ate there.

I dug in my sweatshirt pocket for cash, but the waitress left before I
produced it. I was surprised at her trust, especially considering the way
I was dressed. I wouldn't have served me without seeing the money first.
It must have been my stunning companion that convinced her we were
trustworthy. Sammie looked cool and confident, the savvy government
commando, smiling at me across the table.

"What's the paint for?" I asked, trying to steer the conversation to
her mission in the alley.

The smile faded. "I'm not supposed to tell you."

"Oh, yeah, sorry. I forgot the manual thingy with all the rules," I
said. "How's that working for you?"

Her brow furrowed. "Not so well, now that you mention it." She
looked around for a minute then lowered her voice. "Why were you following me?"

I thought she'd forgotten about my stalking and froze while my
brain scrambled for an answer. "I wasn't following you. I live up that way.
That's how I knew where to find the hardware store. I was just leaving
Starbucks when I saw you. In the store."

Those amber eyes bored into me. "Then why did you walk me back
downtown?"

"Well..." Oh, man, I'd blown it. Sweat dampened my forehead. "You
seemed upset, and I didn't want to abandon you. I figured your agency
probably had offices downtown. In the Federal Building. Or... wherever."

"What were you doing in the alley last night?"

Wow, I wasn't prepared for that, either. I could tell her I was making
a drug buy, or maybe that I was with a hooker. No, too negative. Collecting recyclables? In the middle of the night in the sleet and rain? Too
unbelievable. I began to admire really good liars and wondered how they
did it. Did they rehearse everything in advance? How did they remember
what they'd said? I wiped my brow and rubbed my hand on my jeans.

"I'm the bus boy at Soo Ling's. I found you when I took the garbage out."

She nodded her head, still wrestling with doubts. "I need the paint to leave a message for my team."

In a moment of conversational brilliance, I spluttered, "What?"

She looked flustered, and her eyes slid away. "I need to put a message on the wall in the alley telling my team where to find me."

It occurred to me that perhaps her team and the black robes had all escaped from the same mental hospital together and shared some mass delusion about being spies. That didn't explain how they knew I'd be in the alley, though. Maybe I'd been in the hospital with them and didn't remember?

"Um... no cell phones?" I asked.

Her face reddened. "My... watch was my phone."

"Oh." I fiddled with my silverware and wondered whether the device she'd worn actually told the time at all. "There's a pay phone across the street at the gas station."

She glanced out the window toward the station and stalled by fiddling with her own silverware. Her rosy color deepened. "Not a secure line."

"So why'd they abandon you? I mean, isn't there some credo or something about not leaving anyone behind?"

"That's the military. We're a government agency." She pulled the napkin from under her silverware and smoothed it on her lap. "Besides, if you ran off with me, then it wasn't them abandoning me, was it?"

"But they left before I grabbed you," I replied.

She pounced. "So you *did* see them."

If she ever revealed what I wanted to know, I swore to myself that I would never tell another lie. How did con artists and scammers keep all this stuff straight?

"No, I *didn't* see them," I said. "And that's why I know that it wasn't because of me taking you that *they* didn't take you. I mean, they'd already gone before I came into the alley. Because I didn't see them. Ever."

The waitress rescued me by bringing our food, along with a fancy wire basket that held three syrup pitchers. *Three*. Was it okay to use that much? I settled on having just maple because I didn't think mixing strawberry and blueberry with the maple would taste good. I poured until the syrup threatened to run over the edge of the plate. When I looked up, Sammie had her hand over her mouth, but I could see the laughter in her eyes. She quickly turned her attention to her egg.

Feeling suddenly three years old, I didn't look up again until I'd finished half the pancakes. Behind Sammie in the corner, a huge television displayed a news report, the sound so low I couldn't hear it. Our waitress leaned on the counter, watching the screen.

The wrecked bus flashed up first, followed by a grainy black-and-white picture of me dressed in the trench coat and bin bags mounting the steps of the bus. The three inches of lank wet hair hanging over my face looked so dark I assumed people would think it was brown instead of blond. When they froze the tape, my mouth hung open in a terrified shout, and my eyes looked wide and wild. Even I'd be afraid of me looking like that. 'Bus killing suspect' blazed across the bottom of the screen along with a phone number for tips. The picture must have come from a security camera on the bus. *Damn.*

"Are you all right?" Sammie asked.

I'd stopped with the fork halfway to my mouth, staring at the screen. She looked over her shoulder as the picture switched back to the bus.

"Bad accident," I stammered, setting the fork down with a clank and looking around. The waitress glanced our way. Did she recognize me? Would Sammie believe me if I told her Black Robe killed the bus driver? Or would she turn me over to the cops? She was, after all, law enforcement of some kind, even if she wasn't eager to contact the local police. How could I have forgotten that? *Stupid, River.* I had to leave town now.

"I should go," I said, reaching for the backpack.

"You haven't finished," Sammie said. "And they haven't brought our bill."

I didn't want to wait for the waitress. If I did, she'd get another close-up look at me. I didn't want to go to jail. Every muscle in my body tensed. Sammie noticed my apprehension.

"You *do* have enough money to pay, don't you?" she asked.

I nearly laughed out loud. Yeah, a hot million, another reason to avoid the cops. I slid out of the booth and fished in my jeans for cash, keeping my back to the waitress. "You think I'd dine and dash?"

I glanced over my shoulder. The waitress pulled a cell phone from her apron pocket and stepped into the kitchen. I shuffled through the bills in my hand. A ten or a hundred. I had nothing in between. I dropped the hundred on the table and walked away.

On the sidewalk, I paused to think. Should I try to leave town now, or hole up somewhere and wait for dark? I'd learned to travel by night. Nothing like a bum on a back country road to send a sheriff into overdrive. I should stick with my usual routine, stop the crazy dangerous impromptu behavior Sammie's arrival in my life had triggered. I'd leave the gym bag in the garage. If I got picked up carrying all that cash, they'd think I robbed a bank. The burned-out pie factory was about ten blocks east and a couple blocks south. I'd wait there until tonight.

I set off down the street, eager to get out of sight of the IHOP before the cops came to investigate the waitress's call. I'd gone a block when I heard footsteps running behind me. I bolted. I never, ever take the time to look back; I just run.

"River, wait up!" Sammie cried.

I stopped for her to catch me, and then set out again adjusting my pace to hers, even though I longed to keep running. She had a wad of bills in her hand and thrust them at me.

"You're a generous tipper," she said. "Here's your change."

"Keep it," I said. "You might need it."

"I need your help, not your money. I don't know the town, and I need a safe place to wait." When I didn't respond, she said, "You showed incredible moxie bailing me out at the hardware store, and now you're Nervous Nellie. Did I say something to offend you?"

"I have to get to school," I replied, speeding up.

"You said it was curriculum day." She broke into a trot beside me. "Why all the cloak and dagger? Why can't you just meet them back at the alley?"

She stopped, but I didn't realize it until I'd gone another couple steps. I turned to face her, tired of her silly spy games and lies and worried that I'd gotten myself into more trouble than running could get me out of. Being a hero had lost its charm, no matter how beautiful the girl or how deep my need to belong somewhere with somebody. She'd stirred up feelings in me that I didn't want to acknowledge, that I'd pushed away and learned to live without.

Her expression was a mix of worry and fear. "My team would never leave me behind. Something went horribly wrong in the alley last night, and I don't know what it is because you won't tell me. Now you want me to wait there and see what happens?"

When her team returned, they'd bring another tracking device, and I wasn't getting caught by *anybody*. But she didn't know how to survive on the streets, and Black Robe could be lurking nearby. She didn't even know what he looked like. *Crap.* My feet glued themselves to the pavement, and I rocked.

Five blocks down the street, a police cruiser turned the corner and headed our way. My heart leaped into my throat. I grabbed Sammie's hand and hauled her after me.

We cut down Washington. I kept us on the opposite side of the street from the mouth of the alley where Sammie's team had parked. Yellow crime-scene tape stretched between the buildings, but I didn't see an officer on guard. The lack of a cop didn't boost my confidence much. I scanned for Black Robe and listened for the ticking of Sammie's device. The sooner we had her message on the wall and got out of there, the better.

We turned on Riverside, and walked along the street across from Soo Ling's. Plywood covered the windows and door, and more yellow tape had been tacked to it. Tiny bits of glass glittered in the gutter between hooded parking meters where someone had done a poor job sweeping up. A few pedestrians passed us, all occupied with the damage to Soo Ling's. None of them noticed me, although I checked out all of them, worried that I might bump into the bagman. He was another good reason to hit the road.

Sammie stopped and stared. "Isn't that where you work? What happened?"

"I told you, they were trying to kill you. He came in through the back and... shot out the windows while I was carrying you out the front." I kept my voice low so none of the passersby would hear me.

She looked at me, her eyes enormous. "The gang banger shot at you while you were carrying me?"

Had he? At the time, I'd been too busy running to think about it. His shots here, at the bus, and after I'd fled the bus, had all just missed me. He'd had no problem with his aim when he'd killed his companion or shot the other cop. He'd fired near-misses hoping to disable me. A chill crept over me, and my eyes swept the street looking for anyone dressed in black.

We continued to the end of the block and crossed Riverside to the corner parking lot. About halfway down the alley, more yellow tape barred the way, but I wasn't going down there. To do that, I'd have to walk by the sparkly wall. I could feel it tug at me, snatching at my chest and urging me forward. My feet dug into the pavement.

"Let's go around again and use the other end," Sammie said. She seemed as uneasy about this end of the alley as I was.

When we reached the other end, I got out the paint and brush. I stood guard while she ducked down the alley a few yards to put her message on the wall. The last thing we needed was to get caught for painting graffiti on a building. Whenever someone got close, I'd whistle a few bars of *Mary Had a Little Lamb* so Sammie could hide behind a dumpster until they passed. I guess I shouldn't criticize the light bulbs. I didn't whistle any better than they sang.

Sammie came back in a few minutes and dragged me into the alley. About fifteen feet in, she'd painted a line of gibberish symbols and numbers on the wall of Soo Ling's, but that wasn't what she wanted me to see. Chalked off on the asphalt in the middle of the alley was a human silhouette, right where I'd seen the cop go down, and another by Soo Ling's door. They only put chalk around dead people.

"What happened?" she asked, her brows drawn together and her finger pointing to the shapes.

"I don't know," I lied. I gestured to Soo Ling's. "I came out to dump the garbage. One of the gang bangers was standing over you getting ready to shoot, and then another one shot him. I didn't wait around to find out what the grievance was. I just grabbed you and ran."

"And you didn't see anything else? You didn't see someone there?" She pointed to the silhouette where the cop's body had lain.

"We need to go," I said, and walked away. If I told her everything I'd seen, first, she'd know I was crazy, and second, she'd know I'd been in the alley the whole time. She still had that big knife, and I wasn't being taken prisoner by her again. My excuses didn't ease my guilt.

We headed south. Sammie walked in cold silence beside me. Maybe I wasn't so good with women. I'd leave her at the pie factory and head out. It was the smart thing to do, and I'd survived as long as I had by being smart.

We were waiting for the light at First when I saw Black Robe to my left, Sammie's device in his hand, half a block away. The lower half of his face showed under the hood, his lips curving in a sudden smile, and then his head raised. His right hand went inside the robe, and the sonic banana gun came out.

I grabbed Sammie's arm and pulled her back the way we'd come. A second later, I heard the boom of Black Robe's gun. Sammie tried to look over her shoulder, but I wouldn't let her stop.

"It's him!" I shouted. "Run!"

"Who? Where?" she asked.

I flapped my hand over my shoulder. We'd be sitting ducks, just a clear shot down the sidewalk when he rounded the corner. I shoved Sammie toward the street. We had four lanes of traffic to cross, and the cars were moving right along. We played chicken getting across the first two lanes going north, but no one gave us a break to cross the south-bound lanes. Rude drivers. Didn't they know they were supposed to stop for pedestrians even if we weren't in the crosswalk?

"I can take him," she said, and fumbled with a flap on the leg of her trousers.

"Keep running," I said, towing her down the center stripe while waiting for a chance to cross. "He tires quickly."

We caught a break and made the far sidewalk. The banana gun boomed, and the shockwave slammed me against the building. My head throbbed, and black lace circled my field of vision. Car alarms went off, but I barely heard them. Across the street, I saw Black Robe taking aim. I lurched at Sammie and knocked her to the pavement. Above us, concrete chipped from the side of the building and rained onto the sidewalk as another boom rang out.

"Come on," I shouted. It sounded like I spoke from under water.

We ran on down the block and turned the corner. I'd gone twenty feet past it before I realized Sammie wasn't beside me. She'd stopped and had her wand out. She must have found it when she was painting her message on the wall. She leaned around the corner, taking aim at Black Robe.

"It won't work! The wands don't work on 'em!" I called.

I ran back and joined her just as she fired. Lightning crackled from the wand and hit Black Robe dead center. He didn't even slow down. I wrapped an arm around her waist, and half-dragged, half-carried her out into the street.

"Let me go!" she screamed.

I spotted a cab coming at us fast. I dug in my sweatshirt for another bill, waved it in my hand, and jumped in front of the cab. The vehicle stopped with a screech an inch from my legs. I opened the back door and shoved Sammie across the seat, then dove in after her.

"Go!" I ordered, dropping a hundred on the seat beside the driver.

"Where?" he asked.

"Centralia Valley Mall. Just go!" I peered out the back window and saw Black Robe come into view. His gaze swiveled both directions. When he didn't spot us, he looked down at the device. Sammie rose up, wand pointed, fury on her face.

"You mean Centerville Valley Mall?" the cabbie asked.

Centerville? When had they renamed the city?

"Yes, yes. Go!"

The cab slid forward. A muffled boom rocked the vehicle. The glass in the car in the next lane over shattered, and the car sideswiped a delivery van in a loading space. Blood spattered what remained of the car's windshield.

"Jesus, what was that?" the cabbie swore. "Was that an explosion?"

To my everlasting joy, he accelerated through a yellow light and made a left toward the freeway. On the corner, the eight-foot tall demon lounged against a lamp post. As pedestrians passed, he dragged a single talon through the tops of their heads, and then he licked little shining drips of goo off the claw. I stared, my tattoos itching like mad.

"Not real," I murmured. "Not real."

5

〜〜〜

66 Why didn't you keep running?" I yelled, unable to get the blood-spat-
tered windshield out of my mind. "We could have gotten away without
anyone getting hurt."

"How did you know my 'wand' wouldn't work?" Sammie shot back.

She crossed her arms and scowled at me. We'd both been too
shocked to say anything on the ride out the freeway, but once the cabbie
dumped us off in the mall parking lot, the fireworks started. I would have
scowled back, but confrontation wasn't my thing.

I dropped down to sit on the concrete curb around a little land-
scaped island of scrawny evergreens. Until last night, I'd seen exactly
one dead person in all my twenty-something years. Now they seemed to
be popping up almost hourly. In too many cases, their blood was on my
hands. I felt sick. I wrapped my arms around my knees and rocked while
I focused on just one word: Ohm. Rocking isn't classic meditation posture, but it worked for me.

I was vaguely aware of Sammie pacing in front of me. She walked
away once, and I thought I'd seen the last of her, but then she came
back. I wanted her to go. Hanging around with her was too dangerous.
I'd drawn more attention to myself, and that was the last thing I needed.
Nothing she knew about me was worth the cost.

"People are dying, River. Time to cut the crap." She sat beside me.

I looked her in the eyes, needing at least another week or two of
meditation before I'd be remotely in control.

"What was your first clue, the brains splattered on the dash? Truth
is a two-way street, Sammie. Are you ready to man up? Er... woman up?"

She bit her lip and looked away. When she looked at me again, confusion mixed with worry. "I grew up a military brat. I'm not supposed to
disobey orders, and my orders say I'm not supposed to reveal anything to
the locals."

I shrugged. "Yeah, we had that discussion earlier. Look, if we're going around in circles again, my circle's heading east out of town."

I rose and tossed the backpack over my shoulder. She blinked up at me and shot to her feet.

"You can't run away! What about your parents? They'll miss you."

I wanted to tell her that no one would miss me, but I choked on the words. I shrugged again and started walking.

"River," she called at my back, her voice cracking. "My brother was with me last night. He wouldn't leave me behind. I have to know what happened."

It felt like she'd run an ice pick through my heart. The moment I turned around, she saw the truth in my eyes. Her face froze, then it shattered into a thousand splinters of grief. She sank to the curb and wept.

I'd had a brother once. Not a real brother by blood, but a brother nonetheless. Although we were the same age, Jimmy had always been bigger and braver. When I started seeing the gargoyles, he slept in my bed for a week so I wouldn't cry. At ten, he slashed his arms with a razor blade and bled out on the bathroom floor. I knew the anguish she felt. All I'd wanted at the time was someone to hold and comfort me. Be careful what you wish for.

I joined Sammie on the curb, wrapped my arms around her, and squeezed her tight. She shook so bad I thought she'd come apart. Her breaths came in terrible gulps, and the sound of her pain shredded my soul.

"It's my fault," she said. "I should have protected him. I should have been a better soldier. I should have waded in, grabbed the talent, and gotten us out of there. But I had to be nice, treat the talent like a frightened animal that could be coaxed out. Now Griff's dead because of it."

"Never underestimate the power of a few kind words," I murmured. "They can save a life, and they sure didn't cause Griff's death. There was nothing you could have done. Hell, your own team abandoned you after he went down."

Her crying slowed, and she pulled away. Her eyes held her accusation: I'd known, and I hadn't told her. But I'd had no choice, had I?

"What really happened?" she whispered.

I couldn't tell her, not and cover my mental illness. What if she realized I was crazy? She'd probably turn me over to the police. I spread my hands in a helpless gesture. "You won't believe me."

"That's a cop-out," she snapped, glaring at me. She'd gone all military, putting aside her loss for the mission.

"Alright, fine, I'll tell you, and it won't make any sense," I said, resigned. "Your team was scrounging in the alley. Out of nowhere, our friend Black Robe and his buddies arrived with sonic banana guns and started shooting. The first blast was a near-miss and knocked you out.

The second hit your brother."

Her breath sucked in. She bunched her fists and nodded. "Keep going."

She had guts, I'd give her that.

"Your older guy fired his... wand... thing... whatever it was, but it didn't do anything to the black robes. Someone up at the end of the alley called a retreat, and I heard him run away. Then Black Robe fired again, but I couldn't see if he hit anything."

I expected her to tell me what a loon I was describing wands and banana guns. It had to be some bent hallucination, didn't it? Didn't it? She'd want to get away from me, get some place safe, leave the mentally defective weirdo behind.

"Stunners," she said. "Not wands, although I think the guy who designed them had delusions of being a wizard. They're top secret technology. But why didn't they work?"

I could practically see the wheels going around in her head. More important, she still sat next to me, her shoulder touching mine. Why hadn't she run screaming from the dangerous crazy guy?

"We were ambushed, and not by any normal gang. How did they know we'd be there?" she muttered more to herself than me.

"Your turn," I said, mystified by her behavior. What did it say about *her* sanity that she'd accepted my insane descriptions? "What were you doing in the alley, and who are the guys in the robes with the... banana guns."

"I didn't get a good look at the one who chased us. You're sure they're men?"

I blinked back at her. "Well, they weren't women, and they were kind of big for kids. What else could they be?"

She ignored my question. "No idea who they are. The 'banana guns' seem to fire sound waves in a concentrated beam. They shake things to bits instead of firing a projectile. I've never seen anything like it. The stunner should have worked. Must be something about the robes that blocks them. But they're gonna pay for killing Griff. My dad will catch them, and when he does..."

She stared off across the parking lot for a minute before asking, "What else did you see?"

I was still struggling with the idea that the wands and sonic weapons were real, and that the bad guys wore lightning-proof robes. Should I tell her about the stone tablet UFO? That *couldn't* be real. Or the demon? And didn't she owe me an answer first? I'd lost track.

"There was, um... *something* at the end of the alley where your other... people were. I didn't get a good look."

She seemed satisfied with that. Or maybe relieved. So what had I seen? More of their top secret high tech? Maybe they had some holographic projector that just made it look like a stone tablet. But why pick something so whacky?

"After the older man retreated, what happened?"

"What happened to the part about taking turns?" I asked, thinking that she acted more like an only child who'd never had to share than one who'd grown up with a sibling.

"I answered your question," she replied, brow furrowing.

"I'm pretty sure you didn't. Why were you in the alley?"

She gazed off across the parking lot again, and I tensed in anticipation of her answer. She plucked at her trousers, and I leaned closer. She frowned and chewed her lip. I thought I'd scream.

"I told you before," she said. "We were on a secret mission that I can't reveal."

I screamed; strangled, but a scream. She pulled away and gave me a worried glance. Oops.

"Look, if you want to hear the rest of what happened, you're going to do better than that," I said. "We're sharing, remember? So there aren't any more surprises, any more bodies?"

"But you don't have the necessary security clearance," she argued.

"Oh, well, yeah, security clearance. Because otherwise I'd go blab everything to the press. I'm sure they'd believe a story about men in black with magic wands shooting it out with hoodlums using sonic banana guns." I grabbed my backpack and stood up, hoping she didn't call my bluff.

She jumped up and planted her hands on her hips, giving me a fearsome frown. "Okay, I'll tell you. But you have to tell me the rest of what happened when I have. And you have to promise never to breathe a word to anyone."

I nodded my agreement and set the backpack at my feet. The *last* thing I'd do is tell anyone this unbelievable story. I'd be back in the mental ward in a heartbeat, but she didn't know that. And who would I tell, anyway? The only person I knew was her.

"We were looking for someone." She paused, but I guess my expression said that it wasn't enough. "Someone from a family that has a particular genetic trait that's very rare and very special. We had information this person would be in the alley."

I turned in a circle trying to take in what she'd said. *A familial connection.* "You mean like a mutant?"

She laughed. "You've been watching too many movies."

In point of fact, I never watched movies. Appliance and video rental stores didn't appreciate having homeless ragamuffins hanging around for hours on end, and I couldn't afford movie admissions. But I could read, and I liked browsing the movie reviews in discarded newspapers. It kept me current on the cultural lingo. No stumping me with a reference to Wolverine.

"So what is it? ESP? Vampirism? They sparkle if they go out in the daytime?" I asked, hungering for more information.

"If they don't receive treatment, it makes them crazy," she replied, dodging my question. She must have seen the shock on my face. "Don't worry, it's strictly genetic. It isn't contagious. If you were close to them, it won't hurt you. Now tell me the rest of what happened."

Makes them crazy? But I already was. Was it too late for me? Was I going to die? Read minds? Lust for blood? Go gibbering, drooling mad? I shoved my hands in my pockets and tried to pull myself together, frightened by the prospect of such a future. Sammie waited.

"Um... one of the black robes took your... watch and was going to kill you. Another black robe, the one who's still chasing us, went to check your brother. The third one..."

We'd gotten to the sticky part. No way the demon was some kind of high tech secret weapon. He'd come straight out of my hallucinations of the Dark Place. Maybe I could just gloss over him. Maybe he and the Dark Place were symptoms of the genetic disorder. My fear climbed. Sammie watched me expectantly.

"The third one went nuts and shot the one next to you. The other black robe shot him."

To my surprise, she didn't question me further about the bizarre behavior of the third black robe. I got the feeling she knew why he'd done it. I sure wished she'd share with me. Any explanation would be better than 'an eight-foot tall ravening demon ate his brain.'

"And?" she asked.

I goggled. "And what?"

"The naked person, the one in the garbage by Soo Ling's. You must have seen him—or her—when you came out the door. You'd practically have stepped on him."

A modicum of relief seeped through me. She still thought I was the bus boy. For reasons I couldn't put my finger on, I wasn't comfortable revealing I was the lurker in the garbage pile. A top secret government agency collecting people off the street with a certain genetic profile? What were they doing with them? Call me a conspiracy nut, but I just didn't trust the government, not when it came to my personal freedom.

"I didn't see any naked person," I said, and technically, since there wasn't a mirror in the alley, I hadn't. Besides, I was appropriately dressed in bin bags by the time they'd arrived, not naked. "What's this trait good for, and how do you know they have it?"

"I can't tell you," she said. "In fact, now that I realize the danger, it would be better if you weren't involved anymore."

"What?!" I shrieked. She couldn't brush me off like that. I had to know what they were doing with the people they collected. "You'd be toast right now if I hadn't saved you."

"River, you're a kid, a minor. I'd be in so much trouble if anything happened to you. And I could never live with myself. I'm very thankful you saved me last night and helped me this morning, but I can't have you around."

She surveyed our surroundings. "Here comes a bus. I'm headed back downtown. I want you to go home, get cleaned up, and get to school. You shouldn't skip. Nothing's more important than a good education."

Of all the— I watched in silent disbelief while she jogged across to the bus stop, taking her secrets with her. Just as well. I'd done fine for twenty-some years without knowing who I was or where I'd come from. What did I care what she knew? All that business about genetic craziness was probably just another one of her lies. *We've come to take you home, my ass.*

I needed to get out of town. The business with the bus driver was serious, and there was the bagman and the stolen money to consider, never mind Black Robe and Sammie's team both trying to take me captive. I rocked, watched the bus pull up to the stop, watched her get on.

What if I did have a genetic disorder, something besides the schizophrenia? I didn't want to miss out on a treatment for my madness—or an opportunity to find my family if Sammie knew who they were. But the risks were too great. Too many people wanted a piece of me. I should put as much distance as I could between Centralia—er, Centerville—and me, and I should do it now.

The next thing I knew, I was flying across the asphalt. I caught the departing bus and banged on the side until the driver stopped again to let me board. He gave me a surly look, but he took my fare and waited for me to sit down before he started up again.

There weren't many passengers that time of the day. Only six or seven people sat scattered around the bus. Sammie sat amidships in a row by herself, looking out the window. When she saw me, her expression said it all: I was in for a fight. I took the aisle seat next to her and dumped my backpack at my feet.

"You don't know where you're going," I said. "You need me to show you where the pie factory is."

"You're going home, young man. You will not trail me around like some lost puppy. I have the address for the pie factory, and I can find it myself." She crossed her arms and glared at me.

"You aren't safe out there alone. You need me to watch your back,"

I argued, stung by her reference to a puppy. Wasn't I the one who saved her life—twice? At least she could have compared me to a heroic dog like Rin Tin Tin. "Black Robe's still running around the streets."

"My team will be here tonight. I'll manage until then." She turned to look out the window, ignoring me.

"You promised you'd share, and you didn't," I whined. Geez, I was starting to *sound* like a sixteen-year-old. I glanced toward the front of the bus, and the driver was staring at us in his visor mirror. He looked away to check traffic and swung the bus up the freeway onramp, accelerating to merge with other vehicles.

Sammie had said something while I was watching the driver, but I didn't catch it.

"I saved your life. I got shot at for you. You owe me," I said. "Tell me what you do with these people you collect."

"Are you even listening to me?" she asked, her voice rising over the noise of the motor.

The bus driver was on his radio. I rarely rode buses. Did they usually call in while they were driving? Wasn't he supposed to have hands-free gear if he did? He looked in his visor mirror again, and quickly looked away when our eyes met. Panic squirmed in my guts. *Shit.*

We were on the freeway. The driver wouldn't be making any stops for a couple of miles. I needed to get off. I scanned for emergency exits and saw a lever below the back window, but it didn't look like the kind of thing that would stop the bus. I didn't want to bounce down the concrete at sixty miles per hour.

Back a mile, I saw flashing lights. A cop car headed our way. *Oh, please, let there be an accident up ahead.* He bore down on us at roughly the speed of a jet fighter. And farther back, I saw another one.

I emptied my pockets into the backpack with hands that suddenly seemed all thumbs, and then kicked the backpack under the seat in front of us.

"River, what are you doing?" Sammie asked.

"Hold onto the backpack for me," I said. The first cop car whipped past, and the bus began to slow. "I need your help."

"What are you talking about?" She craned her neck to see the cop car in front of the bus. Fear froze her expression. "Why are the cops pulling the bus over?"

My back stiffened, and the hair stood up on my arms. We were traveling on the shoulder now, one cop car in front, another behind. No way I'd be able to run.

"Last night, when I was getting away from Black Robe, he killed a bus driver," I said. "The police think I did it."

Her eyes opened wide. "Why didn't you tell me?"

I shrugged. "I wasn't sure you'd believe I was innocent. You hadn't seen Black Robe yet."

From the look she gave me, I wasn't sure she was buying my story even after seeing him, and I desperately needed her to. With her government connections, she could get me out of jail, assuming she hadn't fed me a line of bull about her job. I'd saved her life. She owed me, but was that enough? I needed insurance. I needed her motivated.

"I know where the crazy naked guy is," I said. "I can take you to him."

The bus lurched to a halt. I had to make sure they didn't pick Sammie up so she could work behind the scenes to get me out. But I was sitting with her, and if I traded seats now, it might look suspicious to the driver or the other passengers. The cops were at the doors, guns drawn. I was out of time.

"If you help me, I'll keep you out of this. But you have to get me out of jail," I whispered. "Yell at me. Call me a perv. Push me away."

Sammie looked from the cops to me, but she didn't move. *Crap.* What kind of secret agent was she? Didn't they train her to react quickly? I reached over and grabbed her breast.

I'd expected her to squeal and slap my hand away. Her right cross connected with my jaw, and I flew out of the seat to sprawl in the aisle, dazed. I guess maybe her agency training was better than I thought.

She leaped up and pointed at me, her face contorted in rage. "You pervert! How dare you touch me!"

Atta girl, Sammie. I had time to mouth 'Sorry,' and then the officers were on me.

6

I sat in an interrogation room at the city jail facing a one-way mirror, left wrist shackled to a table that was bolted to the floor. I'd spent my time in the patrol car alternately thinking about my strategy for the upcoming chat with the cops and my stupidity for chasing after Sammie. I needed to act normal until Sammie rescued me. I practiced all the time, but I wouldn't say I was good at it.

I didn't need to worry, even if Sammie didn't come for me, I told myself. After all, there were witnesses to what happened on the bus. The bagman would want me turned loose so he could find out what I'd done with the money—assuming the cops didn't know I'd stolen it. The news hadn't mentioned my theft; the money had to be dirty. And the crazy waitress knew I was innocent. Besides, Sammie seemed like the dependable type. She'd get me out.

I wasn't dressed in bin bags and acting like a lunatic now. They'd believe me when I said Black Robe was shooting at me as well as the others on the bus. I just needed to stay cool and wait for Sammie and the cavalry to arrive. Then I'd ditch her and get out of town as fast as possible. Arizona was lovely this time of year, and I was ready for a vacation.

A burly uniformed officer guarded the door. The overhead light sang *Jailhouse Rock*, but I ignored it. I pressed my back against the chair and scooted it forward until the table nearly cut me in two. I wouldn't rock. I'd gird my loins with ohms and be an ice cube. They'd think I was so cool. They'd never guess I was mentally defective.

A detective balding on top and wearing a rumpled brown suit entered the room and sat down across the table from me. He had deep worry lines in his face and tired brown eyes. This was a career cop who'd seen and heard it all, and he was the enemy. He placed a legal pad, a pencil, and a manila folder on the table between us before starting up a recording device at the end of the table.

"Time is 1:50 p.m. In the room are Officer Wahlkowsky, Lieutenant

Knowles, and—" He glanced across the table at me. "What's your name, kid?"

"River Madden, sir," I replied in a quiet, respectful voice. *Cool, River. Ohm.*

"Mr. Madden, I'd be interested to hear about your activities yesterday evening," he said.

"Well, I was waiting for the bus and—"

He held up a hand. "Let's back up a bit. What were you doing in the alley behind Soo Ling's?"

Crap. Of course they'd ask about Soo Ling's. I'd been seen in the restaurant. I'd been so focused on the bus driver I hadn't thought about the fracas in the alley. Three people died, and Black Robe was the only witness. I was pretty sure he wouldn't come forward to speak for my good character. I hoped I could repeat the lies I'd told Sammie and wouldn't have to make up a bunch of new ones. How would I remember which ones I'd told Sammie and which ones I'd told the cop? Maybe I could borrow his legal pad and make a list.

"Uh... I was going through the dumpsters looking for recyclables—"

"In last night's storm?" he asked. "In the dark?"

Okay, not the most believable story earlier when I'd discarded it, and no better now, but he'd know I wasn't the bus boy at Soo Ling's. Maybe I should have told him I was scrounging for Chinese take-away.

"Some kids in the park stole my shoes, so I needed money to buy new ones." I watched his eyes to see whether he believed me, but I couldn't tell. I needed to make a better impression. "It's the ecologically friendly thing to do. Recycling, that is."

He lifted one eyebrow, then flipped open his folder and ran his eyes down some paperwork. "Recycling, huh? That pay pretty good?"

Breathe, River. Don't let him rattle you. I shrugged. "It's okay."

"That how you got the two hundred you had stashed in your shoes?"

Crap. I'd forgotten about the money in my shoes. They must have found it when they searched me. They hadn't returned my hoodie or watch cap, and the ants were already partying. No more mistakes. I had to hold out until Sammie rescued me, and then I had to run far and fast.

"Look, kid, I got dead bodies stacked up like cord wood, and I'm gonna get to the bottom of what happened. If you had nothing to do with all those folks dying, then you just tell me straight and you'll walk free. But if you lie to me, I'll hit you with everything in the book. Are we clear?"

I nodded and maintained eye contact. I thought he'd be more aggressive, more determined to hang it all on the druggy kid and close the case. By now, I'd expected him to put a confession in front of me for my signature. But maybe he was just trying to put me off my guard by acting fair and reasonable. I wouldn't fall for it.

"So you were in the alley, and then what?" He had his hands folded on top of the tablet. He seemed so relaxed, but there was a sharpness to his eyes that I found disconcerting.

"Some guys dressed in black showed up at the end of the alley, and then some other guys dressed in black showed up at the other end of the alley. The next thing I know, there's a shooting war going on."

"Yeah? What kind of shooting war?"

I stared. Sweat broke out on my forehead. "Um... the kind where people shoot one another?"

"You see their weapons?"

"Well... not really. It was dark." Behind me, I could hear a crowd whispering, and occasionally someone would say my name, but in the mirror, only the guard stood by the door. *Ignore. Not real.*

"Hm," the lieutenant said. "But not too dark to see stuff in the dumpsters."

I opened my mouth to speak, but I'd lost track of where I was in the story. My shoulders ached from holding them rigid so I wouldn't rock.

"How many guys were there?" he asked.

"Six," I said, feeling a surge of confidence that I could be truthful about something. "Yeah, three on each side."

My confidence evaporated. What about the guy in the silly costume and the dog? Did they count? Maybe I'd lied after all. Did he know?

"And what did you do when the shooting started?"

"I hid. And then the door opened, and I ran inside. To get away. Because they were shooting." I was babbling. So much for playing it cool. *Answer the questions, nothing more.*

"You ran inside Soo Ling's? All by yourself?"

"Yeah," I replied without thinking.

"What about the person you were carrying?"

"Carrying?" I scrubbed at my scalp, where the ants did the two-step, and the overhead light taunted me by reciting *Liar, Liar, Pants on Fire.*

"Through the restaurant. Several patrons described a body on your shoulder. Who was it? Where's that person now?"

My heart tried to beat its way out of my chest. I spread my hands, hoping I could bluff, but the way my hands shook, I doubted he was buying it. "I was carrying my bags of recycling on my shoulder. Big black garbage bags. Hey, do I look like a guy who could carry a body?"

He reached in the manila folder, pulled out the picture of me I'd seen on TV, the one from the bus, and placed it in front of me. "I don't see you carrying anything. What'd you do with your stuff?"

"Oh, uh, I dropped it so I could run faster. It wasn't anything worth dying for." I glanced up at the light, which chanted louder with my attention.

Knowles nodded. "We didn't find any bags outside Soo Ling's."

"Somebody must have stolen them."

"In the middle of a running gun battle, on a cold, stormy night, someone stole them."

I wiped a sweaty palm on my jeans. "I guess you didn't find a body, either, huh."

The lieutenant leaned back and ran a hand over his face. "You're not doing yourself any favors, kid."

I squirmed in my chair. The room seemed terribly warm. I wondered who watched behind the mirror. Were they laughing at my fantastic lies? I just wanted out of there. Why hadn't I run when I had the chance? Was Sammie and what she knew worth it? I didn't think so, sitting here in an interrogation room. Where was she?

"You left Soo Ling's, and someone chased you. Who was that?"

"Black Robe," I said. He cocked an eyebrow at me. "That's what I call him because he wears a long black robe and hood. We haven't been formally introduced."

"Describe him," he ordered. He leaned forward, waiting.

I scrubbed at the damn ants. Strands of hair wafted down to the table. "He's about average height and I guess about average build, but it's hard to tell because he has this big black robe on. He's a white guy. I've never seen him close enough to tell you hair or eye color. And it was dark. The people in Soo Ling's must have seen him."

"He shot out the lights before he ran through," he said. "Tell me about the bus."

"I thought I could get away on the bus. I didn't think he'd..." My stomach twisted at the memory of the headless bus driver. My fault. If I'd kept running, he'd still be alive. "But you have the security tape. You know I didn't do anything to the bus driver."

Knowles sighed. "We have a broken camera with a few images of you, and that's it."

"Oh." Not good news. "What about the passengers? They can tell you what happened."

"Old Mrs. Zimosa? When the windows shattered, she hit the floor and lost her glasses. She has no idea after that."

I frowned. "And the waitress? She saw everything."

His eyes narrowed. "What waitress?"

"The one near the back." She'd been psycho, the type who'd want to be quoted in the press and seen on TV describing her terrible fascinating ordeal. She'd probably be telling the story to her grandkids when she was eighty.

"No one else was on the bus when we got there, and no one's come forward in response to our broadcasts for assistance."

I chewed my lip and clawed at my head. Maybe she was camera shy. That the bagman had disappeared didn't surprise me. Should I mention him? Hell, in for a penny, in for a pound.

"A businessman sat right behind the driver."

"Another mysterious passenger, eh?"

"Your Mrs. Zimosa must have seen them, too. They were already on the bus when I got on." It must have been Mrs. Zimosa who got on at the same stop as me. If it was, she hadn't been on the bus long before it all went sideways. Maybe she hadn't noticed the waitress sitting at the back, but she'd walked right past the bagman. So much for eye-witness testimony.

"She doesn't remember anyone else. Can you describe them?"

From the tone of his voice, he wasn't believing my story about the other passengers. Hell, maybe the waitress had been a hallucination and wasn't on the bus at all. I hadn't considered that. But the bagman had been there. I just couldn't be sure whether he'd admit it if the cops asked.

Where was Sammie? I'd expected her to spring me by now after what I'd told her. The detective was losing patience. I needed to keep him happy for a little bit longer. I didn't want a trip to the room with the hot light and rubber hoses.

"Can I use your pad?" I asked. "And your pencil?"

Knowles rubbed his hand over his chin. "Why?"

"You want to know what they look like or not?"

He folded over the top page where he'd jotted some notes, and passed me the paper and pencil. I closed my eyes for a moment, calling up Black Robe the way I'd seen him that morning in the daylight. Then I set to work.

In five minutes, I had a sketch of Black Robe done, right down to his crooked teeth and black hood. I'd never forget that smile, or the coldness in his eyes. Whatever drove him, I didn't want to know about it. He was at least as crazy as me. I passed the sketch to the lieutenant.

Both brows rose this time. "You're pretty good. This is the one you call Black Robe, the one who shot up the bus?"

I nodded, hoping I was piling up veracity points. "And I can do the two passengers, too."

He tore off the drawing of Black Robe, handed it to Wahlkowsky, and told him to get it distributed at once. Then he folded his hands on the table and leaned closer while I worked on the waitress. In a minute, the silent Wahlkowsky was back guarding the door.

"That's her," I said, tearing off the sketch. "She's average height and has blonde hair. Oh, and she wears too much makeup."

Knowles put the sketch aside, and I started on the bagman. It didn't take me long. I didn't bother tearing off the page. I just pushed the pad back to the detective, along with the pencil. He stared at it for what seemed a very long time.

"He was on the bus?" he asked without looking up.

I didn't like the undercurrent of tension I heard in his voice. Had something happened to the bagman? He'd left the bus before the police got there, so he couldn't have been injured too badly. Did Knowles recognize him?

"Yep," I said.

The detective cocked an eyebrow at me, and all the goodwill I'd built with the sketches slide away. *Shit.* Maybe I shouldn't have mentioned the passengers after all.

"You said this Black Robe character was part of a gang. Any of them with him when he shot up the bus?"

I frowned and shook my head, wondering why he asked. The hair on the back of my neck rose. *Where was Sammie?*

He put the sketch of the waitress on top of the folder and asked, "After you left the bus, where'd you go?"

"I ran away southwest," I lied. "Black Robe followed me, but I lost him."

"And then?"

"Um... I hid in a garage until morning." And then I'd run into Black Robe again. But if Knowles didn't bring it up, I sure wasn't going to. I'd fabricated enough for one day. Besides, I'd already helped him by providing the sketches.

The lieutenant flipped open the manila folder, shuffled through the contents, and pulled out a photo of the dead bus driver slumped in his seat. He slapped it on the table in front of me. "Did it occur to you that maybe you should contact the police, especially since you can identify the perp?"

I looked away, my stomach shifting uneasily. I had no love for the cops. They'd never done anything but hassle me. It would never enter my head to ask them for help. Without Sammie in the equation, I'd be halfway to the next town south by now. All I ever had from cops was pain, and the more I thought about it, the more angry I got. Anger felt a lot better than the guilt eating through my stomach.

I raised my shackled wrist and shook it at the lieutenant. "What, so you could beat a confession out of me, the crazy druggy kid they talked about on the news?"

Knowles' hands curled into fists. He took a couple deep breaths, and then said, "The press embellished. We never said we were looking for you as a suspect. We need to get the bastard who was shooting at you before he does this to anyone else."

My anger drained away. I shoved the photo back at him. "Can I go now?"

"I'd like to keep you in protective custody," the detective said. "You're safer off the streets until we catch Black Robe."

"Oh, uh... thanks, but I'm good," I said. I'd be plenty safe in Arizona.

Knowles tapped the sketch of the businessman. "And you don't know this guy?"

"Never saw him before in my life."

"Because we fished his body out of the river this morning, gunshot wound to the head."

I blinked down at the sketch. I'd taken his money, and then someone killed him. It couldn't be coincidence. Another death on my conscience. I wiped my hand over my mouth and swallowed. Knowles stared hard at me.

"Is there anything else you can tell me? Did you hear any of these people speak? Call one another by name? Accents? Anything?"

I could hear the desperation in his voice, and I wished I could tell him everything. But he'd think I was crazy. Then there'd be the trip to the state hospital for the psych eval, and I'd fail. What good would come from telling him all I'd seen if he didn't believe me?

"No, nothing," I said.

"Interview terminated, 2:05 p.m." He punched the stop button on the recorder and released my shackled wrist. "You've been very helpful, Mr. Madden. Leave your contact information, and you're free to go."

I stood, working hard to keep my relief hidden and contain my desire to bolt for the door. I was free, and I hadn't needed any help from Sammie. Good thing since she'd left me out in the cold.

A uniformed office came in, blocking my escape, and said, "Lieutenant, the coroner just sent word. She's got a victim from that accident this morning with the same cause of death as the three last night."

Shit. It had to be the driver of the car that Black Robe offed while he was chasing Sammie and me. I held my breath and tried to worm past the uniform.

"And we've got a cabbie who says he picked up this guy," he gestured to me, "and his girl friend at the scene of the accident."

Knowles swung his gaze on me, and I felt like I'd been skewered by twin laser beams. His brow lowered.

"I think, Mr. Madden, that we have more to talk about."

The light sang *The Ants Go Marching*, and the ant feet on my head stepped up to a frenzied pace, apparently fans of the light. I'd be tearing away chunks of scalp soon.

I'd been waiting an hour for Knowles to return. He'd left me in the custody of Officer Wahlkowsky, the big brute by the door, while he'd gone to investigate Black Robe's latest appearance. I tried to focus on what I'd tell him—and what I wouldn't—without success. I was coming unglued. *Where the* hell *was Sammie?*

I glared up at the lights and muttered, "Shut up."

The door opened, and Knowles returned. He didn't bother with social niceties. He just slammed the photo of the dead woman from the car on the table in front of me. It wasn't a pretty picture.

"Interview resumes 3:10 p.m. Officer Wahlkowsky, Lieutenant Knowles, and River Madden present," he said. Anger swirled in his eyes. "Well?"

Fear buzzed through me. "Black Robe shot at us and hit her instead."

"*Us?*" He leaned over me, placing his hand on the table beside mine. No more Mr. Nice Guy from him. "Who was with you?"

Shit. I should have kept my mouth shut and refused to answer his questions. We were in the cab when Black Robe killed the woman. That gave me a rock-solid alibi.

He took his place on the opposite side of the table, smoldering. "A witness places you at the death of Ms. Jones, and he says you were accompanied by a female. Who were you with?"

"I don't know," I muttered, trying to keep my eyes anywhere but on the photo of the dead woman. The light sang *The Ants Crawl In* in a high pitched voice that hurt my ears and grated on my frayed nerves.

"You shared a taxi with her, but you didn't know who she was?"

"I just met her. On the street this morning."

I looked past him into the mirror. The table wasn't a table anymore; it was a coffin. When I looked directly at the table, the dead woman filled the coffin and leaked blood onto the white satin lining.

I leaped up so fast that I knocked my chair over. I was two steps back and gasping before I realized it had to be a hallucination. I thanked my lucky stars they hadn't shackled me to the table again. I probably would have broken my wrist. Officer Wahlkowsky grabbed my arm in a vice grip, and Knowles' eyes narrowed.

"Sorry," I said, voice shaking. "Sorry. I thought I saw a spider on the cof—on the table."

Wahlkowsky righted my chair and sat me in it. I struggled to slow my breathing, kept my eyes glued to Knowles, and folded my hands in my lap. I wouldn't see the coffin and its occupant. They didn't exist, at least not in this room. *Not real, not real.*

"Tell me about the girl," the lieutenant ordered.

"I was walking along the street, and she started walking with me.

We struck up a conversation, and then Black Robe started shooting. I've never seen her before."

"Look, kid, if you don't stop lying to me, I'm going to slap you with obstruction of justice. The girl you were seen with was dressed just like one of our vics from the alley. I think she's the person you had slung over your shoulder when you ran through Soo Ling's. Now tell me who she is and what's going on."

"I can't," I said, a truthful statement at last. "I don't *know* what's going on."

7

They'd taken me to a holding cell not far from interrogation, I guess so Wahlkowsky could have his dinner break and I could consider my fate. I sat on the metal shelf bolted to the wall, closed my eyes, and rocked, trying to regain my composure. Even if they believed I was sixteen, I'd be headed for adult jail, not some juvenile facility, not with the seriousness of the charges surrounding me.

If the police didn't catch her first, Sammie would meet with her team, and I might never see her again, might never find out what they all knew about me. Would she care that I was rotting in jail? Or a psych ward? Would she try to get me out? I didn't think so. She probably figured I'd lied to her about the naked guy in the alley. Of all the times to have her doubt me, this one couldn't be worse.

Guilt and shame made me feel sick. Maybe Knowles was right. Maybe if I'd come forward last night instead of keeping Sammie's secrets, Ms. Jones wouldn't be dead now. Maybe I wouldn't be sitting in a cell with everyone believing I was mixed up in murder. I'd been a self-centered dunce, smitten by a pretty woman and so absorbed in finding out about my own origins that I hadn't considered who might get hurt.

I heard footsteps approach. As I opened my eyes, a vague, sooty cloud floated toward the ceiling. I'd never hallucinated things from the Dark Place in the real world before this break, and I shivered. Was I going completely mad as Sammie said I would? I looked past the cloud to the man standing in the now-open cell door.

He was a smartly dressed plain-clothes detective in his mid-thirties, his shield hanging from a cord around his neck, and he ran his disapproving gaze over me. The sooty cloud drifted out the door, slid around him, and oozed back in before drifting away out the door again.

"On your feet, hands against the wall."

His voice sounded tense, and he glanced down the corridor. I obeyed. He slapped a cuff on one wrist, cranked it behind my back, and added the other.

"Where are we going?" I asked, dragging my feet as he pushed me out the door. From the hard look on his face, I thought it might be rubber hose time.

"Age verification. I'm transporting you to the hospital."

Crap. I was definitely headed for the Big House if I didn't convince them I had nothing to do with the killings. If they found Sammie, what would she tell them about me? What did she really know?

We didn't take the elevator, thank God. Elevators are death traps, and I knew if I ever rode in one, I'd die. I'm strictly a stair man. We went down a flight of stairs, through another corridor, and emerged in the parking garage under the jail.

My escort had a dark blue sedan waiting. He shoved me in the back seat and climbed behind the wheel. We cruised out of the garage into wan afternoon sunlight and headed north, which seemed odd. Both the hospitals were located south near the freeway. Unless my memory was playing tricks on me again.

"Um... excuse me," I said. "Aren't the hospitals the other way?"

The cop smirked in the mirror. "We're going to a private clinic. Don't worry, though. They'll give you very special treatment."

A chill ran through me. I scooted over to the window and looked out, searching for salvation. I nearly jumped out of my skin when I saw a figure dressed in black on the sidewalk, but it was Sammie, not Black Robe. I pressed my face to the window, wanting her to see me, to save me. She looked my direction, but she wouldn't expect me to be in a car, and even if she did, what could she do? I was on my own, same as always. No point expecting help from others.

We cruised north about six blocks and pulled into another underground parking garage, this time beneath a modern twelve-story glass and steel skyscraper. The sign out front read *The Cantel Building*. I didn't see any signs for doctors' offices or clinics, just the Cantel Insurance Agency, Cantel Mortgage, and Cantel Financial Planners. I had a bad feeling about the place.

The detective parked the car near a bank of elevators. Three of the elevators had green doors and one had a red door. He dragged me in front of a video camera by the red door, and pushed an intercom button. I looked around, wondering if I could outrun the guy with my hands cuffed behind my back. It was worth a try, if he'd just loosen his grip for a second. Too late. Machinery whirred, and the red elevator opened.

I screamed and kicked, trying to get away, trying to go anywhere but in the elevator. He smacked my head against the wall so I saw stars, and then he pushed me in. I fell on the floor, and before I could get up, the doors closed on us. I charged the doors, bashed my shoulder against them, and kicked furiously to no avail. I had to get out. The cable would fray, the motor would fail. We'd plunge to our deaths. Didn't this idiot know about elevators? The cop laughed all the way up.

When the doors finally opened on the twelfth floor, I was soaked in sweat and panting hard. Whatever they wanted to know, whatever confession they wanted me to sign, I'd do it, as long as they didn't make me ride in an elevator again.

The cop dragged me down a hall past a lot of vacant offices. The whole floor had an empty air, like the tenants hadn't moved in yet. He stopped at an office furnished with a desk, a nice leather swivel chair, a straight-backed chair with arms, and two thugs. A collection of stainless steel instruments were artfully displayed on the desk blotter. I'd arrived at the 'medical' clinic.

The two thugs reminded me of Abbott and Costello: one round-faced and pudgy, the other suave and thin. Somehow, I didn't think I was there to critique their comedy routine. The cop uncuffed me. Abbott shoved me into the straight-backed chair, and Costello used duct tape to bind my wrists to the armrests and ankles to the legs. I resolved to tell them whatever they wanted to know—quickly.

"Detective Thurston, I see you've delivered the package," said an oily voice behind me.

"He's all yours, Mr. Cantel," replied the cop.

"You'd better run along to the hospital, detective. You don't want to explain why you were so slow to report your prisoner's escape."

Oh, hell. If the police didn't think I was guilty before, they would now. Not that it would matter. I had the feeling I wouldn't be seeing the inside of a jail cell again in my lifetime. I tensed against the tape.

The door closed, and Mr. Cantel took the comfortable chair at the desk. He was about fifty and should have gone with hair plugs instead of a toupee. His suit must have cost a bundle, and he wore a flashy gold watch and ruby-studded ring—not that I'm an expert. It might have been cubic zirconium. He withdrew a shiny silver gun strapped in a carved leather holster from a desk drawer and set it next to the instruments on the blotter.

"Let's introduce ourselves, shall we? I'm Mr. Cantel, and you're... ?"

Uh-oh, he'd told me his name *and* let me see his face. That didn't bode well. I needed us to be friends. I needed him to trust that I'd never tell anyone about him if he let me go—preferably physically intact. *Grovel, River.*

"River Madden. Pleased to meet you, Mr. Cantel," I nodded, trying to look friendly and cooperative despite my trembling and sweating. "Is there something I can do for you?"

The two thugs seemed mildly unhappy at my response. If I told

Cantel right off what he wanted to know, I'd spoil all their fun... unless Cantel let them play with me after he had what he wanted. *Oh, please, let him be a humanitarian crime boss.*

"Mr. Madden." Cantel's smile showed a gold-capped front tooth. He rocked back in the chair. "I believe you have some property of mine, and I want it returned."

As I'd thought, the owner of the gym bag had caught up to me. Would he be satisfied with a few broken limbs in payment for the couple thou I'd lifted from the bag? Or maybe I could work off my debt mowing his lawn or shoveling snow from his walks. With my luck, he probably lived in a penthouse apartment and didn't need a lackey for yard chores.

"I didn't know what it was! If I'd known it was yours, I wouldn't have touched it. Honest."

I hoped he'd be mollified. I'd never heard of him, but if he had a cop in his pocket and minions running around with mountains of cash, he was someone important. And he'd already murdered the bagman.

"I'm glad to see you're so accommodating, Mr. Madden. You just tell my friends here where to find the bag, and they'll pick it up." He gave me a cheery grin.

"Um... I don't know the address, but I could take you there. Or your friends, I mean, because I'm sure you're too busy to run errands." I shivered, even though the office seemed uncomfortably warm.

The grin vanished and one eyebrow quirked up. "Tell me something, Mr. Madden. Who sent you to assault the bus?"

Why did everyone think I assaulted the bus? I was just a homeless guy dressed in bin bags, for Christ's sake. Did they think I'd hidden a bazooka under the trench coat?

"Look, I think there's been a mistake. It wasn't me who attacked the bus. It was some... uh... " How *was* I going to describe Black Robe? "Well, there was this guy in the alley behind Soo Ling's, and I guess he has something against buses, because I'd just gotten on board when all hell broke loose."

Cantel sniffed, leaned forward, and folded his hands on the desk, taking his time examining the instruments. His fingers brushed engraving inlaid with gold on the pearl handle of the gun, and a fond smile touched his lips. The action wasn't lost on me. I gulped.

"I'd been mugged, you see. Someone stole my shoes. And when I saw the gym bag, I thought it might contain some. Shoes, that is. If you ask Lt. Knowles, he can give you a copy of the sketch I did of the man you want. For the bus job. Or Thurston should have it."

The crime boss picked up the gun and sighted down the barrel, moving it slowly from left to right until it came to a stop pointed at my head. I sucked in a breath and gulped.

"See this gun? It used to belong to the last guy who ran Centerville. I won it off him in a shooting match, you might say." He chuckled. "Had my name and the date engraved on the grip to commemorate the... event. And these notches? They mark the men who've gotten in my way since. I'll be adding a new one for John. You remember John, don't you?"

"Oh, uh... I don't think so," I replied, my voice shaking.

"John, the courier you took the money from?" He made a little popping noise and jerked the muzzle up like he'd fired at me. "Maybe I'll need to add two notches."

I struggled against the tape, but it was a useless gesture. The ants marched to my forehead and back to the nape of my neck before reversing course again. Under the binding, my tattoos prickled. I glanced up at the ceiling, but for once, I wasn't hallucinating nightmare clouds.

Cantel seemed to take my squirming for an admission of guilt. "I'm sorry to see that you're not more helpful, Mr. Madden. I'd really hoped we could have a pleasant chat in which you told me who you worked for. I run a tight ship here in Centerville, and I don't appreciate it when others try to cut in on my business. But I'm sure you'll tell me what I want to know... given a little time."

With that, Cantel replaced the gun in the desk drawer, nodded at Abbott and Costello, and walked out. Abbott pulled a pack of cigarettes out of his shirt pocket and lit up before tossing the pack onto the desk. I guess he didn't believe those warnings on the label. Costello gave him a disdainful look and grazed his fingers over a pair of pliers. Maybe he was a non-smoker. My tattoos flared into the worst possible itching.

"What do you say, Mr. Madden?" Abbott leaned his generous behind against the desk and blew smoke rings toward the ceiling. "You want to give us that name and address?"

I shrank back in the chair. "Really, I'm just a bum in the wrong place at the wrong time. I wasn't working for anyone. The guy you want is the guy who shot up the bus. I don't know his name, and I don't know the address where I left the money, but I can take you there. I'd love to take you there."

Abbott smiled and touched the end of his cigarette against my forearm. I writhed and squealed. It hurt like hell. Cold sweat broke out on my brow, and I shook all over, hard. Abbott puffed a few more times, and applied the cigarette again. I screamed and rocked hard enough to tip over the chair. While Abbott righted it, Costello wrinkled his nose at the smell of my burning flesh and picked up the pliers.

"Who'd you say you worked for?" Abbott asked, but I got the sense he didn't really want me to answer, at least not yet.

"I'll take you to the money," I panted. A bottomless black pit of despair opened inside me. "I will, I promise. Please don't burn me again."

"What's that? I didn't catch the name," Abbott said.

"Look, it's a million in cash. I'll give it to you. You don't have to work for Cantel anymore. You can take the money and retire on some tropical island."

Abbott chuckled and Costello snorted.

"Nobody double-crosses Mr. Cantel," Costello said. "John learned that the hard way."

That's when the demon stepped into my sight. He had to duck to avoid scraping the suspended ceiling. He watched with interest while Abbott burned another hole in my arm, and with rapt fascination when Abbott paused to blow a smoke ring. He raised his snout and tried to imitate the thug's ethereal donuts without success. Then he extended his enormous hand and stuck a talon into my head. It burned almost as bad as Abbott's cigarette, and I screamed. Abbott gave me a queer look.

My fear jumped a thousand percent. In the real world, hallucinations never caused physical pain. No matter how unbelievable, the demon was real. And if he was real, what was the Dark Place? My world tipped upside down.

The big demon held his hand in the air. Black goo stuck to the talon and trailed wisps of smoke. A tarry, smoldering substance crept farther up the talon with each passing second. He shook his hand, but the tar continued its slow crawl. His brows drew down in a frown, and he shook the hand harder without result. His eyes opened wide, and he walked away behind me.

"Demon," I croaked. "Demon. There's a demon behind me. We have to get out of here."

The two thugs exchanged a look and a shrug.

"My turn," Costello said.

"I'm not done with my smoke yet," Abbott replied. "You'll have to wait."

The demon returned, minus a talon, and looked at me with curiosity, as though I were a butterfly pinned on an exhibition board. After a moment, he reached out a claw and dragged it across Abbott's head.

"Look out!" I cried. "He's stealing your... he's eating you!"

The claw came out with the white shiny goo I'd seen before, although I couldn't see any mark on Abbott, and he hadn't reacted to the demon's touch. A broad, pink tongue cleaned the goo from the talon. I hopped and jerked the chair across the floor away from them. Why couldn't they see him? Why couldn't they feel him? Why could I?

"I think he's gone crazy already," Costello said with a frown. "And I haven't gotten a turn yet."

"He's faking it," said his partner. "No one's pain tolerance is that low. Besides, he'll still scream even if he's crazy."

The demon dredged a claw through Costello's head while I gaped and scooted the chair the opposite direction. My heart raced, and I rocked like a granny on speed. One way or another, I was at the end of my short, sad life.

The demon returned to Abbott, leaned down, and whispered in his ear. The round-faced man plucked his cigarettes off the desk and lit a fresh one from the stub of his first. Then the demon shifted to whisper in Costello's ear. Abbott set the still-burning stub on the desk blotter, missing the ashtray completely. I blinked in disbelief.

"Hey," Costello said, "you only get one. Then it's my go."

"Yeah? Says who?" Abbott replied.

He set the new cigarette next to the stub on the blotter and bellied-up to Costello. The other man replaced the pliers on the desk and picked up a scalpel. An instant later, they were grappling. Lazy smoke curled up from the blotter, then a small flame crept across the paper. As they brawled, the blotter was pushed off the desk. The demon watched with undisguised glee.

I freaked. While the two men rolled on the floor, I used my teeth to rip at the duct tape around my right wrist. Smoke rolled up from the blotter on the floor behind the desk and caught the plastic chair upholstery. I freed my right hand and started on my left, terror leaking from me in little whimpers. Flames shot above the desktop. Acrid smoke filled the room. Weren't these modern office buildings supposed to have sprinkler systems? Damn, if I didn't get loose soon, I'd fry.

I developed a hacking cough from the toxic fumes of the now burning carpet. I tore at the tape on my ankles. The demon crouched next to the chair and looked on. I could swear he wanted to offer advice. I cowered away, humping the chair across the floor. Terror gave me strength, and I ripped my left leg loose.

Half the room burned, and still the two thugs fought. Blood streaked their clothes and faces. I wasn't waiting around to see who won. But what if they came after me? I leaped to the desk, ripped open the drawer, and grabbed the gun, thrusting it in my waistband. It lay cold against my skin. I burst out the door and ran for the stairs at the end of the hall.

At the door to the stairwell, I paused to look back. Smoke billowed in the corridor, obscuring the flames shooting from the office. No alarms sounded, and the sprinklers still hadn't come on, although I could see the silver heads dotted along the ceiling. Great. The fire suppression system didn't work.

I dashed back through the smoke about twenty feet to a manual alarm on the wall. It was okay with me if Abbott and Costello roasted, but I didn't know who else might be in the building. I pulled the breaker, and the alarm shrieked. The demon strolled unconcerned in my direction. *Real.* I wasn't staying to thank him for his assistance.

I hit the stairwell door at maximum speed and took the stairs down in big bounds. By the time I reached the ninth floor, people were filing into the stairwell, and I had to slow down. They seemed pretty jovial until the first traces of smoke drifted around them. Then they realized it wasn't a drill, and the leisurely exodus turned into a stampede.

While I didn't want to die in a fire, I also didn't want to get trampled by the panicked tide of office workers pummeling each other to get out of the building. I hung back at the tail end of the crowd and glanced over my head to see if Abbott and Costello followed. I had the gun jammed in my pants, but I wouldn't use it except for show. How could I be sure what I shot at? I caught a glimpse of the demon's ruddy skin and nearly missed my footing.

Smoke scented the air, but it still mostly rose in the stairwell. Sooty black clouds of nightmares roiled above the heads of the mob and drifted purposefully down. It occurred to me that if the demon came from the Dark Place and he was real, the nightmares were real, too. I thought about leaping the handrail and plummeting the remaining six floors. It might be a better way to go than living in what reality had become.

At the fourth floor, a woman with one arm in a sling stood next to a little boy who wore plaster casts on both legs and sat in a wheelchair that partially blocked the landing. The nightmares gathered in a dark knot around the two of them. People pushed and shoved to get past, ignoring her hysterical pleas for help. The boy couldn't be more than six or seven. A tear crept down his cheek, and he wiped it away, determined not to cry. He eyed the stairs, his hands on the wheels of his chair.

The smoke in the stairwell thickened enough to start the woman coughing. The upper floors must be engulfed for it to be this bad. I looked up again and saw the demon a couple of floors above, looking down. He didn't seem in any hurry. I could hear the faint sound of sirens. The fire department must be responding—and the police would, too. I needed to get out of there, but my feet glued themselves to the landing. *Crap.*

"Help us, please," his mother begged. "I have a broken collarbone. I can't carry him."

"Listen, kid," I said kneeling beside the boy's chair amidst the nightmares. "You ever play camel fights with your friends?"

"No," he whispered. "Are you going to help us?"

"Yep," I said, "but you have to do your part. Your mom's gonna help you stand on those awesome casts long enough for you to get on my back. Then you're gonna make like an Arab sheik and ride down the stairs on your camel."

I crouched on the step below his chair. His mom got him up, and he lurched onto my back. I nearly plunged head first down to the next landing. He was heavier than I thought, especially with the casts. He wrapped his arms around my neck so tight I couldn't breathe. He'd make a great WWF wrestler someday. I flagged his mother and pointed to the kid's arms before returning my grip to his leg. She adjusted his strangle hold, and we started down. The nightmares swirled around us and then streaked upward out of sight.

I could have crawled down the stairwell on hands and knees faster than we went. I imagined the demon strolling along behind and dipping his claw into the little boy's head. The thought made my skin ripple. The kid whimpered as the smoke thickened, and we all coughed.

"What's your name?" I asked, leaning against the wall to steady us and taking one careful step at a time.

"Mark," he replied.

"Not much decoration on those casts yet, buddy. You better get on that when you get back to school," I said. "How'd you break them?"

"In a car accident," his mother said. "That's why we're here, fighting with Cantel Insurance to get them to pay. They claim I missed a payment, but I brought bank statements that prove I didn't. Now they say the accident was my fault, but it wasn't. I can't afford to take them to court. Even if I could, there isn't a lawyer in town who will stand up to Mr. Cantel."

"I guess Cantel Insurance is getting their payback today," I choked, wondering if Cantel had insurance on his building. I hoped not.

By the time we reached the second floor landing, the smoke was so thick I had trouble seeing the stairs through my watering eyes. I stumbled and coughed and wasn't sure I'd make the bottom upright. My thighs burned, and I couldn't hold Mark much longer.

"Go for help," I told his mother.

"No," she gasped. "We're all going out together. I won't leave Mark. He's all I've got."

"Go. Get the firemen," I said. "I may not make it all the way."

She wiped her watering eyes, brushed Mark's hair back, her face full of fear, and plunged down the stairs out of sight.

One more flight, but my head spun. Not enough oxygen. Where were the damn firefighters? I'd always admired them, but if they didn't get here soon, I might revise my opinion. I staggered on, going by feel to find the next step. Mark stopped coughing, and his arms loosened around my shoulders. I thought he'd stopped breathing and bent lower to balance him on my back. *Faster, River, or this will all be for nothing.*

I put my foot forward toward the next step, and there wasn't one. We were at the bottom. A door opened, and fresh air rushed in along with two firemen wearing respirators. I stumbled through the door into a glorious sunset, hacking my lungs out. More firemen grabbed Mark off my back, and one rushed forward with an oxygen mask. I waved him away.

Mark's mom stood nearby, a mask over her face, and a fireman holding her back. She shook him off, ran to me, and threw her one good arm around my neck. Her lips brushed my cheek.

"Thank you," she whispered, her voice hoarse from smoke and emotion. "You're a good man."

If only I were. But maybe helping her and her son balanced the scales a little for the death of the bus driver and Ms. Jones.

As she hurried after Mark, I glanced around trying to determine the quickest escape route. I expected to be nabbed any minute, especially after the delay to help Mark and his mother. Across the street, a crowd of people watched the fire, many with their cell phones held at arm's length. Police officers pushed them back, but there were too many gawkers and too few officers.

News vans wearing satellite dishes on their roofs clustered farther down the street. Cameramen filmed reporters who stood with their backs to the burning building while they filed their reports. A lovely dark-haired reporter dragged her cameraman to the ambulance where EMTs worked on Mark, his mother hovering nearby. The reporter shoved a microphone in the woman's face, and a moment later, she pointed my direction. The cameraman pivoted toward me, hand adjusting the lens.

I broke for the crowd on the opposite sidewalk, head down, hoping not to be recognized. When I reached the line of people, a cheer went up. They'd seen me come out with Mark, and many of them were using their cell phones to video me. I threaded between them, feeling hands shaking mine and receiving congratulatory slaps on the back. I could only imagine how differently they'd behave if they recognized me as the madman on the morning news. I needed to get out of town pronto.

I pushed down the sidewalk to the cross-street, too many confusing thoughts swirling through my head. The demon was real. I'd thought the Dark Place only a figment of my demented mind. What if it wasn't? What really happened to me during what I'd thought were psychotic breaks? I needed quiet time to rest and think. As I was getting ready to break into a run, a hand clutched my arm.

"River! Thank God," Sammie said. "Are you okay? What were you doing in there?"

I stiffened and stared at her, worried about how she'd found me. No time now. I glanced back at the crowd and the fire and hurried on.

"The police are looking for us. We need to clear out now."

"We? Why are they looking for me? What did you say to them?" she asked, jogging to match my strides.

"The cabbie told them you were with me when Black Robe shot that woman this morning. They have questions."

I gazed around, thinking about where I was and where I should go next. As soon as the video got out, the cops would be swarming the neighborhood looking for me, and I was in no shape for a foot race with them. Ahead, I saw a sign for a vintage clothing shop. I couldn't go in, not the way I looked and smelled, but I could send Sammie in. And once she'd gotten me new clothes, I'd dump her. After all, what had she done for me?

I pointed to the shop. "They know what we're wearing. I'll wait behind the building. You go in and get me a hat and something with a hood. Use the money in the backpack. Make it quick."

Sammie ran to the shop and disappeared inside. More sirens wailed. I was sure they'd call every police car in the city to join the manhunt. I was too close to the scene and hustled around to the alley. I still had Cantel's gun jammed in my waistband and considered tossing it in a garbage can. I didn't like guns, and I would never shoot anyone. I'd only taken it to scare Abbott and Costello if they came after me. But then I stopped.

Cantel bragged about killing the bagman with this very gun, and it had his name engraved on the grip. There'd be questions about when I came into possession of it, but if he'd used it to kill others, then there'd be a string of open murders attached to it, more than my presence in the city would account for. It might prove useful if Cantel caught up to me again. Or maybe I could trade it to the cops as a get-out-of-jail-free card. To make those scenarios work, I needed a safe place to stash it.

A row of houses lined the opposite side of the alley, and one of them had a twenty-foot tall fir tree crowding the garage at the back of the yard. I fished in garbage cans until I found a suitable black plastic bag, and then I tied it around the gun and hopped the picket fence into the yard. In a minute, I had the gun lashed to the trunk and well hidden in the drooping branches. As a bonus, I came out covered in needles and smelling like a Christmas tree instead of a chimney sweep.

Sammie wasn't in the shop long, but it seemed like forever. She darted into the alley carrying a bulky bag and wearing a long brown suede coat and cloche hat. She opened the bag and pulled out a black hooded sweatshirt emblazoned with the Oakland Raiders logo, along with a black baseball cap. I stared. We were in Kansas, not California. Was this the universe twisting the knife?

"Is it the wrong size?" she asked.

Words wouldn't fit through my throat. I dragged the sweatshirt on, seated the cap tight on my head, and pulled the hood up. The ant feet faded away, giving me one less distraction. Right now, I could use the distraction. I just wanted to run, run from all the memories and unanswered questions.

"Where to?" Sammie asked.

Good question. Away from here. It was Fall, and I'd already started my seasonal migration. I'd head south. She could tag along until we reached the other side of the river and city center. After that, she was on her own.

"Downtown," I said. I headed east at a quick walk, going for the fastest route across the river.

"That's a long way, isn't it?" she asked. "Maybe we should get a cab or grab a bus."

"I don't know about you, but that hasn't been working so well for me lately," I replied, sarcasm oozing through.

"Why were you in that building?"

"How did you know I was there?" I countered.

"I saw you leaving the police station and followed. I would have lost you if he'd gone much farther. Good thing he hit those two red lights." She skip-hopped every few steps to keep up. "The car had police plates. Why'd they take you there?"

"To see my lawyer," I said, convinced she had to know why I'd been taken there. "Even crazy people get a lawyer."

"But..." She trailed off and gave me a hard look. "Don't the lawyers usually come to see *you* when you're in custody?"

"I don't know," I said, anger churning inside me. The burns on my arm pulsed with pain, and I wished she'd stop asking me questions. I needed to think, to focus, to plan my run.

We walked in silence for a block. As soon as I left her behind, I'd travel cross-country, stay off roads, head for Arizona or Southern California. Maybe I'd move to Mexico. If only I spoke Spanish. I guess I could learn. Would the demon follow? Nothing mattered except for survival, and to survive, I had to get away.

"I would have gotten you out," she said in that soft, sincere voice she'd used in the alley. "That's why I followed you."

"Yeah? How would you have done that? With your fancy magic wand?" I glanced around, watching for cop cars and the demon. And Black Robe. And Elvis. I figured I might as well since I was seeing all kinds of other impossible things.

"I don't know, but I would have," she answered. "I'm sorry you're mixed up in this. I'm going to do everything I can to make it right for you."

I cocked an eyebrow at her. *Sure, right after you stun me.*

###

When I looked over my shoulder, smoke still billowed from the Cantel Building into the darkening sky. We'd made it a mile and hadn't seen any roadblocks or prowling cops. I hoped they were just too busy with the fire to realize I'd been there. And the darker it became, the better our chances of not being spotted. I would have taken to the alleys already except they ran east-west and we needed to go south. We stuck to the less-traveled streets, but once we reached the river, we had no choice but to use a major arterial to cross.

"You said you knew where the crazy naked guy was," Sammie said. "You said you could take me to him."

"Yeah, well, that was when I thought you might want to repay me for saving your life by squaring things with the cops, but I guess your super secret mission got in the way."

"I did want to help you. I still do. It isn't that easy. I have to go through channels, I have to wait for my team."

"Yes," I replied bitterly. "God forbid saving someone's life should trump following protocol."

"I don't know why you're so angry at me, but this isn't about you and me. The man needs help. He can't take care of himself. His family wants him back."

"How do you know he can't take care of himself? Maybe he's not that crazy. And if his family cares so damn much, how'd he end up in that alley?"

"River," she said, grabbing my sleeve, "I think Black Robe is after him. It's the only answer that makes sense. And if he has my watch, he can find him. Where is he?"

"Don't worry. I'll make sure he's safe," I assured her. *About five hundred miles from here.*

"He needs treatment, or he could die."

"Don't lay a guilt trip on me, Sammie. I tried to do the right thing and help someone in need, and look what's happened."

I crossed the street, scanning the darkness for threats and wondering if the mysterious genetic condition could really kill me. No, it was all lies. They couldn't tell someone's genetics from half a block away. *And demons weren't real, except I'd met one that was.*

"You don't know where he is," she said. "You lied so I'd get you out of jail. You thought you had to manipulate me to get my help."

"You didn't help even then," I said, covering my shame with anger. I'd been an idiot to think anyone would help me, that anyone would show up to save me. "I'm taking care of me from here on. To hell with everyone else. That's how the world works."

"My brother gave his life for this man. I'm not giving up," she said, voice low and angry.

"Fine. Do whatever makes you happy."

I steered us to the Washington Street bridge. Rush hour traffic whizzed past in both directions, headlights shining in the gloom. People hurrying home to their families, their loved ones, their friends. I'd never be one of them. I shook my head, fighting against a blanket of fatigue. *Focus.*

I didn't see any cops staking out our end of the bridge. We wouldn't be able to see the other side until we were in mid-bridge. By then, it would be too late to double back if they lay in wait for us. Jumping off wasn't an option; we were too high above the water and too close to the falls. Besides, I didn't know how to swim.

We walked the last block and onto the bridge, the only foot traffic. I kept glancing over my shoulder, but no one followed us. We hit the mid-point with no sign of police cars on the opposite shore, and I heaved a sigh, the first deep breath I'd taken since approaching the bridge. We were going to make it across unchallenged, and then I would have to muster up enough strength to run away from Sammie.

With less than fifty feet to go, two men in trench coats appeared in front of us, walking our direction. They could have been businessmen heading to a tavern on the north side of the river, but they weren't carrying briefcases, and the bars on the north side weren't the kind of place where well-dressed office workers hung out. I looked back and saw another trench-coated figure not thirty feet behind us. Where had he come from? I'd checked seconds ago, and no one was on the bridge with us.

I looked around, panicked, ready to abandon Sammie and run into the street. I never got the chance. A black panel van stopped beside us, and the side door rolled open. A guy in a dark suit crouched in the doorway, badge in one hand, gun in the other.

"Federal agent, Mr. Madden. Please get in the van. You, too, Miss."

8

Two of the trench-coated men got in with us. Sammie sat in the back, sandwiched between them. I sat beside the agent with the gun. He drew a curtain across behind the driver so we couldn't see the road, and the driver pulled away into traffic.

I thought the curtain was a joke. We were driving north up Division. It was the only possible route that fit with the turns we'd made. Then it occurred to me that the point of the curtain wasn't to keep us from looking out. No one could see us in the back with the curtain drawn. I wondered if I was scheduled to disappear. If that was the plan, I hoped they made it quick and painless. Sammie railed nonstop about our treatment, but none of the agents responded.

After a twenty-minute drive, we made a couple of quick turns, bounced over a pothole, and pulled to a stop. The side door opened. We were parked in an alley, and I could hear the traffic roaring past on Division in front of the building. A black sedan parked next to the van. Two agents escorted me to the back door of a concrete block building while Sammie protested loudly about them taking me and not her, what with me being underage and her being my guardian. One of my escorts snickered at her diatribe.

Iron bars covered the rear window. I wondered if this was a police substation. Inside, bright fluorescent lights revealed a minor emergency clinic, and for a moment, I thought I was in for another torture session. Or maybe the administration of truth serum.

The agents ordered me to remove my sweatshirt and stand against a wall. I heard equipment hum. Then they let me have the sweatshirt back. As soon as I put it on, they trundled me outside. I thought about making a break for it, letting them put a slug in my back and being done with it. I couldn't summon the energy.

When I got back in the van, Sammie asked whether I was okay, but I didn't answer. I kept track of the turns long enough to figure out we were headed more or less southeast. After that, I zoned out. I was running on empty on all fronts: physically drained from all the running, lack of food or water, and pain from the torture, and emotionally drained by the unpleasant memories breeching in my brain.

I didn't realize we'd stopped until the door slid open again. I'd expected us to be in the Federal Building underground car park. We were in a garage all right, your everyday family garage. Maybe the feds worked from home as part of some Republican plan for smaller government. The black sedan shared the space with the van. They'd shut the big overhead door before letting us out.

They led us into a drafty old house where all the curtains were closed, and down a flight of stairs to a finished basement. Sammie was taken one direction, still voicing her protests, and I was taken the opposite way to a tiny bathroom. The agent stepped in with me, handed me a cup, and ordered me to pee in it. I gave serious thought to filling the cup and dumping it on his shiny shoes, but I practiced restraint. When I'd complied, he pulled a hospital gown out of a cupboard and told me to strip.

"No," I said. I was done being a nice, compliant guy. That strategy had gotten me nowhere. I didn't disrobe in front of strange men. Or friendly men. I'd be like Gandhi—non-violent resistance.

The agent cracked the door open and handed my urine sample to another man. Then he sucker punched me in the gut. I dropped to my knees, gasping. He dragged my sweatshirt, t-shirt, and hat off in one swift motion, shoved my arms through the sleeves of the hospital gown, and tied it behind my neck. I thought he'd probably developed his technique by taking lunch money off his classmates in the schoolyard.

"You want to do the pants yourself?" he asked obligingly.

I nodded, reconsidering my pledge to non-cooperation, and set to work on the knot in my cinch tie belt. Once I got it undone, he lifted me to my feet. I kicked off my shoes and stepped out of the jeans. He didn't remark on my lack of underwear.

"Socks, too," he said.

"Can I have the hat back?" I asked, removing my socks. The ants had gleefully taken up a polka on my head.

"Later."

"Please? I'm having a really bad hair day."

My plea fell on deaf ears. He led me to a windowless bedroom, outfitted with a night table and two narrow beds and abandoned me there. The lock clicked ominously. Did they know that bedrooms with no outside egress were a building code violation? What if the house caught fire? Why had they locked me naked in a bedroom? The implications scared the crap out of me.

The overhead light warbled *The Morning After* off-key. I thought about turning it out, but the place would be pitch black if I did. I worried about what might come out of the darkness given my present state of mind. Sometimes it was better to listen to the lights.

Despite my anxiety, I was falling asleep sitting up when the agent finally brought back my hat, along with the rest of my clothes. He gave me the courtesy of stepping out while I dressed, and then he took me upstairs. A tiny flame of hope ignited in me.

Sammie followed me up, still ranting. I had to give her points for tenacity, and I was a little surprised that she defended me so vociferously. I figured since I refused to tell her where the crazy guy was, she wouldn't have any further use for me. I wondered what they thought of her big knife. I bet once they saw that, they didn't try any sucker punches on her.

A cheap folding banquet table occupied the center of the living room, with six metal chairs arranged around it. A big-screen TV hung on one wall, playing a news channel with the sound muted, and electronic equipment occupied the bookcase below it. Two floor lamps provided light. They hummed *When Johnnie Comes Marching Home*. What I'd thought were window curtains were actually thick wool blankets. Except for the electronic gear, I'd seen flop houses that were furnished nicer. The Republicans really had slashed the budget if this was the best the feds could afford.

Our escorts waved us to chairs on one side of the table, and then they took up posts by the exits. After a minute or two, a woman entered. I noticed right off that she had fit, shapely legs. Not that I'm given to watching women's legs, mind, but since I sketch people a lot, I pay attention to shape and symmetry. She wore a black two-piece suit, the skirt a demure knee length and the jacket covering a conservative white blouse. Her thick black hair was cropped short in a well-shaped style that framed her face. She wore minimal make-up this time, not like when I'd seen her before. The psycho waitress from the bus took a seat opposite me.

"Mr. Madden, I'm Agent Lopez." She placed her badge on the table in front of me. *Federal Criminal Investigation Services*, it said.

Wait a minute. Wasn't it supposed to be Federal *Bureau of Investigation*? Or was this a different agency? And what the hell did the feds want with me? My head pounded, and my arm burned. It didn't matter what group she represented, she was a cop, and I was through talking to them—unless they tortured me. Or beat me up. Or made me ride in an elevator.

"Look, Agent Lopez," Sammie said, "you can't question him without someone from social services or another designated adult present. He's a minor."

"Don't worry, Miss..." Agent Lopez said. "We'll get to you. Mr. Madden, would you care to clear up the confusion over your age?"

"There's no confusion," Sammie argued. "He's sixteen. River, don't answer any of her questions. Don't let her bully you."

The fed smiled. "Well, Mr. Madden, FCIS isn't quite so gullible. Our forensic specialist tells me that the x-ray of your clavicle puts you between twenty-two and thirty. Care to share your age?"

"Your guess is as good as mine." At her scowl, I mumbled, "Twenty-five-ish."

I glanced at Sammie. She stared at me with eyes full of confusion and betrayal. She crossed her arms and frowned, not at me but at Agent Lopez. I made a careful study of the tabletop while heat crept up my face and wondered how many more of my lies and omissions the agent intended to reveal. But what did I care what Sammie thought of me? She was the predator, and I was her prey; that's all that connected us. That and our shared goal to get out of the house. Or maybe since Lopez was a federal sister, she wasn't in a hurry to get away.

The agent looked at me and smiled, the same satisfied look a cat gives a captive mouse. "I can see why you do it. Someone as little and pretty as you goes to prison, he ends up some tough guy's bitch. Juvie's much safer if you can pull it off, and I imagine most of the time, you do."

The memories that had bubbled just below the surface of my consciousness crashed back, swamping me so I couldn't see the room anymore, couldn't breathe. Jimmy on the floor, bleeding out, telling me with his dying breath to run away, that I was next. Me crying in bed after lights out that night, feeling like a part of me died with Jimmy, not understanding how he could leave me. Big Bob, the night attendant at the orphanage, taking me from my bed to join him on late rounds like Jimmy used to do. I'd do Jimmy's job now, he said. Jimmy would want me to.

Rounds over, he taken me to his office and held me in his lap while I cried for Jimmy. Held me like he loved me, like I was his son. Held me while he slipped my pajamas off. Held his hand over my mouth to stifle my scream when he penetrated me. I'd taken Jimmy's advice, one night too late, and I'd run.

I had to get out of there, had to run now. I wouldn't go to prison. I scrambled to my feet, shoving my chair back hard. The men at the exits went on alert, reaching into their suit jackets.

"River?" Sammie said, rising. "Are you okay?"

She laid her hand on my arm, touching the burns under my sweatshirt sleeve. I flinched away, gasping from pain felt and pain remembered.

"Whoa, there, Madden." Lopez came around the table to my side, a cool, concerned intensity in her voice. "Let's see the arm."

If I showed her what Abbott had done, it might give her ideas. I moved away, right into Sammie. She took my hand in hers and peeled back the sleeve.

"My God," she whispered.

"Art, get the first aid kit," the agent ordered, and one of the guards left.

"Did you get burned in the fire?" Sammie asked, her eyes looking into mine.

"Those are cigarette burns," Lopez said. "I'd guess Mr. Cantel had some questions."

"They did this while you were in custody?" Sammie whispered, horror and disbelief in her voice.

Art brought a red plastic box marked with *First Aid*. Agent Lopez dug out a spray can and applied its contents liberally. The burning in my arm stopped; the fire in my brain continued. She put noxious yellow ointment on big pads, placed them over the burns, and wrapped gauze around the dressing. Sammie held my hand and kept her other hand on my back, rubbing slow circles. Waves of calm rippled out from her touch. I told myself her concern didn't mean anything.

The agent sent Art for water and put an aspirin packet on the table. Then she pointed to my chair. I collapsed into it, drained and defenseless. Art brought a glass of water and retreated. My throat felt parched from the smoke, but I was too exhausted to reach for the glass.

"Let's start again," Lopez said. "Is River Madden your real name?"

"What's real?" I asked, thinking she deserved a big dose of enigmatic since she hadn't told us why we were there, although I thought I knew. But I wouldn't help her. Gandhi. Passive resistance. Ohm.

"What's your birth date?"

"Don't know." And really, I couldn't see that it mattered. It wasn't like I had buddies who'd throw a birthday party for me. "I kind of lost track."

Lopez didn't like enigmatic and glared at me. "We've run your prints, and neither of you show up in the system. Who are you? Who do you work for?"

"Don't answer, River," Sammie said. "Unless you're charging us with a crime, we don't have to say anything to you. We want a lawyer."

"You're required to give your name, and Mr. Madden is wanted for fleeing custody."

"I didn't flee," I said, wondering why I bothered. "Well, okay, I did, but not until after I'd left police custody."

I guess since she couldn't make sense of my answers, the agent turned to Sammie.

"If you two don't want to talk to me, I'll turn Madden over to Lt. Knowles, and he can ask the questions."

"You can't let the police have him!" Sammie protested. "You've seen what they did."

Lopez spread her hands and shrugged. Sammie fumed. I ohmed. Sooner or later, we'd get around to the gym bag, and that would be the end of Sammie trying to rescue me. Then the agent would turn me over to the cops, and my life wouldn't be worth a plug nickel. My used-up brain tried to make sense of why that hadn't happened already.

Sammie blinked first. "We're part of a top secret military black op. That's why we don't show up in your system, and why we can't tell you more."

The agent leaned back, smug. "Who should I call to verify that?"

"No one," Sammie replied. "It's called 'deniability,' and it means I'll go down before I reveal anything to you."

"Aren't you the patriot," said Lopez. "What about you, Mr. Madden? Are you prepared to do hard time for murder, or would you like to tell me more?"

"He won't do time, especially since he's not guilty of anything. My superiors will make sure he's set free."

Sammie sat ramrod straight, and her eyes glittered. I couldn't believe what I was hearing. I'd lied, tried to manipulate her, and here she was, defending me against the feds. I was a cad, a real low-life gutter rat. I didn't deserve her support. The least I could do was stand with her and fight.

"We're looking for a cache of prototype weapons stolen from the military," I said, trying to spin my story out of a few threads of truth. "We were supposed to meet someone—an informer. But we were ambushed. In the alley. When we were trying to get them back. The stolen weapons."

Lopez's interest sharpened, although I didn't know what I'd said to make that happen. Or maybe my nose grew a foot, and that's why she stared at me. Sammie gave me an appropriately unhappy look.

"You do that patriot stuff if you want," I said, "but I'm not going to jail."

"What kind of weapons?" the agent asked.

"Um... a new kind," I said. "Very high-tech and special."

"Corporal Madden, I'm ordering you to keep your mouth shut," said Sammie. "You let me handle this."

Corporal Madden? Couldn't she have come up with a better rank than that? I waited, eager to see what rank she'd claim for herself. "Yes, sir. Uh, ma'am."

"And who are you exactly?" Lopez nearly slavered on the table. She thought she had us working against one other. Ha! Little did she know.

Sammie and I were a story-telling dynamo. Then I remembered that Sammie was just as wretched a liar as me, and my jubilation ebbed.

"Talent Second Class Clementine Samuels."

Clementine? Ouch. No wonder she went by Sammie. Or was that her real name? And was a talent higher or lower than a corporal? The light bulb sang, *Oh my darling, oh my darling...*

"I've never heard of that rank," the agent said. "What branch of the service are you with?"

"Sorry," Sammie said. "You don't have appropriate clearance."

"And there weren't any secret high-tech weapons in the alley," Lopez said. "Unless you count the fake wands your people carry."

"You've seen the personal effects from the people killed in the alley?" Sammie asked, leaning over the table.

"FCIS has taken possession of them."

"I need to see them," Sammie said.

"And I need answers to my questions," Lopez said. "What happened in the alley? How were the two men killed?"

"Three," I corrected, without thinking. Oops. "One of them kind of... splattered. A lot. Maybe the rats made off with him. The pieces, I mean."

"If you're part of this team, why weren't you dressed like the others?" she asked, turning her attention back to me.

"Uh..." I looked at Sammie, but she seemed as momentarily stumped as me. "I was undercover. As a homeless person. I was the lookout. I mean the surveillance person."

"You don't seem like the military type," she said, one eyebrow raised. "If it weren't for your clean drug and alcohol tests, I might believe you were exactly what you appear to be—a homeless guy in over your head."

Sweat popped out on my brow. Yeah, I was a great undercover operator. Nerves of steel. "That's why I'm good. Undercover. No one suspects me."

"So what happened in the alley?"

"I think before we tell you anything more, Agent Lopez, we'll need some assurances from you that none of this information will leave this room," Sammie said. "Furthermore, you'll release us so we can continue our assignment without notifying the police about Corporal Madden's whereabouts, and you'll give us a look at what was collected in the alley."

"Convince me of your story, and I'll consider it," the agent said.

I'd tell her anything to get us out of there, but Sammie seemed reluctant. Or maybe she'd run out of fantasies. Since she couldn't really order me around, I continued the fable.

"We were ambushed. We had to retreat. I led the bad guy off. To save my fallen comrades. I got on the bus."

"Uh, huh," Lopez said. "So why'd you take the money?"

"The money?" I said. Sammie looked poleaxed again by my lack of forthrightness. "I didn't know it was money. I just wanted shoes."

"Shoes?" the agent asked, both eyebrows raising.

"I was barefoot. Part of my disguise. As a homeless person." The eyebrows on the guards by the exits raised, and they exchanged a look. I bet they weren't willing to go that far when *they* role-played. I could teach them a thing or two about undercover work—assuming I actually did any.

"I needed the shoes so I could keep ahead of Black Robe," I said. "That's our code name for the perp."

I hoped I had the terminology right. I read a lot of mysteries and thrillers at the library on rainy afternoons, but could I trust fiction writers on the semantic details? I looked at Sammie, who looked like the proverbial deer in the headlights. I didn't want her to think I was a thief. I might tell a tall tale or two, but I never, ever stole anything. I don't know why I worried about what she thought of me, but I did.

"I didn't want the money. I wouldn't have stolen the bag if I hadn't been desperate for shoes so I could stay ahead of Black Robe."

Lopez narrowed her eyes. "You expect me to believe you *accidentally* stole a million dollars?"

Naturally she didn't believe the only truthful part of the whole friggin' story. And Sammie probably didn't, either. Why *wouldn't* a homeless guy want a million bucks? No more starving, no more freezing in the winter and frying in the summer. Why hadn't I thought about that and skipped town with the money? Just how stupid was I? It didn't pay to be honest.

"Yes," Sammie said, "I do expect you to believe it. The corporal informed me of his mistake, but returning the money wasn't high on our priority list. We had an arms dealer to catch, and we needed reinforcements. Those came first."

An idea stirred in my sluggish brain, but I couldn't hang onto it. With effort, I tore open the aspirin, tossed pills in my mouth, and followed them with the entire glass of water, stalling so I could think. By the time I'd put the glass back on the table, a scheme started to blossom.

"You were tailing the money because you want to bust Cantel, and you know he has cops in his pocket. That's why you're hiding out here instead of working out of the Federal Building," I said.

"Mr. Madden," Lopez said, "you're a real problem for me. A cop delivered you to Cantel, but you appear to have escaped and in the process, burned Cantel's building to ash. Despite the obvious signs of torture, which should have hurried you on your way, you took time to rescue a little boy. Yes," she said, waving at the TV, "it's all over the news. You're a hero. Did you tell Cantel where to find the money? Is that how you got out? Was the torch job your revenge for him burning you?"

"You knew he was in there being tortured, and you did nothing?" Sammie asked, seething. "What kind of monsters are you?"

I was surprised by her vehemence. I'd withheld information, outright lied to her, and still she leaped to my defense. Wow. I felt guilty for planning to ditch her.

"They thought I was just another homeless guy, a bum," I explained. "No one would miss me, so why interfere?"

To her credit, Lopez looked uncomfortable. "We were working on a warrant when the fire started."

I laughed. I was on solid ground when it came to knowing how much law enforcement cared about the homeless. "And the moon is made of green cheese."

"Listen, Agent Lopez, let's do a deal," Sammie said. "You give us the items the police retrieved from the alley, and we'll hand over the money. You can go on with your bust of this Cantel person, and we'll get on with rounding up our arms dealer. We both win."

"Show me the money," the agent said.

The last thing I wanted was to meet with Lopez or her agents at some later date to hand over the loot. I didn't trust her not to take me prisoner and turn me in. Maybe Sammie could get the information she needed just by looking at what the feds had. Maybe we didn't need to take the stuff away with us.

"Show us that you've got something we'd be interested in. Then we can talk about exchanges."

Sammie nodded her agreement and folded her arms. I was glad she was on my side. She might be small, but once she got going, she was a fireball. She had more determination than a pit bull chasing a dog catcher, and I bet her bite was worse. I thought we made a darn fine team, even if we were the worst liars in the county. I imitated Sammie and crossed my arms, too. We both looked hard at Lopez.

Agent Lopez scowled at us. She nodded to one of the men, who left the room and returned carrying a large box, which he set on the table. She stood, opened the lid, and pulled out my backpack, which she discarded beside the table. Then she produced a black shirt identical to the one Sammie wore. Sammie's face paled, and her hands trembled.

Lopez set the shirt on the table and added a pair of trousers from the box. She pulled a wand out and placed it on top of the stack. Sammie stared at the pile, eyes glistening. I wanted to hold her hand, or offer her a tissue. I still didn't have any.

The agent dipped in again and brought out the chuckler's black robe. I knew it was his by the blood-soaked tatters of hood, and revulsion stirred in the pit of my stomach. Sammie couldn't take her eyes from Griff's uniform.

Lopez pulled another wand from the box and waved it in front of Sammie. "Maybe next time you go hunting an arms dealer, you can buy some decent weapons before you try to bust him."

Sammie's face hardened. She dragged her eyes from Griff's kit and focused on the robe.

"May I?" she asked.

Lopez hesitated, then slid the garment across the table. Sammie stood and spread it flat, pointedly ignoring Griff's clothes. She smoothed the robe, running her hands over every inch. It looked like some kind of heavy synthetic fabric, a flexible ballistic nylon, probably waterproof. She spent a lot of time examining the ragged edges of the hood, heedless of the blood. Light glinted off silver threads woven into the fabric. Then she turned the whole thing inside-out and went over it again.

"Where's the rest of it?" she asked.

She'd caught Lopez by surprise, something I thought didn't happen often, and my admiration for Sammie rose another notch. The agent pulled a harness out of the box and laid it on top of the robe.

The straps were made of flat nylon punctuated with round metal studs and looked the right size to fit around the chuckler's chest and shoulders. A plastic plate was fitted to the harness so it would ride in the center of the chest. I could see scratches or markings around the edges of the plate. They looked a little like the gibberish Sammie had painted on the wall in the alley. When she examined them more closely, she sucked in her breath.

Her fingers hovered over the plate. She glanced up at Lopez and around at the rest of the agents. The need to know warred with the need to keep secrets. She touched one of the little symbols twice, and the plate glowed to life.

Lopez started. "How'd you do that?"

Sammie shrugged, her eyes glued to the plate. Lines of what might be text in some unusual script appeared one after the other. Her finger traced down the lines without contacting the device, her brow furrowed. She touched another marking on the frame of the plate, and the text vanished, to be replaced by a soft glow from the plate that spread to the robe.

Lopez stepped back, and the agents pulled their weapons, unsure whether to point them at us or the table. The glow crept across the robe, lighting the chest and sleeves, but as it began its spread down the remainder of the skirt, it skipped over the half closest to me. The plate hummed, and the light grew stronger, flickering along the edge of the unlit fabric like sheet lightning in storm clouds, as though it tried to spread but bumped against some invisible barrier. Then the plate flashed, and the light snuffed out.

"Huh," Sammie said. She double-tapped a marking, and the list returned. Satisfied, she touched the plate again, and it went dark.

"What is that thing?" Lopez asked, keeping her distance.

"Sorry, it's need-to-know, and you don't need to know."

"Don't give me that BS. Did we just get exposed to radiation or something?"

"I'll just take this with me," Sammie said. "It's not something you want to play around with if you don't know what you're doing."

"The hell you will," replied the agent. "The only way you're getting the equipment is if I get the million."

Sammie just nodded. "Fine. I'll notify my team leader, and he'll make the necessary arrangements. You'll be hearing from us."

"You'll leave Madden here, as insurance," Lopez said.

My heart stopped. Sammie had what she wanted, and she didn't know where I'd hidden the money. If she walked out without me, she wouldn't be coming back. She grabbed her wand from the table and stowed it in her trousers before looking at me. Uncertainty played across her face. Then she turned to the agent.

"Sorry," she said. "I'm already down a man. I can't afford to lose another operative at a time like this."

I felt like a kid at Christmas. Sammie didn't abandon me. I was walking out with her, and then I was heading out of town posthaste. I'd had enough of cloak and dagger for one life time. I'd never play Good Samaritan again. I'd mind my own business, keep my head down and my nose clean. Johnny Law would never see or hear of me again. I'd go be a hermit in the desert or on a mountain somewhere.

"Madden delivers the money, or you don't get the... whatever this stuff is." Lopez waved a hand at the robe. "Anyone else comes, and the trade is off. You have twenty-four hours."

"Just another bully with a badge, pushing people around," I muttered.

My comment riled Lopez. She leaned forward on the table. "For your information, when you made off with that gym bag, you jeopardized a two-year operation that, if successful, could have seriously curtailed drug trafficking in North America and saved thousands from the health risks, the crime, the poverty that go hand-in-hand with addiction."

"Cantel's an international drug runner? I find that hard to believe," I said, feeling bold enough to sneer.

"Cantel's interesting. He does a lot of business throughout the Midwest, but he's small potatoes. We're after a man called Enrique. He's a lieutenant in the biggest drug ring on the continent. If we can get him, we'll apply a combination of pressure and incentives, and he'll give us more of the upper echelons. But you messed us up when you grabbed the bag."

I felt like I'd wandered into the old proverb about the want of a horseshoe nail and a lost kingdom, only in my case, it was all about a pair of running shoes. How had this come down on me? I was no one important. I certainly wasn't a hero meant to save the country from the evil drug cartel. I just wanted to rebury all the bad memories and survive for another day.

"He'll bring you the money," Sammie said, already heading for the door.

"Unfortunately, it's not just the money that we need," said Lopez. "We need Madden to work directly with Cantel and Enrique. By stealing Cantel's money and burning his building, he's challenged Cantel for control of the territory. Cantel's so pissed he's announced a half-million bounty on Madden. Enrique's watching, waiting to see who's top dog. If Madden approaches Enrique, we're confident he'll agree to let Madden make a buy. We can't catch these guys without Madden."

I stared, open-mouthed. I'd been right—she *was* psycho.

9

~~~

"You're crazy!" I said. "Cantel already thinks someone is trying to take over his organization, and he intends to stop them. And this Enrique person would have hit men after me before you had him booked."

"How would they find you?" Lopez said. "You're part of a super-secret government agency. You don't exist."

Ah, hell. This is why I try never to lie. One way or another, it always comes back to bite me.

"Yeah, and I'm already on a mission," I said. "I don't have time for another one."

"You really believe he's crucial to your operation?" Sammie asked. "You couldn't use a double or something?"

"Not with all the publicity he's had," Lopez said, waving a hand in my direction. "He's the biggest thing on YouTube, a cyber Robin Hood. 'Bus driver suspect escapes police but stops to save small boy.' There must be two dozen videos posted already."

I groaned. I didn't want to be famous. I didn't want to be a hero. I just wanted to go south for the winter, catch a few rays, eat citrus fruit fresh from the tree, and sell sketches to snow birds.

"You can't contact Enrique and say you're a representative of River's?"

Lopez shook her head. "He's too cagey to deal with someone he doesn't know. He'll want to see the real thing."

"And exactly what is it you need him to do?" Sammie asked.

"You're not seriously considering this!" I said, wondering what happened to the champion who'd been protecting me so stridently only a few minutes earlier.

"He needs to set up a meet with Enrique, and then show up with the money. We'll be nearby, ready to move in once we've recorded the buy."

"Wear a wire to a drug deal?" I spluttered. "Because you intend to get him for my murder?"

"Hold on, River," Sammie said, chewing her lip and looking worried. "If this dealer's as important as she says, we should do what we can to get her bust back on track. After all, it's our fault she lost her quarry."

I stared, mouth open. Did she believe her delusion about me being her corporal? I might be crazy, but I wasn't *that* crazy. I didn't belong to any super-secret strike team that would shelter me once the shit hit the fan. I'd be out there on the street, alone, with professional assassins hunting me. I couldn't even leave the country because I couldn't get a passport.

"What about Cantel? How will you take him down?" Sammie asked.

"We'll leak Madden's location. When Cantel tries to make the hit, we'll move on him."

"All right, Agent Lopez. We'll help you, but I'll want the details of both operations. I'm not putting River in jeopardy because you run a sloppy bust. Are we clear? And when we return with the money, we're taking the robe and anything else the police collected."

To my astonishment, Lopez nodded. She pulled a cell phone from her suit pocket and slid it across the table.

"My number is the first one on speed dial. A contact number for Enrique is the second. The local police will still be looking for you. I advise you to set up the meet with Enrique before Cantel takes another run at you. When you have it arranged, call me. You're trying to buy a load of a new drug called 'ghost' that he was supposed to deliver to Cantel. He'll be anxious to get rid of it."

Sammie grabbed the phone off the table, and I scooped the backpack from the floor. Then she followed me to the front door. The agent posted there unlocked it and stepped aside to let us out.

"I'll have someone take you wherever you need to go," Lopez said.

I smiled. "No, thanks, we're good."

We exited into the dark, and I took a deep breath, enjoying the fresh, cold taste of freedom. I looked up at the house number, orienting myself to our location before heading to the street. Even numbers on the north side of the street, odd numbers on the south. We made a right and rolled into a brisk walk through the shabby neighborhood. I'd stick with Sammie for a few blocks just to make sure none of the feds followed, and then I'd run. *Not going to be in Kansas anymore, Toto. Way too many crazy people here.*

The air had a bite, but it also seemed thick and gloomy. My tattoos pricked and itched. It made me uneasy.

"River, I'm so sorry. I had no idea they were torturing you," she said. "If I'd realized, I would have come after you, and to hell with the consequences."

She sounded sincere. I swallowed hard. If she knew I was crazy, would she have blasted her way in? I wasn't sure I wanted an answer.

"You couldn't know," I said. "Sorry I snapped at you."

Sammie flipped the phone open, her face illuminated by the screen.

"We have an hour until the rendezvous at the pie factory," she said, handing the phone to me. "Do you know where we are?"

She talked like we were still a team, and she'd acted like it with the feds, standing up for me despite my lies. Guilt rose up and bit me in the conscience. I couldn't just leave her. I owed her an explanation.

"Sammie, I haven't been entirely honest with you," I said.

"It's okay, I understand," she replied, her voice soft. "You're ashamed of being homeless and didn't want me to know. It happens. People lose their jobs, then their cars, their homes. It doesn't make you a bad person. You just have to pick yourself up and try again.

"But River, you have to help Agent Lopez. It might be the biggest, most important thing you do in your life. It could open doors for you, be your ticket to a new career. It'll give you your self-respect back."

"What?! I'm not ashamed of being homeless, and I'm not looking for a new career. I just... live simply, without the carbon footprint of a huge house or a big car. Kind of like a monk," I said, knowing every word was a lie.

"So you're going to keep the money," she said, disappointment in her tone. "I don't know what you've been through living on the streets. It must be hard, but taking the money isn't the way to get out."

Why did it bother me what she thought? Why did I care that I hadn't met her expectations? From the churning in my gut, I knew I did, and that made me more angry. It didn't matter what anyone thought of how I lived. I was doing the best I could, wasn't I? All that counted was survival. Get through this day, and get on to the next.

"Lopez can have the money. I'll send her a postcard telling her where to find it. But I'm not getting tangled up with a bunch of crooks who can snap their fingers and have me killed." I waved my burned arm at her. "I've had a taste of what they can do, and that's enough."

"I'd be dead now if it weren't for you, and that little boy would, too. I just don't understand how you could be the kind of person who would help the two of us and not help the thousands who are affected by these thugs." Her eyes looked at me with such sadness I couldn't stand it.

Maybe I was too selfish. Or maybe it was because all those thousands were nameless and faceless, whereas Sammie and Mark were living, breathing people I couldn't ignore, right before my eyes. I'd seen plenty of drug addicts on the streets and felt sympathy for their plight. But it seemed to me they'd made a choice at some point, and now they were living with the hellish consequences. How was it my job to fix that? How had I become responsible for thousands when I struggled to be responsible for myself? I drowned in a sudden sense of hopelessness, of impossible weight heaped on my shoulders.

"I'm just one guy, Sammie. I can't fix the world." *I can't even fix me.*

"You're not alone, River," she said, hope returning to her voice. "My team will help. We'll see you're protected. When the operation is over, we can take you to a safe place where Enrique and Cantel can't find you. It's our fault you had to steal that bag. We're prepared to step up."

She sounded sincere, but I knew better. No one could make anyone else safe. Maybe if she lived long enough, she'd learn that. Besides, when she found out who I really was, how interested would she be in letting me solve Lopez's problems?

"Do you have family that might be at risk from these people?" she asked.

I laughed. What a thought!

"I'm a foundling, discovered when I was about two. By a couple of fishermen. Down by the river." I pointed to my Raiders sweatshirt. "The case worker was a Raiders fan, hence the name 'River Madden.'"

"River, I'm so sorry. I should have bought something else," she said, head bowed in embarrassment. "You were never adopted?"

I shook my head, uncomfortable with the topic. Nothing says 'worthless' like being passed over for adoption.

"Well, you should have been. You're bright and funny and clever. And your heart is in the right place. It was their loss."

Their loss? Because they didn't end up with the awkward, schizophrenic runt? Maybe I was hallucinating the conversation. She couldn't have said those things about me. Heck, she barely knew me. She didn't know me, come to that. She didn't know about my mental disorder, and she didn't know it was me in the alley. If those weren't deal breakers for any relationship between us, then I'd be a monkey's uncle.

"I don't suppose you're going to tell me about the black robe equipment," I said.

"No," she said. "I can't."

And that's how it would always be with us. She had her secrets; I had mine. We came from different worlds, and nothing could bridge that gulf. It was time to let go and move on, forget the warmth of her hand on my back, forget the kindness in her voice when she'd said she'd take me home. It was all a pipe dream, a crazy man's impossible desires. The darkness around me mirrored the darkness in my soul.

The street dead-ended at a fence around the log yard of a lumber mill. It was ridiculously stout chain-link, seven feet high, and with barbed wire on top. I hadn't realized that logs were so hard to contain, kind of like buffalo, I guess. It would have made a good prison yard if only they'd had some decent lighting. Instead, we stumbled through the inky blackness, stepping in puddles and potholes around the perimeter of the place while we searched for a proper paved street again.

We followed the fence south and turned west at the corner onto a dirt lane, barely able to see twenty feet in front of us. A big wooden two-story building ran along the south side of the lane, a security light on the side of it supplying a dim pool of illumination. We'd gone a hundred feet before we encountered a set of huge gates that blocked our way. Great, a blind alley.

As I turned around, my tattoos flared into intense itching. Coming towards us was the eight-foot demon, hooves silent on the dirt, his eyes on Sammie. I froze, staring. Beside me, Sammie gasped.

"Stay behind me," I squeaked, stepping in front of her.

"You can see him?" she asked, her voice full of disbelief. She fumbled in her trouser pocket for her wand.

I didn't have time to answer. An eight foot tall demon covers ground quickly even when he's not in a hurry. She stepped around me, and lightning crackled from her wand. It went right through the demon and off into the dark beyond. He smiled and altered course to confront her. I jumped into his path.

"Hold it right there, Smokey," I said, holding out my hand in a stop motion. My heart thudded in my chest, and my hand shook, inches from his stomach. "You can't have her."

Incredibly, the demon stopped. He raised his heavy brows, perplexed. "Why not?"

"Because..." Geez, I was talking to the demon. No, I was ordering the demon around like I expected him to obey. Lordy, what had he asked? Oh, yeah, why he shouldn't stick his talon in Sammie.

"Because it's rude," I blurted.

The demon crouched on his haunches, but he still stood a head taller than me. This close, I could see bristly whiskers on his chin, pink skin inside his nostrils, and the individual hairs of the fine, red hide on his forehead. He gestured toward Sammie. "But Traveler, I need information from the affiliate."

"You can understand him?" Sammie whispered.

"You can't?" Oh, oh, maybe I was hallucinating the conversation. My knees felt weak, and I leaned as far back as I could without falling over.

"I hear a kind of irritating buzz," she said, voice shaky. "I can't make out any words. What does he want?"

The songs of demons, like I heard in the Dark Place. A nightmare cloud drifted out of the dark and oozed over the demon's torso. With a flip of his hand, he swatted at it. It dodged like an annoying fly.

"Shoo, shoo," the demon said, waving an arm at the cloud. The nightmare retreated, but not far. "Tell me, Traveler, how am I to gain the knowledge I desire if I don't sample the affiliate?"

"Uh... you ask. That's how humans do it, and since you're in human space, you have to do as humans do. None of that Dark Place stuff here."

"But she doesn't hear me, and I can't understand her unless I sample." He blew two quick puffs of smoke from his nostrils and furrowed his brows.

I glanced back at Sammie, who stared wide-eyed at the demon, hearing only my side of the conversation. "Then ask me."

"You wish to make a bargain?"

Bargaining with the devil. That never turned out well in the fairy stories, did it? I had to be crazy. No, I knew I was crazy, so what the hell.

"You don't sample, and I answer your question. But you only get one question. And the bargain is for all time, not just until I answer." Had I covered all the caveats? "And you don't get my soul, even if you don't like the answer."

The big bull brows lifted in surprise. "Do you expect to be done with it soon?"

"Never mind," I muttered, unsettled by his reply. "Do I sign something in blood?"

He looked perplexed, spread his enormous hands, and shrugged.

"All right, Smokey, ask," I said.

"I would know why she came for you, Traveler."

Ah, the sixty-four thousand dollar question, one I'd tried all day to get the answer to. If I lied, would he know? If he knew I lied, how would he react? If I told Sammie the demon wanted to know, would she believe me? My head ached despite the aspirin.

"I'll need some time," I said, thinking I should have included additional clauses for unforeseen contingencies. Well, it wasn't every day I dealt with the devil. I'd do better next time. No, scratch that. I didn't want a next time.

"Agreed," he said, and rose to his full height. "Send the messenger to me when you are ready to answer."

"Messenger?" I asked, my voice climbing an octave.

Smokey waved in my direction, and the nightmare swirling near him glided in to hover over my head. Oh, wonderful. The damn things were his personal pets. I felt like a cartoon figure with a black cloud following me around. How the hell was I supposed to use it to send a message? Smoke signals? The demon strode away up the lane.

Sammie collapsed against my shoulder. "My God, how did you get rid of it?"

"Uh—"

"River, you're a talent," she said, bubbling with excitement. "You have to be if you can see demons. Do you know how rare talents are?

And we've never found one except in E-Prime, where I'm from. Wait until I tell the team. But the demon is worrisome. We'll need to bring in the Neans and send it packing. We'd better get moving, or we'll miss the rendezvous."

She hurried away, and I trailed along behind trying to process all she'd said. She might as well have spoken Swahili.

"Maybe you could repeat that, only in English this time," I said.

She grinned, her eyes glittering with excitement. "Sorry, it's just that this is the most momentous discovery anyone—any human—has made since the DPS started."

"English," I reminded her.

"Sorry. I work for Dimensional Protective Services, DPS. I'm a dimension cop; a DC. Everyone always talks about the universe, but really, it isn't. It's a *multi*verse. Way back just after the Big Bang, something happened, and the universe split into two dimensions—or maybe more. There's a lot of competing theories. Anyway, that was the start, and now there's a bunch of alternate dimensions out there, parallel universes with different histories.

"The Raps were the first to figure out how to get from one to another. They had to use robot ships to contact other dimensions because they didn't have shields. But then they found the Neans, and the Neans can shield, so that's when people—well, beings—could actually travel from one dimension to another safely.

"And then the Raps found us. It was an accident really. A new fracture showed up on their monitors, and when they investigated, they discovered it was caused by a super-talent blasting a hole in our dimensional barrier."

"Um... Sammie," I said quietly. "I don't want to offend. It really isn't my business, but... are you off your meds?"

She stopped dead and glared at me. "I'm not crazy. This isn't some science fiction story. My team came to the alley because the Raps detected a new fracture in our dimension and followed the energy trail here. And apparently the guys in the robes did, too."

She resumed walking, but she didn't say anything more for the next block. I guess I shouldn't have asked about her meds. And truth be told, I'd seen a lot of strange things in the alley. What if it were all true?

"So these Raps and Neans?" I prompted.

Sammie scowled at me. "The Raptors rose in an alternate dimension where the Chicxulub asteroid never hit the Earth, and dinosaurs still live. The Raps are the only intelligent species. They have very advanced technology since as a race, they're a lot older than us. They can detect fractures and navigate between them.

"The Neans come from a dimension where modern humans never

developed. The Neanderthals are the only intelligent race. They have a deeply religious bond with the Earth and nature, and their priests can draw a kind of power from things like rock or wood. They raise holy shields that protect living beings when they pass through 'demon space' as they call it, or D-space as we humans call it.

"D-space is the space between the dimensions. When we send unmanned probes into it, we don't see or measure anything. But if un-shielded living beings pass through it, they go insane. They come out the other side gibbering and drooling."

"And naked," I whispered, pieces falling into place.

"Yeah, that too."

"But you weren't naked and insane, and neither were the black robes."

"My team came here to E-4 by platform. It's a big stone that the Raps added propulsion and navigation to, and a Nean priest draws en-ergy from to raise a shield around."

She frowned. "It looks like the black robes have some kind of energy-conducting fibers woven into their robes, and it's powered by the harness they wear under it. That panel on the harness is a control module. It has a list of coordinates for fractures it's been to in the recent past. The first one listed was here. I've never seen the second one before. It must be where they came from. The third was the location of the main fracture in the Rap dimension. Touch the one you want, and away you go, assuming you're standing next to a fracture."

A fracture. So that's what the shimmery wall in the alley was. And I'd caused it. I wasn't sure I was ready to reveal that yet. I still had too many questions.

"What was the glow?" I asked.

"Some kind of built-in shield, although it didn't seem to be work-ing right, possibly because the robe was damaged. I'd heard rumors that the Raps tried technology shields, but the failure rate was too high. Once they found the Neans, they abandoned their shield project. But that plate was Rap technology, I'd swear it. What were the black robes doing with Rap tech? Why do they have the coordinates of R-Prime?"

"And these talents you talk about?"

"A very small number of humans can detect stress points in dimen-sional barriers and apply pressure to create dimensional fractures. The Raps say they're doing quantum geometry in their subconscious brain, and they don't have a good explanation of where the power comes from. Most talents aren't strong enough to fracture all by themselves. The DPS trains them to work together in teams of two or three to create fractures."

I couldn't imagine myself doing quantum geometry. Heck, I couldn't do multiplication or division until another street kid taught me how to use pebbles as a kind of abacus.

"And the crazy naked people?"

"Sometimes, the rare super-talent is strong enough to fracture all on his or her own. When they do, they're swept out the fracture like a blowout in a spaceship, through D-space, and into a corresponding fracture in another dimension. Only talents can pass through fractures unaided. Everyone else needs artificial means to create the right energy resonance to get through."

She frowned. "Except demons. No human has ever seen a demon before. We weren't convinced they existed, but I am now. The Neans claim they use fractures to wreck havoc on dimensions, to steal souls. The Neans can use their magic to heal fractures and drive away demonic beings."

I shoved my hands in my sweatshirt pockets. We'd come to the part that made me apprehensive. "But these lost talents. What do you do with them once you've collected them?"

"They're generally disoriented and frequently combative when we first find them. We can't have them causing a ruckus in D-space. Someone might get knocked off the platform. We typically stun them so we can get home safe."

"And then?" I asked, remembering my days in the mental ward with a shiver.

"We take care of them. They can't feed or dress themselves. Doc's been trying a bunch of different treatments to see if they can make some recovery, but he hasn't had much success. We keep special cuffs on them. Not like handcuffs," she added. "More like bracelets. The cuffs have wiring and a battery that disrupts the harmonics needed to fracture so we don't lose them again. A second unshielded trip kills them.

"And we try to identify them and research their genealogy. Talent seems to be an inherited trait. Most of the talents in the program are relatives of the super-talents. With talents being so rare, it's almost like one big family. They'll want you to join."

Family. Could I be related to some of the DCs? Could my DNA reveal who my parents were? Had they fallen through a fracture and unintentionally left me behind? I had to know. I didn't care one whit about Agent Lopez and her drug cartel. I'd go with Sammie and blow this town in a spectacular way.

Sammie gripped my arm. "Now that you know where I'm from, you'll understand why it's so important to help Agent Lopez."

"Uh..." I said. "You lost me."

"By interfering with her sting, we may have altered the course of this dimension. We don't understand why dimensions appear or why some of them seem to collapse, and we don't want to be responsible for making that happen when we shouldn't have. We have to help bust Cantel and Enrique and get this dimension back on track."

I pondered what she'd said for a block or so.

"When you said you'd keep me safe from Enrique and Cantel, you meant to do it by taking me to another dimension, didn't you?"

Sammie nodded. "There's no way they could get to you if you weren't here."

"But wouldn't there be a chance I could have messed something up in the new dimension? Maybe meet myself or something?"

"When dimensions split, it's like there's a cocoon around them for a while. It's not possible to get into a dimension where there's another version of yourself. And most likely, we would have taken you to E-prime, where we could keep an eye on you. But now that we know you're a talent, everything's changed."

"Oh." *Keep an eye on me?* I didn't like the sound of that. Homelessness had its down side, but at least I was free. Should I tell her the whole truth?

"River," Sammie said, a puzzled frown on her face, "have you seen the demon before?"

"Yeah," I replied. "In the alley last night, on the street this morning, and at Cantel's."

"I'm surprised you didn't say anything about it. I mean, it's not every day you see a demon, is it?" she joked.

"Um..."

Could I fool them long enough to find out whether I was related to any of the other talents? I was a terrible liar. She'd know. She already looked at me with a funny expression.

"I see demons occasionally, especially if I'm tired or stressed. Little gargoyles, though, not big ones like Smokey. And they aren't real." I cleared my throat. She might as well know the rest. "Light bulbs sing to me. If I don't have a hat on, I can feel ants walking on my head, even though I know there aren't any. And there's other weird stuff. I have schizophrenia."

Her expression cycled through surprise into concern. I looked away before she got to pity. I couldn't stand pity.

"I do okay. You don't have to feel sorry for me," I said. "I'll understand if you don't want to go the rest of the way together."

She nearly dislocated my shoulder pulling me to a halt. She pointed a finger at her face. "This isn't an expression of pity. It's an expression of concern. That's what friends do for friends. They worry about one another."

I stood there, speechless. Friends? *Us?* How had that happened? I wasn't friend material. But the warmth of the word grew in my chest until I thought I'd melt into a puddle.

"You aren't afraid of me? Afraid I'll go crazy and try to kill you?" I asked.

"I took a psychology class in college. I know what schizophrenia is, and I know that darn few people who have it become violent and harm others. You clearly have amazing coping skills, and your heart is in the right place or you wouldn't have saved either me or that little boy."

I hoped the cold and dark hid the color crawling up my face. My cheeks must be glowing like Rudolf's nose. "So... we're friends?"

"Yeah," she said, taking my hand and resuming our walk. "Crazy, huh? Oh, sorry. I didn't mean that."

I laughed, delighted with the feel of her hand in mine. "Definitely crazy."

We walked on, working our way into the business district. I thought I must be dreaming and couldn't believe my luck. Me, friends with a gorgeous creature like her. I imagined us working together as partners for the DPS. My whole future changed before my eyes. No more running. I'd have a home.

But not everyone was as open-minded as Sammie. A cold chill replaced the warm moment, and the thought of a happy home evaporated.

"Will the DPS take me? I mean, I'm mentally ill. They must have standards."

She squeezed my hand and grinned. "Believe me, you'll fit right in."

We turned up Perry and walked the final two blocks to the pie factory. I hadn't told her that I was the super-talent they were looking for, and I thought I should. After all, friends confide in friends, and I didn't want her to find out when her team turned the tracker on me. She'd had enough surprises.

"Sammie, there's something I need to tell you."

Black Robe lunged out from the cover of the building corner. He grabbed Sammie by the arm and pressed his banana gun to her side.

"Don't try anything, or I'll waste the girl," he said.

10

I froze. My lungs refused to inflate, and I couldn't tear my eyes from the gun. The nightmare roiled ominously around the two of them. With all my heart, I hoped Smokey would step out of the darkness and sink his talons into Black Robe's head. No such luck.

"Move," Black Robe ordered, nodding in the direction of downtown.

I scanned the surrounding darkness. Where were the DCs? They should be here by now. Had Black Robe killed them? If he'd used the banana gun on them, we should have heard the booms as we approached.

Black Robe poked the gun against Sammie and frowned at me. I got the message and willed my feet to move along the pavement, but I kept glancing to each side.

"They aren't here," Black Robe said. "I arranged a little diversion for them. Walk in front of me, five steps, no more, no less. Don't turn around."

If I didn't turn around, how was I supposed to know when I'd gotten five steps ahead? The thought of losing Sammie made my heart thump double-time.

"You don't need to take her," I said, raising my hands. "I'll go with you, do whatever you want. Just let her go."

"No," Sammie said. "Take me and let him go. He can't help you. He doesn't know anything about dimensional travel or fracturing."

"Shut up, both of you," Black Robe growled. "And put your hands down."

We walked the two blocks back to Third in the gloom, me straining to hear Sammie's footsteps so I'd know if I was getting too far ahead. Cars swished past, but there wasn't much traffic this time of night. If the cops spotted us, would Black Robe shoot Sammie? I thought so and prayed that we'd get wherever he was taking us without being seen.

Up the block, three burly guys rounded a corner and came our direction. Hope blossomed in my brain. I thought maybe they'd provide a diversion, and I could jump Black Robe, although with the distance between us, I wasn't sure I could get to him before he fired. But they stopped at Hoolihan's Bar and went inside. My heart sank into my shoes.

As we passed the place, I could hear juke box music playing. The door scraped, the music volume increased, and I heard extra feet on the sidewalk, scuffling sounds, and some grunts. Then someone big slammed into me and propelled me to the street. Tires screeched to a halt, and powerful hands hauled me through the air. I got a quick look over a brawny shoulder before I was shoved into the back of a limo.

"Sammie!" I shouted, and watched helpless while two other brutes pummeled Black Robe and Sammie against the building. The hair on my arms stood on end. The thug who'd grabbed me slammed the door without getting in, and the limo zoomed away.

Out the back window, I saw the thugs leave Black Robe and Sammie in a heap and leap into another car. Sammie tried to break away, but Black Robe grabbed her arm and waved the banana gun at her. Then we turned a corner, and I lost sight of them.

I reached for the door, determined to get out and run back to Sammie. That's when I noticed the two men sitting opposite me. One had a Saturday Night Special pointed at my chest. Or maybe it was a very expensive little handgun so didn't qualify as a cheap Saturday Night Special. I wasn't a gun expert. I only knew that with each passing second, we were getting farther away from Sammie, and I had to get back to rescue her.

The other man gazed out the window as though he were on a Sunday drive in the country. His slick black hair reflected the street lights, sunglasses hid his eyes despite the gloom, and half a dozen gold chains glittered under his silky red shirt. I gulped.

"Señor Enrique isn't too impressed with your bodyguards, Mr. Madden," said the man with the gun. He was a middle-aged guy with dark hair and grey eyes the same color as his suit. The hint of a scar marred his right cheek. He held the gun as casually as he'd hold a drink. I gulped again.

"They aren't—" *Oh, wait.* If I told them Black Robe had taken us prisoner, I'd look incompetent, and that probably wasn't the way to start a new friendship with someone like Enrique.

"They're junior people. Not fully trained yet," I said, trying really hard not to rock in the plush leather seat. "You know how it is when you're building a new organization. I'll have a word."

Mouthpiece nodded his understanding. "Señor Enrique has noticed your activity here in Centerville, Mr. Madden, and he is interested to know your intentions."

It was my intention to rescue Sammie and get the hell out of Dodge, er, Centerville, but that probably wasn't what Enrique wanted to hear. According to Lopez, the drug lord thought I was trying to take over Cantel's operation. But did he approve? Enrique's face was an unreadable mask—a scary unreadable mask. I shoved my hands between my thighs so they wouldn't see them trembling.

"Well, um... I thought it was time to put the old dog out to pasture," I said, then winced at my mixed metaphor. I hoped Enrique's English wasn't good enough to notice.

"How will you do that?" Mouthpiece asked.

"Oh, uh, I ... took his money so he'd lose face and burned his building down to send him notice that I'm serious," I said, dredging up Lopez's tirade.

"Yes. And then?" he leaned forward, encouraging me.

Shit. What did I know about unseating a gangster? My phenomenal success had all been an accident, a horrible trick of fate. But I had to get out of the car and get back to Sammie. *Think, River.*

"Well... in any hostile takeover, it's a good idea to try to get the share—, er, the invested parties on your side," I said, paraphrasing a business article from a discarded newspaper I'd used as a blanket. "So I'll be working on incentives like, uh, cash bonuses and... broken kneecaps. Then I'll look for efficiencies to make the organization more profitable, maybe sell off some of the underperforming assets... or torch them for the insurance."

Enrique swung his dark glasses my direction, and I held my breath. We drove another two blocks before he tilted his head toward Mouthpiece and gave a tiny nod.

"Señor Enrique had some concerns about you, Mr. Madden, given your youth. He thought you might be too rash and not have a cogent plan," Mouthpiece said. "But he's very impressed with your business savvy. He looks forward to doing business with you—once you've removed Mr. Cantel."

"That's it?" I asked, struggling to keep a straight face.

Mouthpiece rapped on the glass barrier behind me, and the limo glided to the side of the street. "Señor Enrique is not pleased with Mr. Cantel's inability to manage competitors. He welcomes someone with an organized and aggressive business plan. A return to sanity, you might say. He asks your pardon for your earlier treatment."

I blinked a trickle of sweat from my eye. "No problem."

He handed me a business card and said, "When you've taken care of your little problem and you're ready to receive your first shipment, give us a call—but don't wait too long."

The car door opened, and I slid out, shaking all over. The thug who'd accosted me took my place, slammed the door, and the limo glided away into the night, followed by the second carload of bodyguards. I looked at the business card in my hand, blank except for a phone number, and burst into hysterical laughter.

But I didn't have time for laughing. I pocketed the card and got my bearings. Sammie had said that the black robes' devices transported them to a different dimension when they were standing next to a fracture. As far as I knew, Black Robe didn't have a base of operations here, so he must have intended to take me back to his dimension. Would he take Sammie there, or kill her as he'd originally planned? I ran like hell for the alley and the fracture.

I peeked around the corner of the building into the alley. The light above Soo Ling's door didn't do much to illuminate the far end, but I thought I saw shadows moving there. I slipped into the alley, remembering how the DCs had been silhouetted against the lights of the side street. I tried to stay near the wall and tiptoed as far as a dumpster that I could crouch behind.

Something definitely moved down by the fracture. I could creep to more cover closer to that end, but I'd pass by Soo Ling's, and anyone looking my direction could see me. The only other option was to run around the block and come in through the parking lot to the other end.

I backed out and raced around the block, hoping that I didn't run into a police patrol. I thought that with two rounds of shooting so close together downtown, they'd beef up the manpower in the neighborhood, but I was relieved that I didn't see any cops. Maybe they were still looking for me in the vicinity of the Cantel building.

As I moved to the corner of the parking lot, I could feel the tug of the fracture pulling at me. It gave me the willies. I still didn't understand how dimension hopping worked, but I was darn sure I didn't want another trip through the Dark Place unprotected, not if there was another means of transportation available, even if it had a dino for a navigator.

Beside the glistening curtain of the fracture, I could see two black robes, glowing slightly, and I sucked in my breath. He'd gotten reinforcements, and here was me come to the rescue party without any weapons. *Good thinking, River.* I should have asked Mouthpiece if I could borrow his gun. I bet those robes wouldn't stop a bullet like they did the lightning from the wands.

But then I noticed that one of the robed figures was darn short, and the taller one pointed something at the short one. *Sammie!* He hadn't killed her, at least not yet. I nearly wept.

Before I could figure out a plan, Black Robe touched Sammie's chest. One minute she stood there beside the fracture, and the next, there was a blur, a waver in the sparkly field, and then nothing where she'd been. Black Robe touched his own chest, and he too vanished.

I wanted to scream, to shout, to rail against the universe. I was too late. She'd come here because of me, lost her brother because of me. And now Black Robe had her because I hadn't been there to protect her. He'd taken her from me, and I couldn't follow. Sure, I could jump through the fracture, but if I'd understood Sammie, I could come out anywhere, not necessarily at the black robe lair. I paced, four steps left, four steps right.

Sammie's team of DCs were here somewhere, but I didn't know how to find them or what kind of diversion Black Robe arranged. Hell, they might stun me before I could tell them anything. I needed a better plan than waiting around for them to show up. I stopped and rocked.

The feds had the chuckler's robe, and Sammie made it work. I'd watched. An instant later, I was running full tilt east. I made it two blocks before I stopped. Cast-iron Lopez and her stainless steel gorillas wouldn't give me the robe. Well, I'd just have to take it from them. I broke into a run again.

A block later, I pulled up. How would I take it from them? Knock on the door and ask politely for them to hand it over? *Yeah, right.* I stepped into an alley and rocked on my heels. I needed the feds out of the house first. Then I could sneak in and get the robe. I still had the cell phone. I could use it to send them on a wild goose chase across the city. I smiled and set out running again.

One more block, one more stop. I pulled the phone out of my pocket and looked at it. It all seemed too easy. As I reflected on it, I realized Lopez had nearly booted us out of the house. She'd wanted us to go. What fed would let me walk with a million dollars without keeping tabs on me?

How many news articles had I read about lost hikers found by tracing their phones? How many crooks were proved to be in the neighborhood of their crimes by their cell records? For all I knew, she might have an additional tracking bug inside the phone in case I turned it off. If I called from right outside the FCIS house, they'd know I was there. If I set up a rendezvous and the phone didn't move towards it, they'd know something was up.

I guess I could make the call and dump the phone. It seemed the obvious solution; maybe a little too obvious. Lopez was smarter than that. They'd taken all my clothes and my backpack, and they'd had them a very long time before they'd returned them. Bottoms to dollars I was carrying a second bug. I changed course and headed for the park down by the river.

###

The park was a mile-long expanse of grass rolling gently up from the river and dotted with clumps of artfully arranged trees and bushes. In the center, a cluster of sculpted buildings left over from an exposition a couple decades earlier huddled together and served as a meeting place for the city's youth.

I walked the asphalt jogging trail at the river's edge, keeping an eye out for the park police who, between long, long coffee breaks in their cruiser, hassled anyone they didn't like the look of, all in the name of preventing loitering and making the park safe at night. Their efforts were largely ineffective, and many of the city's drug pushers worked the area unperturbed.

But that was in the dimension I'd come from. Here in E-4, two uniformed patrolmen lounged under a street lamp near a small parking area from which a steady flow of cars ebbed and flowed. Two scruffy teenage guys with grocery bags did business with the occupants of the cars, doling out little packets of drugs and taking wads of cash in exchange, the transactions overseen by the cops.

Nearby, three girls who couldn't be more than fifteen huddled together in a tight circle, eyes watching the cars. They were dressed in spiked heels, short ass-hugging skirts, and fur coats that exposed bare midriffs. They'd applied makeup with shovels, but it couldn't hide their cadaverous features or their vacant expressions.

Someone in a black SUV paused in the parking area and whistled. A hand flicked out a half-open tinted window, and all three girls tottered over. After some haggling, one of the girls slid in the passenger side, and the SUV rolled away. The other two returned to their positions.

Watching them made my skin crawl. They were kids. The cops ought to be protecting them, not looking on while they plied their trade. My hands balled into fists while I walked on. I could do nothing to help the girls. But someone ought to.

As I'd expected, several groups of kids hung out by the game arcade farther along the path. I felt like Goldilocks picking my target. Some were too young, some too old, some too big, some looked too much like trouble. I spotted a group of three boys, two of whom had skateboards, and a third who watched his pals with obvious envy. He was smaller than the other two, just about my size. And he wore a lovely watch cap. I eased over, keeping an eye out for cops.

"Hey," I said, nodding to the two with the skateboards. "Cool rides."

The three of them looked me up and down, assessing.

"I used to have one, but then I busted my ankle real bad on a jump," I said.

"Yeah?" the one without the board said. "That's tough."

I shrugged. "You haven't got one?"

"Naw," he said, defenses rising. "I have better ways to spend my money."

"Sure, sure," I said. "Hey, how would you like to make a little cash?"

All three of them pulled back like I had a contagious disease.

"Nothing hinky," I said. "I have this friend, and I want to play a joke on her. She's supposed to meet me later, and I want to do one of those candid camera stunts, you know."

"What kind of stunt?" the largest of them asked, eyes narrowed.

"I want to have someone pretend to be me. You know, go up to her and insist they're me? They'd have to wear my clothes and carry my pack, but I'd pay. And I'd be close by, making a video. It'll be a hit on YouTube."

The little one lifted an eyebrow. "Why can't you get one of your friends to do it?"

"Uh…" I couldn't tell him I didn't have a friend in the world. "She knows all my friends. It has to be someone she hasn't seen before."

"Yeah, how much you willing to pay for this?"

I doubted that any of them could break a hundred, and I didn't have anything smaller. Besides, the kid's clothes were better than mine, and he'd probably be grounded for a week when he lost them. I'd be generous. He could get the skateboard I knew he wanted.

"Two hundred now, and a hundred after the stunt."

Their eyes widened and looks passed between them. For one uncomfortable moment, I thought they might roll me for my cash. Then the little one nodded.

"Deal," he said. "But I have to be home by midnight. Where we meeting this girlfriend of yours?"

"Corner of Ash and Twentieth," I said, thinking about the hot water he'd be in when he got a ride home from a federal officer.

"Not at her place?" the little one asked.

I snorted. "If her folks catch me hanging around, they'll kill me. We meet a block from her house."

That seemed to satisfy them. They asked to see the cash, and then we went into the arcade to use the men's room for the clothing exchange. The little guy wasn't too happy with the prospect of walking a couple of miles in my wretched shoes and soot-stained t-shirt , but I convinced him by adding a hundred to his fee. Before we left the men's room, I pulled out Lopez's phone and dialed her number.

"Hey," I said when she answered. "Can you be at Ash and Twentieth in half an hour?"

"You set up a meet with Enrique already?"

"Not yet," I replied. "But we don't want to lug the bag around. We might get mugged. You can hold onto it for us."

"I'm not giving you the evidence from the alley until after you meet Enrique."

"We're cool with that, and we'll get on the meet real soon. We just have something else to take care of first."

There was a long silence, and then Lopez said, "Let me talk to Samuels."

Paranoid cast-iron bitch. I took a deep breath. "She's not able to come to the phone right now, but she sends her regards."

Another long silence passed. I imagined her checking with her agents to find my location. I wondered if they'd bugged Sammie, too. I bet their bug didn't work too well between dimensions.

"Okay," she said, "Twentieth and Ash in half an hour. Don't be late."

I dropped the phone in the pack, stepped out of the stall, and handed the pack to my doppelganger. He took the three hundred bucks and counted it twice, like he couldn't believe his eyes. I told him I'd follow behind them out of sight. They left, the two bigger ones slapping their friend on the back and advising him about which brand of skateboard he ought to get.

I counted to a hundred, then I slipped out of the men's room, through the arcade, and into the park. I ran flat out along the jogging trail that followed the river until it turned north. Then I continued east, headed for the fed's hideout.

When I reached the fed's house, I stopped across the street in the shadow of a tree and scratched my itchy tattoos while I reconnoitered. By now, I figured the goon squad ought to be on the way to their meeting with my double. I didn't know how many agents they'd take, or how many might still be waiting in the house. Even one would be a problem for me. I was a pacifist; I didn't have any fighting skills. I needed some muscle on my side.

I looked up and saw Smokey's nightmare messenger, barely discernible in the dark. I'd run out of options. It also occurred to me that we hadn't discussed consequences if I failed to answer the demon's question, or whether he could follow Sammie to wherever she'd gone.

"Alright, soot-ball, go tell your master I have what he wants," I whispered.

The nightmare drifted in a lazy circle.

"I haven't got all night," I said. "Shoo!"

I heard a soft chuckle behind me and jumped, spinning around. My blood thundered in my ears, and I couldn't seem to get a proper breath. Smokey stood three feet away. He crouched on his haunches.

"You have my answer, Traveler?"

I put a hand on my chest and gulped air. "Geez, give a guy a heart attack."

"If you wish," he said, rising.

"No, no! Figure of speech," I gasped, wondering if he would really cause a heart attack. He was certainly giving me an aching neck trying to look up at him.

Smokey settled again. "What does the affiliate want with you?"

"To help," I said. "She thought I was damaged when I traveled through... well, where you come from. She wanted to take me back to her dimension."

"For what purpose?"

"If I was damaged, I wouldn't be able to take care of myself. She and her friends would help me."

"Hmmm," he hummed as he frowned. "But for what purpose do they gather those who can break the barriers?"

I thought we'd agreed to one question, and I needed to ask him a favor. On the other hand, I couldn't afford to offend him. The clock was ticking. The feds would be back soon. Besides, I didn't know the answer. Sammie said the DCs collected the crazies who fell through fractures, but she'd also said those people were rare. So what did they do the rest of the time?

"I don't know, and a second question wasn't part of the deal."

"True, Traveler," he said as he rose to his full height and turned to go. "An unfortunate answer."

"Wait a minute. Why is it unfortunate?"

Smokey blew a long stream of smoke from his nostrils. "The Council has noticed the gatherings of those with the power to fracture the barriers. When those with the ability were widely dispersed, they offered no threat.

"But now, they gather together in groups. Either group has sufficient strength to do significant damage, perhaps to begin a multiverse collapse were they to trigger in the right location. This cannot be tolerated. The Council will order recycling of their dimensions."

"'Either group'? So there's more than one?" Sammie hadn't said anything about rival organizations. "And what's this 'recycling' thing?"

"Your affiliate is a member of one group, the larger one. The one who pursues you belongs to another." He sighed. "As for recycling, in human terms, you might call it 'pruning'. It is the purpose of my kind to recycle those dimensions that threaten the multiverse, or those that are weakened by negative energy, such as this one."

My breath stuck in my chest. "You mean destroying, don't you? But you'd kill billions of people!"

"The balance of the multiverse must be maintained or all are at risk. Of course, this dimension can still be saved if you act quickly."

I ran a hand over my face. "If *I* act quickly? You think I can save an entire dimension? How would I do that? I'm not anyone important."

"Ah, Traveler, everyone is important. Everyone makes a difference.

No one is alone." He hunched down by me. "When those who inhabit a dimension choose hate over love, cruelty over kindness, self-interest over the good of all, they generate a kind of destructive energy that weakens the dimensional barriers. The barriers become porous, allowing the nightmares birthed by the beings to pass through to where I come from— Between. The nightmares' passage further weakens the barriers until they lose integrity and all that is, is scattered into Between. The dimension is recycled."

"So what, I'm supposed to think happy thoughts and make everything all better?" I couldn't believe my ears.

"You've already affected the barriers. Those I have sampled worry that crime runs rampant in the city. A bus has been attacked, souls passed on. And so those who occupy the city focus on the negative, on how to protect themselves. Their energy creates nightmares.

"But you also affected the barriers when you carried the young soul from the burning building. You inspired hope. You showed how to care for others. This action had great power; more is needed. There is much negative energy to overcome."

"Great. All I need is an arsonist to torch a few dozen more buildings so I can rescue the occupants," I muttered.

Smokey scratched his chest with six-inch claws. "Your effect can go beyond this dimension. If a soul with the power to fracture, to destroy the barriers, were to bend his will to strengthen them instead, a soul that was part of the group the Council fears, the Council might rethink their recycling decision. The fate of two dimensions is in your hands."

"Two!" We were sliding farther downhill with each passing moment. Hell, I was an uneducated homeless schizophrenic loner. Now I was supposed to save *two* dimensions?

"Two only if you intend to allow the other group to continue with their gathering of those who can fracture. If they aren't stopped, the Council will order the recycling of the dimension they occupy. That would be unfortunate, since they are only visitors there."

"Three? *Three!* You expect me to save *three* dimensions? *All by myself?!*" I walked in a circle. I rocked. Then it occurred to me that Sammie was with that other group in the dimension Smokey said would be recycled. I clung to that. Death on this scale was beyond my comprehension. But I understood the devastating loss of a friend, and I couldn't allow it. I had to get her out of there.

"Tell me about the black robes. Who are they? What are they doing?"

"They live, Traveler, as all souls do." He spread his talons, helpless.

I scrubbed at my head and walked in another circle. "Can the black robes fracture?"

"Those who traveled here cannot. Those who sleep can."

I frowned at him. "Sleep?"

Again he spread his hands. "My sampling of humans has been limited. I learn only what is uppermost in their minds. I lack the necessary understanding to answer you better."

"How many of these sleepers do they have?"

"Four."

I rubbed my ears, certain I'd heard him wrong. "*Four?* And that's enough to destroy the multiverse?"

"You alone could begin a multiverse collapse. In the correct location, a new fracture of sufficient size could begin a cascade of destruction; for example, if the new fracture occurred near an existing fracture in one of the older branches of the multiverse. The black robe I sampled had a single thought uppermost in his mind: revenge."

"I need help," I said. This was all way over my head. I couldn't possible save three dimensions. "Do you know where the DCs are? The group that my affiliate works with? They're supposed to be here somewhere."

Smokey pointed north. "They've opened a fracture far that way."

Wonderful. I needed to get after Sammie, not go roaming around looking for another fracture. I gestured across the street at the feds' house. "Can you help me retrieve something from that house?"

"I am unable to act upon the nonliving," he replied. "And I would need to sample the living to affect their actions. Of course, that would be rude."

Crap. Why couldn't I have thought of some other excuse?

"Okay, look, Smokey, let me explain about cultures. See humans have all these different cultures, and what may be bad manners in one culture is okay in another, like eating with your hands or smiling at strangers."

The demon looked perplexed. "And sampling is permitted in some human cultures?"

"Well... yeah... and the people right across the street in that house are from the 'government' culture. They believe that snooping on people is a good thing, so they won't mind a bit if you sample them."

"Ah," Smokey smiled. "So you wish to make another bargain, Traveler? I will sample the occupants of the house and get information for you? And what will you give in return?"

"Um... I'll need a little more than information. I need you to make them ignore me. If they see me in there, they'll try to kick me out. Can you do that?"

He nodded that big bull head of his and narrowed his eyes. "Such assistance will require a substantial favor in return. Are you prepared to grant my request?"

My blood turned to ice. Making deals with the devil again. Boy, this was getting to be a bad habit. Sooner or later, he'd trick me, and I'd lose my soul, I was sure of it.

"What is it you want in return?" I asked.

"What you do about the other dimensions, I leave to you. You must save this dimension. My master has a vested interest in it and would prefer it not be recycled at this time."

"But..." I walked another circle shaking my head.

"You have arrived at a kairotic moment. That's why your incoming fracture broke through in this location. This dimension is trapped in a negative spiral, where bad news begets bad thoughts and bad deeds. The forces of evil go unchecked. A few—a very few—still fight to turn the tide. You hold the key to their success."

"Aw, no, you don't mean I'm supposed to bring down those two thugs, do you? And that's what you want in exchange for helping me?" I cursed and pounded my fist on the tree under which we stood. I was running out of time. I had to get the robe so I could go after Sammie.

"Okay, fine," I sighed. "It's a deal."

11

〜〜〜〜〜

"When we go in, no violence," I told the demon as we approached the front door. "Make them forget about me and go to the kitchen for a snack or something."

"But Traveler, I cannot exert that kind of influence. I can only reduce their inhibitions to act on desires they already feel and suggest how they might express them."

"Well, try to make it something harmless," I said, remembering Abbott and Costello, soaked in blood, and the chuckler's head exploding out the back of his hood. "Like maybe they need to run to the store for a pack of cigarettes. No maiming their co-workers, okay? And don't take too long. The others will return any minute."

The big demon nodded and stepped onto the porch with me. I rubbed at my itching wrists. They'd be raw soon if I spent much more time with Smokey. The nightmare cloud slithered around us both, and then it sieved itself through the crack around the door.

"Where's it going?" I asked.

"To count the souls inside," he replied. "I hope."

I'd read about how vampires had to be asked in to cross a threshold and wondered why that didn't apply to other denizens of the dark side. "It doesn't need an invitation?"

The demon tilted his head. "It is young and has no manners. It goes where it wishes. Are the newer souls of your world not this way also?"

He had me there. I wished it would run away from home and never come back, like I had. No such luck. A moment later, the sooty cloud squeaked through the door frame and swirled around Smokey's head. He breathed it in, closed his eyes, and then ejected the cloud with something akin to a sneeze. I nearly said 'bless you,' but is that appropriate when addressing a demon? What was the Dark Place equivalent? Curse you?

"Two souls inside," he reported.

I knocked on the door. The sliver of light showing between the blankets covering the windows snuffed out, and then the porch light came on. I hoped that the agents still at the house wouldn't call Lopez before we got inside. I didn't know how long it might take to find the robe, and I didn't want to be there when Lopez got back. If Smokey reduced *her* inhibitions, she'd have me on a rack in a heartbeat. Or maybe she preferred Chinese water torture. The government seemed big on water torture.

The porch light sang *Knock Three Times* all the way through before Art cracked the door open and looked me up and down. He peered into the darkness beyond me without reacting to the demon. Smokey poked a talon into the agent's forehead. I grimaced and studied my shoes. They were nice shoes and fit for once.

"Why are you here?" Art asked, his voice ripe with mistrust. The light sang *Suspicious Minds* in a terrible Elvis impersonation, a sure sign I needed to rest before I tipped over the edge. But rest was a long way off.

"Change of plans," I said. "Too many cops for me to show up at the rendezvous. Can we come in?"

"We?" he asked. "Who's with you?"

"Uh..." *Ah, hell.* I was just terrible at this spy stuff. I looked back as though I expected to see someone. "My team should be here shortly, along with your boss."

Art let us in and turned on a light. It hummed the *Mission: Impossible* theme off-key. I stood there waiting for Smokey to whisper to the agent, but he just gazed around the room. The agent flagged me to a chair at the table and took a position near the front door. The demon strolled away to the kitchen, squeezing to fit through the doorway. I hoped he'd do something soon. Perhaps I hadn't emphasized the time constraints enough, or maybe time worked differently in his world.

The box with Griff's clothes and the robe no longer sat on the table. I tried to recall which direction the agent had come from when he'd brought the box in. I couldn't remember. Would Art let me use the bathroom? If he did, I might get a look at the rest of the house.

Smokey returned, and I gave him a hurry-up hand signal. He stopped on the opposite side of the table, hunched over to avoid scraping the ceiling.

"Are you sure this soul is from a culture that appreciates sharing its private knowledge? He spends great energy to censor his communications."

I glanced at Art and gave the demon a nod.

Smokey's brows furrowed. "I cannot sample you to know your thoughts. How can I be sure you speak as you think?"

Outstanding. Even the damn demon could tell when I lied. And this was hardly the place to explain the philosophy behind choosing the lesser of two evils. In my head, the clock ticked on—literally. It was a big pendulum clock going tick-tock at a volume I couldn't ignore.

"You want your dimension saved or not?" I muttered.

"You wished for non-violence, yes?" the demon asked.

I gave him a tiny nod.

"Then you must stimulate him to change his desires."

I glanced back at Art and then whispered, "What's he thinking about?"

"Twisting you into something called a 'pretzel.' He does not like this place and blames you for his continued stay here."

"What did you say?" the agent asked.

"Nothing," I replied. "Just talking to myself."

"Yeah? About what?"

"Uh... about dinner. Are you hungry?" I asked. My own empty stomach rumbled. "Cause I'm starving. I could go for a nice juicy steak. At a steak house. Downtown. How about you?"

"Not hungry," the agent snapped.

Smokey clopped across the living room. From the corner of my eye, I saw him jab a claw into the agent's head and lick off the white goo. He blew a stream of smoke from his nostrils and shook his head.

"Does it feel cold in here to you?" I said. "It seems kind of chilly. Maybe you need a jacket. A heavy jacket. Gonna be winter soon. Wal-Mart's having a sale. You want to go? I can keep an eye on things."

"You stupid or something?" the agent said. "I don't need a jacket."

The demon sampled again, shook his head. "His hostility toward you grows stronger."

Great. At this rate, we'd never get away before Lopez arrived. I needed the agent to feel some desire, some primal emotion for which I wasn't the object of attention—or frustration.

"You married?" I asked, noticing too late that he wasn't wearing a wedding ring.

His eyes narrowed. Smokey didn't need to interpret for me; he'd climbed the hostility ladder another couple of rungs. I'd exhausted the base levels of Maslow's Hierarchy of Needs. Maybe I should jump to the top and try self-actualization.

"Ever do meditation? I've been thinking about joining a yoga group, and they practice it. I wondered what it was all about."

That got me a cold stare. Hell, he was a tough nut to crack. What else could I try? The weather? Sports? Politics? No, not politics. I was trying to make him less hostile, not more.

"Lopez leave you behind to hold the fort?" I said. I hadn't seen the other agent. I hoped it wasn't the jerk who'd sucker punched me. "Just you here by yourself?"

Art wasn't speaking to me anymore. He crossed his arms and glared.

Smokey dipped a talon in, licked it, and raised his brows. He strode away toward the bedrooms.

In a few minutes, he returned, a happy cow smile on his fat cow lips. Behind him, a young female agent with muzzy hair and a just-woken-up expression entered the room. Her attire looked like a carbon copy of Lopez's wardrobe, and I wondered if they had some rule about everybody wearing black suits. Only this woman's skirt wasn't quite such a demure length. She had great legs. Really. Any artist would want to draw them.

"What's he doing here?" she asked, rubbing her pretty brown eyes and stifling a yawn. She had high cheekbones, a lightly tanned complexion, and an attitude that screamed *I'm a hot babe, and I know it*. I had to give them credit: the feds knew how to pick the beautiful people.

"Waiting for Lopez," the agent said, his gaze drinking her in. "He says his team is right behind him. Have you got your gun in case they try anything dumb?"

Smokey whispered in her ear. She tossed her auburn locks, threw her breasts out, and put one hand on a curvy hip that I hadn't noticed until that moment. She unbuttoned her suit jacket and held it open to display her gun in its shoulder holster, as well as a very trim waist. The demon sidled over to the agent and whispered in his ear. He leered at her.

"What about you?" she asked, batting her eyelashes and giving him a sultry smile. "Want to show me your weapon? I've heard it's a big one."

He slipped his jacket off, dropped it on the floor, and loosened his tie. I could see it wasn't his gun he planned to show her. The woman shed her own jacket, kicked off her sturdy shoes, and unfastened one button of her blouse with each lazy step she took toward him. I had to remind myself to close my mouth before I drooled on the table. The floor lamp belted out *She's a Maneater*.

By the time she'd reached him, their weapon holsters were on the floor with their jackets, and he had his shirt cuffs unbuttoned. His hands slid her blouse off her shoulders and nimbly unfastened her sexy lace bra, liberating generous knockers that took my breath away. Imagine those hiding under that plain black suit. I gulped. She unbuckled his belt and opened his fly, slipping a hand into his shorts. My own nether regions responded big time.

Her soft rounded breasts had erect brown nipples that set my heart to thumping. Art must have appreciated them, too. He bent to take one in his lips while he stripped off her skirt and pantyhose. Oh, oh. Weren't those a no-touch zone? I expected her to clobber him the same way Sammie walloped me.

Instead, her head lolled back, and she groaned. He removed his mouth from her, and she tore his shirt open. Buttons flew through the air. He grinned and latched onto the other nipple. She writhed and groaned louder. Wow! How'd he done that? I had a lot to learn.

I eased out of my chair and tiptoed from the room. I felt like some Peeping Tom, but regretted leaving all the same. I mean, what did I know about seduction? I might never get another chance to see how it was done, and Art was clearly an expert. Geez, I hoped they remembered to have safe sex. Things seemed to be moving pretty fast. I wasn't sure they'd think about it—or anything else.

I rummaged through the bedrooms at light speed. The big box was in the third one I tried. I found the robe and harness. At the last minute, I took Griff's wand, too, and hustled back to the living room where the floor show continued.

I thought I'd missed several vital steps while I was gone. Art and the woman grappled naked on the carpet by the front door, him grunting and thrusting, her moaning and rocking, her long sensuous legs spread wide. Wouldn't they get rug burns from all that friction?

Smokey looked on, fascinated—almost as fascinated as me. After my experience with Big Bob, I'd been repulsed by sex for a long time. But then my hormones kicked in with a vengeance, and I'd become curious— maddeningly curious—with no source of enlightenment, no mentor to explain the birds and the bees, and no hope of an outlet for my libido.

The library didn't carry porn, and the physiology texts from which I'd learned about sex didn't go into much about practical mechanics. They made intercourse sound dry and boring. The two agents didn't seem the least bit bored.

I wished I could trade places with Art, just to see what it was like, just once. No one would ever display that kind of passion toward me. I didn't have broad shoulders, a manly chest, and firm butt like stud-muffin federal agent Art. Smokey should have picked him to save the world. He had the looks for it.

Guilt over invading their privacy got the better of me, and I tore my eyes away. I couldn't get past them to the door, so I trotted into the kitchen. Another door led to the backyard. I pulled open the fridge, and grabbed an open quart of milk. A twinge of guilt for the theft nibbled at my conscience. As I pushed through into the yard, I heard a long squeal of ecstasy and a low rumble of satisfaction from the living room. *Damn. I'd missed the important part.* Well, maybe Art wouldn't be so unhappy now.

A spotlight came on, illuminating the leaf-strewn yard. I sucked down the milk on the way to the rickety back fence and hopped over. In the alley, I dropped the empty carton in a garbage can. I might be a liar, a thief, and a voyeur, but I wasn't a litter bug. Then I raced off to the west to rescue Sammie and save the world. No, wait. *Three* worlds. It was gonna be a busy night.

12

I'd spent my younger years hanging out in Southern California. In my late-teens, I got tired of the summer heat and started migrating seasonally. I'd jog my way to the Pacific Northwest through the Spring, and migrate back to California, Arizona, or New Mexico in the Fall. I'd run forty or fifty miles each night for four nights, and then lay up for a couple days before running again.

This Spring, I'd had the terrible idea to return to my roots. I'd carefully forgotten exactly where I'd come from, but I knew it was somewhere in the Midwest. I'd crossed the Rockies and spent the past six months moving every few weeks from one Kansas, Nebraska, or Iowa town to another, any place with a river, and I couldn't figure out why. I never checked the phone book for orphanages; I didn't care about them. But I jogged miles and miles of riverbanks looking for something I couldn't put my finger on. All that running kept me fit.

I didn't feel fit when I arrived downtown. I'd covered less than twenty miles in the last twenty-four hours, but I felt like I'd run a hundred-mile marathon. I wanted a quiet shelter out of the chill wind and to sleep for a good eight hours. My arm burned, further distracting me, and I needed to think, to pay attention to my surroundings.

I kept to the alleys as I approached the location of the fracture. It was after midnight on a weekday, and Centerville pretty much rolled up the streets this late. The occasional car passed, and most of the traffic lights flashed red instead of cycling normally. I held my breath at each crossing, hoping I'd make it before a police cruiser rolled around a corner. No more trying to walk calmly. I dashed across each street like an Olympic sprinter.

When I was a block away from Soo Ling's and the fracture, I stopped to reconnoiter. I didn't know whether Black Robe had returned after delivering Sammie to his dimension, and I didn't want to run into him. I hoped I might see Sammie's team nearby. I could use some help rescuing her. My plan consisted of turning on the device and getting sucked through to the bad guys' dimension. I had no idea what I'd do when I got there. Surely real cops would come up with a better strategy.

As I looked west down an alley, I could see the tiny light above Soo Ling's door, a block away. Faint illumination came from the fracture, too. Had it glowed like that before? I didn't think so.

I stalked as far as a dumpster and stopped to look and listen. Then I slipped forward another twenty feet. Ahead, I thought I heard a rustle. I jerked to a halt and peered into the darkness. Was the noise real, or just another hallucination? I took a few more steps and paused.

My nerves gave out, and I rocketed from the alley. I stopped just around the corner and counted to fifty. Then I peeked in again. At the far end, something moved in one of the doorways, or I thought it did. I might have heard a voice whispering. On the other hand, I heard indistinct whispering lots of times, like I had during the interrogation with Knowles.

If that was Black Robe, I could outfox him by circling around and coming in from the other end to get to the fracture. I'd have to pass by the light at Soo Ling's, but I'd just have to take that chance. I waited in the shadows of an awning while a car passed, and then I began my circle.

I headed north a block and eased through an alley. When I emerged, the only thing I spotted up Washington was a large U-Haul rental truck parked close to where the stone tablet had been. I kept going west for another block before turning south. When I stopped again, I was looking through a dark alley to Washington and the U-Haul truck.

Time to get dressed. I set the robe on the ground, grabbed the plate, and turned it toward the street light. The little marks around the edge made no sense to me, but I remembered where Sammie pushed. Or I thought I did. I poked at a couple of the them without result, frustration rising.

I was a technophobe at heart, a real Luddite. I mean really, who was I going to call on a cell phone? Where would I charge it? At a currant bush? I hadn't learned to use the free computers at the library because I didn't have a library card for the log on. And now I was trying to activate alien technology. *Great plan, River.*

I gave the plate a good shake. Nothing. Boiling over, I stabbed half a dozen times at the little scratch I was sure Sammie had used to start the device. The screen flashed to life and winked out. I frowned. Dead battery? I poked at the mark again. Still nothing. I poked twice. The screen responded with a dim glow. I grinned. Alien technology wasn't so hard.

A bit of fumbling around, and I had the destination list on the display. Sammie said all I had to do was touch the one I wanted when

I was near the fracture and Bob's your uncle. I wondered how far 'near' was. The thought of walking up to the sparkly wall gave me the willies. I touched the second line of symbols. They pulsed. Was this another one of those double-touch situations? I tapped the text twice. It continued to pulse the same as before.

More fumbling got me to the shield activation. It didn't seem to do anything. Then I remembered that the plate had been in contact with the robe when Sammie started the shield. I shrugged into the harness. It didn't adjust down enough for someone my size. I growled under my breath. I hated being a runt.

I slipped the robe on and tried not to think about the blood and gore on the remnants of the hood. When it came in contact with the plate, it gave a half-hearted wink and remained dark. Good thing I didn't actually need the shield. Except maybe I did if I wasn't going to arrive sans clothing. How embarrassing would that be? *Hi Sammie, your naked, crazy, weaponless hero has come to rescue you.*

I'd taken three steps when I tripped on the robe hem and fell on the pavement. Okay, maybe I was shorter than the average wearer, but really, did it have to be that long? I hitched up the front and tried again. With each stride, the fabric snarled around my legs. No wonder Black Robe couldn't keep up with me.

I began my creep down the alley, the damn robe rustling all the way. I might as well have announced my presence on a bullhorn. I hadn't made the halfway mark when I noticed a lumpy bundle propped in a doorway just a few feet ahead. I froze. Should I bolt back the way I'd come? If that was Black Robe, he would have shot at me by now, wouldn't he? Besides, wasn't he the person in the alley on the other side of the fracture? Had he gotten reinforcements at last?

The bundle shifted, and I heard soft snores. I breathed again. Another homeless person like me slept in the doorway. As I moved slowly forward, I could make out the blanket wrapped around him. Maybe he was the same wino I'd run into the previous evening. Well, I wasn't going to wake him to say hello.

I slipped along a little faster. The sooner I got to the fracture, the sooner this would all be over. I didn't want to think about what might be happening to Sammie while I dithered. She needed me. I'd rescue her, and then she and her team would help me with Enrique and Cantel. We'd work together like one big, happy family.

Something small and hard rammed into my back, a blanketed arm wrapped around my throat, and a male voice said, "Fight me and I'll shoot."

Not a sleeping homeless person. Idiot. I raised my hands. His arm pressed my throat so hard I couldn't speak. I didn't know who he was.

Another of Cantel's goons? A cop? Not Black Robe. The voice wasn't right. One of his compatriots? Icy fingers of fear gripped me.

Two more figures came toward me from the end of the alley, and I nearly wept with relief. They wore the same black uniforms Sammie had. I'd found the DCs. Sammie would be okay. Why were they pointing guns at me?

The one behind me released his hold on my throat, twisted my arm behind my back, and shoved me forward. I tripped on the too-long robe, and he nearly dislocated my shoulder keeping me on my feet. We paused to check that the street was deserted, and then they marched me to the back of the U-Haul truck parked near the alley. The door rose, revealing another man standing inside, but a black curtain hung just beyond him, hiding the interior.

One of my escorts jumped up on the truck bed, making it look like child's play. No wimpy recruits in the DCs, I guessed. Why had Sammie thought I'd fit right in? The other two boosted me up to the two inside. The big overhead door rattled back down, and the two holding me dragged me through the curtain.

The light on the other side blinded me. When I could see, I thought I was hallucinating. At the far end of the twenty-foot long space, three of the short, thick guys in the gold lamé robes and pointy hats stood beside a rack of elaborate equipment being operated by a dog.

Well, not a dog. The elbows were too low on the front legs for a dog, and the ears were little nubs, kind of like how the dog-fight crowd trim their dogs' ears. The paws had very long, flexible toes, and the tail was too thick at the base. Something brown that seemed more like downy feathers than fur covered it. It stood comfortably upright on its hind legs and still didn't reach shoulder height on me. All its movements were quick and darting in a bird-like way.

The dog thing had to be a Rap, and the other three glum fellows must be the Nean priests Sammie mentioned. They glared at me and tapped their staffs against the metallic floor of the truck. Their lips moved, but I couldn't hear words, especially over their annoying racket. Their staffs and robes took on a soft patina, like they were swathed in sunlight.

Behind me, the door rattled up and down, and then more people passed through the curtain. One of them stepped around us and turned to face me. He was six feet tall, with sandy brown hair touched by grey at the temples and a weathered face. His pale blue eyes started at my feet and traveled over every inch of me, coming to rest on my eyes. The intensity of his gaze scared me.

"Strip him," he said.

"What? Wait!" I cried, too late.

Two of the DCs forced me to the floor while a third pulled open the robe. He took Griff's wand from the waistband of my jeans and handed it up to his commander, who handed it to the Rap while I writhed and screamed on the floor. He removed my shoes, socks, and pants. The two holders shifted to my legs and lifted me until only my shoulders touched the floor. The other one pulled off the rest of my clothing. They left me in a heap on the icy metal floor, shaking and terrified, naked and surrounded by men I didn't know and didn't trust. I struggled back to my feet, fear twisting my stomach in knots, and wrapped my arms around my torso.

Their commander pointed to the bandage on my arm. "Remove it."

One of them got out a big knife like the one Sammie carried. He slashed through the gauze wrap and exposed my burned arm. Another soldier gathered up my pile of clothes and began searching them. Terror set my nerves on fire.

"You've got it wrong," I said, shivering in the cold truck. "I need your help."

"The weapon is keyed to Talent First Class Griffith Samuels," the Rap said, its speech filled with clicks and chirps.

The man turned cold eyes on me. In a blur, his hand flew out and clobbered me on the right ear. I hit the deck before I realized I was falling. My head filled with ringing and my vision blurred. He crouched beside me, and his hand gripped my throat. I couldn't breathe, couldn't fight back. They could do whatever they wanted to me, and I couldn't stop them.

"Where are my kids?" he growled.

Sammie's father? She'd said she was a military brat. He wouldn't hurt me, would he? He was supposed to be one of the good guys. He was supposed to help me save her.

"Black Robe has Sammie," I croaked.

He stood and bared his teeth at me. I couldn't understand why he acted so hostile. Maybe I was slow because I was so fatigued. Maybe I was just stupid. But the pieces fell into place at the same time his boot connected with my gut. *They'd found me wearing a robe.*

I grunted as all the air rushed from my lungs and pain shot through my stomach. I rolled into a ball. His next kick slammed into my burned arm, and I howled. I tried to scrabble back, but the inside of the truck spun in dizzy circles.

"No," I pleaded. "Not me. Need help."

Distantly, I heard the door open again. Through bleary eyes, I saw another pair of boots join Sammie's dad.

"You found the talent," a voice said. "Why didn't you call me?"

"He's no talent," Samuels growled. "He's one of those bastards who attacked the platform."

A buzz of static sounded, and the new voice spoke. "He's the talent, all right, and he's running hot. We need to get cuffs on and sedate him before we lose him."

A moment later, an older man bent over me, a hypodermic needle in his hand. He split into two images, doubling the laugh lines around his eyes and mouth, and then merged into one again. He reached cautiously toward me.

"No drugs," I whispered. "Must help Sammie."

He drew back, his eyes wide. Then he looked up at Samuels.

"He's not mad. What's going on here?"

"I told you, he's one of those hoodlums who attacked the platform. He knows where my kids are, and I'm going to have answers."

"What have you done to him?" the kindly man asked in an unfriendly voice. He drew something out of a black bag he carried on a shoulder strap. "Look, son, I need to put some cuffs on you so we don't have an accident. They won't hurt. Will you let me do that without a fight?"

I nodded, or at least I tried to. My head wobbled around like a bobble-head doll. He gently buckled two straps around my right wrist. When he moved to my left arm, he frowned at my burns.

"Who did this to you?" he asked, voice gruff. He tossed Samuels a vile look and buckled two more bracelets on my left wrist.

"Not him," I said, my head beginning to clear.

"I'm Doc," he said. "I'm going to put something on those burns."

He spent a minute applying a cream that took the heat and pain from my arm. Then he retrieved my clothes. He asked if I needed help dressing, and I probably should have agreed, but I freaked out when men touched me, especially if I wasn't wearing clothes, so I declined.

I dressed, and he helped me into a chair. My gut hurt, and I couldn't sit straight. I hunched over and shook. He got a blanket and wrapped it around me before pulling up a chair beside mine. Samuels stood a few feet away, hatred etching his face.

I'd been a fool to want to join the DCs. I was nothing like them and God forbid I ever should be. But what would happen to their dimension if I didn't? I wasn't sure I cared anymore. I wasn't up to saving them. I'd failed Sammie. I wasn't up to saving myself. Smokey picked the wrong hero.

"What's your name, son?"

"River," I said. "Sammie needs help. You have to help her."

"Talent Samuels knows better than to give her name," Samuels growled. "Did you torture her to get it? Where is she? Where's the boy who was with her?"

"Enough," Doc said, holding up an arm to ward him off. "Let me handle this."

"We caught him headed toward the fracture. He wore a robe exactly like the priest described. He's one of them. Coddling won't get the truth out of him."

"Killing him won't either." Doc threw a look at the priests still banging away in the corner and lowered his voice. "Aren't they supposed to be out there closing the fracture? I can't think with that racket going on."

Samuels glowered at him, but left to speak to the priests. They frowned and pointed at me while they argued with the commander. I guess Samuels won the argument because the three priests filed toward the curtain.

As they approached me, the light in their robes flickered and went out. They looked at one another, and then at me, their eyes wide with fear. They backed away, rapping their staffs in a staccato rhythm and chanting loudly. The staffs sputtered, and their fear turned to panic. One of them pointed his staff at me. A weak beam of light reached my direction, but it stopped a couple of feet away and hung in the air. I'd never seen anything like it, and I guess they hadn't either.

"Demon!" one of them shouted in a Germanic accent. They huddled together and edged past me out the curtain.

"What the hell was all that?" Doc asked.

"Please," I said, placing my hand on his wrist. One of Samuels' men had his gun out of its holster so fast I thought he was a gunslinger from the Old West. I jerked my hand back.

"River, tell me what happened," Doc said.

I couldn't cope and started to rock. "They have Sammie. We have to get her back."

"Where's Sammie?" he asked.

"Black Robe took her through the fracture. I have to go after her."

"I can't let you go until you've told me what's going on," he said in a quiet voice. "I want to help Sammie, but we need to understand. How do you know Sammie?"

"I'm the talent. The one she came for. Only she doesn't know that."

"It's all lies," Samuels spat. "If he were the talent, he'd be crazy, and he's not."

"I am too crazy," I argued. *Oh, shit.* That wasn't what I meant to say. If I told them about the schizophrenia, they'd never believe me about anything else. They'd never let me go after Sammie.

"I don't think you're the kind of crazy we mean," the doctor replied. "Tell me what happened when her team was attacked. Were you there? Did you see it?"

"They used sonic banana—sonic weapons. Sammie got knocked down. Her brother..." I couldn't look at Sammie's dad, so I told Doc instead. "Griff was killed."

Rage purpled Samuels' face, and he charged over to stand before me. "No! It's more of your lies."

I drew back and held up my hands, expecting another beating. Doc jumped between us. After a moment, Samuels stepped away. Doc resumed his seat beside me.

"Is that when the men in the black robes took Sammie?"

"There's only one now. Unless more came through." I rubbed my head, trying to think despite the splitting headache that throbbed between my temples. "He caught us at the rendezvous. Why weren't you there?"

"What rendezvous?" asked Samuels, taking a step toward me.

"Sammie put a message on the wall." I waved a hand in the direction of the alley. "You didn't come."

"There wasn't any message. You're lying."

Anger bubbled up. "I helped her buy the paint. She put a message on the wall. I can show you."

Doc looked from me to Samuels. "Well, captain, maybe we should have another look in the alley."

13

The doctor made them pull out the loading ramp so I could walk down instead of jumping. If they'd made me jump, I would have needed a parachute. I couldn't quite stand straight. I worried that I might have internal bleeding.

Down by the fracture, the three priests tapped their staffs and waved their hands while they chanted. Warm light *drifted* from them to the rip in the dimensional barrier, like a tangible living sheet, not a cold beam of energy. High above the alley, an enormous group of nightmare clouds swirled, and the sight of them chilled me further. By the time we reached Soo Ling's, I could see the fracture clearly, double its previous size. I stopped and stared.

"Why's it getting bigger?" I asked, afraid I already knew the answer. How much time did I have?

"You can see it?" Doc asked.

"You can't?"

"We left all the talents at the landing site. It's getting too dangerous near the fracture. There's too much dimensional instability. Or at least that's what the Raps tell us."

"Where's this so-called message?" the captain said. He had his arms folded over his chest, and a smug look on his face.

I turned away from the fracture and roved my eyes over Soo Ling's wall. The message wasn't there. I pivoted in a circle looking for it. I'd seen it. It hadn't made any sense, but it had been there. I *had* seen it, hadn't I? Sammie said she was putting it there, so it must be real. Why wasn't it there now?

I walked closer to Soo Ling's door and spotted the flecks of white paint where the message had been. Someone had obliterated it, but I could see bits of it. Splatters of fresh paint spotted the garbage bags at the base of the wall.

"Right there," I said, pointing. "Only someone scratched it out."

Samuels joined me by the wall. "Bullshit. That's just old graffiti that someone's tried to remove."

"Is not," I replied. "See the paint on the bags?"

Doc joined us and shone a flashlight on the wall and bags. "He's got a point. The bags haven't been here that long."

"That's how he knew," I muttered. "He read the message, erased it, and met us at the rendezvous."

"Impossible," Samuels said. "The messages are written in code. Only a DC could read it."

I thought about Sammie's assertion that she'd been ambushed and got an uncomfortable feeling in my gut. A second uncomfortable feeling. Who would know they were coming here? Who could read a coded message? The DCs must have a mole in their midst.

"Where were you tonight?" I asked.

"I don't answer your questions, you answer mine. Got it?"

Doc rubbed a hand across his chin. "You say you're not one of the people who attacked our team, but we found you wearing their device."

I sighed. "I stole it. From the feds. Who got it from the local cops. So I could rescue Sammie."

Both men gave me a long look. I guess they didn't think I could best the feds.

"How'd you know what it was, how it worked?"

"Sammie showed me." We didn't have all night, and the story only got messier. "She said it was Rap technology. Where were you earlier?"

Doc looked at Samuels, but when the captain didn't answer, he did.

"We were following Sammie's tracker, ten miles east of here. We couldn't pick up Griff's signal."

"Then you found Black Robe?" I could only hope they'd taken the villain down and given him a taste of the greeting I'd received. Well, maybe not. Karma. Gandhi. Forgiveness. Ohm.

"No, we found a dog with her tracker strapped to its neck."

Of course, Black Robe's distraction. He kept everyone away from the rendezvous while he set a trap for us. And we walked right into it despite Sammie's fears about an ambush. *Dumb, River.*

"Easy enough to check your claim about the robe being Rap technology," Samuels said. "We'll ask the Rap."

"You can't tell by looking at it?" I asked, getting more worried by the moment.

Doc shifted, uneasy. "The Raps don't share much technical knowledge with us. They won't teach us their language and strictly limit what equipment they let us see or use. Sammie's good with languages. She's been picking up quite a bit, probably more than they realized. She's as close as we have to a Rap expert."

Were the Raps working with two groups of humans, and the DCs didn't know about the other one? To what end? I walked in a tight circle, thinking. Should I tell Doc what Smokey told me? No, he'd want to know my source, which he surely wouldn't believe. And what did I know? Only that there were two groups, both of which could travel between dimensions with the aid of the Raps and both had people who could fracture. Who should I trust?

"Let's get back inside before the cops cruise by again," said Doc.

We went back to the truck. Samuels picked up the harness and robe and approached the Rap. The Rap took them in those long-toed paws and turned them every which direction for a very long time. I didn't know anything about their race, but I knew stalling when I saw it. My mistrust of the Rap grew.

"This is not Rap," it chirped and whistled at last. "The script is similar to Rap, but different. Perhaps it comes from an offshoot dimension we have not discovered yet."

"I told you he was lying," Samuels said, making an angry gesture at me.

I stared at the Rap. Sammie said the third set of coordinates were for the Rap dimension. If I were going to bet, it would be on Sammie having the right end of the stick.

Doc passed a hand over his thinning hair. He didn't believe me. They weren't letting me go after Sammie. No one was going after Sammie. And if I didn't get back here soon to meet Enrique and Cantel, this dimension would be recycled.

"I think we should take him back to E-Prime for further questioning," Doc said.

"You can't!" I yelped. "Who's going to help Sammie? You can't let the black robes have her."

Samuels turned to the Rap. "If these criminals have been traversing between here and their base of operations, can you trace them through D-space?"

"Having one of their devices may prove useful, but it will require time to analyze, and I am not hopeful. The energy signature is quite small. I'm sorry. I should return with this to R-Prime as soon as possible." The Rap turned its all-black eyes on me and blinked. It gave me a creepy sensation, like worms crawling under my skin.

"Get the priests in here," Samuels ordered one of his men. "And gather up the rest of the scouts. We're leaving for the landing site."

"No!" I wailed. "You can't abandon your daughter."

Samuels grabbed my shirt front and pulled me against his well-muscled chest, snarling down into my face. "Mention my daughter again, and I'll kill you where you stand."

He shoved me back hard. I thumped against the side of the truck, whacking my head. Doc moved to support me before I slid to the deck. Samuels strode out through the curtain.

Doc helped me into a chair and sat beside me. I held the back of my head and rocked. *Shit.* Nothing was going right. For a moment, I wished I'd never seen Sammie, never rescued her. Then I remembered the feel of her soft hand in mine when she'd said we were friends. I had to do something.

"What's your diagnosis?" Doc asked in a low voice.

I stopped rocking and frowned at him.

"Did Sammie tell you about super-talents who drop through fractures unshielded?"

"Yeah," I said, and resumed rocking. What did it matter if he knew I was crazy? At least I'd be calmer.

"I'm a psychiatrist. I take care of the super-talents we've recovered. You say you're crazy, but you're not crazy like they're crazy. If you really have been through a fracture with no protection, I have to wonder why that is. Maybe if I can figure out why you're still sane, I can help those in my charge."

I laughed, bitter. "I doubt I'll be any help. I was crazy before I went in."

He gave me a blank look.

"I'm schizophrenic," I said. "I see things that aren't real every day."

I thought that would put him off. He'd figure I hallucinated going through a fracture, that I pulled the wool over Sammie's eyes, and that's why I wasn't insane. Instead, he leaned closer.

"When you were in D-space, what did you see? What happened to you?"

"Do you trust the Raps?" I whispered, watching for his reaction.

He remained quietly composed and didn't so much as glance at the dinosaur fiddling with the equipment on the rack.

"Paranoid schizophrenic?" he asked.

Ah, hell. Now I'd done it. He figured I was some conspiracy freak, and I had no credibility with him. I would have been better off lying and trying to act normal.

Outside, we heard raised voices. The door opened and Samuels returned.

"Eagle, I need you. The Neans refuse to take him back on a platform."

Samuels stepped back through the curtain with the Rap in his wake. Doc and I followed, my armed guard close behind. The wind cut me to the bone, and I wrapped the blanket tighter. Or maybe I was bleeding out, and that's why I felt so cold.

The Neans stood on the sidewalk talking amongst themselves. When they saw me, they moved well back and began their chant, raising a blinding light shield around themselves. The Rap walked stork-like on his hind legs down the ramp and approached the group. One of the priests broke off chanting long enough to speak to Eagle. They must have used Nean—or whatever they called their language. It didn't sound like English. The Rap returned to the truck.

"The priests say he is a demon, he has the marks on his wrists. They won't travel with him inside their shields in D-space. They think he will try to sabotage the platform and take everyone's souls."

"That's nonsense," Samuels said. "He's a human. We have to get him back to E-Prime for interrogation."

"It is a moot point in any case," said Eagle. "For whatever reason, they are unable to maintain their shields in proximity to him."

Samuels looked like he wanted to hit someone, and I edged away until I bumped the wall. My guard narrowed his eyes, and I froze.

"Then we'll take him to the landing site and question him there. We're too exposed here. Doc, do you have interrogation drugs with you?"

The corners of Doc's mouth pulled down. "We won't get anything more with drugs than we would without them. In fact, with his mental illness, if we drug him, we might get nothing intelligible at all."

"Look, Doc," Samuels said, hands on hips. "We can use your drugs, or we can use my interrogation methods, but we're going to get the truth out of him, one way or another."

I shook harder. Why had I thought I wanted to join these people? Let the demons recycle their dimension. They'd get what they deserved. But then I thought about Sammie, about how she'd been revolted by what Abbott had done to me. And Doc seemed like an okay guy, too. It was all so confusing.

"There may be another option," the Rap said, and all eyes turned toward it. "The language of the device is enough like ours that I may be able to program it to take the captive to E-Prime. Then you can question him at your leisure."

"Are you sure you understand how it works?" Doc asked. "We don't want to take any chances with him."

"There are always risks to travel in D-space," Eagle replied. "Besides, the structural integrity of this dimension declines rapidly. It would be safest if we all returned to E-Prime immediately, and then I can take the device on to R-Prime."

"But I can save this dimension." I said. "I have to save this dimension."

Doc gave me a kindly look and said, "It'll be okay, River. We'll take you back to E-Prime and get you treatment."

"I'm not delusional!" Not exactly true, but I wasn't delusional about saving the dimension. "I screwed things up. I have to make it right. Even Sammie said so. She said she'd help. She said the DCs would help."

A car cruised down Washington. It slowed as it approached our strange little group, and then it sped past. A low rumbling of displeasure came from Samuels.

"All right. Get him in the robe and send him to E-Prime. Everyone else get packed up. We're leaving for the landing site as soon as he's gone."

"No!" I shouted, but it did no good. No one listened to me.

A nightmare dipped down from the sky, swirled around Samuels, and spun past me. It hovered nearby. The DCs didn't seem to notice, nor did the Nean priests. They were too busy chanting and pounding their staffs on the ground. What the hell. Doc already thought I was a loon. I might as well do the whole schizophrenic shtick and talk to things he couldn't see.

"Get Smokey," I commanded. "I need help."

The cloud shifted and danced, but it didn't move away. I frowned at it. A soldier brought the harness to the Rap, who tapped on it for a moment and handed it back. Two soldiers pulled my blanket off and strapped on the harness. Doc watched me, concerned.

"Tell me what you see," he said.

"Now," I ordered, ignoring him. "Shoo! Shoo!"

The cloud hung motionless for a moment, and then continued it's slow inside-out roll. From the corner of my eye, another nightmare streaked away toward the far end of the alley. Great. I'd addressed the wrong one. How did I tell them apart? They all looked like soot-balls to me. And would Smokey come? Sammie said the Neans could see demons—and that they could get rid of them. Maybe sending for him wasn't such a good idea, but I was desperate. I had to get to Sammie, no matter what it took.

The two soldiers forced my arms into the robe and dragged me along behind the Rap into the alley. I kicked and screamed to no avail. They were big dudes, and I was a wimp. The Neans moved a respectable distance away as I passed, never missing a beat of whatever they recited, but even then, their light dimmed.

We passed Soo Ling's, and my tattoos itched like crazy. Smokey stepped from the darkness to stand before the fracture, the nightmare wrapping his chest. He waved it away with a flick of his talons and studied my little group with narrowed eyes.

From behind me, a blinding beam of light split the darkness, illuminating the entire alley, and spearing for Smokey's chest. Eagle jumped sideways with a squawk, and my guards jammed on the brakes, gripping my arms so hard I thought they'd snap.

The beam never touched the big demon. He twisted one hand and transformed the light into a spinning rainbow medallion, ten feet across, a translucent wall between us and the fracture. I glanced over my shoulder and saw two of the Nean priests pointing their staffs our direction, providing the power for the beam. They grimaced and growled, and the beam strengthened, but the only effect was to increase the size and speed of the disk.

"Woohoo!" I cried. My guards looked on, open-mouthed. "You rock, Smokey!"

"You wish to make another bargain, Traveler?" the big demon said.

"Make them let me go," I said.

"But you haven't fulfilled our last agreement."

"I'm trying; they're getting in my way."

Eagle approached me and tapped on the plate, oblivious to my conversation with the demon. The robe flickered, winked, and remained dull black. He wrinkled his snout and clacked his jaws in what I interpreted to be an evil laugh, then flipped up what remained of the hood. He'd solve a lot of problems for himself if I came out the other end of my journey stark raving mad.

He stepped back and motioned the guards to take me closer. The beam blinked out, and the huge psychedelic medallion vanished with it. The guards looked at one another, clenched their teeth, and pulled me forward.

"The unholy children have much to learn," Smokey said, looking past me to the group at the other end of the alley. He snorted contempt.

"I'll give you whatever you want," I pleaded, dragging my heels across the pavement. "You can have my soul. Just don't let them send me to E-Prime!"

His brows drew lower. "But Traveler, that's not your destination."

14

I plunged through a curtain of glitter. A thousand razor blades peeled my flesh away, one microscopic layer at a time. My blood formed a misty fog that I breathed, and it drowned me. Monsters of every ilk passed before my eyes, and I whirled through an abstract landscape my brain refused to take in.

When my soft tissue was gone, unseen grinders started at my toes and pulverized my bones to dust, an inch at a time. They advanced as far as my hips, and then I smacked down on a hard surface, nauseous and gasping. My head throbbed. I'd arrived fully dressed. Otherwise, I saw no advantage to travel by robe; it was as exhausting, disturbing, and painful as ever. Just my luck.

I heard the soft patter of feet and looked up. I was in a big, window-less building with white walls and a composite floor. One corner was taken up by a stone platform like Sammie's team used, and a long rack stacked with miniature flying saucers stood against a wall. A good-sized fracture shimmered behind me, flanked by metallic obelisks. In front of me, sunlight streamed in through a broad door. Across an open space outside, a tall, solid fence blocked my view. It was punctuated by a guard tower.

A Rap stood nearby, its head tilted to one side while it studied me. It wore a belt draped with mysterious gadgets. Beyond it, a couple more of them pointed gun-like weapons my direction. I waited, and so did they. The floor was cold and hard, and I grew tired of laying on it, so I clambered to my feet and raised my hands in surrender.

The Rap clacked it jaws and said, "Is this a joke, Twelve?"

The other two Raps lowered their weapons and turned away, squeaking and whistling to one another. The one in front of me moved closer and peered up at my damaged hood, which now hung around my neck. I tried to make sense of where I was.

"You may be amused by our anxiety when you delay your sanity check, but we are not." Its paw reached to touch my hood. "It's damaged."

"Um... yeah," I said. "Sorry. Is this E-Prime?"

The Rap froze, staring at me. "Another joke to make me question your mental state?"

"Sorry," I repeated, feeling like Alice in Wonderland.

"Come," it said, walking away. "Travel with a damaged robe is dangerous. We will replace it. What have you come for?"

"Uh..." Who did the Rap think I was? How long could I fool it? Long enough to get back through the fracture to the black robe dimension? Unless *this* was the black robe dimension. Oh, I was so confused!

"A new robe," I said. "I came for a new robe."

The little dino glanced over its shoulder. "Next time, borrow an undamaged robe until you can get a new one. Is your navigation console intact?"

"Seems to be," I said.

In a moment of inspiration, I poked at my chest plate until it displayed the list of destinations. Still the same three as before, listed in the same order. None glowed helpfully to tell me where I'd arrived. So Eagle hadn't entered the E-Prime coordinates. He'd sent me to one of the other two already programmed portals. But which one? And how much time did I have until he sent word about who I really was?

We walked into the sunshine, and I raised a hand to shield my eyes. The Rap turned left toward a structure that soared into the sky, all glittering metal and glass. I craned my neck back trying to see the top. I hoped we weren't going in there. It must have the elevator from Hell.

Beyond it, similar but smaller buildings dotted the interior of the fenced compound. Unfamiliar species of trees sprouted around the area, and the vegetation covering the ground had a distinct bluish hue.

To my relief, we passed by the skyscraper and entered the next, single-story building. For once, I was glad to be a runt. Rap ceilings were a good foot lower than standard human ceilings. They gave the space a cramped feeling I didn't like. As with the exterior, the interior walls were metal, and our footsteps echoed against them.

The Rap stopped before a blank space on the wall and chirped. A panel swished up, and it led me into a storeroom. Shelving marched in rows across the generous space, and all the shelves were crammed with robes. There must have been a thousand of them. Were they planning an invasion? If the black robes were the smaller group, how many DCs were there?

The dino walked between the rows, plucked a robe from a shelf, and brought it to me. I removed the tattered robe and pulled on the new one. It was just as inconveniently long as the old one. Must be a one-size-fits-none marketing strategy. I sighed.

"What else do you require?" the Rap asked.

"Oh, uh, I think that's it." What I really needed to know was whether I was in R-Prime or the black robe dimension, but I couldn't think of a way to ask without giving away my ignorance.

"In future, please adhere to your expected schedule. Arrivals at other times might prove problematic."

"Right, right," I said. "Why is that?"

The Rap did a slow turn to face me, and its black eyes squinted. "Perhaps, Twelve, we should do a scan to ensure that you didn't suffer damage while traveling."

"I'm good," I said, holding up my hands. Sweat trickled down my ribs. "It's just... well... the schedule isn't always convenient."

The little dino nodded and retraced our steps. "When your research is complete and you can open a second fracture to our dimension, you may come and go as needed. Until then, you must follow the schedule."

"Sure. Of course. Follow the schedule. Got it," I replied, thinking furiously.

From what the Rap said, I had to be in R-Prime, and the Raps were working with the black robes to create a second fracture. If they wanted a second one, why didn't they ask the DCs to make it? Something smelled rotten in the Rap dimension.

What should I do next? I wanted to go after Sammie, but what if the black robes invaded E-Prime while I was doing that? I couldn't stop an invasion all by myself. I thought I should tell the DCs about the room with all the robes—and that Eagle wasn't the trustworthy team member they thought he was. Would they believe me? Another chat with Capt. Samuels wasn't something I looked forward to. I resolved to go on to the black robe dimension by myself.

As we neared the building that housed the fracture, another Rap came out, talking with someone behind him—someone wearing a robe just like mine. I looked for an escape route, somewhere to duck out of sight. Too late. The man's hazel eyes widened in surprise, and my pulse pounded in my ears. Did he have a banana gun hidden under his robe? What would the Raps do if he started shooting?

The Rap escorting me pulled a gadget from its belt, pointed it at the stranger, and read the display before returning the little device to the belt.

"One," my Rap said, "I have just explained to Twelve the importance of adherence to the travel schedule."

"Beg pardon," One said, giving the Rap a little bow without taking his eyes from me. "I must talk to the flight leader on a matter of some importance, a matter that could not wait until the next travel interval.

Perhaps Twelve can join us, and then we can go back together."

Why hadn't he blown the whistle on me? From his expression, he knew I wasn't part of his merry band, but he didn't seem inclined to admit that to the Raps. What crazy game was he playing?

"Oh, uh, got to go," I said. "Tick, tock. Burning daylight."

"This won't take a moment," One assured me, flipping back his hood to expose a head of thick brown hair worn shoulder length and topping a craggy face with bushy brows, a long, straight nose, and a pointed chin. He wrapped his arm around my shoulders in a fatherly way and propelled me along with him, his eyes burning holes in the side of my face. My skin crawled from his touch.

He slowed his steps so our Rap escort pulled away and whispered, "Don't worry, I'll protect you. If the Raps find out you're not Twelve, you're dead."

"Who are you?" I asked.

"Shh," he warned. "I'll explain everything when we're alone."

We entered the skyscraper, and I stiffened. *Not an elevator. Please not an elevator.* The Rap waved us into a sunny atrium while it walked away into the bowels of the building, and I let out a little sigh of relief. I pulled loose, and One faced me.

"Listen to me. We only have a few minutes," he said, voice urgent. "I assume you're a DC investigating the terrible incident in the dimension you call E-4. If the Raps find out you're a DC masquerading as Twelve, they'll kill you. They don't want the DCs to know about us."

"How come they can't tell I'm not Twelve?" I asked.

"To Raps, all humans look alike, especially when we're wearing robes. They use the transponders in our harnesses to determine who we are. You're wearing harness twelve, and therefore, you're Twelve. Just keep quiet, and I'll get you out of here alive. There's been too much killing already."

"But—"

"Shh," he said, as our escort returned.

"The flight leader will see you now," the Rap said. It waved us down a hallway.

One held my elbow while we threaded through a labyrinth of hallways until we turned into a little cul-de-sac that ended in a small round room no more than six feet across. Our escort stopped but waved us forward. I couldn't see where we were supposed to go, unless the back wall was another of those invisible doors. There wasn't a ceiling, and the shaft seemed to go right to the top of the building. I had a sudden bad feeling.

One dragged me in, turned us around, and pressed a silver plate beside the opening. The next thing I knew, my stomach turned somersaults, and we floated rapidly upward. I panicked and thrashed.

"Relax," he advised. "And don't look down."

Ah, hell. Why'd he say that? As soon as he did, I had to look. There was nothing but a lot of empty space under us, and more of it with each passing second. I hyperventilated and hoped we could use the stairs on the way down. Raps had stairs, didn't they?

We reached an opening in the side of the tube, and One pulled us through onto solid floor where gravity worked normally.

"Say nothing," he whispered, like I could stop panting long enough to make conversation.

He walked into a large, dimly lit chamber. Through the smoked glass windows, I could see a city in the far distance, all spindly skyscrapers like this one, glinting in the sun over the top of a leafy green jungle that seemed to go on forever. I didn't see any doors that might lead to stairs.

"Flight leader," said One, making a little bow. "I'm sorry to disturb you at this hour."

The flight leader sat on a stool at a desk with a smooth glowing top. He waved a paw toward two stools on our side of the desk. One bowed again and took a stool. He looked at me and tipped his head toward the other. I sat.

The stool was too short, even for someone my height, and it canted uncomfortably forward. I didn't know whether it was supposed to be uncomfortable so visitors wouldn't linger, or whether it was designed for Rap physiology and didn't fit humans well. I did know that if I didn't get out of there soon, Eagle would arrive to tell the Raps who I really was. The stool made it difficult, but I managed a teeny-weeny rock all the same.

"I have bad news, flight leader," One said, tipping his head forward in deference. "A few of my clan have been unable to resist the urges of the flesh. They have used the gift of travel you generously provided us to go to another dimension and seek females to assure the continuation of our species."

The Rap bared his teeth. "Indeed, this is bad news. Our medical staff will provide pharmaceuticals to prevent such behavior in the future."

I shifted on my stool, wondering whether I'd been wrong, and Sammie had always been the target of Black Robe. But that didn't make sense. He'd told the chuckler to kill her and look for me.

"Thank you, flight leader. As always, we appreciate your guidance and assistance." One gave another little bow. "Unfortunately, while the men were hunting females, they came upon a group of humans from another dimension, and a misunderstanding ensued."

The flight leader went very still. "What was the result of this misunderstanding?"

"I am uncertain. I still seek those who are responsible, but when I find them, they will be suitably punished. I came to assure you that only a handful of renegades took this action. The rest toil as assigned."

His groveling sickened me. What kind of warped relationship did these humans have with the Raps? 'Toil as assigned' sounded a lot like code for slave labor. Samuels hadn't acted like this with Eagle. Is that why the Raps were working with a second group of humans? Did the E-Prime humans refuse to engage in this kind of master-servant relationship?

The Rap moved his paws over the desktop. Lines of symbols scrawled across the surface. He studied them for a minute before turning his attention to One.

"What progress have you made on your research?" he asked.

One cast a quick glance my direction before answering. "The test results are promising. We're very close to a breakthrough."

The flight leader stared at the human. "This is the same report you gave a moon ago, and the moon before that. We cannot continue to provide endless materials unless we see progress."

"These things take time. We don't want another containment failure." One had an edge to his voice that he couldn't disguise.

The Rap rocked back and folded his paws on his belly. "Is there danger from containment failure? I thought you'd changed your containment methods?"

"Of course, flight leader. And we're taking every precaution to ensure control of the process."

"When do you anticipate you'll be able to create a fracture large enough to travel through?"

One smiled. "Very soon, flight leader. Very, very soon. Believe me, you'll be the first to know when we've succeeded. In the meantime, I request extra supply pallets be sent through to Beta."

"What kind of supplies?" the flight leader asked.

"The weather worsens. We've used more fuel than expected this moon, and we require replenishment if we're to keep the facility running." One leaned forward. "If this is a problem, we could evacuate the facility until Spring, but of course, that would delay our progress."

The Rap tapped lists on his desk, and one section displayed a graph with a jagged line climbing sharply upward. He focused his black eyes on One, and I didn't think it was a friendly look.

"Fuel use far exceeds projections," he said. "More than can be explained by weather."

"I believe the projections were made before the expansion of the lab facilities, flight leader. Do you wish us to close the new section so we may conserve fuel? Doing so shouldn't extend our schedule more than twenty-five or thirty percent."

The flight leader bared his teeth. "Delays are unacceptable. I will arrange additional fuel deliveries."

"Many thanks, flight leader. As always, we are at your service."

One rose, bowed, and walked back to the tube thing we'd come up in. I lagged behind, wondering whether I was better off telling the Rap who I was or going with One. He didn't seem like a bloodthirsty, cold-hearted killer. If anything, he reminded me of a harried administrator trying to do the best possible job with limited resources and an impossible schedule. He was good at it, too, the way he'd wheedled the extra fuel out of the flight leader. Maybe he didn't know why Black Robe and his friends had gone to E-4. How did he know about DCs?

One offered to protect me from the Raps, and he said he'd go after Black Robe for what he'd done. If he was black robe law enforcement, he should help me get Sammie back. And he hadn't tried to shoot me, stun me, or beat me up, which gave him bonus points in my book. My hope for the mission surged.

If only I didn't have to take that damn tube to get back to the fracture. It was infinitely worse than an elevator, and I didn't even have any delusions associated with it. I stopped beside One at the edge of the evil contraption.

"How do you know it's working?" I asked, wiping the back of my hand across my mouth and peering down, down, down. "I don't see any indicators."

"Raps can detect the energy field through their skin," he said.

"Can you?"

"No."

He grinned, grabbed my arm, and dragged me into the tube with him. I yelped and flailed and drifted steadily down the shaft beside him. *Homicidal maniac,* I cursed silently, fighting not to retch.

When we reached the bottom, a Rap waited for us. One bowed to it, and I did the same.

"I need to speak to the supply master," One said.

Our escort gestured us to follow and led us to another low building behind the main fracture building. It chirped at a section of wall, a door slid back, and we entered another large warehouse jammed with supply pallets that were stacked with boxes, cylinders, and a lot of stuff I couldn't begin to name.

A Rap rose from a desk inside a little cubicle in one corner and approached us. One bowed, and the new Rap dismissed our escort with a wave of its paw.

"What brings you to R-Prime today, One?" the Rap asked. It was the first plump individual of its kind that I'd seen. I wondered if the gray around its muzzle and up its cheeks indicated age, or whether that was just its usual coloring. It was otherwise a uniform dark blue.

One glanced around the warehouse, opened his robe, and drew out two metal cylinders each the size of a thermos. He handed them over to the Rap, who also looked around the space before taking them.

"Two?" it asked.

"For twice the usual service," One replied with a smile and another little bow. I dipped, too, unsure of the protocol. The Rap turned its muzzle toward me.

"Who is this?" it asked.

"Twelve," One replied. "He's learning my routines so he can come when I am unavailable."

"Twelve?" The supply master ran its eyes up and down me. "It seems small for Twelve."

"Uh, new diet," I said. "I've lost a few pounds."

I bowed, twice. Bowing was a lot like rocking, and in a strange way, it felt pretty good.

The Rap carried the cylinders to the desk and placed them in a sack, which it shoved out of sight before returning to us.

"The flight leader has approved additional supplies of fuel," One said. "I would like to include it in our delivery today. Can you please ship immediately? We're expecting a bad storm to arrive in a few hours, and I would like to get the goods situated in the depot before it hits."

The supply master nodded. "This can be arranged."

"Also, since we may be locked down in a whiteout for the next several days, it would be helpful to receive the technology pallets immediately after the fuel and in place of our usual food shipment. The flight leader is concerned that we remain on schedule, and we need the parts on the pallet if we're to do that."

"You have sufficient food supplies?" the Rap asked, tilting its head to one side.

"Thank you for your concern, supply master. We prefer to tighten our belts and deliver our research results on time rather than feed our bellies, and we need the spare parts to continue," One said, bowing again. I did the same. "May I mark the pallets for immediate delivery?"

The supply master went to its desk and returned with a pad of red stickers.

"Place these on the pallets you want to receive today," it instructed.

One and I bowed a few more times, and then we threaded our way amongst the pallets in the warehouse while the supply master went back to his desk. One seemed able to determine the contents of the pallets based on their labels. The Raps must have shared more about their lan-

guage with the black robes than they'd shared with the DCs. He plastered stickers on the occasional pallet as we meandered between them.

"What was that you gave to the Rap?" I asked in a low voice.

He glanced back the way we'd come before speaking. "It's a harmless recreational drug. There's a black market in it, but the supply
master prefers to get it from us so he doesn't have to worry about getting caught in a sting operation. In return, he sees to it that we receive
supplemental equipment, food, and fuel that makes our life in the Beta
dimension bearable. We'd rather not be involved, but life at the Beta
colony is harsh, so we do what we must to survive."

I could understand the realities of survival and doing what had to
be done, although I wasn't sure I'd be able to justify dealing drugs in any
circumstances. Maybe they were harmless as he said. Maybe it was no
different than running moonshine during Prohibition. Still, I felt uneasy.

"Who are you?" I asked.

"I and my friends are the sole survivors from a dimension destroyed
by the Raps." He slapped a sticker on a pallet and moved down the row.
"They sent their machines to contact our dimension four years ago after
some experiments of ours attracted their attention."

My eyes grew wide. "They destroyed your dimension? How? Why?"

"When news of Rap contact got out, my country's enemies feared
that with Rap support, we could overrun them, so they launched a nuclear first strike. Of course, my country retaliated. We plunged into global
warfare.

"The Raps provided my country with technology so we could survive
long enough to evacuate at least some of our people, but it failed with
catastrophic results. Our dimensional barriers weakened and collapsed.
Instead of saving thousands, the Raps saved just thirty-seven of us. And
they placed conditions on our rescue."

One threaded between more of the pallets, placing stickers as he
went. I followed behind.

"There aren't any other humans in your dimension?"

"No," he said. "No humans, no other intelligent life. We've seen ancient ruins of a past civilization, but they're all that remains of their creators. We're alone in a hostile environment and dependent on the Raps.
We've lost a third of our members already."

He selected all the pallets containing large white metal tanks, as
well as a smattering of other things.

"What are these?" I asked.

"Propane to fuel our generator," he said. "Are you a DC?"

I didn't know what to tell him. Sammie said they'd take me, but
after their reception at the fracture, I wasn't so sure I wanted to sign
on. But Smokey said I had to be one of them to save their dimension. Of

course, saving their dimension assumed I saved E-4. The overwhelming sense of hopelessness returned. I needed help. I needed Sammie.

"Yeah," I said. "What's this research you do for the Raps?"

One glanced around again. "They believe we're working to create a device capable of fracturing dimensional barriers in a controlled way. In truth, we're working on a device capable of sealing dimensional fractures. When we succeed, we'll seal the Raps in their own dimension so they can't destroy anyone else."

"Oh," I said, frowning. It seemed a drastic measure to take, and wouldn't the Raps eventually figure out how to break barriers anyway? Wouldn't they be pretty pissed off when they did?

"Um... maybe you should work with the DCs to rein in the Raps," I said. "The Neans can close fractures already. Or I think they can."

He eyes turned on me, and his look sharpened. "The Raps don't want the other races to know what they've done or what they're researching. They'll wipe us out before they'll let our existence be discovered. And if your DCs do learn about us, the Raps will destroy your world and probably the Neans' world, too. Imagine the annihilation wrought by delivering a nuclear device through a fracture."

I shuddered at the very idea. The Raps didn't seem like very nice people, er, dinos. "So what's your plan? The DCs and the Raps know your people were on E-4. One of your guys took my partner, a DC, captive. I think the secrecy train already left the station."

"But the Raps don't know you're here," he countered, his brow drawing down.

"They will as soon as Eagle gets back. He was supposed to send me to E-Prime."

"Why?" One asked.

"Oh, uh..." I stammered. "Well, it was a test of the device. Eagle said it wasn't Rap technology."

He rubbed a hand over his pointy chin. "But why send anyone with the device? Why not take it back on a platform?"

"Um, overcrowding," I said. "E-4 seems to be failing. Lot of stuff to get back to E-Prime."

"They still hope to cover our existence," he muttered, more to himself than to me.

"Listen, not to rush you or anything, but I need to find my partner. Do you know where your guy took her?"

One plastered another sticker on a pallet and headed toward the front of the building. "I had no idea anyone was taken. Of course we'll do anything we can to ensure her safety and return her to you. We're anxious to build a relationship with fellow humans and find a dimension where we'll be welcomed by our own kind."

In the back of my head, a niggling little worry squirmed. I was terrible at math, but something didn't add up.

"You knew they'd gone, but you didn't know Black Robe brought someone back?"

One looked at me levelly. "How do you know someone was kidnapped? How did you get the equipment you now wear? So many unanswered questions, but we have very little time. I must warn my people and move them away from the fracture in case the Raps take action against us. Then we can sort out what happened on E-4."

He hurried on to the supply master's cubicle, where he again reminded the Rap of the approaching storm and the need to speed the delivery through to his camp. It walked us back to the fracture building, where the guards lounged, inattentive. One headed across the floor toward the sparkling fracture.

"We'll go through together," One said. "When we've reached Beta and I've warned everyone, we'll look for your missing DC. There aren't many places to hide her."

We stopped halfway across the room. One pulled back his robe and tapped his plate. I could see his selected destination pulse, and then he switched over to his shield control. When he activated it, it gave a weak flash and went out. He frowned down at the plate.

The murky became clear. It wasn't some failing of my damaged robe that prevented the shields from working; it was me. I negated the robe shields the same way I knocked out the Nean shields. Wonderful. If One got too close to me as we entered the fracture, he'd come out the other end a vegetable. I couldn't be responsible for that.

I tapped my plate to life, selected the black robe dimension, kicked on the shield just in case that was what kept me clothed, and trotted toward the fracture.

"Wait!" One called. "Your shield! It hasn't activated."

I waved a hand without looking back and jogged on.

15

I plunged into the Dark Place, and it felt like every molecular bond in my body was assaulted by deafening sound waves. One by one, microscopic layers of my flesh peeled away as atoms separated. My bones, already reduced to dust, burst free from any remaining connective tissue and rose in a cloud that choked and blinded me. Despite my lack of sight, I could still see all the crazy, impossible creatures and their bizarre, unimaginable surrounding.

"Not real, not real," I chanted, but now that I knew it was a lie, the chant didn't provide the comfort it used to. Fear that I might go permanently mad hit me like a bolt of lightning, intensifying my pain.

"Find Sammie," I growled. "Save Sammie. Ohm."

Then my chest whacked into the floor, more of that Rap composite stuff that was just as hard as any asphalt or concrete I'd ever had the misfortune to fall on. And freezing cold besides. My hands chilled where they touched it. My stomach arrived an instant later, but I didn't barf, maybe because I hadn't eaten anything for hours. I couldn't remember feeling so tired in all my life. I wanted to crawl into a warm bed and stay there for a couple of days. Two men dressed in blue coveralls pointed sonic banana guns at me, which made me feel right at home somehow.

I was in another warehouse kind of place, this one a third full of Rap pallets. Light filtered through translucent panels near the ceiling. No electric lights. Hooray! I wouldn't be subjected to their off-key singing. A trace of snow coated the floor in front of a big door at one end. The fracture glimmered at the other end.

A moment later, One arrived, looking worried. Of course, he was on his feet. I'd have to ask him how he did that. He rushed over to me. Embarrassed, I scrambled to get up. The guards tracked me with their weapons.

"You're not crazy," One said, staring.

"Well... no more than usual," I said, panting. I wiped a dribble of blood from my nose and thanked my lucky stars that I'd arrived clothed even if I did have a splitting headache. I wasn't keen on standing naked in front of a bunch of strangers, and the place was near Arctic temperature.

One's eyes opened wide. "You're the super-talent Two's been chasing, the one who can travel unprotected without going mad."

I froze. If he knew about me, then he knew a lot more than he'd let on. I'd believed he was a good guy, and now I'd walked into a trap. I looked around for an escape route, but the two men with the banana guns had the drop on me. I'd trusted him. His betrayal tasted like ash in my mouth.

"Fascinating," One said. "I thought Two must be mistaken, but I see it's true. How do you do it? Do you have some kind of device? Or do you create a shield from your mind the way the Neans do? I must know."

I had the queasy feeling I'd become something less than human in his eyes, something more like a specimen, to be probed and experimented on. He shared that same cold, mad look that Black Robe had. Maybe it was something about traveling by robe. Maybe it didn't completely shield the wearer and over time, they went crazy. Or maybe they were both nuts in the first place. Birds of a feather and all. Why hadn't I seen it on R-Prime? Was I so desperate for help that I'd thrown all my survival instincts out the window? What the hell was I thinking?

"Uh, it's a talent," I said, backing slowly away. "I should really get the DC I came for and be on my way. I'll be missed. Soon. Very soon."

"Our plan has changed," he said, addressing the two armed guards. "We no longer have time to perfect the fracture bombs. As supplies come through, move them to the bunker, and get all the fuel from the depot to the bunker as well. We'll prepare the sleepers and use them to destroy R-Prime."

"What?! You can't!" I cried. "You'll cause a multiverse collapse if you destroy an old dimension like that."

One stepped closer and narrowed his eyes. "What do you know of dimensional collapse? Have you witnessed one?"

"Well... no," I said, taking another step back. "But a very reliable source warned me it could happen."

He closed in again, his eyes intent on mine. "What source? What dimension do you come from that they have this knowledge?"

"It's... uh... an extra-dimensional source with experience in these things." I inched back and sideways, trying to put him between me and the closest guard. "You might say his whole purpose for being is dimensional collapse."

"Tell me about your source," he said, looming over me. "What research has he done?"

"Well... he's from the Dark Place, and dimensional collapse is their stock in trade so to speak."

"Dark Place? You mean D-space?" He threw back his head and laughed. "Pah! I don't believe the fairytales and myths about demons that the Neans spread. They're children afraid of their own shadows and use lies about creatures of the night to keep their priests in power. Neither they nor anyone else has seen these boogey men they claim come through fractures."

"Just because you can't see it doesn't mean it doesn't exist," I argued, edging back more and fighting the urge to run screaming from the madman in front of me. "I mean, what about microbes and... and... air? You can't see them, but you'd die without them. Well, without air. And some microbes, too. But I've seen them. Demons, not microbes."

"You'll prove an interesting subject when I have more time," he said, turning away. "We have work to do."

"What about him?" one of them asked.

"He'll be our special guest," One replied. "Take him to the bunker and see that he's handled carefully. I don't want him damaged."

I tried to break and run, but the guards were on me in a heartbeat. They grabbed my arms and stripped the robe and device off me before dragging me away. One of them released me long enough to heave the door up, and icy wind buffeted me. I stared out at a winter landscape. *This must be Siberia.*

The camp stood in a thin spot in an otherwise dense evergreen forest. Another two-story metal building stood fifty feet away. It had a couple of regular people-sized doors on the ground floor and rows of windows along the upper story. Farther away, three log cabins stood in a row, smoke curling from their stone chimneys and enormous stacks of firewood banked against their walls. Farther down the row, the bleating of goats and the crow of a rooster came from a log barn. Pole corrals surrounded it.

In the opposite direction, a vertical axis windmill rose into the sky and turned lazy circles. Next to it, I heard the rumble of an engine coming from a small shed. A pallet of propane cylinders sat beside it. Power lines were strung from the shed through trees around the compound, and then to the two metal buildings. I guess those living in the cabins didn't rate electricity. A foot of snow covered everything and drifted in clouds off rooftops and tree branches with each gust of wind. Dressed as I was in jeans, sneakers, and sweatshirt, bolting from my two escorts looked less like a survival plan and more like suicide in the frigid temperature.

They hauled me to one of the Rap floating freight platforms. It was an eight-foot by twenty-foot metal slab with a windowed box at one end that was about the size of a pickup truck cab. One guard opened the cab and pulled a piece of rope from behind the two canted stools bolted to the floor. He bound my wrists behind me and shoved me in behind the stools. A control panel with a bunch of Rap scratches and a view screen stretched across the compartment in front of the stools. I heard lots of clunking and banging, but I couldn't see out the windows from where I lay.

I was shaking from the cold before one of the guards got in and perched on a stool. His hands played over the control panel, and blessed heat flooded the compartment. The floor vibrated, and then we were moving. Out the window, the tops of trees dropped from sight as we rose above them. I tried to keep track of which way we were going based on the direction of the sun without success. The guard pulled a ration bar out of his pocket and gnawed on it for the duration of our journey, paying no attention to the control panel or the vehicle. It didn't inspire great confidence.

"So you on board with this destroying the Rap dimension thing your boss wants to do?" I asked.

He turned glazed green eyes on me, and I wondered if it was only the Raps using drugs brewed up by One.

"I don't think it's such a hot idea," I said. "Nothing like destroying a dimension to make people cranky with you—never mind the potential for multiverse collapse."

He snorted and went back to watching the landscape glide by. I wormed every which way I could, but I couldn't get the ropes loosened up enough to slip them off my wrists. Jimmy and I used to tie one another up for fun when we were playing cowboys and Indians, or cops and robbers, just to see how long it would take to get free. I guess I should have kept up my practice.

"Listen, if you help me, I can put in the good word for you. With the DCs. They're going to come looking for me real soon."

He laughed. "Not soon enough."

I gulped. "What are you going to do with me?"

"You'll dream," he said. "Like you've never dreamed before." He smiled, and it scared the crap out of me.

I pulled at my bonds and peered around the compartment. The light streaming through the front window dimmed for a second, but when I looked up, I didn't see anything to cause it. I chalked it up to the sun slipping behind a cloud and focused on the damn rope.

I'd made exactly zero progress toward getting loose when the platform descended and trees came into view again out the windows. We set down with a thunk, and then my guard got out. He dragged me out feet first, and I fell in the snow with my own thunk.

"What's this?" a male voice asked.

"Another super-talent, the one Two's been after. The Master says to make him comfortable. Be careful. He isn't like the others. We'll be hauling all the supplies here asap, and then we're headed to the Rap dimension. Get the sleepers ready to go to the fracture."

I managed to roll to my feet and faced another guard with a banana gun in a holster on his hip and blue eyes this time, but that same glazed look. Did One have them all drugged or under some kind of hypnosis? Why else would they follow him? They had to see he was insane, didn't they?

"Why's he taking the sleepers?" the new guard asked.

"No time left. If we don't destroy the Raps first, they'll come here and kill us all," my escort said. "He'll wake the sleepers and make them fracture, and we'll have revenge at last."

"You can't let him do that!" I shouted. "He's nuts! He'll start a multiverse collapse that will destroy all the dimensions. You have to stop him. The DCs will protect you from the Raps. They'll take you in."

Blue Eyes spat into the snow. "You DCs are in bed with the Raps. You can't do anything without their technology. When we're done with those uppity lizards, we'll come for your dimension. We'll cull the filth, get rid of the criminals, the retards, the perverts. Then we'll make sure non-human dimensions are bombed back to the Stone Age and repopulated with humans like they should be. Earth wasn't meant to be ruled by animals."

They were *all* crazy, I realized, all a bunch of demented racist bigots bent on destroying the multiverse. My blood ran cold, partly because it was frickin freezing standing there in the snow. I didn't see any buildings, just a lot of trees and brush. Maybe they planned to turn me into an icicle and keep me in suspended animation. Maybe the sleepers were popsicle talents. What had they done to Sammie?

Blue Eyes pushed me ahead of him toward an open patch on a hillock twenty feet away. When we reached the top, I looked down a ramp descending underground. A nightmare lurked in the darkness below, and as I watched, another one glided in from the sky, looped around us, and joined its compatriot in the tunnel. I saw a few more lurking in the boughs of the trees. My tattoos pricked ever so slightly. I hadn't noticed because of the rope tied around them. Was Smokey here? Hope burned in my chest.

The driver used a remote control to float one of the pallets from the platform up the hill. Blue Eyes dragged me down the ramp, and the driver and pallet followed. The ramp was coated with snow and ice, and I had to watch my step or risk sliding down on my rump. Hadn't these turkeys heard of rock salt? Traction sand? Something? No Labor & Industry safety inspectors here.

Blue Eyes clicked on a flashlight and led us deeper. When the snow petered out, we walked on a ceramic tile floor strewn with mud and pine needles. Apparently they didn't have janitorial staff. More tiles lined the walls, and I could make out a landscape mosaic in the pattern. Or at least I thought that's what I saw. I sometimes made patterns out of random nonsense.

A few tree roots pierced the ceiling, which rapidly disappeared into the darkness overhead as we descended. The place smelled of earth and mold, and the nightmares drifted ahead, staying at the edge of the light. It reminded me of the entrance to a subway station—a very old, abandoned subway station.

The tunnel opened into a larger space where it was still as cold as a grave but without the biting wind that blew above ground. Tunnels led away in three directions. A few pallets were parked in one corner. My driver added his to the group and joined us. He pulled a grimy rag from his pocket and shook it out.

"We don't need that," Blue Eyes said. "Where's he going to run even if he does make it out?"

"Better safe than sorry," the driver said. He tied the filthy strip of cloth around my eyes. "Be quick about bringing the sleepers. I have to get back for another load."

Blue Eyes grunted agreement and dragged me away down the passage. Our footsteps echoed in the space. I tripped over unexpected lumps and wondered whether the place was structurally sound. A cave-in was probably the least of my worries. I tried to count steps and keep track of turns. In minutes, I had them hopelessly confused. My tattoos itched more, but not enough to indicate Smokey's presence.

After a lot of tripping and turning, Blue Eyes stopped me. I heard clanking, and then he pushed me forward again. Wherever we were, it was warm, almost stifling, which made the smell even worse. Urine predominated, backed by feces and a rotting, infected-flesh stench. It burned my nose and turned my stomach. He pulled the blindfold off my eyes.

We were in a room the size of a small boutique shop at a mall. The door we'd come through was glass, and most of the remainder of the front wall was also glass that showed a wide, dark corridor beyond. A propane heater glowed at the far end of the space. The walls were water-strained and streaked with mold. Cartons of medical supplies were stacked haphazardly in a corner up front, and a few IV poles were scattered around the space. One of them supported a propane camping lantern. I stared transfixed at the horror before me.

Four naked humans lay on gurneys lined up along one wall. All of them had shaved heads. The two men at the far end of the row lay as still as death, chests barely rising with each slow, rattling breath. Their hands and toes curled tight despite their unconsciousness.

The eyes of the woman in the next bed moved under the lids, and little groans escaped her lips. One hand twitched against the filthy bed sheet she lay on. Her legs were spread in a way that reminded me of how the female agent under Art looked when he'd been on top of her. I choked on bile that rushed up from my stomach.

The final man lay curled in a fetal position. Strange sharp cries broke from him every few seconds. His back and buttocks were a mass of open, oozing sores, and urine puddled on the floor under his bed. All of them were as thin as Auschwitz survivors. Nightmares drifted over and around them.

"River!"

I jerked around, and there was Sammie, still in her DC uniform and strapped to another gurney on the opposite wall. An electrical charge of relief ripped through my chest. They hadn't hurt her, at least not yet.

Blue Eyes flipped me onto an empty gurney next to her and attached straps to my ankles. Then he smacked me hard across the face, and I saw stars. By the time they'd cleared, he had the rope off my wrists and my hands in restraints fastened to the gurney rails.

He began rearranging the sleepers, stacking them like so much garbage onto a single gurney, piling one on top of another none too gently. He tossed a blanket over the heap of humanity and rolled them to the door.

"Don't worry, honey," he said, leering at Sammie. "I'll be back for you soon."

He pushed the gurney into the hallway. A knot of nightmares trailed out after him. A single dark cloud drifted into the room and glided around Sammie and me.

"River, what are you doing here?"

"Hey, Sammie." I smiled weakly. "I came to rescue you."

"All by yourself?" she asked, staring. "Where's my team? Didn't you find them? How did you get here?"

"Uh…" Maybe now wasn't the time to tell her about my experience with her dad. "We have to stop One. He's taking the sleepers to the Rap dimension where he'll make them fracture. It'll cause a multiverse collapse."

"He can't," she replied. "There's no predictable way to force them all to fracture at the same time."

"He seemed pretty confident."

"With the state they're in, I can't imagine they'll muster enough energy to create even a small fracture. We have to rescue them, get them back to E-Prime. God knows, they won't last much longer here, not with the treatment they've had."

"Okay," I said. "We'll rescue the sleepers."

Sammie gave me the "you're crazy" look I deserved. "I've been pulling at these straps for hours, and I've made no progress."

"Well, uh..." I hoped my skills with hospital restraints hadn't become as rusty as my rope work. I scooted toward my right hand until I wedged my shackled wrist between the guard rail strut and my hip. Then I flexed and squirmed until my hand pulled out of the restraint. I reached over to unbuckle the one on my left wrist.

Sammie's eyes opened wide. "How'd you do that?"

"Practice," I said.

Six months in a mental hospital and I'd learned a number of useful talents that I'd hoped I'd never need again. Once I had my legs undone, I hopped off my gurney and unstrapped Sammie. She rolled off the mattress and into my arms.

"Thank you," she breathed, squeezing the daylights out of me, her tiny frame shaking. "I had to watch while the attendant—" She gestured toward the space where the woman had been.

"Yeah, I thought he might be—" I couldn't finish the sentence and hugged her close. "We'll get her back, I promise."

"All I could think about was why I was here, what I'd done with my life, what I *hadn't* done. I've tried to be a good trooper, someone my father would approve of. Even the men I dated were soldiers, because I knew that's what he wanted. Now here I am, in the worst trouble of my life, and where are the trained warriors? Nowhere. Instead I'm rescued by—" She gazed up into my eyes.

"Yeah," I said, feeling awkward as hell. "The crazy guy, who showed up without a plan."

She gave me a sad smile and shook her head. "No. By the kindest, gentlest, bravest man I've ever met, which just proves heroes don't have to be soldiers. I'm done pleasing my father. When we get out of here, I'm going to follow my own dreams, not his."

"Good idea. Um, do you know how to get back to the surface?" I asked.

"No," she said. "Do you?"

16

"There's about two dozen of them," I said, "and everyone is busy getting things locked down before they head to the Rap dimension. They think the Raps will come here to kill them when they find out about... well, about what the black robes have been doing."

Sammie dug through the boxes of medical supplies. They'd taken her knife, and she didn't seem to be finding a replacement weapon or a flashlight. I retrieved the lantern off the IV pole. I should tell her I was the super-talent. I wondered if she'd be mad that I hadn't told her sooner.

"What is this place?" I asked instead.

"It must be ruins left by the previous civilization. It's too old to be anything the black robes built. It's an archeological gold mine. When the scientists hear about it, they'll all want to come."

Assuming we got out of here to tell them. The place wasn't exactly rife with artillery, and we'd be going up against those sonic banana guns. Even if we found our way to the surface, how would we get back to the fracture? I didn't relish the idea of a long walk through snowy woods, especially since we didn't know which way to go. We could freeze to death in the first hour.

"Look at this," Sammie said. She held up a black uniform shirt just like her own. "Where did they get it?"

"One knew about DCs," I said. "He knew what they were called. Back on E-4, Black Robe read your message and obliterated it. That's how he knew where to find us. You said you thought you'd been ambushed. The black robes must have infiltrated the DCs."

She frowned at the shirt for a minute. Then she reached into a box and pulled out one of the golden robes the Neans wore.

"I think they captured a platform crew. The black robes might pass for an E-Prime human, but they couldn't get by as a Nean priest, and the Neans would never let anyone have their ceremonial dress. We lost a retrieval crew about eight months ago. The platform returned empty. Everyone assumed something happened in D-space, that the priest lost his shield, and the crew didn't make it back. We haven't had a retrieval since then. I bet the black robes jumped them, just like they did us, and that's how they learned about DCs. They must have Rap technology that lets them monitor D-space for new fractures."

The nightmare cloud drifted around me for about the fourteenth time, and I waved a hand at it. Dumb. It wasn't like I could make physical contact with it.

"Shoo," I said. "Get lost."

It drifted to the door and hung in the air before it. Sammie looked up from her scrounging.

"Excuse me?"

"Nothing," I said. "Just a nuisance nightmare that won't leave me alone."

"I don't see anything," she said, frowning at me before she returned to her search. "If it's like the demon, I should be able to see it, shouldn't I? Are you sure it isn't a hallucination?"

"If it is, it's damned annoying," I replied. "Look, maybe we can find some weapons along the way. We need to be out of here before that guy comes back."

"That's one alternative," Sammie said. Her eyes narrowed, and she peered out the front window. "It's pretty dark out there. We could ambush him when he returns and take his gun."

I hated violence. With a little luck, we might sneak out without encountering anyone. The last thing I wanted was a confrontation with Blue Eyes. I was no fighter, and while Sammie had a mean right cross, she wasn't very big. He could end up beating the stuffing out of us both. The nightmare circled me again.

"Be gone," I said. I held up my fingers in a cross. "I exorcise you."

It drifted back to the door and hovered there. I ground my teeth. Sammie rose and put her hands on her hips.

"There's nothing useful here. Let's set up a trap in the corridor."

"What if he doesn't come back right away?" I asked, shifting uncomfortably from one foot to the other. "One could get away with the sleepers before we catch him."

"We don't know where we're going," she said. "We could force him to tell us how to get out of here."

"We could?" I said, thinking of the beating I'd had at her father's hands. I felt suddenly chilled despite the overheated temperature of the room. Had I misjudged Sammie? I hadn't thought she was capable of that kind of brutality.

She got a little crease between her brows, and then she said, "Okay, maybe not. But we need his weapon. We know which way he went. We can start that direction and find a suitable place to waylay him."

"Right," I said, leaping for the door, lantern in hand.

Sammie cannibalized one of the IV poles to give us each a metal rod a couple feet long. I wasn't sure what I was supposed to do with it. Was it meant to be a club? A sword? Some lethal spinning ninja weapon? Maybe I could be the spear bearer and let her do the clever weapons stuff. But what kind of man would that make me, letting the woman do the fighting? I bet Gandhi never had to make these kinds of decisions.

"Leave the lantern here," she said. "It'll give us away."

"But..." I peered through the glass into inky blackness. "It's dark out there. Really dark. Totally dark."

Sammie joined me at the door and looked out. "Damn. Okay, turn it down as far as it will go. I'll get a blanket to mask it."

She picked up a blanket, and we ventured out the door together, just the three of us: me, Sammie, and the damn nightmare. Maybe that's all it had been waiting for. Maybe it couldn't fit through the crack around the edge, although the space looked plenty big enough to me. I wished it would go away. I had enough to think about.

Sammie walked holding the blanket spread out in front of us so the light couldn't be seen by anyone approaching, or at least not seen as well. I was sure light shone beyond the edges, and in the pitch black of the corridor, we might as well be wearing a neon sign. At least the lantern didn't sing.

We eased past another glass store front. I held the light up to see what was inside, but it was empty except for a couple of propane cylinders. The place reminded me of an underground city or shopping mall. But if these were shops, where were the signs? Had they taken all the goods with them, or had the black robes cleaned them out? They were uniformly bare.

We'd passed only three shops when we hit an intersection. Sammie held up her hand in a stop motion and eased forward to check the cross-corridor. The nightmare circled my head twice, the lantern three times, and then drifted away to the left. Unfortunately, it didn't go far before floating back to repeat the procedure. I batted at it ineffectually.

"Shh," Sammie warned. She pointed to the right. "Someone's coming this way."

"Now what?" I whispered.

She looked around, decisive. "You go back that way about ten feet. When he comes around the corner, let him see the light. I'm going to sneak up behind him."

She tossed me the blanket and disappeared across the intersection. I backtracked the way we'd come, hoping her plan would work. I put the lantern on the ground and draped the blanket loosely in front of it. The nightmare whirled around me like a dervish gone crazy. I let go of one corner of the blanket to bat at it.

A moment later, bright light blinded me. The blanket went up with a whoosh, ignited by the hot glass of the lantern. I squeaked and tossed it away, right into the face of Blue Eyes, who'd just turned the corner. As he fended it off, Sammie rushed up behind him and whacked him over the head with her metal rod. He dropped to the tile unconscious. I stared, open-mouthed. *It can't be that easy.*

"Great distraction," she said, pulling the banana gun from Blue Eyes' holster and scooping his flashlight from the tile.

She found a pocket knife in his coveralls and sliced up his shirt. Then she gagged him and tied his hands behind his back with the cloth. Together, we dragged him into the nearest shop. For one uneasy moment, she looked down on him, bound and gagged, and I thought she might be contemplating some revenge for his rape of the sleeper. But she bit her lip and left him unmolested.

We exited the shop, and I picked up the lantern, being careful to keep it away from my leg. I had enough burns for this lifetime.

"I guess we go this way," she said, pointing off the way Blue Eyes had come.

The nightmare lashed around us at tornado speed and flew off the opposite direction. Then it rocketed back and flattened itself on my face. I turned away, swinging my arms and gagging on nothing.

"Stop it!" I commanded. The nightmare did. I blinked. "Are you Smokey's... friend?"

The little soot-ball hovered. I scrubbed at my head.

"Okay, if the answer is yes, float up and down. If the answer is no, float side to side. Got it?"

The black cloud drifted up and down. I moaned. Why me?

"River, there's nothing there. You're hallucinating," Sammie said.

That was a distinct possibility, of course. I had no independent verification that the nightmare was real, and off in the darkness around us, I was hearing lots of things I didn't think were real. Maybe Smokey was somewhere nearby. If Sammie could see him, then we'd know what was real and what wasn't.

"Is Smokey in this dimension?" I asked.

The nightmare drifted left and right. *Shit.*

"Do you know how to get out of here?" No, wait, it could pass through tiny cracks we'd never fit through. "Do you know a way that we can go to get out of here?"

The cloud indicated it did, and drifted to the left again.

"I'm not following something I can't see," Sammie said. "The attendant came from this direction, and that's the way we should go."

I walked in a circle, caught between the two of them. "If we go your direction, then what? We only know the first little bit. There were a lot of turns. I think we should follow the nightmare. It can take us all the way."

Sammie looked askance. "Making deals with demons, following nightmares? They're evil. You can't trust them."

Were they evil and untrustworthy? I wasn't so sure. Hadn't Smokey asked me to save E-4, to fight the tide of darkness there? And if I'd learned anything since meeting Sammie, I'd learned that sometimes I couldn't go it alone. Sometimes I needed to ask for help. Right now, help took the form of a soot-ball.

"I'm going with the nightmare," I said.

Sammie's lips formed a straight, hard line, and she glared at me. I shrugged and followed the cloud down the left corridor. Before I'd gone ten steps, she joined me, banana gun in one hand, flashlight in the other.

"I just know I'm going to regret this," she muttered. "Talking to demons, traipsing after nightmares. So not in the manual."

I grinned. "Maybe you should rewrite the manual."

"No," she said. "I'm going to toss the damn manual. No more military manuals for me."

Our soot-ball guide seemed in something of a hurry. It sped ahead to the edge of the light and slipped in and out of the darkness around us. Not having great familiarity with the species, I couldn't tell whether it was happy-excited or agitated-excited, but it bounced around like an ADHD kid on a sugar high. Did demons have mental illnesses and personality disorders?

Whoever built the ruins we traversed must have had a thing against straight lines. Or maybe the looping curves the corridors took were their version of speed bumps. In any case, the twists worked to our advantage. Our light couldn't be seen from more than fifty feet in any direction.

From the darkness, we heard scuttling noises, but nothing came close enough for us to see. The sounds raised the hair on the back of my neck. In places, puddles formed from water dripping somewhere over our heads. At one of these spots, a big drum caught the leakage. It made me wonder how the former occupants of the ruins lived. We hadn't seen any plumbing, or even any signs of lights or light fixtures. Just acres and acres of tile and glass.

The soot-ball sped around a corner ahead, and I hurried to catch up. That noisy pendulum clock was ticking in my head again. The sooner we rescued the sleepers and left this dimension, the sooner I'd stop hearing it. The nightmare and I collided as it raced back to me. I slammed on the brakes.

"What is it?" Sammie asked in a hushed whisper.

"I don't know," I replied, just as quietly. "It doubled back."

"Great," she muttered. "Now your hallucination is lost, too."

She slipped up to the corner and peered both directions. Then she jerked back, waving me to douse the light. I cranked the knob, and the lantern dimmed. She picked her way back to me.

"There's light ahead, coming from inside a room. We can't go this way."

Hell. With fuel supplies crucial to their survival, I didn't think they'd leave the lights on if someone wasn't in the room, and it might be a group of someones. We had one banana gun and the element of surprise. That didn't seem like great odds to me. The nightmare drifted between us and the corner.

"Listen, you little soot-ball, we can't go that way. There must be another way you can take us."

The cloud glided around us and back to the corner where it waited. I sighed.

"What's wrong?" Sammie asked.

"Communications breakdown," I said.

"We shouldn't have followed it. We were better off on our own." She started back the way we'd come.

Her assessment stung. What did I know about secret missions and sneaking out of the enemy camp? I'd followed a friggin' nightmare. Hell, it might be nothing more than a hallucination, and now we were more lost than ever. *Dumb, River.* I trailed after her, despair and a sense of failure gnawing at my insides.

The little nightmare went crazy. It flew by, then turned around and did a kamikaze run at my face. It backed away and flung itself at my chest. It swirled around my head until I got dizzy trying to watch it. I stopped.

If it were a hallucination, how had it known about the lights around the corner? I couldn't see them, but it warned us they were there. Lights. Not people, just lights. We'd assumed there were people, and we shouldn't go that direction. I looked at the cloud that now hovered a few inches in front of my face.

"We really have to go that direction?" I asked.

The cloud vibrated up and down and slid past me toward the corner. I turned around and watched it disappear into the dark. It was back in a moment.

"Are there bad guys ahead?"

The nightmare drifted, aimless. We'd hit another communications snag. How had Smokey talked about humans?

"Are there souls ahead? Souls where the light is?"

The nightmare floated up, down.

"River, what are you doing?" Sammie whispered, at my side again.

"How many?" I asked.

The nightmare drifted up, down, and then it moved closer to the corner. I rubbed my watch cap. Was that one or two? I guess it didn't matter if we could sneak past without being detected. I padded to the corner and looked around.

At the center of the next curve, light streamed out through glass. I couldn't see anyone moving, but from this angle, they'd have to be standing right next to the windows before I could spot them. On the other hand, if I couldn't see them, they couldn't see us.

"The nightmare says there's only one," I said. "Or maybe two. If we pick them off now, it improves our odds when we get to the surface, right?"

Sammie frowned at me. "Or we might blow our element of surprise, and they'll all be waiting for us at the surface."

"If we get lost down here, we won't get to the surface in time to save anyone," I argued. "We did okay with ol' Blue Eyes, didn't we?"

She shook her head. "Beginner's luck."

"We've got the banana gun, er, the sonic weapon."

"Yeah, and we're going to avoid using it. We don't want to bring down the ceiling on our heads. There's no telling how unstable these ruins are."

I hadn't thought of that. The only tactics I'd ever practiced consisted of deciding whether to run away at high speed or very high speed. The whole confrontation thing was new to me. I had a lot to learn.

"So we do it like last time? I'll be the distraction, and you whack him from behind?" It seemed like the chivalrous solution. He'd be pointing his weapon at me, not her. And besides, I wasn't sure I could bring myself to hit another human hard enough to knock him out, whereas she seemed pretty good at it.

Sammie and I crept around the corner and up the corridor. There wasn't enough light, and we both tripped over heaved places in the tile and fallen chunks of ceiling. I worried that we were making so much noise our target would know we were coming. When we got closer, I could see that the door was closed, and I breathed a sigh of relief.

The nightmare hovered briefly in the light shining through the window, and then it drifted past. I lost sight of it as it disappeared into the darkness. Sammie plastered herself to the wall and inched up to the window. I tiptoed beside her. I could hear wailing and moaning coming through the glass. It reminded me of the sounds the loonies at the mental ward made when they were getting close to time for their next dose of meds.

She peered in the window and froze. All the color drained from her face, and her lips parted in a silent intake of breath. She stared for ten or fifteen seconds, and then she pushed past me up the corridor before falling to her knees and vomiting on the tile.

Distant muffled screams reached my ears. I sidled to the edge of the window and looked in, my back stiff and my hands shaking.

A black robe sat at a console watching one of a dozen monitors in a cramped room filled with computers, control panels, and digital readouts. In a video displayed on the monitor, a man dressed in one of those enviro suits used a scalpel to carve designs in the flesh of a naked man strapped to a stainless steel table. The victim had a plastic bubble around his head, and wires led from it into the wall, as they did for the dozen other people similarly restrained. The victim screamed and writhed while the others looked on in panic and struggled against their bonds. The scalpel wielder laughed, and One's minion at the console laughed with him.

17

"They're sick," Sammie whispered, her face screwed up in horror.

I wiped a hand across my mouth and wished I had water to rinse the taste of my own vomit away. I'd never forget those images. They'd haunt me the rest of my life. How could anyone do that to another human being? *Why* were they doing it? I was more terrified now than I'd ever been during my stay in the mental ward. The black robes were seriously psycho. My craziness didn't hold a candle to theirs.

"What should we do?" I asked.

"Same as before," she said with new determination. "We take him out so we don't have to deal with him later."

"Okay," I said. "How?"

"We catch him unawares when we burst in the door. I'll threaten him with the gun. He doesn't know I won't shoot. Then you can tie him up." She held the banana gun in one hand and the open pocketknife in the other. I felt like a caveman with the length of IV pole in one hand and the flashlight in the other.

We edged up to the window and then walked boldly to the door. Sammie pushed through, gun at the ready. Inside the room, the increased volume of the screams on the video made my nerves jangle.

The man at the console spun a lazy circle to face us. When he saw who we were, he leaped up, the chair ricocheting back against the console. After a moment's hesitation, he went for his holster, his eyes locked on Sammie.

This wasn't a scenario we'd discussed. He was supposed to give up peaceably, not draw his own weapon. What was wrong with him? Didn't he know he'd already lost? *Shit!* I charged him.

We smashed back against the console, him still trying to fumble his gun out and me trying to keep his arms locked to his side. He was a pretty big guy, and strong. He got his hands against my chest and pushed. I flew back and smacked against the window. My head whacked the glass.

I heard a crunch, and then things got dim.

When the lights came back on, Sammie leaned over me, fear etching a pale face speckled with red. Everything in the room danced the hula. I closed my eyes, opened them again, and things steadied. The red speckles registered in my consciousness.

"Sammie! Are you okay?"

I struggled from the floor and stared at the wet stain splattered across her black shirt. I seized her hand, slick with dark, sticky liquid. *No.* My mouth fell open, and my eyes searched for a tear in her shirt.

"His blood," she mumbled, and the pocket knife clattered to the floor. "Are you okay?"

I looked around for our opponent. He lay sprawled on the floor, a pool of blood spreading across his chest. He wasn't breathing.

Sammie glanced his direction and looked away. "I've never killed anyone before, but he was going to shoot you."

I thought about that big knife she carried and realized it wasn't just for show. She knew exactly how to use it, even if she didn't want to. Unlike me, she'd proved she could do it if she needed to. A shiver crawled up my spine. I was useless, nothing but excess baggage. I'd probably get her killed before we got out of here. It was me who needed to be rescued, not her.

"You should go," I said. "Leave me. Get to the fracture and get help."

"We go together," she said, putting a hand on my cheek. "Friends don't leave friends behind."

The warmth of her touch flooded through me, and I lurched forward. She grabbed my arm and held onto me until things stopped spinning.

"You have cuffs." She pushed up my sweatshirt sleeves. "Two pair."

She had that look again, the confused one where she'd bumped into another of my lies. Her eyes looked into mine, and she went very still.

"Why are you wearing them?" she asked.

"I met your team. At the fracture. On E-4." She was going to be mad and hurt, and I didn't want her to feel like that. I didn't know what to do, but I had to tell her the truth.

"I'm the one," I blurted. "The one you've been looking for."

"I know," she said, the hint of a wan smile touching her lips. She squeezed my hand. "I've been looking for you for a very long time; I just didn't know it."

We must have different definitions of 'long.' We'd met less than twenty-four hours ago. I was missing something, but I couldn't figure out what. The headache, the fatigue, the stress were messing with my brain. I didn't usually feel this stupid. Or maybe it was her warm, soft hand in mine causing the mental short circuit.

The smile left her face. "But that doesn't explain the cuffs."

"Uh... I'm the super-talent you came to retrieve," I said, cringing inside. "Doc put these on so I wouldn't have an accident."

Geez, that made me sound like a dog that wasn't house-trained yet, and she'd already compared me to a puppy following her around. Heat spread up my face, and I stared at my shoes.

"You can't be," she said at last. "You're not crazy."

I cocked one eyebrow and waved my hand at the room. "Yeah? Then what am I doing following a nightmare through Hell and taking on guys twice my size when I don't even know how to fight?"

"Not crazy," Sammie said. "Amazing."

"Crazy," I muttered, "*and* stupid."

She left me leaning against the door jamb and turned to the console. She messed with the computer and stopped the video. Then she slid into the chair and did I don't know what. I had no idea how computers worked, but she watched the screen with intensity and single-minded purpose.

"This seems to be his primary research lab," she said. "He probably keeps his research hidden in case the Raps visit. Let's see what he's been up to."

The nightmare floated around me and back to the door. It repeated the pattern a couple of times. A second nightmare drifted in, and then a third. In a moment, I couldn't tell which one was which.

"Oh my God," Sammie breathed.

She had more horrific video up on one monitor, and writing on another, which she scanned quickly. In the video, a hundred people who were crammed in a tiny room were misted from overhead sprinklers with something that turned their skin bright red on contact. Even with the sound muted, I could tell they were screaming. My stomach flip-flopped, and I looked away.

"He stumbled over a fracture some years ago, and he's been studying the energy fields around it ever since. He's been researching something he calls 'negative energy' that's responsible for keeping the fracture open. Mentally disturbed people generate it, and his government gave him permission to experiment with them. But he couldn't get enough test subjects from institutions, so then he got 'volunteers' from prisons. He found if he put them 'under duress,' they gave off more energy."

She scrolled text quickly across the screen. "Eventually he figured out a containment system for the energy he collected, but the first system failed, causing a fracture. That's when the Raps contacted his dimension. He told them he could build a device that could create fractures on demand."

"And the Raps went for it, even though it was powered by pain and torture. Bastards." I spat on the floor.

"I don't think he revealed how he got the energy in the first place. He's too paranoid to trust them. They provided new power sources so he could build a stronger containment system." She flicked through diagrams, then brought up another batch of text.

"To create the power, he tortured people to death. Here's a list of—" She stopped abruptly. An endless trail of text ran down the screen. She looked up at me, eyes hollow. "There's over a hundred thousand names on this list. And his government sanctioned it."

Sammie cleared her throat. She wiped tears from her eyes and continued scanning the text. Minutes passed in silence while the nightmares hovered around us.

"Eventually, he realized that if he kept his sources alive, he could continue to harvest them indefinitely," Sammie said at last. "He developed a drug, a psychedelic that causes terrifying, vivid dreams. Repeated doses drive the subject permanently mad, but that only increases their usefulness. The formula, the dosage, the time interval from administration to maximum output—it's all here in his notes."

"He said his dimension collapsed, and it was the Raps' fault," I said, watching the three nightmares swirl and dance over our heads. This horror couldn't be real.

"Not exactly. The dimensional barriers in his dimension were already thinning. The Raps warned him they'd fail soon. They made evacuation plans, but then the containment failed, causing an enormous fracture. In a matter of hours, the dimension collapsed. He blames the Rap power supply, but the power required for containment was growing exponentially, way more than can be explained by what he collected. No power source could provide what he needed."

Sammie moved to another monitor and flipped it on. It displayed a small room like the one we were in, jammed with more equipment, and beyond it through a glass wall, a much larger room with curved metal struts rising from the floor to form a huge ball fifteen feet high. The interior of the ball was empty space.

"He's done it again," she whispered. "It's a containment device."

"Of course," I said, pieces falling into place. "He doesn't have enough people here to gather sufficient energy, so he's been grabbing super-talents and harvesting them."

She spun around toward me, a frightened 'ah ha' expression on her face. "He'll get them to fracture at the same time by using his drug cocktail on them. They'll be a lot stronger than they would otherwise be. It'll work. He'll destroy the Rap dimension."

"And the multiverse with it. We'd better get going."

"River, wait." She put a hand on my arm. "We can't leave this here. If we succeed, others will come here to explore. They'll get his research.

Someone might try this again. We have to destroy it."

I glanced around the room. "How? Short out the electronic equipment?"

"Not good enough. Someone might recover the hard drives."

I had no idea what she was talking about, but I figured it meant we needed to do some major destruction. I didn't see a lot of options.

"Blast it with your gun?" I asked. "No, that might make the roof fall in."

I spied a couple of gallon jugs and a pack of cleaning clothes under the desk and hauled them out. They looked promising.

"Which of these things are the computers that we need to wreck?"

Sammie pointed to two boxes on the desktop and three more under the console. I looked around a bit more and decided there was nothing for it. We'd need the dead black robe.

"Bring the lantern in here," I said while I grabbed the first computer from the desk. I ripped cords out of the back and laid it against the body. By the time Sammie got back with the lantern, I'd added two more. She helped me with the last two.

I opened one of the jugs and took a sniff. Yep, cleaning alcohol, just like the label said. I tucked all the cleaning rags but one around the computers, and then I emptied the jugs over the rags, the computers, and the dead black robe's clothing. I used the lantern to ignite the final cleaning rag and tossed it on the pile.

The pyre went up in an impressive whoosh that nearly singed my eyebrows. The sudden heat drove us through the door. We stood outside the glass for a minute just to be sure it worked as well as I hoped, but the smell of burning flesh got to us, so we moved on, grim determination carrying us forward. Two down, twenty-two to go, and One's research now history. Damn, we were good.

Sammie put a hand on my arm. "River, the knowledge of how to do what he did is still in his head, and there are people who would forgive all this if he agreed to work for them. If we get the chance, we have to kill One."

I gulped and nodded, not at all sure I was cut out to be a DC.

Our guide-nightmare and its two new companions led us along the corridor. They seemed delirious; drunk on one another's company. I hadn't seen nightmares act like that before, not that I was an expert on nightmare behavior. We stopped at the next intersection. The nightmares slewed around to the left. Sammie looked right.

"Smell that?" she asked.

I sniffed. The damp earth and mold smell seemed a little less strong, overridden by clean pine scent.

"The entrance is this way," she said, and started away.

"But the nightmare went the other way," I said.

"We don't need the nightmare now. We know how to get out. Come on."

I took a couple of steps her direction. The nightmare darted in front of me, frantic again, swirling and leading off the opposite way. I stopped and rocked while Sammie's flashlight receded up the corridor.

"Wait!" I called. "I think we need to check this out first."

"River, he's going to get away with the super-talents if we don't hurry. We can come back later and explore. Right now, we have more important things to do."

I rocked a moment more as the soot-ball zoomed around me.

"You go ahead," I said. "I'll catch up."

I walked away after the nightmare, my hand clenched on the lantern. I had a banana gun tucked in my waistband, but I doubted I'd use it. I didn't have killer instincts. The black robes did. If I encountered them without Sammie, it would all be over in a heartbeat. Some days, being a pacifist sucked.

Footsteps pattered from behind me, and Sammie walked at my side. Her scowl could have scared the pants off a whole division of Navy Seals. I didn't like having her mad at me, but the nightmare hadn't led us wrong. I had to know why it wanted us to go this way. It wove in and out with its new friends, all five of them.

Five? When did the other three join the pack? I recalled the monster cloud of nightmares roiling in the sky near the E-4 fracture. Smokey said they were caused by humans, that they migrated out through dimensional barriers, weakening them as they went. So what were these doing here? If they'd been created by the sleepers, they should be inside the containment field. I had an uneasy feeling in the pit of my stomach.

We went another hundred feet or so and saw a dim glow coming from a window ahead. We both stopped. The nightmares continued, boiling into a knot as they jockeyed to squeeze round the edges of the door. Two more nightmares drifted past, on course to join the others. Sammie clicked her light off, and I set the lantern on the tile.

"How many?" she asked.

"A lot," I replied, thinking she meant the nightmares. "Too many."

"Then we should go back. We can't take on an army with two weapons. Let's get to the fracture while they're still here." She turned on her light and walked away.

I stood and rocked and caught the first snatches of demon song over the purring noise of a generator. My tattoos escalated from prickling to downright itching. Another nightmare floated past. My chest tightened so I couldn't breathe. A soot-ball squeezed out the door and did lazy loop-the-loops until it reached me.

"How many souls?"

The cloud drew snaky lines left and right, like it had been on an all-night bender. The wiggles matched the beats in the eerie, grating music that clawed at my nerves and made me shudder. It both called and repulsed me.

"Are you coming?" Sammie said, beside me.

I shook my head and followed the little nightmare toward the light.

18

I stood before the glass and looked into a tiny room clogged with nightmares. The dim light came from the dials on the control panel. They reflected in the glass of the window that separated the first room from the larger chamber beyond.

In that second room, curtains of colored illumination undulated between the metal fingers that formed the containment ball, rippling like the Northern Lights in a winter sky. I might have thought them pretty had I paid attention, but I couldn't take my eyes from the roiling mass of black in the center of the ball.

Not a group of nightmares, but one huge, dark creature slowly twisting itself inside out, over and over. In that shifting blackness, images surfaced, horrible, sick sights created by a mad mind; an external view on a Dark Place transit, I realized, recognizing the destructive processes acting on the all-too-human shapes that wheeled by.

"The containment facility," Sammie breathed. She reached for the door.

"No!" I grabbed her arm. "Don't go in."

"It's empty," she said. "We should destroy it, too."

She shook off my grip and pushed through the door before I could stop her. The nightmares swirled around her in a renewed frenzy. I pressed my hands to the glass, willing her to leave the room. She looked over the controls, running her fingertips along the symbols under the dials. She stopped at a display screen showing a rising, jagged line. Then she turned to the window and waved me to join her. I swallowed hard and forced myself through the door. Three more nightmares surged in with me.

"The energy level is too high," Sammie said. She tapped one of the dials. "And it's rising."

In the next chamber, a nightmare glided into view. It flitted around the containment ball the way a moth dances around a candle. As I approached the window to watch, the light between the struts flickered. I jumped back. The little nightmare thinned itself to an almost invisible cloud and plunged through the light curtain.

"Wow," Sammie said. "What caused that?"

I looked to where she indicated, but the readings on the dials made no sense.

"What?" I said, fearing I knew the answer.

"Momentary power drop in the containment field," she said. She looked at the ball. "I don't see anything, do you?"

I backed away from the window separating the two rooms, certain that I was the cause of the drop. I affected the containment the same way I affected shields.

"We should destroy this, too," she said, looking around for a means.

"No! We can't let it loose. It could destroy this dimension, same as before."

Sammie frowned, looked at the controls, and looked into the chamber.

"If the energy continues to skyrocket, containment will fail in another day anyway. Better to trigger now before it gets worse." She tapped a gauge. "I don't understand why the energy is growing. One isn't harvesting the super-talents now, but look at the graph. It's risen continuously over the last hour."

The intruding nightmare swooned around its larger cousin. The demon song slowed to a lull, and the movements of all the nightmares—both the one inside the containment and those in the room with us—calmed. The intruder hung motionless and serene, and the monster cloud engulfed it.

I thought I heard a scream, but maybe I just imagined it. The nightmares in the control room charged for the door, sieving themselves through the cracks until only one remained with us. It quivered and pulsed before me, and I quivered, too.

"Another spike up," Sammie said.

"It's feeding."

"'It'? There's nothing out there."

"It wants out, and it's eating other nightmares to get strong enough to break the shields."

The little soot-ball floated up and down. The demon song started again, quiet at first, and then louder. I covered my ears, not that it did any good. Our guide drifted toward the window, unable to resist the call.

"Come back here," I ordered. "You have a job to do."

Our nightmare stopped, but another one wafted past to flatten itself against the window.

"Can I talk to it?" I asked.

The nightmare drifted in an unhelpful circle. What did that mean? Maybe smoke signals *would* have been easier.

"Can it hear me?"

The cloud indicated yes.

"Can it understand me?"

Left, right. *Crap.* So much for reasoning with it.

"Can it understand you?"

Up, down. Hooray! Progress at last.

"Tell it I understand what it wants. I'm going to help it get out. But I have to prepare the way first so it gets away without being seen. It has to stop singing, and it has to stop eating the other nightmares, or it'll get too big and be too conspicuous. If it tries to get out without my help and preparation, it'll…" Geez, did demons die? How did I threaten a demon? Was a nightmare even a demon? "It'll get eaten by a really big, mean demon."

The nightmare drifted to the window where it got in a shoving match with the one hogging the space already. I guess my buddy won. The other nightmare yielded and sank under the console. After a minute, the demon song stopped.

"Yes!" I said, grinning.

I turned to Sammie, and the grin slid from my face. She had that little crease between her eyebrows, and I could tell she was trying to decide just how crazy I might be.

"We have to destroy this place," she said.

"And we will, but we have to figure out how to do it without destroying this dimension."

Her jaw set in a determined line, and she put her hands on her hips, unyielding.

"Our priority is One," I said. "We'll stop him first, save the sleepers, and then we'll take care of this, okay?"

Sammie didn't look happy, but she led me back the way we'd come. In another few minutes, we heard voices ahead. We abandoned the lantern, shut off the flashlight, and inched forward as quietly as we could.

At the next junction, rows of pallets sat haphazardly in the corridor. Somewhere beyond them, the voices of three men approached. All three of them levitated pallets down a side corridor, and Sammie and I ran on tiptoes for the junction, barely able to see by the lights they carried away with them. We made it to the cover of a pallet and heard footsteps approaching in front of us.

Two more voices discussed the merits of goat meat versus chicken and how much they both wanted a thick, juicy Angus steak. Pallets clunked on the floor, and footsteps started away.

"Hey! You can't leave those there," one of the men in the first group hollered. "Take 'em down with the others."

To my horror, the pallet we hid behind lifted off the ground and floated away. Sammie jumped for it and clung to the side away from the men. She'd given herself maybe an extra ten seconds before discovery. I didn't know what to do, so I followed Rule #1: Don't look back; just run.

I sprinted in the opposite direction they'd taken the pallets, hoping that my diversion would give Sammie time to get to cover, or maybe even to get out of the damn tunnels.

"Shit! Intruder!" someone shouted.

"No, you fool!" someone else called. "Don't shoot that thing in here. You'll bring the whole place down."

Footsteps echoed behind me. I didn't think they could match my speed. On the other hand, I was running in the dark. Their waving flashlights gave me glimpses of what lay ahead, but I didn't know where I was going. I could be running into a dead end. Or into more bad guys. Or a wall. At least as long as I ran, I still had a chance.

I took a right at the next intersection, thinking that I might be able to loop around and get back to where we started, but I'd forgotten that I'd have no light to see by once I turned the corner. I ran with my hand brushing the rows of windows until they ran out and kept taking rights until the entrance was directly ahead. My feet pounded the tiles, and my fingers ached where they touched the cold glass.

A flashlight beam blinded me, my foot landed on something lumpy and unstable that squeaked, and I pitched head over heels onto the floor. My shoulder crunched into the tile, my burn hit next, and then I was swearing a blue streak and rolling forward to throttle whoever had that light.

"River, come on!" Sammie called shining her light down the corridor.

"Told you he'd go around," a voice said from my right. "Hey, what's with the pallets?"

Sammie pulled me to my feet and flashed her light toward the right-hand tunnel. She'd blocked it with the pallets while I'd been running, preventing my pursuers from backtracking to cut me off. I whooped and leaped in the air. That was my Sammie. Then a head appeared over the top of a pallet.

Sammie aimed her banana gun up into the darkness and let off a shot. Dirt, rock, and tile rained down onto the pallets, and someone screamed. She fired again, deeper into the tunnel, her teeth gritted.

"Let's go!" I cried, pushing her ahead of me.

More lights flashed on us from farther down the corridor I'd just come through. We had a head start, but we'd be in trouble when we got outside. We ran on, the air getting fresher with every stride, until we burst into the room at the base of the ramp. Feet clomped close behind, and fear drove me faster.

I could see daylight up the ramp, but the darn thing was slippery as all heck. One's minions closed on us while we scrambled up. A boom deafened me, and ice sprayed in my face. Sammie dropped and rolled to her back to return fire. She aimed at the ceiling just in front of them. Her shot brought dirt and rock down on the rest of the group, but the front-runner had been too quick for her. He swung his weapon up.

My snowball hit him square in the nose. Okay, I admit I packed the snow around a rock just to give it a little extra oomph, but I figured since he had a real gun, it wasn't cheating. His hand jerked up as he fired, collapsing more of the ceiling. He stumbled back and disappeared under an avalanche of debris, his scream cut off by a sudden silence.

Sammie stared at me, open mouthed. "A *snowball*? What if you'd missed? He would have killed me."

My jubilation at our escape evaporated. She was right. I was useless in a fight. Couldn't she see that? What did she want me to do?

"Sorry," I said. "I'm not much good at being a hero. I don't have what it takes to get us out of here."

She looked back at the debris that buried the minions, then she drew in a deep breath and blew it out.

"Look how far you've come already. There's no stopping you—even if you have to fight with snowballs."

I perked up. We *had* come a long way, hadn't we? Maybe I *could* do this. But I was glad to have Sammie's help. We were a team.

We scrambled up the ramp. The wind cut me to the bone. I wished I had that heavy Raiders sweatshirt she'd bought me instead of the thin one I'd traded for. And a mug of that creamy IHOP hot chocolate. I hated the cold.

She squatted at the top of the ramp, weapon up, scanning the area around the tunnel mouth. Satisfied that no one waited to ambush us, she sprinted to one of the two vehicles. I trailed behind, watching our backs. The little soot-ball spun in lazy circles over my head.

"We need a plan," Sammie said. "We can't just charge into camp."

"Right. Plan. Aren't you freezing?" I asked, shivering and rubbing my arms.

She grinned and plucked at her shirt. "Rap nanotech. Never too hot, never too cold, as long as things don't get too extreme. Get in the cab."

I climbed in and sat on one of the uncomfortable stools. A robe and harness lay on the floor behind me, the property of the driver, no doubt. I wrapped the robe around myself, but it didn't help much. Sammie took the other stool. She spent a minute inspecting the controls, and then she did her technology magic and heat poured through vents in the floor.

"It sounds like One intended to take everyone with him to the Rap dimension," she said. "I can't think why he'd do that."

"Probably to take out the Rap fracture guards and protect the sleepers until they fracture. Smokey said they had to be positioned correctly to destroy the dimensional barrier."

"He'll use his own people for cannon fodder," she said, disgust in her voice.

"We need to get the sleepers away. Without them, his plan falls apart." I looked down at the robe I wore. "Can you program a harness to go to E-Prime instead of R-Prime?"

"I think so, but I'll need some time to do it. Why?"

"I'll create a diversion to draw everyone's attention. While they're busy chasing me, you go into camp wearing a robe and take the super-talents to E-Prime."

Sammie's brow wrinkled, and she chewed her lip. "I don't like your idea, but I can't think of a better one. I promise I'll be back as quick as I can."

"Take these," I said, pushing up my sleeves and unbuckling the cuffs. "If he's already dosed the sleepers, you have to stop them from fracturing, or you could endanger any dimension you went to."

"But River, what if *you* fracture? I don't want to lose you."

I gave her a grin I didn't really feel. "You tracked me down once. You can do it again. But promise me you won't go near me around a fracture."

"Why?"

"Because something about me knocks out the shields when I'm close to them." I laughed. "The Neans claim it's because I'm a demon."

"You've been traveling through D-space without working shields?" Her face paled.

I shrugged. "Hard to go crazy when you already are."

She gritted her teeth. "How will you distract them?"

"Oh, uh..." She had me there. This planning stuff was harder than it looked. One seemed most worried about his fuel supply, and it didn't look like they'd brought that much to the ruins. There must be more still at the camp.

"Don't worry," I said. "I've got an idea."

19

"It's easy," Sammie said, pointing to the platform's control board. "Think of it as a video game but with multiple joysticks."

I stared at her in disbelief. "It isn't a game. It flies. Off the ground."

"It's dead simple, and you can get away faster and safer in one of these than you can on foot. It's not like there's any air traffic or sky-scrapers. What can you hit?" she said. "You can practice on the way to the camp."

Me, *flying*. It didn't get any crazier than that. I'd never even driven the riding lawn mower at the orphanage. But she had a point about the fast getaway, and besides, I'd be warmer inside the cab. Still, the controls intimidated the heck out of me. What if I hit the wrong one at a crucial moment? A crash landing wasn't the distraction I planned.

"This lever controls your altitude and can tilt the platform a few degrees each direction to accommodate an unbalanced load. This one is your speed. Set your direction with this one. Think of it like an outboard motor. You point the propeller the direction you want to go, but that means you turn the handle the opposite direction."

I'd already forgotten which knob was which and wished for some nice, printed labels under each. And what the heck was an 'outboard mo-tor'? I felt like a fool and didn't ask.

"What about all the touch-pad thingys?" I asked, scanning the nu-merous little rough squares scattered across the dash.

"Those program the computer, but you'll be on manual, so you don't need them. Go ahead," she said, patting my back. "Give it a try."

I placed a sweaty palm on the altitude control and pushed it forward a fraction of an inch. The platform didn't move. In the space behind our seats, a crowd murmured in disapproving voices. Just what I needed: a chorus of imaginary back-seat drivers. The nightmare hovered over my right shoulder.

"Other way," Sammie advised. "Back to get off the ground."

I shifted my grip on the knob and eased it back to center. Holding my breath, I slipped it back a quarter inch. The platform rose and hovered a few feet off the ground. Hooray! I'd done it. A smattering of applause punctuated with exclamations of wonder came from the group behind the seats. I let out a sigh and reached for the speed control.

"You'll need more altitude first. You won't clear the trees."

"Uh... right." I bumped the altitude knob another fraction, and we rose a few more feet.

"You have to be more aggressive with the controls, or we'll never get there."

Sweat beaded on my forehead. I tried to put on a brave face, but I don't think I fooled Sammie. I grabbed the knob and gave it a vicious yank, determined to be the master of the damn machine. A high-pitch whine filled the cabin, hurting my ears. I whipped my hands off the control panel, sure the platform would explode.

Sammie grabbed the knob I'd moved and eased it back to its starting position. "That's the speed control. And before you give it more gas, you'll need to indicate a direction."

Great. Not only did I have to remember which one was which, I had to remember in what order to adjust them. I wiped my hand on my jeans and reached for the altitude control while the crowd muttered a litany to a dozen different deities. She put her hand over mine, and together we eased it back. The platform rose above the tree-tops and swayed a little in the gusting wind. My stomach flipped over, and my shoulders tensed. The trees were darn tall.

Sammie touched one of the pads, and a screen lit up. In the upper-right corner, an arrow pulsed.

"The camp's that way," she said, pointing out the window the same direction the arrow indicated. "Bring us around until the arrow is straight ahead. Then set your speed."

I reached for a knob, then hesitated. Where's a felt-tipped pen when you need one? "This one, right?"

She smiled and patted my shoulder. "You can do this."

With teeth gritted, I fiddled with the direction control, turning it the wrong way on the first try, and overshooting when I cranked us back. I felt a little seasick. How had the minion done this when he'd brought me to the ruins? He'd looked asleep at the controls.

Sammie fiddled with the touch pads while I zigzagged the platform toward the camp and muttered my own litany. If humans were meant to fly, we'd have wings—and no fear of heights. When she finished, she pointed to one of the touch pads.

"Press this, and the platform will return to the ruins on autopilot. Press the one next to it, and the platform will head for the base camp. If you get lost, you can get back to somewhere familiar, provided you aren't out of radio range."

"So I didn't need to fly this thing?" I asked, shooting her an incredulous look.

"You never know when the autopilot might fail," she said. "You need to be able to run it on manual, just in case. Besides, we don't want to go straight into camp."

Not far ahead, I saw smoke curling into the air. Sammie indicated that I should circle around to the right and had me take the platform so low we were brushing treetops. I found a clear space two hundred yards from the camp and set the platform down.

"River, be careful," she said, squeezing my hand. "Don't take any unnecessary risks. If you have to shoot someone to save yourself, do it. You're a better person than any of them."

"I'll be fine," I replied, struggling to accept her assessment of me. "You be careful, too."

Sammie donned the harness and robe and hopped out.

"I'll be back with the cavalry," she promised, and gave me a confident grin.

She shut the door and headed off. When she'd gone twenty feet, she gave me a last wave, but she turned away before I could wave back. Then she slogged through the snow toward the camp and disappeared into the trees. A sharp pang twisted in my gut, but I didn't have time to worry. I had a mission to complete.

My plan was to set the autopilot for the glide through the camp and use the banana gun to shoot one of the propane pallets before veering off. The resulting explosion should get everyone's attention and convince them that the camp was under attack. They'd all come running.

Then I'd circle over the trees on the side of the camp farthest from the fracture building and lure the black robes into chasing me. Sammie would make a getaway with the sleepers, and I'd keep clear of the camp until she returned with reinforcements. With surprise on my side, it should be pretty simple.

I got the platform off the ground, and like some drunk, pointed the platform back the way we'd come.

"Destination?" a sultry female voice asked from the dash.

I frowned. Was the platform really speaking to me? I didn't think I'd brushed the autopilot control. Voice steering would be a lot easier than messing with the damn joysticks.

"Um... can you fly this thing?"

"Can you?" the dashboard replied. The noise from the back seat drivers stopped while they all hung on my reply. *Shit.*

"Not real," I cursed under my breath, and the chorus bubbled with apprehension.

"Destination?" the dashboard nagged.

I set the platform to treetop level and maximum speed. I didn't want Sammie sneaking into camp before I'd started my diversion, and I didn't think she'd wait long. I needed to swing around and come in from the south, over the barn and away from the fracture building.

"At your current course and speed, you will run out of fuel in two point three minutes," the dashboard intoned. "Would you like me to locate a fueling station?"

Maybe I wasn't hallucinating the voice. Run out of fuel? Sammie hadn't said anything about fuel, and I didn't see a fuel gauge. Two minutes would put me right over the camp when the tank ran dry. Crap, not the place to run out of gas. The whispers of the chorus grew louder, and I heard *crash*, *explosion*, and *dead* rise above the indiscernible chatter. I swallowed hard and pulled the banana gun from my belt.

The platform rocked in the breeze, worsening my queasy stomach. The treetops scraped and scratched the bottom. The banana gun slipped in my sweaty hand. I was a hundred yards from the clearing and coming in fast—scary fast.

I pointed my craft over the barn and the tops of the cabins so I could shoot across the clearing at the propane. If I could get one pallet to go, it should take the rest in a chain reaction. When it exploded, I didn't want to be too close.

I tapped the autopilot. The platform slowed to a crawl, rose up from the treetops, and altered course toward the landing area by the supply pallets, only one of which was propane. They'd been busy while we were wandering the tunnels. *Shit. Screwed already.*

I pushed the speed knob forward before remembering that I needed to pull it back, but the platform didn't respond to either movement.

"To change speed while the autopilot is engaged," the dashboard said, "realign the ventral Jefferies tubes."

"Jefferies tubes? Aren't those from Star Trek?" I bit my tongue. Never engage with a hallucination—it just encourages them.

But maybe it was a rough translation from Rap to human. Or someone designing the autopilot had a terrible sense of humor. How could I know for sure?

I tapped the autopilot again to turn it off and wondered how I was supposed to hang out the door blasting my target if I also had to fly the damn vehicle. And where had all those trees come from? I'd thought the space the camp occupied was more open, but I could see now that a perfectly straight line through the area wasn't possible, especially in something as big as the platform and moving at my current speed. This might be more complicated than I thought.

Ahead, another platform stacked with equipment and propane pallets lifted into the air and came my direction. We were on a collision course. *Aw, hell.*

"Danger! Danger!" the dashboard shrilled. "Collision imminent! Turn right immediately."

I grabbed the directional control and pushed. Except it was the altitude control, and I was bumping along in the tops of the trees before I realized it. The console bleeped, and lights flashed. I jerked the control back in a panic and soared up out of the timber, my heart beating fast.

The oncoming platform swerved to my left. We passed so close, I could see the driver shake a fist at me. Then his eyes grew wide and his mouth opened in a silent shout before he vanished from sight.

Crap. There went my element of surprise. I grabbed a knob to correct my direction, and the platform canted over, nearly throwing me off the stool. I slapped it back and grabbed another. The platform slid right, aiming me at a tree. I jammed it the other way, got the right lever to drop the platform down to ten or so feet off the ground, and increased to full speed, which seemed way too fast for threading between the trees and building roofs scattered around the area.

I grabbed the door latch and gave it a yank. Nothing happened. I tried again. *Damn!* It had some kind of lock to prevent it from opening in flight. Why hadn't I checked that sooner? While I struggled with it, I sailed past the pallet I intended to blast and on toward a tall tree in the middle of the compound.

"Danger! Danger!" the dash shrilled again. "Collision imminent! Turn left in five feet."

I slammed the direction knob left, and the platform made a right. It wouldn't clear the tree, and this close, I could see the power line strung through it leading to the fracture building.

"No, *fool*, your other left," the dash pronounced. "Fuel supply critical! Turn toward the light!"

Too late to correct back to the left. I climbed higher and clipped branches. The chorus behind me rustled, and *parachute, electrocution,* and *extra-crispy chicken wings* became topics of conversation. A black cable slapped against the windshield, followed by a popping sound. The platform rocked hard before stabilizing. The soot-ball whirled around the compartment. Out the back window, I could see one end of the cable sparking and gyrating in the tree branches. Had it fried the electronics in the platform? The autopilot voice had fallen ominously silent, but the platform flew on. Maybe that wasn't a bad thing.

I continued to climb and started a gradual left turn over the two-story metal building, intending to find a landing site from which I could begin an assault. A flying attack was beyond nuts. I needed to have sneakers on the snow if I was going to do anything effective.

A loud bang echoed through the compartment, and my platform dropped out from under me. Motion in the corner of my eye caught my attention. I looked out the back window.

"Danger! Danger!" the dash screamed. "Crash imminent! Turn right, proceed for fifty-seven light-seconds. Turn back time, proceed to Big Bang!"

The other platform was parked on my empty flatbed and forced me toward the ground. I freaked and jerked my altitude control back. We stopped our downward flight, but my power plant screamed.

"Fuel critical! Power plant temperature critical! Explosion imminent! Increase reverse manifold polarization! Eject warp core! Turn left last Tuesday!"

"Shut up!" I yelled.

I dropped the banana gun in my lap and put both hands on the controls. With my right, I pushed the altitude control forward, and with my left on the directional control, I cut left. At least, that was the plan. The platform dropped a few feet and shot forward. I clipped the stone chimney on the second cabin, but I'd lost my passenger. I cursed, switched knobs, and steered off to the left. The other platform followed, the pilot grim as he pursued the psychotic random particle that was River Madden. I caught a glimpse of men by the supply pallets pointing my direction.

I ducked and dodged and swung past the first cabin headed toward the barn, but not because I intended to. I was a shit driver and couldn't go in a straight line if my life depended on it. The other guy drove a lot better than me. He was soon smacking against my empty flatbed, forcing me down. I rammed the corral fence, and goats fled every which way.

"Turn right in ten feet," the dash commanded. "No, sorry. Ascend to three thousand feet. I lost my bearings there for a minute."

I zigzagged from under my pursuer and gained altitude. As I came around for another run over the cabins, I saw flames shooting through the roof where I'd knocked over the chimney. Men with buckets ran toward the fire. *Oops.* It wasn't the diversion I'd intended, but anything would do in a pinch.

The other platform cruised up beside me, and my eyes opened wide. The driver had his banana gun out and pointed my direction. I squealed and fumbled with the knobs.

"Set jibs and stuns'ls, and steady as she goes," the dash pronounced. "Right at the next tree."

I didn't care which way I went as long as it was away from the other platform. I slapped at the controls, and my platform made a stationary ninety degree turn as the driver's banana gun boomed. His side door shot through the space I'd occupied a second earlier. My tail swung around and clobbered the pallets on his flatbed. Two of them tumbled off and dropped through the roof of the first cabin.

We continued parallel to each other, him moving forward and me going backward while we drifted through the smoke of the fire from the second cabin. We were aimed more or less at the two-story building. He was leaning way out of his compartment trying to get a clear shot at me. I swung my nose around until I was perpendicular across his flat bed. Then I hit my speed control.

For once I got the right knob and moved it the right direction on the first try. The side of my flatbed slammed against the back of his compartment, and I kept the power on, driving his nose hard toward the two-story building. He was so engrossed lining up his shot that he never saw the wall coming. The platform buried itself in the second-floor with a screech and a groan. The driver's shot went wild and hit a tree that toppled on the remaining intact cabin, flatting most of the roof and extending into the flames leaping from the second cabin. I whooped with glee. Maybe I wasn't so bad at this flying stuff.

A boom rocked my platform, whacking it against the building roof. Three black robes ran my direction, weapons drawn. I accelerated up the roof and dropped over the other side, putting the building between us while I devised a plan. I'd drawn them up the compound close to the fracture building, and that was the last place I wanted them to be. I needed to take them back the other way, and I needed to be able to use my own gun.

"Fuel level critical. To see a list of fuel outlets, press one. To see a list of fuel outlets that sell beverages, press two. To reset expectations, press three. To speak to the autopilot, press star zero."

Star zero? *Not real.* I turned my attention to the compartment door. The other driver had blown out his door so he could shoot at me. If it worked for him, it would work for me. As I continued away from the two-story building, I took careful aim at the far side door and fired.

The noise inside the tiny compartment deafened me. The windshield fractured. The door blew away at speed—until it crashed into the windmill. The fins bent and twisted but continued rotating as the axis doubled over in slow motion. *Oops. Didn't see that there.*

The windmill crashed down on the generator shack and the propane tanks stacked beside it. Sparks flew where the metal fins scraped the metal tanks, and a moment later, the propane went up with a whoosh that quickly spread to the nearest trees. I stared. How the hell had I done that?

"Warning! Fire suppression systems offline!" the dash said. "Continue straight to repair facility."

Frigid air streamed in the door, and I shivered. I turned away from the fracture building and headed around behind the line of cabins trying to keep them between me and the baddies. The second cabin was fully engulfed, and the fire had spread via the fallen tree to the cabin nearest the two-story building. I hadn't noticed before, but the tree I'd brushed through in the center of the compound also blazed. Smoke obscured most of the area.

My platform rocked with booms from banana guns, knocking me to the floor. I reached up a hand and scrabbled at the controls, hoping to turn out over the forest. I must have hit the autopilot. The platform turned into the smoke billowing from the cabins and dipped toward the center of the clearing. *Stupid ass controls.*

"Take the second star on the right, and then continue on until morning," the dash chirped.

No time to correct course, and even if I did, I was well within banana gun range. I choked on the smoke and wiped at my stinging eyes. Then I crawled across to the open door, and when we'd crossed the burn line, I slid out.

"I want him alive!" One screamed over the noise of the roaring fires.

I hit the ground in the thick of the smoke and way too close to the fire. The heat of it singed my sweatshirt, and I rolled over in the slush. Then I scampered away toward the barn, trying to get a shot at the remaining pallet. I hit it, too, and pumped a fist in the air.

Propane cylinders burst from the protective plastic wrap that kept them on the pallet, and they skidded across the ice like balls on a billiard table. Absolutely none of them caught fire or exploded. I wanted to scream.

Seconds later, I heard three muffled booms coming from inside the fracture building, and my heart stopped. Had Sammie been discovered? Had she been captured? Or killed?

Another gun boomed much closer, and I was on my chest sliding across the snow, my head ringing. I tried to rise, to run on, but my ears ached. I couldn't keep my balance, and my feet slipped out from under me. Someone tackled me, pinning me to the ground. Another one landed hard on top of us. A third minion skidded to a halt and held his gun on me. The other two rolled off and jerked me to my feet.

One approached, his look thunderous. He backhanded me hard across the face, and I reeled against my captors, the blow adding to my general dizziness. He'd raised his hand to strike again when another of his men ran up.

"Sir," the minion said, terror paling his face, "the sleepers are gone."

Hope exploded in me. Sammie got away. We'd won.

"Woohoo!" I shouted, not caring whether One hit me again.

One turned his next blow on the messenger, who fell backwards into the snow, his nose gushing blood.

"Idiots!" He pointed his gun at the minion, who cowered back and wet himself. Then One seemed to think better of his actions and put the gun away.

"Bring him," he ordered the others and headed to the fracture building. I looked over my shoulder, amazed at my handiwork. A couple of supply pallets burned, ignited by the fire in the central tree. Flames rose from the first and second cabins and threatened to spread to the third. The tree nearest the generator fire still blazed, and the twisted and charred remains of the windmill lay on the ground next to it. Not a bad day's work. If only I hadn't gotten caught.

My guards dragged me into the fracture building. Two men lay dead on the floor. One barely glanced at them. He crossed to the gurney that had held the sleepers and now stood empty near the fracture. He gave it a vicious kick that sent it crashing into the wall. His fists balled at his sides, and he turned his angry eyes on me.

"You might as well give up," I said. "You can't destroy the Rap dimension now, and the DCs will be here very soon."

He strode back to me, and I thought he might hit me again, but he stopped short. His eyes narrowed, and an evil smile spread across his face.

"Two tells me you're a powerful super-talent. The fracture you tore at E-4 was much larger than any the other sleepers created. Perhaps I don't need them."

A chill raced up my back, and I shivered. "I'm not like your sleepers. You can't make me fracture. I'm already crazy."

"Let's test that theory, shall we?" he said. He retrieved a vial and a hypodermic syringe from a nearby table. "Usual dose: one cc. Your dose: three cc's."

He plunged the needle into my arm and injected the yellow fluid. It burned like a hot poker, and I writhed against my captors.

"Bring everyone. We're going now," he said to a waiting minion. He extracted robes and harnesses from a cupboard, donned a set himself, and handed one to his minions to strap on me.

Heat spread over my arms and torso despite the cold and my wet sweatshirt. The light in the room became more intense and winkled off microscopic dust motes that drifted in the air. *Microscopic?* How could I see something that small? Before I could sort it out, I smelled roses. No, carnations. No, feces, feces and cigar smoke. Foreboding rose in me.

I watched from outer space as an endless river of black robes poured into the building. The color ran from their cloaks and spread over the floor and up the walls so that the dust motes became stars twinkling in a night sky. Then the stars expanded into drops of pearly white that swirled with the black to form yin and yang circles that rotated slowly.

Not real. Not real. Think, River. Survive. I should break free from my captors and run for the fracture, but I had no strength. No gravity held me to the Earth, no rules of physics applied. My eyes could see through the minions' bodies to their dark and twisted souls. They were creatures from Hell, and they were taking me with them to their own Dark Place, from which cigar smoke wafted. The hair stood up on the back of my neck.

A death's head grinned in front of me, and One's voice said, "Good. His pupils have dilated. We're ready. Send through the first wave."

The patter of feet running across the floor sounded like the booming of timpani drums. I wanted to cover my ears, but I couldn't find them. I couldn't find my body. I was sure I had one, but I'd misplaced it. I panicked. I had to find my body. Bad things could happen to it while I was gone. The scent of cigar smoke grew stronger.

"Second wave away," One's voice called from across the universe.

A stampede of feet echoed in my head, and I was surrounded by enormous black spiders that charged toward a yawning, sparkly mouth ringed with shark teeth. I jerked, trying to shrink away, but I was enmeshed by strands of silk from the biggest spider of all. A burst of static deafened me.

"Excellent," the spider said, towering over me. "You're right on time. Shall we go?"

We surged forward toward the hungry, sparkly mouth. Something tapped against my chest, the spider growled, and the cigar smoke thickened.

"What's wrong with these damn shields?" the spider said. "No time to change harnesses. You'll have to go without me, I'm afraid. Don't worry, I'll be along shortly."

The dread in my chest threatened to explode my rib cage. He pushed me forward again. I mustn't pass through that ring of teeth into Hell. It tugged at me as I moved closer, sucked at my body like a starving vampire. The songs of demons hummed in my head. Dense cigar smoke swirled around me. I focused all my paltry remaining will and grabbed the spider.

20

The screams of a madman filled my ears. One's, mine, I don't know which. Maybe both. The already incomprehensible structure of the Dark Place twisted and writhed around us, crystal and fire and fairy-tale legends in vivid colors like nothing I'd experienced before.

One's eyes rolled back in his head, and he dissolved in my hands, only to reassemble inside out, and then disassemble and reassemble again in his original form, but blue, all-over blue. His face contorted in a mask of incomprehensible horror. Scream after panicked scream issued from his mouth as a black cloud of snakes, flailing and striking at him before slithering away into the void around us. His form changed again to that of the spider.

I clung to him and shrieked, "Not real! Not real!"

My own body dissolved in a burst of flames, and my essence scattered over the whole of the universe, dark and light together. Time stood still, or rather, I saw all of Time at once. Dimensions grew like enchanted vines, splitting and intertwining until they filled the Dark Place, and then they withered and died and shattered just as I had. The dimensions, the Dark Place, and I were one and the same.

Just as quickly as I'd scattered, I coalesced, still gripping One. The mad creatures of the Dark Place zeroed in on us, gathering One's screams and gulping them down like sweetmeats as they followed our trajectory, their hungry eyes lusting for us. The scent of cigar smoke strengthened. Dread bubbled in my chest.

A storm of silver glitter swirled around us. We burst from the Dark Place into a new, infinitely more terrifying location. One whimpered beside me on the floor of the Rap fracture building. Somewhere in the distance, banana guns boomed and were answered with the rat-a-tat of machine-gun fire. A stone platform glided past on my right, and Sammie's voice called a warning I could neither understand nor obey.

But that reality was a dream. In my own personal reality, I stood in the doorway of a huge office, as though I'd entered a kingdom of giants. Soft light from a lamp on the desk illuminated a file cabinet, a desk with a credenza to one side, and a battered and stained old couch near the door. Next to a lumpy form on the desk, a cigar burned in the ashtray. The smell of it made my chest constrict and my shoulders stiffen. Demon song rose in a slow crescendo in the background.

Three hundred pounds, thinning grey hair, huge meaty hands, and a rumpled tan uniform shirt, Big Bob sat in the chair behind the desk, smiling and beckoning me in. I resisted but was compelled to enter, powerless. The door slammed behind me, and my heart pounded. Big Bob's smile warped into a leer, and he beckoned again.

I stood rooted, unable to breathe. He pushed up, ten feet tall, and unzipped his fly to liberate his enormous erection, which he stroked while he grinned at me. Demon song rose, louder and discordant. I trembled and gasped.

"Come in, River, and feel my love," he said.

His hand reached down to the object on the desk. He dangled Jimmy's limp, bloodless body by the neck, the cut marks on Jimmy's arms a livid red against his alabaster skin. He pumped the body up and down, threw back his head, and groaned with pleasure. Then he turned his leer on me again and took a step my direction. I screamed, and the demon song screamed with me.

"Run, River," Jimmy's dead lips whispered. "Run, or you're next."

Big Bob frowned at Jimmy and tossed his body into the corner like he tossed garbage into the bin. He stroked himself and took another step closer, lechery glowing in his inhuman eyes.

"Don't you want to be loved?" he asked.

Run, River. They can't get you if you just keep running, the voices in my head echoed. But I couldn't run. I didn't have the strength. I didn't have the will. And I wanted love—someone to care about me—more than anything in the world. *Be careful what you wish for,* the voices whispered.

My head ached, filled to overflowing with the screech of the demon song. I was mad, completely gone, trapped in a nightmare I couldn't escape while a battle between the black robes and the DCs raged around me like a dreamscape overlaying the reality of the office. The walls began to crack, and the cracks leaked silver glitter. Banana guns boomed. Doc scrabbled toward me, cuffs in his hands, but sonic booms drove him to cover before he reached me.

"Run, River," Jimmy croaked, lying crumpled in the corner. "Save Sammie. Save them all."

Big Bob snarled at Jimmy and lunged for me. I backpedaled, staggering across the floor and bursting through the closed door. The boom from a banana gun bent the pylon to my left. My hand touched my chest, and I fell into the fracture.

I passed through a blizzard of glitter and into the Dark Place, the monstrous Big Bob close behind. His beefy hands reached for me. The cacophony of demon music blotted out my thoughts, and I was paralyzed, unable to escape my pursuer or defend myself. His erection grew to an impossible size, and abject terror filled me.

My head exploded with the music of the demons. My own voice joined their song, now a cathedral chorus singing with divine inspiration. I was both in my body and outside it, seeing the Dark Place through my own eyes and through the eyes of every demon who inhabited it. I'd never felt such power. I could do anything—except face Big Bob.

I focused my will and transformed into a pronghorn antelope, a trifling feat. I raced through the Dark Place, my hooves striking with a force that sundered the crystalline structures across which I ran. Nightmare clouds scudded away, and demons scattered before me, carried on seismic waves caused by my every leap.

I charged on, but despite my speed, I couldn't outstrip Big Bob. He gained ground, laughing and leering as he pursued. In a panic, I transformed again, into a swift, and flew across the Dark Place. My wings beat in a blur that created tornadoes, which wrecked havoc on everything they touched. The demon chorus became disjointed, the voices out of sync.

My strength ebbed, but I needed to flee faster, much faster than the little swift I'd become, so I morphed again, into the Flash, complete with sleek red suit and yellow lightning bolts on my masked hood. The sound barrier fell before me. Shock waves spun out, and crystal spires shattered and crumbled. Retreating demons burst like punctured balloons, the substance of their beings spraying out in amorphous black clouds.

And still Big Bob closed on me. Exhausted and unable to outrun him, I had no choice but to stop. I stood trembling before him.

"Come and feel my love," he said, opening his hairy arms wide. "It's what you said you wanted. Who else will love you?"

"No!" I shouted, raising my hands in defense. "I don't believe you. You never loved me. It's all lies. You're a monster."

"All lies?" he asked. "I'm the only one who cared about you, the only one who comforted you. I showed you what love really is."

A little nightmare cloud drifted between us, fighting the raging winds I'd created by my passing. It wasn't much, a smudge of soot and smoke, but it moved with determination and purpose. It roiled and thrashed and became a translucent ghost of Jimmy.

"I love you, River," Jimmy said.

Big Bob roared. A straight razor as large as a battle ax appeared in his hand, and he sliced Jimmy in two. Jimmy dispersed into the nightmare and was blown away in the storm.

"Jimmy didn't love you," Big Bob spat. "If he'd loved you, he would have shared you with me. He was jealous, afraid I'd love you more than him."

His words swirled in my brain, making a kind of sick sense. Jimmy, jealous? Could it be? Had he hogged all the affection for himself? Is that why he'd never let me go along with him and Big Bob even when I'd begged? That's what I'd thought.

No. Big Bob had it wrong. *I* was the one who'd been jealous, jealous of the special attention Big Bob gave Jimmy. I'd wanted the same for myself. Jimmy protected me for as long as he could. He knew I'd never run away without him, and he wasn't the type who ran from anything. With sudden clarity, I realized why Jimmy killed himself. He'd done it to sever my ties to the orphanage, so there'd be nothing to keep me within Big Bob's grasp. In his final act, he'd tried once more to save me from a bully.

"Jimmy loved me more than life itself," I said, my voice choked with the sacrifice my best friend made. "Nothing you say will ever change that."

Big Bob scowled. "Jimmy's dead. You have no love but mine now. Who will comfort you and keep you safe?"

I thought about Sammie's warm, soft hand in mine, about her words of praise. Words of my own rose from my heart, words that I believed.

"I have a friend, and I'll make more. I'm a good person, a person of worth. I have important things to do, people to help."

Big Bob flinched back. The words I'd spoken fell like rain on a snowman. He melted and changed, features running, his form shrinking from an impossible giant to a runty ten-year old boy. Pale blue eyes, brimming with tears, looked into mine.

"It was my fault," my ten-year old self whispered. "I wanted him to love me. I asked for it."

The demon song rose again, harmonious in my ears. My outward appearance shifted to resonate with it, taking on a form not my own. I enveloped my younger self with the scruffy, much-patched arms of my beloved stuffed rabbit, the companion who comforted me through all the lonely nights, who I'd accidentally left behind when I'd run away. Little River threw arms around my bunny waist and sobbed against my chest.

"Not your fault," I said, my long floppy ears brushing his head. "You'll be okay now. He'll never hurt you again."

Then a storm of glitter surrounded me, and I smacked down on a pile of garbage.

21

―――~~~―――

"Traveler, what have you done?"

I rolled over on the garbage pile and squinted up at Smokey, who did not look happy. The whole of the alley reeled around me, but I suppose it was my head reeling—and throbbing—and not the buildings. My wrists itched like crazy. Somewhere nearby, a bird sang. The sound hurt my ears. I wanted it to stop. In the faint dawn light, too vivid colors blinded me.

What *had* I done? The episode in the Dark Place had been a hallucination, a product of the drug, hadn't it? Hadn't it? Jimmy was dead. He hadn't spoken to me from beyond the grave. And I couldn't have turned into animals, birds, and a comic book super-hero. But I'd confronted Big Bob and all he represented, and I'd beaten him. That much felt true. He'd never haunt my nightmares again.

"Uh..." I mumbled, struggling to sit up. My stomach arrived, late as always, and I retched onto the garbage beside me. Wiping my mouth, I asked, "Did I save the multiverse?"

Smokey snorted a billowing cloud of smoke. "No being has ever unleashed such energy Between. Repercussions will be large, consequences unknown."

"But the Rap dimension survived?" I asked, worried about Sammie. "Sammie... the affiliate is okay?"

"Impossible to say. Much destruction has been done. The Council will not be happy."

"It wasn't my fault," I whined, desperately tired. "One drugged me."

The big demon frowned down, hands on hips. He didn't seem mollified.

"Thanks for sending your nightmare to help. We couldn't have gotten away without it."

Smokey's frown deepened. "It isn't my nightmare, Traveler. It's yours. You created it. It opened the fractures that brought you here."

I blinked up at him, horrified.

"When you fracture, souls like you and the affiliate release negative energy in sufficient quantities to create cohesive entities. They have an affinity for interaction with their creators, but because your kind aren't aware of them, they soon become bored and migrate to Between."

"Where is it now?" I asked, twisting my head around in search of it.

"It has not returned. Perhaps it has been absorbed by another."

I thought about the big nightmare in the containment field, how it used its siren song to call smaller clouds and pounce on them. I hoped that hadn't happened to my little soot-ball. It was a pain, but I couldn't have saved the Rap dimension without it. And it had done its valiant best to help me while I'd battled Big Bob.

"What becomes of nightmares when they go to Between?"

"Demons sustain themselves on energy from your dimension. Think of it like your sunlight. Energy that coalesces into entities is akin to your plants and animals."

I frowned at Smokey. "You think my nightmare's been eaten?"

"Possibly, although it is wily and clever, much like its creator."

"If it hasn't, will it come back?"

"Let us hope not. Your space is ultimately toxic to my kind."

"So it's dead either way," I said. I was nuts to worry about the little soot-ball when I had a whole dimension to save.

"It may mature into a higher being."

Hope rose in me. "Into a demon? What are the odds of that?"

"Odds?" Smokey furrowed his brow. "What are those?"

"How likely is it that the little guy will grow up to be like you?" I had visions of a cute little baby version of Smokey, complete with tiny horns and diaper.

"Very few are like me, Traveler. I am a soul keeper, which is why I am able to come to you through the barrier."

Fear bubbled up in me.

"When I said I'd give you my soul if you'd help... well, you didn't, so I don't think we had a bargain."

Smokey snorted a huge black cloud. "Soul keepers collect the souls of those who leave their existence before their time. We shelter them until they can be transferred to a new container. Like your affiliate, Jimmy."

My breath came in short gulps. "You took Jimmy's soul?"

"For a while. Now you must keep your promise and save this place."

Jimmy dead but not dead. I couldn't wrap my tired brain around it. But Smokey was right. I needed to focus on the job ahead and think about all the crazy, impossible stuff later.

"Are the DCs coming?"

"Between is impassable because of the tempest you caused."

Great. So much for getting help from the DCs. I looked toward the fracture and sucked in a breath. The sparkly area now covered the back wall of two buildings.

"How long do I have?"

Smokey squinted at the fracture. "Integrity is lost more quickly near the end. Already the barrier approaches the point of no return. You must act immediately."

I slumped forward, head in hands. I wasn't sure I could walk to the end of the alley, let alone save a dimension. I needed food and sleep and a really good plan.

"You are not safe here, Traveler. You must go elsewhere."

I looked up in alarm. "Not safe? From what?"

"From your own kind—and from mine. You have drawn much attention."

I dragged myself out of the garbage, grateful to have arrived fully clothed, and staggered to the end of the alley. I looked back to see if Smokey intended to accompany me, but the big demon was gone. I shrugged out of the robe and wrapped it into a bundle tied by the harness.

The chill wind cut through my thin sweatshirt, and I shivered. My stomach rumbled, and my mouth was as dry as the Sahara. I stood there on the deserted street in the wan light and considered my next move. I had to help Lopez bust Cantel and Enrique, but that would take time to arrange, and the fracture looked bad. The city needed a shot of good news, and I had an idea, but Cantel had that bounty on my head. I couldn't afford to get caught. I needed a disguise.

I headed off at a slow jog, the best I could manage. In a few blocks, I reached the parking lots that stretched for half a mile under the elevated freeway. Three or four flash cars parked in the otherwise empty lot, and about two dozen women milled around them or chatted in small groups. I thought they must be freezing in their micro-miniskirts and their short jackets hanging open to expose thin sweaters or skimpy blouses with plunging necklines. I'd arrived at the rendezvous point where the ladies of the night squared up with their pimps. I slipped behind a concrete pylon to watch.

At the edge of the group, a buxom blonde whipped off her long, silky wig and offered it to another woman to try on. The second hooker couldn't make it fit over her own generous head of hair and handed it back with a laugh. She bummed a cigarette from the wig owner, and they both lit up. *Eww.* Well, sometimes when you're out to save the universe— er, multiverse, you have to make sacrifices. I flipped up my hood and sidled up to the two women, keeping my back to the rest of the group.

"Uh... hey," I said, trying not to stare at the wig owner's cleavage.

The second hooker looked me up and down, grinned at her friend, and walked away. The wig owner gave me the same head to toe appraisal and sighed.

"Sorry, kid, business hours are over. Come back in about five years," she said with a husky voice. She took a final drag on her cigarette, stubbed it out on the pavement, and turned to go.

"Oh, uh, I didn't want that," I stammered. I pulled a wad of bills from my pocket. "I mean... I want to buy your wig. If you'll sell it."

She stopped in her tracks and turned. One carefully plucked eyebrow raised at the sight of the cash. "You shittin' me?"

"No, ma'am."

She tipped her head on one side and squinted at me. Then she glanced around, gestured me to follow, and walked away to the far end of the lot.

"You're that kid, ain't you? The one that shot up the bus?"

I froze. My pulse thumped in my ears. She was close enough to grab me, and I was in no shape to sprint away. Would a hooker call the cops? Or Cantel?

"I'm a pacifist," I said, easing away and holding out my hands. "No weapons. Ever."

"The same one who saved that little boy from the fire?" she asked, following me. "I seen your picture on TV."

"You have me confused with someone else." I lengthened my stride, figuring she couldn't keep up in her stiletto heels.

She matched my steps and put a hand on my arm. "Tell me the truth."

Running was a tough habit to break, and lying was nothing more than another way of running. But I wasn't running away anymore. I stopped and faced her.

"I wish I'd never gotten on that bus. Someone was shooting at me and hit the driver. I didn't kill him, but I feel guilty all the same."

"You start the fire at Cantel's building?"

"Nothing to do with it. Absolutely wasn't me," I swore, drawing an X over my heart while tucking crossed fingers behind my thigh. Technically Abbott's cigarette started the fire, so I wasn't *really* lying.

She studied my face for a long time, and then she said, "Two hundred."

My eyebrows shot up. "For a used wig?"

"Honey, you're gonna need more than a hair piece. Besides, it's quality, made from the real thing."

I grumbled under my breath and counted bills.

"Not here," she said, voice low.

We walked across Fourth and up a block to an alley. I wondered if she planned to mug me now that she'd seen the cash. Instead, she set her enormous purse on a dumpster lid and stripped off her jacket.

"Take off your sweatshirt, and if you got a shirt on, take that off, too," she ordered.

"Hey, I just want the wig," I said, backing away.

"Honey, Mr. Slime-ball Cantel put a fat bounty on your head. If you don't want to get caught, you do as I tell you." She had her hands on her hips and her lips drawn into a pout. "Well? Do you want a disguise or not?"

I glanced around before reluctantly pulling off my sweatshirt. She shimmied her skin-tight red sweater over her head, revealing a lacy black bra filled by hefty knockers. She caught me staring and glared. My face turned into a three-alarm blaze, and I worked on removing my t-shirt. By the time I had it off, she'd removed her bra and pulled her sweater back on, not that it did much to cover what she had underneath.

She strapped me up in her bra and filled the cups with litter from the alley. I pulled on my shirt, which stretched tight over my phony mammary glands. My sweatshirt wasn't cut as large, and I could only zip it halfway, accentuating my new-found curves.

While I dressed, she dug out bottles and compacts and tubes of stuff I thought I probably didn't want to ask about. She made me sit on a garbage can, and then she smeared a horrible thick liquid all over my face. She added a covering of beige powder on top, pink powder to my cheeks and matching pink lipstick on my lips, dark pencil around my eyes, and a dusting of pearly silver to my eyelids. The wig went on last, in place of my watch hat. I had some concerns about whether it would keep the dancing ants at bay, but it seemed to work. When she'd finished, she scanned me again.

"You'll do," she said, grinning.

She held a mirror in front of me. A comely young woman looked back. I smiled. No one would recognize me now. Then I frowned. Had the transformation been that easy? Did I look like a girl?

"Don't worry," she laughed. "Looks don't make the man. It takes a tough guy to poke somebody like Cantel."

"Thanks," I said, and handed her the two hundred. On impulse, I handed her another one. "For the makeup."

She took the bills and rubbed them together. "This some of Cantel's money?"

I stopped breathing.

She laughed again. "When you're running this city, remember Ruby helped you."

Ruby tucked the money in her purse and strolled away down the alley. I'd never realized prostitutes could be so nice and resolved to think better of them in the future.

I hunkered against the chill wind and headed east on Third. Stores wouldn't open for another hour, and I wanted out of the cold. My next stop was the Starbucks on Division. They were already getting busy. The trendy set needed their caffeine fix before heading into the office to make war on their competitors.

I ordered a large hot chocolate, and the male barista handed it over with a lascivious wink that made me uncomfortable. I also got one of their turkey and egg breakfast sandwiches. I grabbed a table away from the drafty door, my back to the room.

I'd been there forty-five minutes when the FCIS agents came in. *Shit.* I bent over my hot chocolate and hoped they got an order to go. No such luck. The one who'd sucker punched me took the table next to mine.

Puncher lounged in his chair, long legs stretched under the table and eyes on me. He smiled in an inviting kind of way. I turned my face away and tried not to shake. I had the bundled robe and harness on my lap under the table. A second agent joined him.

"I can't believe it," said Puncher. "Art and Cindy. I didn't see that coming, did you?"

"I thought they hated one another," the second agent grunted.

Guilt whistled up my spine. Art and his heartthrob must have gotten caught. He'd lost me and the evidence. I'd probably tanked his career. Both their careers. Lopez would never believe they'd been influenced by a demon. Shame waltzed with my guilt.

"California," Puncher said. "Art's a stuffed-shirt New Yorker. What's he going to do in California?"

What *did* the FCIS do with agents who screwed up? Were they going to San Quentin for dereliction of duty? Hard labor on California truck farms?

"Surf and dive shop, I heard," the other agent replied.

Surf and dive shop? Was that code for concrete overshoes and a burial at sea? Lopez was a lunatic, but she wouldn't go that far, would she?

"There's something fishy about that scrawny wimp getting the drop on them," Puncher said. "And making them strip before he handcuffed them to that radiator was low. If I ever see him again, I'll teach him respect."

Handcuffed to a radiator? Wait a minute. The last I'd seen of Art, he was on the floor—well, on top of Cindy on the floor—in the living room, and the living room didn't have any radiator. And I hadn't made them strip. They'd wanted to do it. Smokey just helped them along.

"Lopez sure was pissed when they handed in their resignations."

"I wouldn't have the guts to quit in the middle of an investigation,"

Puncher said. "Not one of hers, anyway. What are you getting them for a wedding present?"

I spewed a mouthful of hot chocolate, and Puncher gave me a curious look before returning his attention to his partner. The lights warbled *Here Comes the Bride*—off-key and with highly inappropriate lyrics.

"We'll pass the hat and buy a gift certificate," his companion replied, rising from the table.

Art and Cindy *getting married*? Smokey wasn't your typical matchmaker, but he'd said he couldn't force people to do anything they weren't already thinking about. Married. Wow. I smiled. Maybe I wasn't such a bad guy. I ditched my empty cup and headed out.

22

I hit St. Vincent's Thrift Store first, but this time I shopped indoors. I found a warm parka suitable for another trip to the Beta dimension, which reminded me I needed to talk to Smokey about how to safely release the nightmare. And that set me thinking about the soot-ball instead of what I'd come to buy so I had to walk around the entire store three times before I remembered to get everything. Some days being schizophrenic sucked.

I left with the coat, gloves, and a new backpack. Then I dropped into a gas station convenience store for a bottle of water, half a dozen granola bars, another rain poncho and space blanket, and a pre-paid cell phone. I felt naked without the weight of my usual Swiss army knife and camping supplies, but once the feds collared Cantel and Enrique, I'd be headed for my new home with the DCs and wouldn't need them. That thought got me worrying about Sammie again.

Outside, the morning remained gloomy and grim. Swirling clouds of nightmares dimmed the sky. The big pendulum clock tick-tocked in my brain and periodically gonged. I winced at the sound. On the way to the garage where I'd stashed the money, I called Lopez.

"I wasn't amused by your little stunt, Madden," a sulky voice said after one ring.

"Hey, Agent Lopez," I replied, stifling a laugh. "I'm ready to set up the meet."

"Where are you?" she asked.

"Oh, uh, running errands," I said, wondering how quickly she could trace my phone. I wasn't more than ten minutes' drive from her safe house.

"Stay out of sight and wait for us. Everyone in the city's looking for you."

"Sorry, things to do, places to go," I said, walking faster. "We'll meet at the burned-out pie factory, Fifth and Perry, eight tonight. That'll give you time to set up."

"Look, Madden, Cantel's determined to find you. He beat up Mrs. Schmidt, that woman whose kid you rescued, trying to get information about where you'd gone. He made her tell the press you did it when you robbed her last night. You're not a hero anymore. Someone will turn you in for the reward."

My hand tightened on the phone. "Is she okay?"

"Bruised and battered, but she wouldn't see a doctor."

I snapped the phone off and walked a circle. It was one thing for Cantel to come after me. Knocking around innocent women was something else again. I headed for the garage at a brisk jog. Time to bring this city an angel of hope and Cantel crashing down.

"I don't know what to say," Father Rodriguez said, wiping his glistening eyes. A fan of cash lay on the desk between us. "Thank you, child. Bless you."

"Thank River Madden, Father. I'm just his messenger," I said, trying for an octave above my usual register and flashing a demur smile.

I made a hasty exit from the St. Joan Shelter for Battered Women before the old priest could ask questions. It was late afternoon, and the sky looked a smidge lighter. I grinned and jogged away. I'd doled out Cantel's cash at the Gospel Mission, the Centerville Sunrise Drug Rehab Center, Safe Haven for Animals, the YMCA, and the local Children's Hospital, and called the media after each visit.

I'd caught a newscast at the IHOP when I'd broken at midday for a hot chocolate. The press crisscrossed the city behind me, reporting on the unexpected good fortune of Centerville's charities. My name was on everyone's lips. I was a hero again, and the dimensional barriers seemed more stable. *Take that, Mr. Cantel.*

I pulled Enrique's number from pocket, opened my phone, and dialed.

"Si," Mouthpiece's voice said.

"Hey, Mr.—" I said, flummoxed about what to call him. "It's River Madden. I'm ready to do a deal."

"You've taken care of your little problem?"

"It's in the works as we speak."

"When we have proof, we'll contact you."

"Wait!" I cried. "I'll have it with me tonight. If we can't do a deal then, everything's off."

I heard a long moment of heavy breathing, and then Mouthpiece said, "There's a cabinet factory at Sullivan and Wellesley. You know where that is? We'll meet you there at midnight. Bring the proof and the money. If we're satisfied with both, we'll call for delivery of the product."

Drat! I needed them to come to me, not the other way around. I should have asked Lopez how to arrange the buy. *Think, River. Would an experienced hood agree to such a thing?*

"Sorry," I replied. "You'll need to bring the product to the old pie factory at Fifth and Perry at 8 p.m."

I disconnected before he could argue and hoped Enrique would be impressed with my decisiveness and not pissed off. I jogged five blocks east, in case Lopez was tracking my phone, and dialed another number.

"Centerville Police, Narcotics Division," a perky female voice answered.

"Detective Thurston, please."

The operator put me on hold, and I fumed, worried that I might run out of minutes before he answered.

"Thurston."

"Hey, detective, River Madden," I said. "How would you like to work for the new boss in Centerville?"

"Where are you?" he asked, his voice a hoarse whisper.

"Crazy, not stupid. If you want to work for me, I have a little job for you. Do it right, and you can play on my team. I'll up your cut by twenty percent. Are you in or out?"

He waited so long to reply that I thought he was tracing the call.

"What do I have to do?"

"Bring your former boss to a meet tonight."

"And then?" he asked.

"We don't talk about these things on an open line," I said.

"What do I tell him so he'll come?"

I laughed. "Tell him you're meeting me."

I gave him the details. Then I headed north. I had two more stops to make before I reported to the pie factory.

The street lay dark and quiet before me. Leaves from the big maples that lined the sidewalks had been raked off the yellowed lawns, and the cars in the driveways were no more than a couple years old.

In the middle of the block, the windows of a blue two-story house glowed with soft lamplight. I strolled up the front walk, across a wooden porch, and knocked on the sparkling white door. The porch light winked on, and a silhouette peeked out the front picture window. The light hummed *Homeward Bound*. A moment later, the door cracked open.

"If you're from the press, I have nothing to say," Mark's mother said, her blackened eyes squinting out at me.

"Hey, Mrs. Schmidt, River Madden. I helped you and Mark down the stairs. Can I come in?"

She opened the door another foot and scanned the street behind me, brows drawn into a frown. Then she gestured me in and closed the door.

I stood in a cramped vestibule facing carpeted stairs leading up to the second floor. An archway opened into a fifteen-foot square living room furnished with a comfortable brown and green striped couch and arm chair. Green brocade drapes covered the windows. Matching brown lamps that sat on mahogany end-tables lit the space. A door led into a kitchen. Two bulging suitcases stood in the middle of the room.

"I'm sorry about what happened to you," I said as we stepped into the living room. "Did you report it to the police?"

She gave a humorless laughed. "And have them hurt Mark?"

"Are you leaving?" I asked, gesturing at the suitcases.

"What else can I do?"

I slipped off my backpack and dropped it at my feet. When I un-zipped it, Cantel's shiny gun slid onto the floor. I thrust it back inside and drew out fifty thousand dollars, which I offered to her.

She stared first at the money, and then at the backpack. "I don't want your stolen money. You're no different than he is."

"It's to cover your medical bills, the ones your insurance won't pay," I said. "And to make up for what happened."

"He said you're a thug, a mobster trying to take over Centerville. He claims you set the fire."

She wrapped her arms around her chest and looked at me with swollen, suspicious brown eyes. A nasty bruise colored her jawbone, and red finger marks showed on her throat where she'd been strangled.

"I'm not," I said, frowning. "I'm just a homeless guy who happened to be in the wrong place at the wrong time."

"You have the money." Her voice dripped with loathing. "And you're carrying a gun."

"All right, I admit I stole the money, but I didn't mean to," I said. "A crazy guy was trying to kill me, and I'd... lost my shoes. I took the money by accident while trying to steal some. Shoes. Now I'm trying to stop Cantel."

She wasn't believing a word of it. "A homeless man with a gun? Do you plan to shoot him?"

My storytelling skills hadn't improved despite their truthful content. I had no way to convince her. I set the stack of bills on an end-table and headed for the door. I heard her gasp and turned to see her staring out the front window.

"It's him," she hissed, her hand covering her mouth and her face white as alabaster. "The one who came with Cantel when he beat me up."

Shit. I threw the deadbolt on the door and retreated to the living room where I closed the drapes.

"You have a gun," she said. "You can shoot him."

"You know how to use a gun?" I asked.

"Not really," she whispered, eyes wide with terror.

"Me either," I said. "Where's Mark?"

She stared at me, unblinking. He couldn't be upstairs, not with those casts. He had to be on the main floor. I held the backpack out to her.

"Take the gun and go to Mark. Barricade the door and stay away from the windows. Call Lieutenant Knowles. There's a cell phone in the pack."

"You can't just shoot him?" she said.

"I'm a pacifist."

I pushed the pack into her arms and shoved her toward the back of the house. She'd just cleared the living room when the first thump hit the front door. The second one bashed it open, ripping the trim loose from the inside wall. Thurston stood in the doorway, tie loosened, snub-nosed gun in hand. His eyebrows rose when he recognized me.

"Madden. So you're the angel spreading good cheer." He chuckled.

"Good evening, Detective Thurston. Nice to see you again." I wondered how long I needed to stall him until Knowles arrived. We were ten minutes from the police station, but maybe Knowles had gone home for the night. And maybe Knowles was just as dirty as Thurston.

He waved me back and closed the door. "Where's the woman?"

"She's not here," I lied. "But I'm expecting her soon."

Thurston glanced at the suitcases. "Leaving town?"

"Me?" I said, struggling to keep my voice calm. "Lord, no. Lots to do still, getting the organization up and running. Did you consider my offer?"

He laughed. His eyes ran up and down my body. "Work for you? You must be joking."

"You won't get a better offer," I said. "This is your chance to get in on the ground floor, grow with the company."

"Mrs. Schmidt," Thurston yelled. "If I have to find you, I'll make you watch while I carve up your kid, and then I'll do the same to you. Come out now, and I promise to make it quick and painless."

My hands shook, and sweat popped out on my brow. I thought about an article I'd ready in Psychology Today on motivational style. "You could help me build my team, make sure we're one big, happy family, that everyone gets along."

"I'm counting to ten, Mrs. Schmidt. One, two—"

Okay, so he wasn't an affiliate personality type. "You'd be the leader, the big cheese, the one everyone looked up to. You'd get the gold star."

The cop gave me a cold stare. "Five, six, seven—"

Yikes, so not an achiever, either. This wasn't going well at all. "Cantel's a loser. Look how easily I've turned his world upside down. You don't want to live upside down, do you? You want things orderly, logical, predictable. Cantel's a loose cannon."

Thurston's eyes slid from the door to the kitchen to me. Bingo! An organizer.

"Enrique's already agreed that I have a superior business plan for reaching full potential," I said. "I'll keep everyone in step and marching toward the same goal."

The detective raised one eyebrow, but he stopped counting, uncertainty crinkling his brow.

"The feds are interested in Cantel," I said. "If they bust him—and it won't be hard with all the mistakes he's made—he'll take you down, too."

"How do you know the feds are onto him?" he asked, suddenly suspicious.

"Oh, uh... I have an informant on the inside. Of the FCIS."

"Cantel's on his way here," the cop said, looking worried. His hand clenched and unclenched on the gun.

"Oh," I replied, my nerves on fire. Where were the feds when you needed them? "Maybe you could get the drop on him, and we could take him for a ride?"

"People who cross Cantel tend to end up dead."

I shuffled my feet and tried not to rock. The clock bonged again in my head, tolling the minutes left in my life and this dimension's existence. I needed to close the sale.

"Did I mention I'm part of a much bigger East Coast cartel? They know all about your relationship to Cantel. If anything happens to me, they'll come looking for you." I swallowed hard. "They aren't very nice people."

The door swung open, and Cantel huffed in. His toupee was slightly awry, his gold watch flashed in the lamplight, and he'd replaced his shiny gun with a miniature cannon that barely fit in his beefy hand, the black barrel pointed at me.

"I knew he'd be back," Cantel snarled. "Cuff him, and then go find a blanket to wrap him in so you can carry him out to the car."

"We should finish him here," Thurston said.

"He's going to be a long time dying." When Thurston didn't move, Cantel snapped, "Do as I say."

I needed to stall. I needed Knowles to show up. Lopez knew Cantel beat up Mrs. Schmidt. Did they have the house under surveillance? I needed her agents to burst in the door. Or were they all busy at the meet site? This was my last chance to sway the detective.

"A quick kill here and now is the smart thing, right Thurston?" I said. "Neat, clean, orderly. That's the way it should go. Before my friends come looking for me. Or the feds take an interest."

Thurston frowned at me, and then at Cantel. Just like that, he made his decision. The muzzle of his gun swung, and he fired twice into Cantel's chest. The mobster's eyes opened wide, and then he dropped to the floor, the cannon bouncing away. I stared at the body leaking blood on Mrs. Schmidt's nice braided rug. *Shit.* At least it was him, not me, but how would I explain Cantel's death to Agent Lopez?

"We need to find the Schmidt woman and get rid of her and the boy," Thurston said.

"Hold it right there," Mrs. Schmidt said, voice wavering. She peeked around the kitchen doorway, Cantel's gun shaking in her hand. "Put your gun down."

Thurston swung toward her, but she'd positioned herself well. He couldn't get a clear shot, whereas she couldn't miss. I leaped between them.

"It's okay," I said, raising my hands to Thurston. "She's part of my gang."

Thurston squinted at her, his smoking gun pointing at my gut. "She knows I killed Cantel. She has to go."

"Hey, she didn't rat me out even when you beat her up, did she? Your secret's safe with her." I glanced over my shoulder and saw her mouth drop open. "She's my torch. You know, the one who set the fire in Cantel's building."

He lowered his gun.

I turned to Mrs. Schmidt and eased Cantel's gun from her hand. "Thanks, I can take it from here."

"What about him?" The cop pointed to the body.

"What time is it?" I asked, concerned I might miss my meeting with Enrique.

"Seven-thirty."

We were a good twenty minutes from the pie factory on the other side of town. Enrique wanted proof I'd taken care of Cantel, and now I had it, although it was never my intention to kill him.

"Get your trunk open," I said, bending down to roll the rug around the body.

Thurston hurried out.

"Sorry about all this," I said. "You and Mark will be safe now."

"Lieutenant Knowles is on his way," she said. "Shouldn't you wait for him?"

Of course the cavalry would arrive when I didn't want it to. I had to get the body to the meet, not stand around trying to convince Knowles that Thurston shot Cantel.

"I'm running late for an appointment," I said. "And I think it's better for Mark if we get Mr. Cantel out of here right away."

"What should I tell the detective?" she asked, incredulous.

"Give him my regards and tell him someone will be in touch," I said as Thurston returned.

I stifled hysterical laughter on the way to the car. What a cliché—two guys hauling a dead body wrapped in a rug. We dumped Cantel in the trunk of the unmarked police car, and Thurston roared off to the meet. When we were a block or two away from the Schmidt house, we heard sirens. A moment later, we were passed by two cruisers, lights flashing blue against the darkness. Thurston turned on the radio and listened to reports of gunshots.

"How'd they hear so fast?" he asked, frowning at me.

"Probably the neighbors called it in," I said, wiping my hands on my jeans. Now that I had time to think about it, the idea of hauling Cantel's body into the pie factory made my stomach do handsprings. Plus, I was headed for a drug buy and had no clue what to do. Agent Lopez better have her people in position to cover me. Otherwise, I was dead meat.

Thurston wove through traffic at a good fifteen miles per hour over the speed limit. I guess he was anxious to make a getaway. Since I was still Centerville's most wanted person, I had no problem with his driving.

We got to the pie factory with ten minutes to spare. Getting a dead body out of a trunk turned out to be a lot harder than getting one in, and the clock in my head tick-tocked in double time.

As we struggled through the loose piece of plywood that covered the door, the lights came on inside. Thurston looked up in surprise at the cavernous space, two-stories high, fifty feet wide by a hundred fifty long, the ceiling open to the sky and crisscrossed with huge, dark beams. Scorched conveyor lines and soot-covered processing tables ringed an open space lighted by a single overhead bulb.

"Who's here?" he asked, dropping his end of the rug and drawing his gun.

"Oh, uh, no one," I said looking around. "The light's rigged with a motion detector."

Thurston frowned at me, but he picked up Cantel and helped carry him to where the light created a pool of illumination. Handling the bloody bundle made my skin crawl. I didn't see either agents or cameras.

We arranged Cantel face up. He looked awful. We'd lost his toupee, and blood soaked his expensive gray business suit. I wondered if I should lay his hands over his chest in a proper pose. Was he religious? Should I say a few words? What was the protocol for mob hits? The overhead light belted out *Amazing Grace* off-key, and a crowd of mourners murmured behind me. I picked up my backpack and stepped away, ignoring the hallucinations.

"Hold it right there," a voice said behind us.

Thurston and I spun around. Lieutenant Knowles stood at the edge of the light, pointing his service revolver at us. He didn't seem surprised at my disguise or my companion. Mrs. Schmidt must have spilled the beans. *Damn.* Thurston's hand strayed towards his gun.

"I wouldn't," Knowles said. "Put your hands behind your heads, both of you, and then turn around."

A car motor rumbled outside, and lights flashed across the broken-out windows set high in the factory walls. Knowles glanced up, and Thurston made his move. His gun came clear of his holster and started its swing toward the lieutenant. At the same time, I tossed the backpack. It connected with Thurston's head, knocking him sideways. His gun fired wide, and Knowles' gun answered. Blood blossomed on Thurston's chest. He was dead by the time he hit the floor. Knowles' swung toward me. Car doors slammed.

"Quick!" I yelped. "Put your gun away."

With a creak and a snap, the plywood over the door ripped off, and two thugs carrying mean-looking rifles with fat magazines came in, followed by Mouthpiece. The thugs flanked left and right and pointed their weapons at Knowles. The lieutenant could see he was out-gunned but continued to hold his weapon on me.

Mouthpiece stared at me before moving his gaze to the two bodies on the floor, and finally to Knowles. "Have we interrupted something, Mr. Madden?"

I hoped the sweat trickling down my face wasn't making my makeup run. Knowles adjusted his grip on his gun, his face sweating as bad as mine. He didn't know whether to watch me or the thugs.

"Everything's under control," I said.

"Then why is that man pointing a gun at you?" Mouthpiece asked. "And why are there two unmarked police cars outside?"

More lies to spin. I had to stop doing this. Soon.

"This is my enforcer, Lt. Knowles," I said, gesturing to the cop. His gun pointed steadily at me, and I caught *the end of times* muttered by the chorus.

Mouthpiece raised a brow. "He's a police officer?"

"One of the city's finest, but I don't hold that against him," I replied. I stared hard at Knowles. "I try to learn from my elders. Mr. Cantel found it useful to have an officer on his payroll. I thought I'd do the same. Unfortunately, Detective Thurston wasn't interested in the position."

The detective glanced at the two guys with the scary rifles and lowered his gun, confusion in his eyes.

"A wise move," Mouthpiece said.

He flipped a hand, and one of the goons slipped out to return a moment later with Enrique. Knowles' eyes widened, and he looked at me, fear stiffening his jaw. A bit of soot drifted down from the beams overhead and soiled his shoulder. He glanced at it before returning his gaze to me, surprise lighting his eyes.

"Señor Enrique," I said, bowing low.

Enrique still wore those damn sunglasses and wasn't any more talkative than before. I wondered if he and Mouthpiece used telepathy. After a moment, he shrugged.

"Señor Enrique is pleased that you've taken care of your little problem. He's prepared to do business with you," Mouthpiece interpreted.

I moved carefully over to the backpack and picked it up. Knowles watched my face, his body tense.

"We've heard that you've been busy today, Mr. Madden," said Mouthpiece. "Centerville's charities have received surprising donations."

"Building goodwill while greasing the wheels," I replied. I clutched the backpack strap so hard my nails bit into my palm.

"In light of your generosity, you won't mind if we count the money before we call for the delivery," Mouthpiece said.

Knowles looked at my face, and then at the backpack. I was such a bad liar. His eyes flicked up to the darkness overhead. Then his lips set in a straight, hard line. He walked over and took the pack out of my grasp. He weighed it in his hand, grimaced at me, and turned to Mouthpiece.

"The money stays in our possession until we verify the quality of the delivery. But you can have a peek," the lieutenant said as he held the backpack out at arm's length, drawing Mouthpiece and Enrique into the circle of light. When they were standing before him, he opened the zipper a few inches and allowed Mouthpiece to look in.

Mouthpiece frowned. "That's not sufficient."

Knowles pulled the zipper closed and held up the bag. "Check the weight."

Mouthpiece took one of the straps and hefted the bag while Knowles kept a grip on the other. I held my breath. Would Cantel's gun, the robe, and a few granola bars make up for all the missing cash? After what seemed a very long time, he let go. He pulled a phone from his pocket, spoke a few words, and snapped it shut again.

Knowles stepped back beside me and handed me the backpack. I fought the urge to scream at the light, which had given up on church hymns and belted out gangsta rap at a deafening volume in time to the gonging of the pendulum clock.

In minutes, another vehicle pulled up at the factory, and two more thugs came in, one of them carrying a paper-wrapped bundle, which he handed to Mouthpiece. Mouthpiece transferred the bundle to Knowles, who unwrapped it to reveal a plastic bag filled with a bright red powder.

Was this the part where I was supposed to pull out a knife, slit the bundle, and rub some on my gums? In this day of forensic chemistry, was I supposed to have a portable lab to test the drugs? More important, if I accepted the shipment, Enrique would want the money, and I was about seven hundred thousand short. I'd figured once the drugs arrived, the feds would burst in and arrest everyone before any counting got done. Sweat poured down my ribs, and my hands shook.

Knowles looked around the burned-out interior. Then he gestured for me to move to one of the solid stainless steel prep tables. He herded me to the far side so we could keep an eye on Enrique, placed the bundle on the grimy surface, and reached in his pocket for a pen knife. He made a slit in the bag, bent over, and waved his hand over the slit while he inhaled.

"Definitely ghost," he said. "Give them the payment."

This was it. I'd toss them the bag, they'd figure out I'd cheated them, and then we were toast. When I didn't move, Knowles nudged me with his elbow. I grabbed the backpack in both hands and heaved it at Mouthpiece. He caught it, unzipped the main compartment, and spread it wide. It didn't take him long to realize he'd been cheated.

"Is this a joke, Mr. Madden?" Mouthpiece asked.

"No joke," Knowles said, placing his hand on my collar. "You're all under arrest. Put your weapons on the ground and your hands behind your heads."

I don't know why Knowles thought Enrique's men would comply. He hadn't even drawn his gun. Mouthpiece pointed at us, Knowles flipped the table forward and jerked me down behind it, and a million bullets filled the air, not that I stopped to count. Knowles threw himself over the top of me while the rat-a-tat of those vicious rifles deafened us. But it lasted no more than a split second.

When the shooting stopped, Knowles helped me to my feet. I didn't think my legs would support me and looked down at the gritty, bullet-pocked surface of the prep table, glad none of the shells found their mark.

Enrique's four goons sprawled on the floor, neat holes through their foreheads. Mouthpiece held his bleeding thigh and groaned. A federal agent dressed in black fatigues stood over him, pointing a gun at his face. Enrique was on his knees, unharmed, another agent cuffing his wrists behind him. Three more agents rappelled down from the overhead beams, sniper rifles slung over their backs. Lopez strode in through the door, a satisfied smile on her face. She marched up to Knowles.

"Agent Lopez," she said, waving her ID. "When did you figure it out?"

Knowles gave me a sideways look and muttered, "Waitress, huh?"

My cheeks warmed, and I scuffed my sneakers on the floor.

To Lopez he said, "I couldn't see why Madden would prevent Thurston from killing me, or why he'd tell Enrique I worked for him if he were really a new crime boss moving in on Cantel's operation. Then soot drifted down from overhead, and I knew there were people on the beams. It had to be a bust."

"Lucky for Madden that you did. Amateurs!" Lopez arched an eyebrow at me. "Nice disguise, Madden."

My face burning, I walked to the backpack, scooped it off the floor, and dug out my phone. I punched speed dial and connected to a local TV station.

"Hey, I'm down here at Fifth and Perry, the old pie factory. There's shooting. I think Mr. Cantel might be dead."

I hung up and was joined by Knowles and Lopez. She relieved me of the remaining cash with a wag of her finger to let me know what a naughty boy I'd been spending Cantel's money. The agents escorted Enrique out, and we followed. Two police cruisers pulled up at the curb. A news van arrived hot on their heels, and I could hear more sirens in the distance. Spectators appeared out of the shadows. Nothing like a good shoot-out and drug bust to wake up the neighbors.

"Where does Black Robe fit in all this?" Knowles asked.

"Well... he doesn't. I mean, if he hadn't been chasing me, I wouldn't have hopped the bus or accidently stolen Cantel's money." At his narrowed eyes, I rushed on. "Yeah, sorry, I probably should have mentioned the money before. I have this gut feeling that Black Robe won't be back."

A moving van pulled up half a block down the street, and people got out. With the poor lighting, it was hard to tell who they were, but one of them was quite a bit shorter than the others. My chest tightened, and I blinked back tears. Sammie was okay. I wanted to fly down the street to her.

"What were you doing in the alley?"

He knew how to ask the tough questions, and I rubbed my hands on my jeans.

"I don't know. I'm schizophrenic, and sometimes I have psychotic episodes. I woke up there. Then the fight started, and I ran."

"With someone on your shoulder."

I shrugged and looked over to where another TV van pulled up.

"Agent Lopez can explain." I dug Cantel's gun from the backpack and handed it over. "The ballistics on this might help you close a few unsolved cases."

Knowles took the gun. When he read the inscription on the handle, his brows rose. The group from the moving van stood across the street, unrecognizable in the shadows. I hoped Capt. Samuels wasn't with them.

"So what happens to me?" I asked. "Am I free to go?"

Knowles took a deep breath and let it out. "You don't know where Black Robe is?"

I shook my head. I'd been so spaced out on the drug that I couldn't say for certain whether he'd joined the raid on the Rap dimension.

Knowles ran a hand over the stubble on his cheeks. He looked done in. "Yeah, you can go."

I glanced at the DCs. "The young guy who died in the alley? His family would like to take his body."

The cop pursed his lips while he thought. "Why do I get the feeling there's a lot more you're not telling me?"

I shrugged again. He pulled a business card from his pants and scribbled a note on it.

"The morgue's up the hill. Here's the address." He held out the card. "I'll let them know you're coming."

I took the card, nodded my thanks, and headed away from the lights and cameras and toward my new life. One shape separated from the others in the shadows and came forward to meet me. I heard the click of a tracker, and Doc held out cuffs. Behind him, I could make out Sammie, her father's hand on her arm restraining her. I strapped the cuffs on, and she burst away to join me.

"River, are you okay?"

"Hey, Sammie," I said, uncertain about what I should say. I wanted to tell her how glad I was to see her, how much I'd missed her, how I hoped I'd be with her every day for the rest of my life. But her dad glared at me so fiercely that I couldn't open my mouth. I stepped around her and walked over to Capt. Samuels. She fell in beside me.

"The police agreed to release Griff's body," I said. I held out the card. "Here's the address."

We all stood there in awkward silence for a century or so, and then Samuels took the card. He blinked a few times and walked away. Sammie squeezed my hand.

"Thanks," she said. "Come on. It's time to go home."

It sounded so wonderful the way she said it. But I had miles to go before I could rest. I dug the harness and robe out of the backpack.

"Program the E-Prime coordinates, and I'll join you there later," I said, handing her the harness.

"Aren't you coming with us?" she asked, incredulous.

"I made a promise, and I have to keep it."

"To a hallucination. It's nothing more than a ball of energy, and if the containment fails while you're there, you might not make it back."

She'd never believe in nightmares, even though we'd followed one in the tunnels. But I knew about the poor, sick creature trapped on Beta, and I couldn't in good conscience leave it there. Besides, if I tried to rescue it, maybe Smokey's demon council would look more favorably on the DCs and not recycle their dimension—especially after the mess I'd caused in D-space.

"I'm going to ask Smokey to help. Maybe we can save the Beta dimension."

"You've done enough," she argued. "You saved R-Prime and brought down a drug lord. Don't take foolish risks."

"If I'm going to be a DC, taking risks comes with the territory, doesn't it?" I gazed down into her amber eyes and saw her concern looking back. It gave me a warm, fuzzy feeling. "I won't do anything stupid, I promise."

Sammie programmed my harness, gave me a rib-crushing bear hug, and ran after her father without saying another word. Doc watched her go.

"I'm sorry," he said. "I misjudged you. I assumed you were delusional without proof. I like to think I'm a better man than that. I hope you'll give me a chance to prove it."

"Um... I *am* delusional. Just not about the black robes," I said, making a careful study of my trainers. "Or that Rap, Eagle."

Doc laughed. "Life will be interesting with you around. I look forward to getting to know you. Good luck on your mission."

He offered a handshake, and I took it. His grip was warm and firm and his smile sincere. I thought it possible that I'd made a second friend, which seemed beyond belief. Then he walked to the moving van and got in. I stared at the van's taillights until it turned south toward the hospital, sinking loneliness filling my chest.

I guzzled the rest of my water and munched a granola bar as I jogged to the fracture. The sooner I completed my mission, the sooner I could go home, too, and that's where I wanted to be.

23

I stood back from the sparkly wall and shrugged the harness on over my parka. The cuffs cut the undertow, but I didn't want to be too close all the same. It looked less shiny, and if I stared at the edge long enough, bits of red brick gradually replaced the vague images beyond. I hoped that meant I'd acted in time.

A translucent black cloud zoomed around me and stopped in the air three feet away. A grin split my face.

"Hey, soot-ball, you made it!" The little nightmare jittered up and down like a drug addict in need of a fix. My tattoos warned of an approaching demon.

"Yes," Smokey said from behind me, resignation in his voice. "It seems most resilient."

I spun around, glad to see him, too. "Will it be okay?"

"It cannot last long if it remains with you, and it seems loathe to leave."

"Oh," I said, worry replacing my elation. "Is there anything I can do?"

"Order it away, and then ignore it."

I glanced at the nightmare and frowned. I hadn't intended to create it, but I had, and I felt responsible for it. Kicking it into the Dark Place to survive or die didn't seem right.

"Can you take care of it for me? As a favor? So it doesn't get eaten? So it grows up to be a demon?"

Smokey's brows drew down. "Favor? I am not familiar with that concept."

I sighed. "It's where you agree to do something for someone, but you don't know what you'll get in return, except that if you need to ask for a favor in the future, the person you did the favor for has some obligation to help you."

The demon spread his arms. "This seems like a poor bargain. Why would creatures agree to such an uncertain thing?"

I mulled that one over for a minute. "Because they're friends, and they trust one another."

"Ah, *friends*," he said. "Like the souls I sampled to help you get the robe."

"Oh, uh, not exactly. More like the affiliate and me." I took a deep breath. "Or like you and me."

"You and me, Traveler? We're friends?"

"Well... yeah," I replied, thinking I might have gotten myself into hot water again. I really needed to rein in the bargaining with demons stuff. "You helped me get the robe, and I saved this dimension for you."

"For my master," Smokey said.

"For your master. But that helps you, doesn't it? You'll get a raise or a bonus or something?"

His fat cow lips twisted into a smile. "My master will satiate his hunger with another instead of me."

"If I didn't save this dimension, he'd *eat* you? Why was he so keen on saving this dimension anyway? Don't demons specialize in recycling?"

He laughed. "When dimensions are recycled, new space is created. My master controls a large, desirable area near this dimension. Were there to be a glut of new space available, demons would migrate away, and my master's power would diminish."

I stared, unable to believe my ears. "Saving this dimension was all about *real estate prices*?"

"Power drives all things, Traveler, in your world and in mine." He turned his eyes on my soot-ball. "You wish me to mentor your nightmare? And in the future, you'll do something I ask?"

"Within reason," I hedged. He frowned at me. "I mean, it can't be morally objectionable, like killing someone. Or myself."

The big demon used his long, sharp talons to scratch his well-muscled bovine cheek while he contemplated. "It is like its creator—willful and clever. It will require much work. But I will do this for you."

His eyes showed a disconcerting eagerness. I'd missed something. He'd gotten the better deal, and I'd been hoodwinked. *Damn.* I resolved to have no further bargains with him despite my claims to friendship. I turned to the soot-ball.

"I know you want to stay with me," I said, "but you can't."

The nightmare slipped away, seemly stung by my words.

"You can't live in my world, and I don't want you to starve. Or be eaten. You go with Smokey. He'll take care of you. And teach you."

It looped around in circles, indecisive.

"I appreciate how much you've helped me. I won't forget you, I promise. But you have to go with Smokey and do what he tells you. Go on. Go to Smokey."

The soot-ball floated to Smokey, circled once, and slumped near his left shoulder. It broke my heart, but we both had to move on. At least I hadn't abandoned it.

"The black robes trapped a nightmare," I said. "It's big and getting bigger. I promised I would get it out, but I don't know how to do that without destroying the dimension."

Smokey's brows lowered. "If it's large but still has no form, the danger of collapse is great. To save the dimension, it must be sundered before it attempts to breach the barrier."

"Sundered?" I asked, guilt riding my conscience. Hadn't I promised the nightmare that I'd keep it safe?

"And the pieces managed as they flee to minimize damage. Such an operation is fraught with danger. I will require help."

"What can I do?"

"Not you, Traveler. I must find others of my kind to undertake the task."

"Other demons?" Boy, the crowd I ran with these days.

"Other soul keepers. Only they have the ability to survive in your space." Smokey strode toward the fracture. "I will gather them and meet you there."

He stepped through the sparkly wall and was gone. I tapped my chest plate and followed.

The Dark Place was a mess. The demon chorus seemed both harmonious and discordant at the same time. The usual cast of bizarre creatures moved amid the devastated landscape, but they retreated from my passing. I was broken down in a billion component atoms and reassembled, like I imagined the Star Trek transporters must work, only it took place a million times before I emerged—on my chest—in the Beta dimension fracture building.

The floor was just as cold and hard as ever, but I didn't feel it through my warm coat. Once my stomach arrived, I climbed to my feet and did my usual checklist to make sure I'd materialized with all my body parts.

The Beta dimension wasn't getting any warmer—or any lighter. Faint moonlight shone through the translucent panels near the ceiling. I could make out shapes, but little else. I groped around the shelves where the robes were kept and found a flashlight before I cracked open the door.

Outside, the moon reflected off new-fallen snow that covered the burned-out hulk of the three cabins, the charred trunk and limbs of the tree in the center of the compound, and the skeleton of the windmill. I smiled. I'd done a darn good job distracting everyone while Sammie got away with the sleepers. Then guilt crept over me. I shouldn't take pleasure in wanton destruction.

The cargo hauler was just visible under its layer of snow, and I was glad for that. Even with my new parka to keep me warm, I didn't think I could make the ruins on foot, at least not before the nightmare broke loose. Somewhere out there a canine voice howled, and another answered. I shivered. Definitely not going on foot.

A cold wind whistled in the door. No point standing around freezing when I didn't know how long I might have to wait for Smokey. I trudged through knee-high drifts to the platform. When I got there, I remembered that I'd blown off the door. *Crap.* So much for a warm ride to the ruins. I scooped snow from the cab.

"We're ready, Traveler," Smokey intoned.

I jerked and whacked my head on the cabin roof as my tattoos burned. When I turned around, I jerked again.

Smokey stood beside the platform with two companions, both of whom towered over him. One was an ogre with a twisted face covered in boils, uneven eyes, misshapen shoulders, a bent back, and heavy legs that ended in enormous flat feet. The other was a troll, all pointy teeth, chimpanzee ears, fur-covered body, and talons that rivaled Smokey's.

My heart raced. Were a friend's friends automatically my friends, too? I hoped not. But wait, if they weren't my friends, did that make them my enemies? With friends like the three of them, who *needed* enemies. I gulped.

"Um, we won't all fit inside," I said, gesturing at the cab.

"Unfortunate," Smokey said. "They wish to converse with you to better understand your kind."

Sweat broke out on my forehead. "Maybe you can ride on the back? We can talk while we walk through the ruins."

Smokey nodded and climbed on the flatbed. The two companions joined him. They did not look happy, but who was I to say what constituted a normal demon expression?

The soot-ball zoomed into the cab with me. I got the impression it didn't like Smokey's friends any better than I did. I began to question sending it to live with the big demon. How well did I know him? Did I want my nightmare raised in an environment with ogres and trolls? Then I chastised myself for judging others by their appearance. Maybe they were perfectly nice hideous demons. Heck, in their world, they might be considered handsome.

In no time, we came to rest at the entrance to the ruins. By the light of the moon, I could see an arm protruding from the debris cluttering the bottom of the ramp. My gorge rose, and I turned away, swallowing hard.

Smokey's posse joined me, and we walked down the ramp together, the soot-ball racing ahead into the darkness, and then tearing back again like a yo-yo on a long tether. I switched on the flashlight as we descended deeper into the tunnels where no moonlight reached.

The faint sound of the trapped nightmare's siren song swirled in my brain. *Shit.* I hoped it hadn't been feeding again. We might not reach it before it grew strong enough to break the containment field. I broke into a run, envious of the demons' long legs; they strolled easily beside me, although Smokey's brows were drawn down.

We twisted and turned through the tunnels, following the soot-ball until it reached the containment control room. I stopped outside, and the demons scrunched down to look through the window. The troll rumbled and the ogre hissed his displeasure. Maybe it wasn't such a good idea coming here.

"What evil is this?" Smokey asked. Smoke billowed from his nostrils.

I thought it was a rhetorical question and didn't answer, but they all glared at me. I felt suddenly very small standing in their midst. The soot-ball whirled around them before coming to rest between them and me.

"It's okay," I told it. "I can handle this. They're on my turf."

Smokey arched an eyebrow. "You believe we cannot harm you?"

A chill crept up my spine. "No, uh, what I meant is I can explain."

The big demon crossed his arms, and the other two loomed closer. The siren call of the trapped nightmare rose to a scream.

"The black robes did this. They're all dead or crazy now. The affiliate and I destroyed the knowledge so no one can do it again. Ever," I babbled, terrified of what the demons might do to me. "What they did was wrong, and that's why I asked for your help. So I could do what's right. Because this isn't. Right, I mean."

Smokey's eyes narrowed. He looked from me to the containment chamber.

"This is much worse than expected. It is ten times the size of the one that destroyed the black robe dimension. When we have dealt with the abomination, you must destroy all of this and never allow it to be created again."

"Absolutely," I agreed. "For sure. No problem. Everything destroyed. Just let me know when you're ready to have me turn it loose."

"If we fail to sunder the abomination and direct its energy to a single small fracture, it will create a massive weak area in the barrier as it exits to Between. The weak area will develop small tears first, then burst, causing a catastrophic collapse.

"I tell you this as warning," the demon admonished. "Neither we nor you can survive the destructive power at the core of a full collapse. Should one start, you must leave this place as soon as fractures large enough to accommodate you open. That is your only hope for survival."

"Got it," I said, shaking in my trainers. "If that thing gets loose, run."

"We will prepare." The three of them disappeared into the darkness.

I pulled open the door to the control room and stepped inside to await Smokey's signal but stayed well back from the glass. The control panel winked with a handful of red lights scattered among the green. Had there been that many before?

The trapped nightmare screeched louder and roiled like a huge storm cloud. Maybe it had seen the three demons or sensed their presence. I wished I hadn't threatened it with being eaten. I felt like a traitor. It threw itself at the curtains of light surrounding it. Miniature lightning bolts shot out from the contact, and the curtains wavered.

I heard footsteps behind me and turned. Black Robe pulled the control room door open, banana gun pointed at my chest.

"So you're a deviant as well as a super-talent," he said, his eyes alight with anger as he scanned me from head to toe.

My cheeks flamed. He probably couldn't see it under the powder. I resented his assumption that I was a drag queen just because I was dressed in a wig, fake boobs, and makeup.

He glanced over the panels, tossed his robe on the back of a chair, and waved me away from the controls.

"Give yourself up," I said with more confidence than I felt. "The rest of your people are dead or in custody, and One's gone mad, not that he wasn't already. I destroyed his research. No one will do this again."

Black Robe laughed, and surprisingly, it didn't sound mad, which made it all the more chilling.

"What do I care about One? He was merely a political puppet, a minion meant to clear red tape for my research. This is *my* work, not his. As long as I live, my research lives." He reached into his pocket and drew out a square of plastic that he waved in the air. "Besides, I have a back-up copy of everything."

Anger boiled in my stomach, and I clenched my teeth. "Even if you get away, you won't have the sleepers to create another nightmare."

"I don't need them," he replied, grinning. "I have you. You're the most powerful super-talent I've seen. And you're more durable, too. As soon as I've added the latest data from the containment computer, we'll be on our way to E-4."

He plugged the plastic square into a slot on the computer under the desk and tapped on the keyboard while keeping an eye on me. My little soot-ball writhed and twisted around him, its contortions a mirror for my own frustration.

What had I done? If he succeeded, he'd do this again. Millions more would suffer. I hadn't saved E-4 just so he could destroy it. I couldn't let him get away, but throwing myself on his banana gun didn't seem like a sensible solution. I looked around the room, taking in the nightmare and the robe on the chair beside me. I asked myself what price I was willing to pay to make sure he never harmed anyone—or any demon—again.

"Tell Smokey to go now," I said to the soot-ball in a low voice. "And you go with him."

"What?" Black Robe asked, looking at me.

The little nightmare hovered a moment, then flew out the crack around the door.

"I said it's over."

I took two quick steps to the containment window and pressed my hand against it. The curtains of light vanished, and the nightmare exploded past the pylons of the containment field. It whirled and seethed around the room, looking for a way out.

In the control room, all the lights flashed red, and an alarm wailed at an ear-shattering level. Black Robe turned to check the same panel Sammie had when the field flickered, just as I'd hoped. I stepped up behind him, grabbed the banana gun from his grasp, and fired at his robe. It and the chair blasted through the glass window and bounced away into the corridor, tatters of robe trailing behind. Black Robe twisted toward me, but the gun kept him back.

My tattoos flared, and I eased back to where I could keep an eye on Black Robe and look into the corridor.

"Traveler, why did you release the abomination?"

"Hey, Smokey," I replied as he strode into the light. "No choice."

The big nightmare went nuts, sieved through around the control room window, and boiled on out into the corridor. It flowed around the big demon, who slashed at it with his talons, which only seemed to make it roil faster. His ruddy skin paled, and he shrank six inches while the nightmare grew more dense. With a gasp, I realized the nightmare was *eating* Smokey.

The ogre and the troll stepped out of the darkness and waded in. The twisted faces and mutilated bodies of screaming humans writhed inside the nightmare, and the two demons sliced and diced, separating pieces that swirled away toward the ceiling.

The nightmare responded with a brief attack on the newcomers, but it must have known it would lose. It swelled suddenly spreading itself thin, and then it was gone. Thousands of sparkling cracks lit the space for as far as I could see. In seconds, they began to gap open and tear wider. The troll and the ogre stepped to the nearest and slipped through, even though they were much too big to fit. A seven-foot tall Smokey wobbled to the shattered wall of the control room, eyes dulled.

"We have failed. Go now, Traveler, or die," Smokey intoned, and then he, too, slid through a crack and was gone.

Black Robe had sidled closer while I'd watched the battle with the nightmare. I waved him back and moved toward the door, putting more space between us.

"The dimension is collapsing. Set your destination and get out. You don't have much time."

"Without a robe?" he asked, eying the gun. "I'd go mad."

"Too late, you already are," I said, tapping at my own plate. "At least you'll still be alive."

"Give me your robe. You don't need it to survive. I have a bad heart. Traveling without a robe will kill me. You'll be a murderer. Can you live with that?"

Hell. I'd thought offering him alive and mad or dead would absolve me of guilt for the consequences of his choice. But he'd turned the tables so the choice—and the consequences—were all on me. If I sent him to E-4 with a robe, could I count on Knowles to keep him locked up forever? What if he got off on a technicality? He'd be right back to his dirty tricks.

The multitude of fractures widened and brightened, and one behind me gapped ominously. The tug of the Dark Placed pulled at me like a riptide. How long until we'd passed the point of no return and the dimension shattered?

"You made your choice when you tortured your first victim," I said.

He lunged at me but didn't connect. I'd already been sucked through the widening fracture behind me.

24

The turbulence in the Dark Place tumbled me like a load of aggregate in a cement mixer. I'd been blasted to smithereens, burned by fires, frozen, broken, eaten. None of it matched this trip. I'd always been vividly aware of my surroundings, but this time, I was battered to near unconsciousness. Had I left it too long? Was this my final crossing? My sense of self ran away from my brain like water through a sieve. I clung to life with desperation.

And then I slammed down on a concrete floor. No garbage pile. No soft-by-comparison composite. Good old-fashioned rock-hard concrete. My stomach cannonballed into my aching guts. I spewed blood-tinged vomit onto the floor.

When I looked up, the room spun a little. Two soldiers stood over me pointing rifles at my head. Some things never change. I didn't bother getting up. Someone would drag me away sooner or later.

"Stand down," Doc's voice ordered. "He's one of ours."

The soldiers stepped back and lowered their aim about six inches, but they remained alert. Maybe it was the robe. Or maybe they'd never seen a drag queen before.

Doc crouched beside me. His fingers found my pulse.

"Are you okay?" he asked, looking at his watch.

"Um... yeah. Great," I croaked. "Never better."

He frowned but helped me up. When he reached for my robe, I flinched away. Old habits die hard.

"Sorry," he said. "You'll need to leave the equipment here. We keep everything under lock and key."

He stood back while I stripped off the robe, and struggled out of the harness. One of the soldiers took everything away. The other remained, watching me.

"I'll need to frisk you," Doc said. "And search your pack. It's regulations."

For a moment, I thought about asking for the robe and harness back. I'd saved two dimensions. Did they think I intended to sabotage this one? I gave Doc an icy glare and handed over the backpack. He unzipped it, gave a cursory glance inside, and closed it again.

"Looks good," he said. His hands barely touched me when he frisked my pockets. He didn't bother with my legs or the small of my back where I'd seen so many thugs carry a gun.

"No weapons," he announced. "Let's get you to your quarters. You look like you could use some rest."

I took a wobbly step, and he stopped short.

"Should I get a wheelchair?"

Wheelchair? I shook my head and did my best to steady up. I didn't want anyone to think I was a sissy. Bad enough I looked like a girl. That got me thinking.

"This is a disguise," I said. "You know that, right?"

"Damn fine one," he said, a twinkle in his eye. "The soot's a nice touch. Adds to the 'damsel in distress' look."

The big room seemed incredibly warm all of a sudden, and I wished I'd kept my mouth shut.

"You can shower when you get up to your quarters."

I wanted to ask a zillion questions, but I decided to get the lay of the land before I said anything more. I'd made enough of a fool of myself for one day.

We went through large double doors and walked an institutional gray hallway that ended at two elevators. One was a huge shaft with an empty open freight elevator parked in it; the other was a conventional human conveyance. I lurched to a halt and sweat blossomed on my forehead.

"Claustrophobic?" Doc asked. "We can take the freight elevator if it'll help."

"Are there stairs?" I asked.

"Are you sure you can make it?"

"I could use the exercise," I lied.

Doc's eyes narrowed. "You have a delusion associated with elevators."

I felt like he'd stripped me naked and waited for him to laugh. After all, being afraid of elevators was crazy.

"Sorry to hear that," he said. "We're three flights down. Stairs are over here. Lean on me if you need to."

I followed him to the stairs, amazed at his casual acceptance of my lunacy. To cover my embarrassment, I said, "Three flights down from where?"

"Our fracture's underground, in an old mine. The rest of the facility is on the surface. After the mine went bust last century, a group of monks built a monastery on the site and used the tunnels to age wine. Then the place got turned into a boarding school, and now the locals think it's a military school. Not a bad cover."

We made our way up, up, up until we emerged in a small room where two armed soldiers stood guard. One of them unlocked heavy steel doors that opened into another small room with more guards and more steel doors. The place seemed more like a prison than a school, and foreboding crept up my spine.

We came out into crisp, cold air, a night sky dusted with stars, and a full moon spreading its light on an open courtyard surrounded by three-story stone buildings. Mountains etched a jagged line across the horizon on one side, and reflected city lights glowed against the sky on the other.

"Where are we?" I asked.

"Northern Idaho," Doc said. "Hope you like snow."

We crossed the quad, entered one of the buildings, and went up one flight of stairs. Doc opened a door near the end, flipped on an overhead light, and waved me in. The light warbled *Home* off-key and made me want to cover my ears.

"This is your room while you're in training, or until high command decides to play musical chairs with the room assignments again," he said. "I guessed at your clothing size. If anything doesn't fit, let me know, and we'll get something that does. We'll try on boots tomorrow. Just wear your running shoes until then."

I ran my hand over the single bed along one wall. The bedding included a soft pillow, real sheets, and a scratchy green blanket, all done up with fancy military corners and pleats. I wasn't sure I could make it look that good again and thought I might sleep on the floor so I wouldn't mess it up.

A lamp stood on a scarred wooden desk next to a battered wardrobe. The lamp hummed *Swing Low, Sweet Chariot* off-key, even though it wasn't turned on. Doc opened the wardrobe to show me a row of shirts and pants hung neat as a pin and drawers with brand new briefs and socks. It would take me weeks to pay for it all, assuming they'd let me leave the grounds to earn money.

"This is more than I need. Maybe you could take some of it back?"

"Don't let the bean counters hear you," Doc said in a mock whisper. At my puzzled look, he continued, "It's part of your benefits, along with free health care and paid vacations."

"Oh, yeah, benefits," I said, trying to sound like a normal person who knew all about these things.

He opened another door to a bathroom with a sink, toilet, and shower. My eyes nearly popped out of my head. Fluffy white towels hung on the rack, and a full-size bar of soap rested in a little dimple on the sink. More benefits, I guessed. How could the government afford all this decadence? This must be why it was going broke.

A window in the main room looked out on the moonlit quad—and there weren't any bars on it. Not a bad view. My creeping case of jangled nerves ebbed a bit.

"It's all mine?" I asked. I'd never had a room to myself in my life, except for when I'd slept in garden sheds or rickety long-abandoned farm houses, and even those I'd shared with mice and spiders. "I don't have a roommate?"

Doc chuckled. "You're the first to think it's big enough to share. You'll have a full day tomorrow, so get a good night's rest. Someone will come by in the morning to take you to breakfast."

With that, he left me to my own devices.

I stood in the middle of the room and turned around three times trying to take it all in. Maybe it was a hallucination. It seemed too good to be true. A home. A place I belonged. Or at least I thought I did. I wished I'd asked Doc more questions about what happened next. Too late now.

What to do? I stripped off my clothes, removed the wig, and put on my watch cap. Then I tried out the shower. There was more soap on a ledge, and a bottle of shampoo, too. I scrubbed every inch of me twice, except for my scalp. A quick once-over was all I could stand before I jammed the cap back on. Ants don't like shampoo. It makes them dance twice as fast.

Curious to see how I'd look as a real DC, I put on the new clothes. Doc did a pretty good job with the size. I gazed in the mirror, and a homeless schizophrenic playing dress-up stared back. I guess clothes didn't make the DC.

At loose ends again, I wondered what I should do next. I ought to get some sleep, but I was too wound up. The overhead light sang *Wasting Away in Margaritaville*, and the desk lamp added off-key harmony. I switched the overhead light out, but the two bulbs sang on, undaunted.

Refusing to be bested by a pair of light bulbs, I dragged the desk into position under the overhead light, stood on it in my bare feet, and removed the bulb. I shoved the desk back and unscrewed the desk lamp bulb. Both bulbs got marched to the bathroom and stashed in the medicine cabinet above the sink. When I left, I slammed the door behind me. *Take that, you losers.*

I don't know how long I stood by the window staring out at the stars. I slept outdoors quite often, and the stars at least felt familiar. Nothing else did. Maybe I'd wake up in the morning and discover the last couple days were all some psychotic episode. What a cruel joke that would be.

The door opened a crack, and light flooded in. I blinked and held up a hand to shield my eyes. Sammie stood in the doorway.

"Sorry," she said. "I knocked but you didn't answer. I was worried about you. Can I come in?"

"Oh... uh... sure," I said, words catching in my throat.

She flipped the light switch by the door without result. "Your bulb's burnt out."

Undeterred, she walked to the desk and tried the lamp. When it didn't work either, she swiveled it toward the door and frowned.

"The bulb's missing."

I winced. "Um, they're having a timeout. In the bathroom."

She stared at me a moment. Then she turned away to look around the room while she struggled not to smile. My cheeks warmed. I gestured toward the window.

"The moonlight's nice," I said. "And environmentally friendly."

Sammie closed the door and joined me in the silvery pool of light. It made her look all the more magical and beautiful. I was stumped for what to say.

"How're you doing?" she asked.

"Oh, um, I have my own room. And new clothes. And there's a shower with hot water." I gazed down at her smiling up at me, and I wasn't sure she was listening. "And... it's all kind of strange and scary."

She stepped in close, wrapped her arms around my neck, and kissed me. On the lips. I froze. She lurched back, worry and confusion on her face.

"I shouldn't have done that. I thought when you mentioned the moonlight, you meant— I'm sorry. It won't happen again," she assured me.

Won't happen again? No!

"It's not you. It's just, I've never done that before. Kissed. I guess I'm not very good at it. Kissing, I mean." I hung my head, heat shooting up my face. I touched my fingers to my lips where they still tingled. "It was... wow."

Sammie gave me a hesitant smile. "You'd get better with practice. Would you like to practice?"

Of course I wanted to practice kissing with Sammie. Who wouldn't? But what if I screwed it up? She'd might never want to kiss me again. Ever. My chin took matters into its own hands and nodded while my mind churned over all the potential disaster scenarios.

She stepped close and put her arms around me. Then ever so slowly, she raised her lips to mine. With trepidation, I put my arms around her, careful to touch only the middle of her back. Her lips were warm and soft and inviting. My fear faded away, and so did my fatigue.

We practiced there in the moonlight for quite a long time, until Sammie decided we'd practiced enough. She smiled up at me with sparkling eyes and brushed my cheek with her fingers.

"River, would you like to be with me?"

She had me flummoxed. I was with her now, wasn't I? Boy, did I need that manual.

"Um, we *are* together, aren't we?"

She dropped her eyes with an embarrassed grin. Then she squared her shoulders and looked straight at me.

"Do you want to make love with me?"

I hadn't seen that coming. All my social anxiety rushed back and turned me to stone. What if I did it wrong? What if I touched something I shouldn't? Was I destined for another right cross? Would I get kicked out of the DCs?

"I haven't done that before, either," I stammered.

"I figured," she said, a beguiling smile curving her lips.

She led me to the bed and unbuttoned my shirt. She slipped it off and dropped it in a heap on the floor. I worried that it might get wrinkled, and I didn't have an iron. Maybe I could steam the wrinkles out in the shower. I stopped worrying about my shirt when she unzipped my fly and dropped my pants around my ankles.

I felt like I ought to be participating more, but I didn't want to fumble her buttons with my shaking fingers. Sammie solved my problem by unbuttoning her own shirt and adding it to the growing pile of clothing on the floor. For such a dedicated soldier, she wore a surprisingly lacy black bra. A moment later she'd kicked off her boots, shed her socks, and unstrapped her knife from her leg. She dropped her drawers to reveal black lace panties that matched her bra.

The room seemed too well lit for further disrobing unless we turned our backs. Before I could suggest that, Sammie unclasped her bra and revealed soft mounded breasts in perfect proportion with her trim body. I admit it—I stared. She caught me. My face became an inferno to rival a supernova.

"It's okay to look," she said, laughing.

Her panties went next, and my breath came in ragged gulps. Then she pulled down my spiffy new briefs. The waistband caught on my rock hard erection. I thought she'd be disgusted. She gave me a pleased grin and pushed me between the sheets. I didn't have a clue about women.

She slid in beside me, all soft and warm. Her fingers set my skin on fire. Her soft voice encouraged me to touch, to taste, to explore. When I didn't think it could get any better, she took me inside her, and I learned how amazing touch can be. How two can be one, whole and complete.

Afterward, she snuggled against my shoulder, her warm breath soughing across my chest. I wrapped my arms around her and wanted to hold her forever.

"Friends," I said, savoring the word.

She squeezed my ribs and said, "Lovers."

Lovers. Joy exploded in me. I could never go back to the loneliness of the road, never again deny that yawning black chasm of emptiness that only love could fill. Not after feeling this. I'd thought home was a place. I'd had it wrong. Sammie was the home I needed. I basked in her warmth.

And then I chilled. What if this was all a hallucination? Light bulbs didn't sing when they were turned off, but they'd sung tonight. What if Sammie weren't here with me? What if we weren't lovers? I needed independent verification, but where would I get it?

"Sammie, will you still be here in the morning?"

"Not this time," she replied. "Dad and I have an early flight. We're taking Griff home for burial."

She must have picked up on my worry. She propped herself on an elbow and watched me.

"What's wrong?"

I scrunched down my brows, thinking hard. "How will I know it's real?"

Her eyes opened wide. "You think this is a hallucination?"

"Or a vivid dream. I have them sometimes, especially if I'm stressed or over-tired."

Her lips set in a straight line while she stared off at the wall. Then she looked back.

"How do you usually tell what's real?"

"Pain." At her puzzled look I said, "Real things hurt. Hallucinations don't."

Insight flashed in her eyes, and she grinned. "Don't worry, you'll know."

She put her head on my shoulder and patted my chest.

"I'll stay until you fall asleep."

I resolved to remain awake the rest of the night. I wanted to imprint every moment with Sammie in my memory. I wouldn't waste a single second. I'd meditate to push my worry away. I'd relax. I'd focus on her soft fingers stroking my chest, her warm body pressing against mine, the rhythm of her breathing, the scent of her body, the...

###

I awoke with a jerk to the sound of knuckles rapping on wood.

"Let's go, Madden," a voice called through the door. "Breakfast in fifteen."

I looked around disoriented. I was naked, and I always slept fully clothed, never knowing when I might need to run. Had I slipped through a fracture? No, wait, I still wore my watch cap.

Groggy, I swung my feet over the edge of the bed and sat up. The promise of sunrise glimmered through the window.

The window. The light.

Had Sammie really been here? I'd acknowledged my need for love, and now I couldn't live without it, at least not as anything more than the worthless husk of a man. How could I know? She'd promised me I would.

My eyes searched the room. My clothes were neatly folded on the corner of the desk. But I could have put them there. Being a neat freak was a coping mechanism against the schizophrenia. Nothing else looked out of place in a room where nothing seemed familiar.

Except for Sammie's big knife on the bedside table.

I stared, afraid to touch it. Was it a cruel trick of my brain? I reached for the handle, stopped inches away. Maybe I didn't need proof. Maybe it was better to believe a lie than discover the truth. But I had to know. I grasped the knife.

The rubberized handle felt cool against my fingers. I held the knife before my eyes. Light glinted off the blade. I raised a forefinger and pressed it against the tip. It pricked my skin, and blood welled from the tiny cut.

"Real," I whispered, my eyes misting.

"*Real.*"

Coming March 2013

Undercover Madness

K S Ferguson

Light bulbs still serenade River Madden, but at least the hapless schizophrenic has a job now. As the newest recruit at Dimensional Protective Service, River's anxious to prove himself. His first assignment: rescue a scientist who's been lost in D-space. When River finds his target, the man's dead. The Neans claim a demon did it. The FBI and the CIA think River's the culprit. The light bulbs aren't talking. Can River unravel the web of lies and spies to find a mole and stop a madman before the demons destroy the human and Nean dimensions?

For more information, visit http://www.ksferguson.net

Also by K S Ferguson

Calculated
RISK

Rafe McTavish, charming self-made businessman, owns the most successful private security firm in the galaxy. Estranged from his family since his wife's bloody suicide fourteen years earlier, he's nevertheless honor-bound to find out why his brother-in-law, CEO of the mega-corporation EcoMech, has placed his reputation and the company's future in jeopardy by purchasing a dilapidated deep-space mining station.

Kama Bhatia, outlaw computer hacker and corporate spy, works for socialistic non-profit corporation Oasis, in opposition to the ruthless mega-corporations that control society. She has a mission of her own at the mining station: retrieve a secret document accidentally leaked to the station manager—before he can sell it to Oasis' rivals. If she fails, Oasis loses its best hope to rescue the masses from under the iron boot of the mega-corporations.

But at the station, the crooked manager is missing, and the locals are far from friendly. Rafe takes a savage beating from miners who blame him and his corporate employers for fraud perpetrated against them. His safety relies on Kama, an ally no fonder of corporate executives than he is of criminals. With their own lives and the welfare of millions at stake, can they put aside their mutual attraction and distrust to unravel fraud, blackmail, and murder before the tide of violence overtakes them?

For more information, visit http://www.ksferguson.net/.

Calculated Risk: Excerpt

1

The giant swordsman thrust Rafe's short sword aside, thumping the blade against the steel bulkhead. Rafe ducked another strike. His forehead glanced off his assailant's knee, blurring his vision. He'd thought he could take on two at once. He was better-trained, more experienced, and at thirty, still as quick as he'd ever be—and *damned* if he was going to lose this fight. But these guys were built like gorillas and quicker than he'd expected. Each topped six feet by several inches, while Rafe barely made a lithe five foot ten. They'd kill him.

Rafe shook stars from his eyes. He feinted to the left, dove into a forward roll down the EcoMech space yacht's companionway, spun, and thrust a killing strike to the kidneys of one of the men. The other surged forward, his shoulder taking Rafe in the chest. Rafe fell hard and rolled left as his adversary's sword crashed down. His opponent loomed over him. He kicked out, catching the man in the knee and unsettling his balance long enough for a last, desperate thrust to the throat.

"Ow!" shouted his opponent, clapping his hand to his neck.

Rafe scrambled to his feet. "Sorry, Cookie. I got carried away. You okay?"

The ship's cook laughed and placed the rubberized practice sword into Rafe's hand, then tapped on his nanocom gauntlet. "All right, Mr. McTavish, you've won the bet. I'll upload my chili recipe to your account."

"Rafe. Call me Rafe. Don't forget any secret ingredients." He grinned and pushed sweat-dampened hair off his forehead. His own nanocom chimed, and an unopened mail announcement replaced the date and time on the tiny screen—23:45, 11 March, 2040.

The cook's assistant handed over his sword and clapped Rafe on the shoulder. "Thanks for the sparring match. Haven't had so much fun since I left the service. You're strong for a little guy."

The backhanded compliment brought back fond memories from when Rafe led a squad of mercenaries in the field instead of languishing behind a CEO's desk. He couldn't remember now why he'd thought that running his own security company would be more satisfying than commanding a close-knit combat team for Earth Authority.

The vibration of the ship's engines changed pitch, and a second

later, Rafe felt the bang of a docking collar. The other two registered the
change and glanced down the companionway toward the cargo bays and
airlock. They exchanged a wary look and turned away.

"What's up?" Rafe asked. "I thought once we cleared the Earth-to-
asteroid-belt jump gate, we were going straight through to the mining
station?"

Cookie spoke over his shoulder. "Captain Benson didn't tell you?
We're picking up passengers at the jump gate station."

The men disappeared into the ship's galley. Little prickles raised the
hairs on Rafe's arms. He could think of only one person with the authority to divert his borrowed ride. The hatch at the end of the companionway
banged back.

As Rafe feared, Leon Goldman, the subject of his stealth investigation, stamped through. He looked fifteen years older than Rafe, even
though only four years separated them. His brown hair was swept back
and plastered with too much hair gel. A stylish business suit did nothing
to enhance his pudgy shape. Even at a distance, the chunky gold wedding ring on his left hand and the diamond studded band on his right
flashed in the light. His beefy cheeks and bulbous nose glowed pink, like
he'd had one too many drinks, but his walk was sure and swift, and his
hazel eyes promised trouble.

Captain Benson, the yacht's commander, trailed in Leon's wake,
his normal upright posture slightly bent in deference to the EcoMech
CEO. Rafe steeled himself for the coming confrontation, uncomfortable in
Leon's presence, but confident he could suffer through.

Leon's wife, Amaya, clattered down the companionway next, the
flared legs of a black pantsuit swishing around her swollen ankles, her
skin more yellow than Rafe remembered. In the dim light, her slanted
brown eyes appeared sunken, and her black hair hung straight and
unadorned to her waist. Her expression made his breath catch; the same
sour, judgmental air she'd had since she was ten.

The blood curdled in Rafe's veins, and the temperature in the companionway dropped ten degrees. He hadn't seen his sister-in-law since
his wife's death, fourteen years ago. Amaya leaned on the arm of a young
Adonis, Leon's eleven-year-old son, Gabe. His bright blue eyes darted
around the ship, awe on his face. The sight of the boy chafed at old
wounds in Rafe's heart. He forced his gaze back to his brother-in-law.

Leon slammed open the hatch to the executive suite and glanced
inside. "Benson! Clear this room and get our things in here."

"Sir, Mr. McTavish is using—"

"This isn't a debate. Get it done."

Benson's eyes communicated apology, and Rafe shrugged. The captain flagged a crewman loaded with luggage into the suite.

Leon advanced along the companionway.

"Still playing pretend I see."

Rafe glanced at his practice swords. His cheeks warmed, the only source of heat in the suddenly chilly space. *Focus. Breathe. Speak.* He sucked in air, but his lungs seemed unwilling to inflate. "Hello, Leon."

"What brings you way out here, McTavish?" The man's smug eyes glittered like a crocodile's. He folded his arms across his chest.

Crap, he knows. So much for conducting a quiet investigation. Still, Rafe had an obligation to finish what he'd started. "I've been hired to check out this mining station EcoMech wants to purchase. The onsite inspection needs to be completed before the sale goes through."

"And you're such an expert on asteroid mining that you're qualified to do it?" Leon sneered. "Anyway, you're on a fool's errand. I signed the purchase papers yesterday. You can run along home now, back to your toy soldiers and war games."

Rafe counted a slow five and fought the urge to bunch his fists. "Sorry, I have a contract to fulfill, and this is my ride, provided by your father."

Leon's pink face reddened. He stepped closer and dropped his hands to his sides. "You think you're so hot building your little company from your momma's money, living the high life, fast women and faster flyers, a real playboy. Do those mercs you lead know what a coward you are? How you couldn't be bothered to show up for your wife's funeral? Don't tell me you don't break contracts."

Rafe's nerves burned like he'd been poked with a taser. He wanted to run from Leon's accusations, but his muscles wouldn't respond. Fourteen years vanished in a heartbeat, and he stood again in his wife's bedroom. Blood spattered the yellow walls and soaked the lacy white coverlet on the bed. Congealing blood oozed between his bare toes. The scent of slaughter poisoned the air. The memory made his stomach float as if he were in zero gravity. He thought he might vomit on Leon's fancy Italian shoes. The CEO's face glowed with victory.

Rafe jerked closer and smelled the bourbon on Leon's breath. "I follow your father's orders, not yours." His voice came out barely louder than a whisper.

Leon's muscles tensed, and he shook with the effort to maintain his composure. Rafe felt sure a punch was coming, almost hoped for it. His brother-in-law frowned, his control returning but his rage undimmed.

"You won't find anything." Leon grabbed Gabe by the shoulders and dragged him away, ruffling the boy's hair. "Come on, son. Let's go kill some orcs. I've got a new strategy I want to try in that *Galaxy at War* game."

Rafe stared after Leon. Amaya stood by the open door to the executive suite, an icy glare frosting the air between them. She waited. He didn't know what to say, still couldn't express the grief aloud, make the apology he should have made fourteen years ago. With a snort, she disappeared inside and slammed the hatch.

2

Kamala Bhatia slid silently along the empty mining station corridor in the dim half-light of the artificial night. If she hadn't lost her way, the administrative section was just around the corner. She'd spent the last hour trying to access the business server from the safety of her rat hole cabin before determining it was offline.

Damned administrators shutting off the computer at night. How was any self-respecting hacker supposed to crack it when they'd powered it down? She'd find the computer closet, pick the lock, and power it up. A few more minutes decoding the log-on credentials, and she'd plant her search-and-destroy program. Maybe she'd have time to go back to bed for an hour before that bear of a smelter supervisor, Browning, came for her. She hated managers, especially when she'd had less than four hours' sleep.

The lights brightened without warning, and chimes echoed. Kama's heart jumped. In the distance, she heard hinges creak, male voices mumble and complain, and the thump of boots on decks. She focused bleary eyes on the nanocom on her wrist. *Vishnu preserve us, they start at 5:00 a.m.?* She couldn't risk breaking into the computer now.

With all the aplomb she could muster, she slung her duffel bag of computer tools over her shoulder and strolled back the way she'd come. As she walked, she set her nanocom to play *They're Coming to Take Me Away* and chanted along under her breath. It didn't take long for a crowd of miners to gather up ahead. She chided herself for not paying more attention to the station layout and avoiding the living quarters. The wolf whistles and cat calls began at once.

Damn! These guys looked more desperate for female companionship than she'd anticipated, and here she was parading through the thick of them. She never wore makeup, always hid her shapely figure under baggy Oasis Corp coveralls, and pulled her hair back in a business-like ponytail at the base of her neck. And still men swarmed toward her like bees to a butterfly bush.

Kama embedded plugs in her ears. A touch to her nanocom and "heavy metal" droned from the speakers. Another touch and the volume rose loud enough to rattle her teeth. She hooted and stamped down the corridor to the grinding beat of the bass like some lunatic fresh from the asylum. The miners fled. Excellent. She hated using the backup plan: a little vial of *eau du road kill.*

A hand touched her shoulder, and she pivoted to see Edgar Browning, a short, black-skinned man with close-cropped hair, a pugnacious face, and an enormous upper body. He was dressed in work-stained overalls and thick boots. She guessed he was about forty-five—old for a miner. Two tattoos covered his dark forearm, one a crudely-drawn dragon, the other a stenciled prison serial number. He pointed to her nano-com and shouted something. Kama silenced the noise and removed her ear plugs.

"What didn't you understand about 'stay in your quarters until I come for you'?" his gravelly voice scolded. "The last thing I need is you distracting the guys or getting yourself lost. Out here, inattention can kill."

She bristled. Just because she hadn't gotten where she was going didn't mean she was lost. She did her best to feign contrition. "Sorry. My boss likes to know I'm earning my pay, so I thought I'd give him a shout."

"Long range com's down again. Miss Patty'll check it later." Browning gestured to the man beside him."This is Yuri Roshal, our shipping manager."

About forty, immensely tall and thin, with darting eyes and enormous bony hands, Roshal had dark hair and a Slavic cast to his face. He wore cargo pants and a garish yellow t-shirt emblazoned with a sports logo obscured by blotchy red stains. A fidgety man full of nervous energy, he didn't look much better rested than Browning.

Kama nodded and shook the cool hand he offered.

"Mr. Levine around?" she asked.

Browning grimaced. "Admin side don't start the same time as the rest of us. Got something to fill your time, though. Urgent job's come up, and we could use your help."

She froze. Buying Levine's silence and recovering that bloody lost contract was her mission, not helping the two hundred workers at this owner-operated startup.

"Can't start until I check in with the manager. Have to get a rundown of my duties, sign forms, yada, yada..."

Browning's brow furrowed. "Your duties are to do what I damn well need doing," he muttered, rubbing his temples. "Look, it won't take long. Yuri here can give you the lowdown, then you can see Mr. Levine once he's up and about."

"We've got a mass spectrometer array that's acting twitchy," Roshal put in. "We haven't got the tech skills to fix it."

Kama checked the time. She figured she could repair a mass spectrometer in about five minutes and be knocking on Levine's door within ten.

"It can't wait," Browning said. "We stand to strike out on an asteroid claim and can't afford to lose it."

"R. S. Steele's sniffing around it," Roshal added.

Browning's muscular shoulders quivered, and he got a worried look. "Those bloody cowboys. How the hell do they always know when we make a good find?"

Guilt rose in Kama's chest. Whatever her private objectives, however many faceless thousands counted on her, these people were counting on her right here, right now. They weren't powerful executives or company drones; they were independent people trying to make their own way on the backs of their skills. Just the kind of people she and Oasis said they wanted to help.

"All right," she said. "Just the one job. Then I'll need to see Mr. Levine."

Browning broke into a smile, all the more charming for his missing canine tooth. "Thanks, Miss Bhatia! Levine'll be flattered when he finds out how keen you are to meet him. Yuri here will ferry you out to the ship."

"No problem," Roshal chimed in. "I only stopped here to pick up some parts. I'll drop you off on the way to my tug."

Kama did a double-take. "Ship?"

Browning nodded. "Yeah. You know, the ship with the mass spec? Got a prospecting team heading out in a couple hours, and they won't be much good without a working mass spec."

Kama's stomach gnawed on itself, and she struggled not to swear. Five minutes' work, but probably half an hour's journey to and from some isolated ship, and no possibility of an early return. She hoped she wouldn't be too late getting to Levine, or the failure of the entire Sharma Network project might fall on her shoulders.

3

Rafe drilled the little rubber ball to the floor and caught it as it rico-cheted off the far wall. Someone tapped on his cabin door, but he ignored them and threw the ball again. No matter which way he turned the mining station purchase, it didn't add up. He'd traipse around the station with his brother-in-law, send his report to Aaron Goldman, Chairman of EcoMech and Leon's father, and take the first vessel headed home to Earth—as long as it wasn't this one. Not a satisfactory repayment of the debt he owed Aaron, but it would have to do.

The tapping became loud, insistent rapping. Rafe pocketed the ball and sighed. He took the two steps across the cramped cabin and opened the door.

His dead brother Miguel stood in the companionway. The sight stole his breath. On second reflection, he realized that this boy stood at least three inches taller and couldn't be more than seventeen or eighteen, not the twenty-five Miguel had been at his death. Endowed with the same curly black hair and cobalt blue eyes the McTavish men all shared, he wore an ill-fitting business suit and wiped one hand against his trouser leg. The other hand held a filmie.

"Uncle Rafe? I'm Greg." He shuffled his feet and ducked his head. When Rafe didn't step back to let him in, he continued. "You know, Shannon's kid? Your sister? Can I come in?"

Rafe gave the boy his best smile but didn't open the door. "Greg, yes, how nice to see you. Unfortunately, you've come at a bad time. We're arriving at the station soon, and I have to prepare. Perhaps we can talk later."

"Mom has a message for you." Greg glanced down the corridor and lowered his voice. "She doesn't want Mr. Goldman to know about it."

Rafe felt like a violin string—dug out of something's guts and stretched far too tight. He didn't want cryptic messages from his sister. He didn't want anything but for this trip to be over, for the mystery of Leon's inexplicable purchase to quit rattling around inside his head. He waved the boy inside.

Greg glanced around the interior, and Rafe saw it through his eyes. Untidy stacks of filmies tottered on the desk and bedside table, a few sheets already scattered on the floor. A pair of trousers and a shirt hung over the back of the chair. One workout shoe lay in the middle of the floor, and the other—where was the other? His canvas hold-all was kicked against one wall, the practice swords piled on top. Perhaps they should have used Greg's cabin.

Greg seized one of the swords and swished it through the air. "Wow, Gabe told me you had swords. You must go to those Renaissance fair reenactments. Do you have armor? You know, chainmail, or maybe real plate?"

Rafe grabbed the sword and put it back on the hold-all, glad he'd tucked the real sword and off-hand dueling dagger away at the bottom of the bag. "They aren't toys. In space, energy or projectile weapons are no one's friend. Soldiers on ships and orbital stations favor close quarter weapons—knives, swords, nunchucks, batons. Why are you here?"

"Gramps thought I should do an internship with Mr. Goldman. I didn't want to, but Mom said I could help her get information she need-ed. Goldman doesn't like me much."

Rafe lifted an eyebrow. He wondered if the boy used 'Gramps' to the old man's face. "I meant, what's the message?"

"Oh, yeah." He handed over the filmie. "Hey, I know you don't probably remember me, but maybe I could do an internship with you? I mean, with you being a CEO of your own company and all, I could work for you? I bet you're a better boss than Goldman any day. And besides, you're family."

Which is exactly why I'd never hire you. Rafe added Greg's filmie to the pile on the desk. He didn't intend to read it, at least not before he was in his own office on Earth, away from Leon, EcoMech, and his annoying nephew. He took the boy's arm and propelled him toward the door.

"Now isn't the best time. Let me think on it, and we'll talk later."

"You mean it? Thanks! But I can't go unless I have a reply for Mom. She said it was urgent."

Rafe bit back the response he wanted to make, resisted the urge to throw Greg into the corridor, and returned to the filmie:

> *Rafe,*
>
> *I've found corporate documents crediting Dad with push-ing through the purchase of this mining station you're visiting, as though it was all his idea. I've seen the figures. The purchase is a disaster with serious repercussions for EcoMech. When the whole venture fails, Dad will be blamed. He'll have to step down from his position on the board. That'll kill him.*
>
> *We both know this is Leon's doing. I need your help.*
> *Shannon*

He crushed the filmie in his fist and dropped onto the bed, rage spreading like fire through his blood. Couldn't his family understand that he'd disowned them? Why should he rescue a man who hated him, for whom he'd never been good enough?

"Are you all right, Uncle Rafe? You look kind of pale." Greg shuffled his feet. "What should I tell Mom?"

"Tell her..."

He reread the filmie. The CEO's purpose for purchasing the station suddenly became clear: he didn't want to share power with the McTavish family anymore. With Cullen McTavish off the board, only the Goldmans would remain to control EcoMech. Had Aaron Goldman known—or at least suspected—that Leon intended to frame Cullen when he'd coerced Rafe to investigate the purchase? Rafe had questions. Leon had answers.

He pushed past Greg and strode down the cramped hallway. Anger boiling inside him, he swept the dimly lit lounge looking for his brother-in-law. View screens that emulated windows showed the tiny sparks of distant suns scattered over blackness. A thick green carpet damped the constant throb of the ship's engines. Comfortable armchairs or couches were bolted to the deck.

He found Leon seated alone in the corner on a wing-back chair, a tall glass of bourbon on a table by his elbow. From the rheumy look in the man's eyes, it wasn't his first drink. He didn't seem surprised to see Rafe.

"So Shannon's little mole has delivered her message." He smiled at Rafe's astonishment. "What, you thought you were the only one doing any spying?"

"You know the mining station is a white elephant, and you're using it to destroy my father. You want EcoMech all for yourself, you selfish, greedy bastard."

Leon reached for his drink and took a noisy sip. "Grow up, McTavish. Your family's influence at EcoMech is nil. Your father's only a figurehead, and a piece of piss to manipulate. Shannon won't speak to me, and you won't come within a light-year of the company. Miguel was the only one with both balls and brains. Too bad he splattered himself on a mountainside."

"Then why are you framing my father? Buying the station makes no sense in any other context."

Leon gave him a grim smile. "I'm in a war, and Cullen is collateral damage. I like your old man, I really do, but if I'm to win, he had to be sacrificed."

Rafe stepped back, perplexed by the easy admission. "What war?"

"One for family honor and position at EcoMech. But what would you know about that?" Leon drained the rest of the bourbon. "You disgraced your family long ago."

Before Rafe could drag Leon from the chair and pound the daylights out of him, Captain Benson knocked on the hatch frame and stepped in.

"Excuse me, gentlemen." Benson looked uncomfortable, his eyes flicking to Rafe before settling on Leon. "We've arrived at the station."

Leon rose. "I didn't hear the docking collar."

"There's been a communications snafu, sir. The station's long-range com has been down all night. We've just reached them via ship-to-ship radio."

The CEO straightened his jacket, ignoring Rafe. "Typical. Well, get on with the docking. We don't have all day."

"They won't allow us to dock, sir. They say they weren't expecting us." Benson fell back in Leon's wake as the pudgy man steamrolled through the hatch into the companionway, cussing out everyone and vowing to take care of the matter himself.

Rafe remained behind, sucking in deep breaths to regain his composure. Mind racing, he drew the ball from his pocket and bounced it against the deck. None of what Leon said made sense, nor did it give him any ideas for how to extricate his father from the mess he'd gotten himself into. Shannon wanted his help, but what could he do?

He needed to get inside his brother-in-law's thick skull to find out more about this war. Short of kidnapping and torture, the only way he could see to do that was to chain himself to the vile man until he got answers.

Rafe pocketed the ball and went after the CEO, who stormed around screaming at everyone. Benson ducked into the com room, presumably to convince the station to let them dock. Leon ordered Greg and his assistant, Bob, to wait for him at the airlock, then he disappeared into the executive suite.

When Leon emerged, he was the sharp, self-confident CEO ready to do business. He wore a fresh suit, and he'd rinsed his mouth with some minty product that masked the smell of the bourbon. As he headed for the airlock, Rafe grabbed his arm and kept his voice low.

"A good general knows not to fight a war on two fronts, Leon. Tell me what's going on. Or shut me out and have me on your flank. It's your choice."

Leon's eyes flashed. "What's this? The runt of the litter challenging the big dog? You're all bark and no bite, same as you always were."

The docking collar clanged against the ship, and the CEO pulled away. Rafe followed him to the airlock, seething from his rebuke. Leon bounced on the balls of his feet. Bob stood placidly behind his boss, and Greg fidgeted next to Rafe. The hatch opened with a squeal of metal.

The docking bay was just a metal cube with a bench along one wall, a rack of spacesuits, and a tool locker. Rows of indicator lights punctuated a non-slip floor, the bay number scrawled in yellow paint on each wall. Two men and a woman waited for them. No one smiled.

"Leon Goldman, CEO, EcoMech Corporation." Leon extended his hand to the one he'd somehow determined must be in charge, a short, black man with broad shoulders and a challenging gaze. He didn't bother introducing Rafe, Bob, or Greg.

The miner eyed Leon before extending a beefy hand of his own. "Edgar Browning, smelter supervisor. This is Miss Patty Hertzog, assistant to our manager, Donald Levine, and Yuri Roshal, shipping manager."

An unlikely team, Rafe thought. About sixty, blonde, and heavily made-up, Hertzog wore an old-fashioned, ankle-length dress and heels. Roshal reminded him of a scarecrow stirred by a breeze, in his garish yellow shirt splattered with a huge red stain and dirty black trousers bagging on a stick-figure frame. Distrust oozed from their tense faces and rigid postures. Rafe glanced around the docking bay, automatically evaluating its defensibility.

"And where is Mr. Levine?" asked Leon.

"He's not available," Roshal said, his gaze sliding to the entrance of the docking bay. Rafe followed his lead and spotted a security camera above the door.

"Before we continue, can you give us any proof of who you are or your claims to ownership of this facility?" Browning stood, hands on hips, blocking their passage. His belligerent, bull-necked posture reminded Rafe of the troll under the bridge in the children's story.

Leon stared at Browning as though he were a naked madman spouting Shakespeare. "The Galaxy Mining home office has informed Mr. Levine of the transfer of ownership."

"And that's a problem, Mr. Goldman, because we believe that we own this station, not Galaxy. Or you," Browning said, huffing up. His biceps strained against the material of his shirt. Rafe's unease ratcheted up.

Leon shifted to a more aggressive stance, while Greg wandered over to peer up at the security camera. Boots drummed on the deck outside the docking bay.

A gruff voice shouted, "In here. Get em, boys!"

A rough-looking man dressed in an old work shirt, worn-out jeans, and heavy boots stepped through the door. He carried an enormous wrench. Behind him, another lout swung a length of pipe against the door frame, testing its strength. More men crowded behind the first two. Browning's dark face morphed from a scowl to naked aggression.

Rafe shoved Leon toward the spaceship hatch. "Run!"

Leon sprinted across the decking, followed by Bob. Greg froze. Rafe grabbed him by the collar and half threw him toward the airlock before turning to meet the attack of the man wielding the wrench. The manager's assistant, Miss Hertzog, screamed.

Rafe sidestepped a crunching overhead swing and paid the over-eager miner with an uppercut under the ribs. The man had a stomach like a steel plate, but the blow still doubled him over. A knee to the miner's face finished the job.

He stepped inside a swing from the lout with the pipe, locked the man's arm, and rammed a thumb into his Adam's apple. The miner went down, choking, and the pipe was Rafe's.

The mob fought their way through the doorway, but it was too tight for them to rush him *en masse*. A fist swung at Rafe, then the owner howled as knuckles landed full-force on the unyielding pipe. Two miners dashed past him, lunging for Greg who lay terrified a few yards from the hatch. Rafe landed a boot on one's kneecap, then jabbed the end of the pipe into the other's groin and sent him tumbling with a shove.

Someone picked up the fallen wrench, and Rafe was driven to his knees as he parried a massive swing with the pipe braced above his head. His counterblow with an elbow to another rock-solid gut didn't cause so much as an eyebrow twitch. He lowered his weapon to invite a horizontal swing at his skull, wormed his way under it, and used the pipe as a lever to send the miner tumbling under the feet of his fellows, scattering them.

Rafe grabbed Greg's belt and hauled him across the deck, slinging him through the yawning hatchway as something cannoned into the back of his legs. The deck rushed up to meet him. He landed hard, smacking his head against the unyielding surface. Fear sent fresh energy coursing through him, and he scrambled to rise.

The metal hatchway sang as Rafe's escape route slammed closed. Dazed and terrified, he rolled into a ball while the group of men kicked and punched him. He wondered briefly how long it would take them to beat him to death and what he'd done to deserve it. Then something heavy and unforgiving connected with his skull, and the world went black.